THE AWAKENING

OTHER NOVELS BY ANGELA HUNT

The Debt
The Canopy
The Pearl
The Justice
The Note
The Immortal
The Shadow Women
The Truth Teller
The Silver Sword
The Golden Cross
The Velvet Shadow
The Emerald Isle
Dreamers
Brothers
Journey
With Lori Copeland:
The Island of Heavenly Daze
Grace in Autumn
A Warmth in Winter
A Perfect Love
Hearts at Home

www.angelahuntbooks.com

THE AWAKENING

A Novel of Discovery

Angela Hunt

WESTBOW
PRESS

A Division of Thomas Nelson Publishers
Since 1798

visit us at www.westbowpress.com

Published by WestBow Press, a division of Thomas Nelson, Inc., P.O. Box 141000, Nashville, Tennessee 37214, in association with the literary agency of Alive Communications, Inc., 7680 Goddard Street, Suite 200, Colorado Springs, Colorado 80920. All rights reserved. No portion of this book may be reproduced, stored in a retrieval system, or transmitted in any form or by any means—electronic, mechanical, photocopy, recording, or any other—except for brief quotation in printed reviews, without prior permission of the publisher.

This is a work of fiction. Names, characters, places, and incidents are either the product of the author's imagination or are used fictitiously.

Scriptures quoted are from the following Bible translations:

THE NEW KING JAMES VERSION. Copyright © 1979, 1980, 1982, Thomas Nelson, Inc.

The Holy Bible, New Living Translation (NLT), copyright © 1996. Used by permission of Tyndale House Publishers, Inc., Wheaton, Illinois 60189. All rights reserved.

Library of Congress Cataloging-in-Publication Data

Hunt, Angela Elwell, 1957–
    The awakening : a novel of discovery / Angela Hunt.
      p. cm.
    ISBN: 0-8499-4481-3 (trade paper)
    I. Title.
  PS3558.U46747A98 2004
  813'.54—dc22   2004005040

Printed in the United States of America

04 05 06 07 PHX 9 8 7 6 5 4 3 2 1

For Sherri

But God speaks again and again,
though people do not recognize it.
He speaks in dreams, in visions of the night
when deep sleep falls on people as they lie in bed.
He whispers in their ear and terrifies them with his warning.

Job 33:14–16 (NLT)

1

THE WESTBURY ARMS, APARTMENT 15A

My mother is dead and I can't seem to feel the least bit sad about it.

I didn't go to the memorial service. Aunt Clara sighed heavily when I told her I couldn't go, but she didn't protest. "Don't worry yourself," she said, plucking at the veil over her smooth white hair as she preened in the mirror. "It's not like you didn't give your mother respect while she lived."

Now an assortment of strangers and dimly remembered faces are milling about in the apartment. I don't like having all these people in my home, but what can I do? Mother would expect me to be gracious.

Murmuring in solicitous tones, our guests wander through the living room, graze at the groaning table in the dining room, then zoom in on the bar manned by Clara's latest boyfriend. I lean against the wall and frown, trying to remember the man's name. Arthur Somebody-or-Other, a banker from the Wall Street district. The latest in a string of dignified elderly escorts Clara keeps on hand for fund-raisers and funerals.

I shake my head, grateful that Clara—who is bound to me by circumstance, not blood—has remained a constant in my life.

She has taken care of all the terrifying details. From the time I pounded on her door Monday afternoon until now, she has been completely in charge. She came and examined my mother's body; she called the funeral home; she spoke with a minister to arrange the memorial service. She even managed to find the envelope containing my mother's final wishes among the crowded drawers in the antique desk.

"Your mother left nothing to our imaginations," she said, holding up the envelope and the letter. "She is to be cremated and interred in her niche at the columbarium . . . and everything's been prepaid, of course. Reverend Jennings of St. John's is to lead the service, which should be short and sweet, with no eulogies. She wants Giorgio's to cater the wake because they always do a wonderful job, and later I'm to go through her papers and get rid of anything you don't want to keep. Everything she owned is now yours, a copy of her will is on file with her lawyer . . . so you see, dear, she thought of everything."

In that moment, I felt the burden of responsibility shift from my shoulders to my mother's. Everything I've done for the last ten years has been focused on making her life easier; I had no idea what to do for her in death. The hospice nurse had tried to explain certain procedures, but I'd been so convinced Mother would live many more years that I didn't listen.

Mother must have known I wouldn't want to let her go.

Clara stopped by this morning to check on preparations for the wake. "You understand why I can't go to the funeral, don't you?" I'd asked.

"Of course I do, darling." She took my hand and led me out of the kitchen, where the caterers were unpacking their coolers. "Mary Elizabeth would understand, too. And trust me—once she realized she was sick, she decided she wanted people to remember her as she was before the illness destroyed her mind. I've spoken to the minister, and he's agreed that the service will be simple, only a brief gesture, really."

I nodded in relief. Mary Elizabeth Wentworth Norquest would want her burial handled with the same no-nonsense approach with which she managed her business affairs . . . and at that moment I'd been too numb to fully appreciate how much work she'd spared me.

A weakened heart had taken my mother's life two weeks after her seventieth birthday, but dementia had begun to erode her personality years before. The detailed funeral instructions Clara found had to have been written in '94 or '95 . . . back when Mother could still remember who and where she was.

In those days, she could even remember who I was—her daughter, not her enemy.

I close my eyes, momentarily reliving the pain of those final years, then turn from Arthur the banker/bartender and wander to the windows on the south side of the dining room. Through the sunny arch of glass, I see Manhattan rising around me, the black tarpaper rooftops of neighboring buildings mingling with patches of green from terrace gardens and the metallic reflection of a majestic copper dome. Far below, near the street I can't see beyond the stony ridge of my window sill, a pair of twin spires rises from a church that once hoped to impress city dwellers with its architecture.

But time changes things. That church, which once lorded over nearly everything in this block of Manhattan, now squats amid more imposing structures like a poor relation awaiting a handout.

A woman touches my arm and whispers. Her voice can't compete with Arthur's gregarious chatter, but I smile as if I've understood every word.

"Mary Elizabeth was a strong woman." The stranger raises her voice and taps my arm as if to anchor me until she's delivered her cargo of sympathy. "We will miss her."

I resist the urge to bark in laughter. My mother hasn't left this apartment in years; Clara and I are the only ones who will miss her.

I am already aware of her absence. My mind keeps rushing to fill the void, and I find myself catching glimpses of Mother from the corner of my eye—I see her hunched at the kitchen counter, her long braids unraveled, her gaze vacant, her hands aimlessly searching for some object she can't identify. Last night I thought I saw her swaying in her bedroom doorway, but when I turned, the only movement was the subtle stir of curtains at her window.

I smile at the departing stranger, then turn back toward the view, grudgingly making room for the guilt that has attached itself to me like a shadow. As heartless as it seems, I don't think I'll miss my mother once the funeral has passed and I've adjusted to living alone. Does a woman with a migraine miss the pain when it ends? The last decade of my life has been filled with countless trays of oatmeal and soup, piles of filthy laundry, boxes of adult diapers. Apart from Clara and my invalid mother, my only companions have been small shames, frequent reproaches, and constant weariness.

Despair lived with us in this apartment, and I hope—desperately—that it died with my mother.

As another woman accepts a drink from Arthur and turns in my direction, I move away from the window. If I appear to be on a mission of some sort, perhaps people will think twice before speaking to me. The solitude of the last few years has left me feeling self-conscious and uncomfortable with strangers. I've never been a brilliant conversationalist, but today I don't think I could manage a coherent conversation about the weather.

My mother, however, could talk to anyone about anything. If she were here and healthy, she would be standing by the bar, making quiet tsking sounds as she studied me. "Chin up, Aurora," she would say, a hair of irritation in her voice. "You are the equal or better of anyone in this room."

I wander to the bar and lean on it, seeking Arthur's attention. "White wine." I lower my gaze from the banker's broad smile. "Please."

Arthur What's-His-Name is kind enough to remain silent, probably mistaking my discomfort for heartfelt grief. He slides a glass toward me and I take it, thanking him with a nod before I cross the room on a diagonal, pretending to be on an urgent errand.

When I reach the opening to the living room, I lean against the doorframe and sip my wine, keeping my gaze low lest it snag someone else's and invite conversation.

Before she became ill, my mother never tolerated my conversational weakness. Mary Elizabeth—M.E. to her friends—wore strength like a tiara. She could stride into a room of strangers, greet everyone from the butler to the host with the proper *bon mot*, and command the respect of every observer.

When I was old enough to stay up and be introduced at Mother's parties, I used to sit on a settee in the living room and watch as she reigned over a gathering of New York's finest families. The mayor and his wife would often sit at her left elbow, while the chairman of the Greater Manhattan Committee for the Arts would stand at her right, nodding like a puppet as Mother waved an elegant hand over her assembled guests. She would introduce me, bask for a moment in comments about what a dear child I was, insist I say a few polite words, then send me off to bed.

I almost always crept back down the long gallery to watch from the shadows.

Even as a woman with no husband, Mary Elizabeth ruled with grace and dignity. Hindsight and intuition have led me to believe she held sway because she exuded old money and prestige, but in my younger days I thought her power sprang solely from her beauty, poise, and charm. Handsome men circled her at every opportunity, and the nouveau riche yearned for the stamp of respectability an invitation from Mary Elizabeth Wentworth Norquest could bestow.

I suspect that stamp had begun to lose its luster by the time I became a brief fixture at Mother's illustrious parties because she could no longer deny she had a child . . . the offspring of a brilliant novelist and a horrible man.

I never knew my father, but numerous eavesdropping occasions assured me that he had been lured away by the light of some European beauty. He could have kept the Englishwoman as his mistress, but when my mother announced she was expecting, he chose to abandon her in the fragility of pregnancy. The divorce lawyers had finished their battles by the time I was born. While hiding beneath a Louis XIV chair one night, I learned that my father had returned to America to finalize his divorce the same month I was christened. Theodore Norquest scandalized my mother's friends when he appeared in Manhattan only long enough to sign the necessary paperwork and catch a jet back to London.

"You must be Mary Elizabeth's daughter." A hoarse voice jars me from my memories. I turn and see a gaunt man with a shiny head. His flesh, dotted with age spots, hangs from his jaw like skin from a soup bone.

"I am."

"So sorry for your loss. Your mother was an exceptionally lovely woman." The man squeezes my hand with surprising strength, then moves away without bothering to introduce himself.

His flesh felt dry and creepy against my skin, reminding me of dead flesh. My thoughts flash back to a book I read on the ancient Romans—one of their torture techniques involved strapping a criminal to a freshly deceased body. As the forces of decay began to break down the corpse, they began to attack the living body, too.

I wipe my hand on my skirt, shivering at the thoughts of malevolent bacteria and viruses. The apartment stirs with strange smells and unfamiliar noises and whispered conversations like the buzz of angry bees.

I want these people out. I need to be alone.

I swipe hair from my damp brow, then set my half-empty glass on a table and move through the foyer, heading toward the bathroom off the gallery. When I find it empty, I slip inside, close the door, and lock it with trembling fingers. I lower the toilet lid and sit down to stare at the monogrammed towels on the rack.

M.E.N.: Mary Elizabeth Norquest.

I breathe deeply, trying to calm the rise of frustration in my breast. This ritual must be endured; the wake is the final farewell. When it is over and these people are gone, surely the last dregs of despair will go with them.

This apartment has known so much private unhappiness. In my early years, my mother must have abhorred the thought of being a divorcée. Divorce was common enough in the early seventies, but not among women of Mother's status. Clara has told me that for the first year or two of my life Mother completely withdrew from her social circle, only reappearing when Charley, Clara's husband, offered to shelter her under his cloak of respectability.

Clara doesn't like to talk about those years, but faded photographs from my mother's albums speak volumes. In these collections I've seen Mother, Clara, and Charley in frozen moments at dinners, at the beach, at balls and museum openings. Charles Bellingham apparently acted as an escort to both women until a heart attack felled him in 1982.

I knew Charley as a doting uncle. When he died the winter I turned thirteen, I remember being shocked when the *Times* obituary didn't list me and Mother among his survivors. Blood might be thicker than water, but in my mother's circle, shared champagne bound people more closely than blood. I will always appreciate Clara and Charley because they took pity on a husbandless friend and allowed Mother to resume her life.

I have searched those photo albums many times, but never found a picture of my father.

I lift my head as someone raps on the bathroom door. "Aurora?"

"Clara?"

"Are you all right, dear?"

Releasing a deep sigh, I tunnel my fingers through my hair. "I'm fine."

"Will you open the door, please? Several people would like to pay their respects to you."

Somehow I rise and unlock the door, then open it. Clara stands in the hall, one hand absently stroking her sable collar, the other firmly on the doorknob. "Thank you, dear. I know this is hard for you, but it'll be over soon enough."

"It's just . . . so many people. I don't know any of them."

Clara's bejeweled hand pats my arm. "They're your mother's friends."

"But we haven't seen them in years."

"How could they visit your mother in her condition? Be grateful they came today. M.E., God rest her, deserved such a send-off."

She's right—and I know this can't be easy for her, either. Smiling in acquiescence, I cross my arms and study my mother's dearest friend. A succession of face-lifts has tightened the skin around Clara's forehead and mouth, but an unusual worry line has worked its way into the flesh between her brows.

"Mother would be happy to know so many of her old friends came."

"Indeed she would—so come out and mingle a bit more, would you?" She turns slightly to survey the crowd in the living room at the end of the gallery, then rises on tiptoe as a stranger enters the foyer. "Excuse me, dear, that must be the writer for the *Times*. I promised to give him details—but goodness, I wish he had chosen a more appropriate coat. To wear tweed to a funeral . . ."

Shaking her head, she glides away to intercept a young man in glasses and a rumpled sports jacket. I draw a deep breath, then spy an empty seat on the bench in the foyer. If I can traverse the gallery without being noticed . . .

Pressing my lips together, I stride down the long hallway, then slide into my favorite seat. When no one approaches, I turn to watch the mingling guests in the living room. Some of the faces are familiar—the director of the New York Symphony is here, with a new wife dangling from his arm. (I've never met the woman, but I read the account of their wedding in last month's Sunday *Times*.) Dr. Montrose Helgrin, my mother's physician, has come, and with him are two men who seem more determined to empty their buffet plates than make conversation.

When Dr. Helgrin glances my way, I stand and hurry back through the gallery. The kitchen is filled with caterers; I've been expelled from the bathroom; the storage room is a mess—I dart into the next open doorway, which leads to the library. A trio of older women stands in this room, heads together as they sip from their teacups. A fourth woman stands aloof from the others and idly runs her fingertips over an Incan fertility statue, one of Mother's favorite treasures.

I turn toward the bookshelves as if I'm desperately searching for something. I run my finger over the leather-bound spines as a spasm of irritation tenses my nerves.

"You can see M.E.'s sense of style everywhere," one of the trio says. "She was really something."

"Wasn't she? Such passion and grace."

"And her wit—no one could ever get the better of her. Trust me, you didn't want to get on M.E.'s blacklist. The woman had a memory like an elephant."

"I'll say. Remember her ex-husband? I always said that if ever a man deserved forgiving, Theodore Norquest must be that man. Not only was he handsome, I hear he's worth millions."

From the corner of my eye, I see the tallest woman stroke her throat and laugh. "Billions, my dear. He's richer than the queen of England. Almost as wealthy as that British woman who invented Harry Potter."

"Yet he didn't provide a penny for Mary Elizabeth or the girl?"

The tall woman glances around the room and meets my curious gaze. I am certain she will blush and stammer out an apology, but she only looks at her friends and lowers her voice. "Mary Elizabeth said she would never take money from a louse. She didn't need it—the Wentworth fortune provided more than enough for her and her daughter."

After a startled instant I realize these women don't know who I am. I am a stranger in a black dress, a face they didn't see at the funeral—why, they probably think I'm a maid!

"I'm surprised she kept his name," another woman adds. "Hating him the way she did."

"She did despise him, but she had to think of the child. And I think she rather enjoyed the association with his fame."

"She possessed a remarkable sense of pride," says the third woman, her eyes skimming over me as if I'm no more than furniture. "So few women do these days."

An inadvertent smile crosses my face as I linger beside the bookshelves. Though my mother's Manhattan has faded from the pages of the *Times'* Fashion and Style section, these older women remember who and what she was. They have come not only to mourn my mother, but also to pay homage to a lost way of life. They have come to step on Mother's plush woolen carpets, inhale the scents of her leather-bound books, and handle the delicate Wentworth china. Later, around their dinner tables, they will eat carry-out from cardboard takeout boxes and strain to make themselves heard above the rumble of the television. They will tell their husbands or significant others that today they attended a matriarch's funeral. They will say an era passed with Mary Elizabeth Wentworth Norquest.

Reaching the end of the bookshelf, I turn to negotiate another pass through the apartment. No one, I notice upon reentering the gallery, has ventured back to Mother's sickroom. Though the door stands ajar, our guests avoid it as carefully as they avoided her in her last years.

A small woman with silver hair and bright blue eyes stops me, her face lighting with recognition. "Lenora? Can it be you?"

"Aurora." I force a smile. "Yes, it is me."

"My goodness, child, how you've changed. Where have you been keeping yourself? I remember hearing you were engaged, so I'm sure you've gone off somewhere to raise a family by now."

I shake my head. "The engagement didn't work out. So I've been here, taking care of Mother."

"Oh! What a dear girl you must be." Her eyes crinkle at the corners as she touches my cheek. "You must have brought great joy to your mother. I know she loved you dearly."

Then she is off, moving past me into the storage room where the women have hung fur coats and deposited neat little handbags. I watch her go, then thread my way through the crowded kitchen and dining room, smiling at Aunt Clara, Arthur the banker, and a pair of pleat-thin older women I have never seen before.

Clara said people wanted to pay their respects, but no one else stops me. When I have made one complete pass through the public rooms, I return to the gallery and walk at a quick pace until I have reached the corner bedroom my mother used—the one room no one has entered to exclaim over Mary Elizabeth's impeccable taste.

I close the door and stand behind it, my palms pressed to the painted wood. This door has not been closed in years, because closing it meant I might miss some signal that something had gone terribly wrong. Yet even with the open door and a baby monitor beside Mother's bed, I heard nothing the afternoon a heart attack took her without warning.

I lower my forehead to the door. I ought to be weeping, I ought to feel some loss, but I feel . . . nothing. Are my emotions frozen because dementia robbed me of my mother long before the heart attack, or am I too exhausted to feel anything? Maybe I'm experiencing the mental equivalent of the physical shock that occurs after a traumatic injury.

I back away from the door and turn, catching a glimpse of myself in the mirror over the antique dresser. The brown eyes looking back at me must be my father's, because they have nothing in common with my mother's eyes of icy blue. A mass of dark hair creeps below my shoulders in raveled hanks; my mother's natural color was honey blond. In her latter years she let it go silver gray and wore it in a sleek chignon. Even in the sickroom, I took pains to keep her hair braided and neat. I could not risk having her wander into a public hallway looking like anyone less than Mary Elizabeth Wentworth Norquest.

A wry smile tugs at my lips. My mother and I were about as alike as mustard and custard, so I'm not surprised few of the guests recognized me. If I had worn a white apron over this simple black dress, no one would have looked at me twice.

I lift my head as someone coughs outside the door.

"Aurora? Darling, are you all right?"

I glance back at the mirror. The woman in the looking glass certainly *seems* all right. Her eyes are clear, her cheeks dry, and her mouth is still tinged with a faint tint of pink lipstick.

From a deep reserve of willpower, I find my voice. "I'm fine, Clara. Do you need me?"

She opens the door and peers at me, then the ghost of a smile touches her mouth with ruefulness. "I can't keep chasing you out of hiding places, dear heart. Is this really too much for you?"

"I'm sorry. It's just . . . uncomfortable for me out there."

Her cloudy blue eyes sink into nets of fine wrinkles as she smiles. "Then don't worry about a thing. If you need time to yourself, you should take it. I'm only wondering if—well, this feels a little awkward."

I sink to the edge of the hospital bed. "What is it?"

Her brow furrows as she steps into the room. "I hate to bother you like this, but you and I both know your mother was a complete pack rat. Since so many of her dearest friends are here, I was wondering— would you mind terribly if I gave a few small things away? I think Esther would adore the little Limoges box on the dining room mantel, and Gloria would love to have the cut-glass paperweight from the desk. They were your mother's friends, and I know they'd love to have some little token to remind them of her."

Something stirs in my soul—a dim memory of Mother's hand curled around that paperweight as she worked through a stack of personal correspondence. For an instant I want to cling to it, then I remember I never write letters.

"If Gloria wants the paperweight"—I meet Clara's eyes—"Gloria should have it."

"That's very sweet of you, dear." Clara's birdlike hand squeezes my wrist. "Has this completely exhausted you?"

"I only need a few minutes to gather my thoughts."

"You take as long as you need. I'll stay until the last guest leaves if you want to rest."

I nod and close my eyes, but a sudden thought makes me look up. "How long will the caterers be?"

Clara glances down the hallway, then shrugs. "I don't know, dear. Maybe an hour after the guests have gone. These are good people; they'll put everything back to rights—"

"Ask them to leave with the guests, will you? I'll clean up."

She narrows her eyes until they almost disappear in her taut cheeks. "That's not necessary, dear. Cleaning is part of their job."

"I want to be alone, Clara."

Clara stares at me as if I've suddenly taken leave of my senses, then she nods and closes the door. I am overcome with weariness, but I would never nap on this hospital bed. I slip from the mattress and curl into the recliner by the window. This chair knows me; over the years it has shifted to accommodate the curves of my hips and the jut of my bones.

In the compliant embrace of the recliner, my pulse slows, my nerves relax. I pull back the heavy curtains and study the familiar skyline. In the rooftop garden across the street, the bearded man's Japanese maple has nearly lost all its leaves. Autumn has advanced, announcing her inexorable arrival with shorter days, threadbare trees, and steel gray clouds that obscure the taller Manhattan rooftops.

I lift my gaze to the ceiling, where a water stain has formed on the plaster. I will have to call George, the building superintendent, to check for a leak . . . when I find the energy.

A wave of self-pity threatens to engulf me, but I push it back. I am fine. My mother is dead, but for years the essence of Mary Elizabeth Wentworth Norquest has been fading like a spent flower. I have given ten years of my life to nurse her, but she sacrificed far more than that to care for the child of a successful novelist and despicable man.

We are even. All debts are paid. Tomorrow, *my* life can begin.

I lean back and push the chair into a reclining position. I grimace when the soles of my black pumps touch the upholstered footrest—even in the fog of dementia, Mother railed against the sight of shoes on the furniture.

But she is no longer lying in the bed next to me, and this chair is destined for the nearest thrift store.

And I am ten years tired.

2

APARTMENT 15A

I dream. I know I am dreaming because when I look in the mirror I see myself as a fresh-faced twenty-year-old, not the woman of thirty-five I know myself to be. I am no longer wearing my black dress, but jeans and a Sweet Briar College sweatshirt.

Apart from the alterations in my face and clothing, nothing else in the room has changed. From behind the closed bedroom door I can still hear the distant tinkle of silver and china. The wake must still be in progress.

I climb out of the recliner—still wearing my black pumps—and cross the room, then turn the doorknob. No one moves in the gallery beyond, but voices pour from the dining room, sprinkled with laughter. Once I enter the hall, I press my back to the wall and slide along it, darting past the entrances to the library, the storage room, and the kitchen. Each step brings me closer to the noisy gathering.

"Honestly, Mary Elizabeth, how can you think such a thing?"

I recognize Clara's voice, though it is warmer and more vibrant than a few moments ago.

"Theodore Norquest is quite possibly one of the greatest novelists of our time; how can you argue with his reputation?"

My forearms pebble with goose flesh when my mother chuckles. "Because I know the truth—he is a pig."

A flutter of delighted gasps punctuates this remark, and no one is more surprised than I am to hear Mother utter a coherent sentence.

I quicken my pace, moving cautiously through the foyer and into the living room. From the double doors there I can peer into the dining room and not be seen.

The crystal chandelier spills gilded light over a festive gathering. My mother, in a blue silk evening gown that matches her eyes, sits at the head of the table, the marble fireplace looming behind her. One shoulder is bare; an oversized silk rose adorns the other. Her honey-colored hair has been swept up, emphasizing her wide forehead, while a single golden strand curls at the nape of her neck.

She is breathtakingly beautiful.

Clara sits to Mother's left; an older gentleman in a tuxedo sits at Mother's right. He glances up and sees me standing by the French doors; oddly enough, he says nothing.

Perhaps I am as invisible in this world of dreams as I am in reality.

"Theodore Norquest is a pig," my mother repeats, "and I know this because I lived with the man fifteen years. I think that experience gives me the right to express my opinion, don't you?"

The man in the tuxedo swirls amber liquid in his glass. "His work is highly regarded in literary circles, which is astounding given his commercial success. Some say his understanding of human nature is sheer genius."

My mother waves the remark away as if it were a bad smell. "Public opinion is one thing; reality is something else altogether. Tell me, Mr. Johnson—who but a pig would abandon a woman who has just discovered she is expecting his baby? Yet this is what Theodore Norquest did. Not only did he abandon me when I needed him most, he fled the country and went to live in Europe with his tootsie. I gave birth to his daughter with no one but Clara in attendance."

Clara's head dips in agreement. "Charley and I both liked Theodore at first, but Mary Elizabeth is quite right. Ask her how many times the man has returned to visit his child."

Mr. Johnson wears a look of polite shock as he obeys: "How many?"

"None." Mother's voice is clipped. "Not one visit, not one call on the child's behalf. Yet in the divorce proceedings he had the gall to declare his undying love for the child."

The man at the table lifts his head. "Is that the girl?"

My blood chills as he meets my gaze. The fly on the wall has been spotted. If I can be spotted, perhaps I can be swatted.

My mother's eyes follow his. "Yes." She regards me with the unflinching interest she might employ to appraise a piece of art. "That is Aurora. She is a dear girl, but I see little of myself in her."

Suddenly an entire roomful of strangers are probing me with eyes like cold needles. My knees tremble and my heart thumps beneath my college sweatshirt as I run for my room. I should be only steps from safety, but the gallery stretches as I run, growing longer and darker with each pounding footfall—

"Aurora!" my mother calls, her voice reverberating against my eardrums.

"Auroraaaaa?" Her voice changes—no longer is it the strong instrument with which she commanded scores of dinner parties, but the broken, crackling cry of a woman who can't remember whether it's Friday or Monday, the year 2000 or 1979.

I gasp and sit up in the recliner while the world shifts dizzily before my eyes. My heart is pounding like a timpani, my palms are damp, and the old panic has begun to bloom in my chest.

Then I look down and see my black dress. I'm not wearing my college sweatshirt. I'm not twenty years old. I am thirty-five and my mother is not holding court in the dining room, but resting in an urn at the Cathedral Church of St. John the Divine.

Only a dream. And dreams can't hurt me.

Can they?

After gulping several deep breaths, I lower my shaky legs to the floor. Outside the room, the noise has faded considerably.

I cross to the bureau and glance at the clock—it is nearly four, so more than an hour has passed since my leaving the gathering.

I pick up the brush from the dresser, pull a handful of tangled gray strands from its teeth, then swipe at my frazzled hair. The effort is wasted upon my wiry curls, but it gives me an excuse to murder minutes. When the clock strikes four, I wipe my clammy hands on my dress, then glance at the mirror one last time.

Everyone should be gone by now. If I appear, somber eyed and pale faced, perhaps any stragglers will clear out and allow me to get on with my life.

A blanket of silence lies upon the apartment when I step through the bedroom doorway and creep down the long, windowless gallery. The kitchen is empty and the dining area deserted, though the table is littered with the remains of the funeral feast. Half the bibelots that once occupied the buffet are gone; tiny shiny circles mark the dust field where they stood an hour ago.

I lift a brow, more concerned about the dust than the missing trinkets. On Monday I told Mildred, our housekeeper, not to come again unless I called for her, and after that dusting never crossed my mind. I hope no one noticed this sign of my incompetence, but my mother's sharp-eyed friends notice everything.

The living room is empty as well, but someone has taped a note to the silver basket Mother kept on the desk.

> *Get some sleep, darling. I sent the catering people home so you can call Mildred to clean up. Be sure to knock if you need help going through your mother's papers. I'm sure you'll want to clear out a few things to make a fresh start.*
>
> *—Clara*

I resist the urge to laugh as I drop the card into the basket. Clear out my mother's things? If I got rid of all her belongings, I'd have nothing left. Everything in this apartment reflects my mother, from the paintings on the walls to the furnishings in each room. She chose the draperies, the kitchenware, the carpets, even the paint color in my small bedroom. When I came back from college, I was too focused on my upcoming wedding to think about changing anything; after Mother became dependent, I never had the time or the energy.

And I will never call Mildred again. I welcomed her help when Mother was ill, but right now I have this unyielding urge to clean the place myself . . .

I wave my hand before my nose as I wander through the apartment. The place still smells of perfume and cigars, the scents of well-heeled scavengers. The glass shelves of the étagère in the living room have the picked-over look of a clearance sale, and indignation fires my blood when I realize how many of Mother's treasures have vanished.

I close my eyes, dreading the thought of confronting Clara about her presumptive generosity. But why am I upset? I cared nothing for Mother's expensive little ornaments; I ought to be grateful for fewer items to dust. Besides, I could never be angry with Clara. When Mother fell ill, Clara provided the support I needed. She proved to be as much my friend as Mother's, and I will always be grateful for her.

I can't stop a smile. Sometime last year I watched a television special on international adoption. The news crew followed a group of prospective parents through the home study process, trips to INS, and finally to the airport where the couples met their new children. Without fail, the first thing those parents did after hugging the new arrivals was tug off the babies' old clothes, scrub their little bodies with baby wipes, and dress them in new outfits.

Maybe that's what I need to do. Clara has already helped me rid the place of a few old things. Now I'll clean, and maybe these walls will begin to feel like *my* home . . .

I grab a garbage bag from a kitchen cabinet and begin to clear the dining room. After dumping runny deviled eggs, stale canapés, and chewed chicken bones into the trash, I twist the top of the bag, tie it, and drag it toward the foyer. Nearly two dozen china teacups and a fistful of silver are waiting to be hand-washed, but they will keep.

Organic trash, however, will not. Mindful that my mother could not abide the sight or stench of refuse, I pause to grab the key from the foyer table and slip it into my pocket. Mother has lived in this building since 1952, but I didn't summon the courage to install two additional deadbolts without asking her permission until three years ago.

With the key in my pocket, I step outside the door and drag the trash bag onto the worn hallway carpet. Three residences occupy each floor of the Westbury Arms, which is little more than a huge square with a courtyard carved out of the center. Clara's place occupies the southeast corner of the building; mine takes up the entire west side. The third apartment, located at the far end of the public hallway, occupies the northeast corner. This third suite, the smallest of the three, abuts with my apartment on the west, Clara's on the south.

When I look up, I see a man standing before that far apartment. A wave of curiosity stirs my dull melancholy—this man is not Mr. Williamson, the man who has occupied that suite of rooms for the last twenty years. Nor does he look like any of Mr. Williamson's assorted relatives, who are as short and round as this man is tall and thin.

As I bend to lift the bulging trash bag, from the corner of my eye I see the stranger turn.

"Can I help you with that?" he calls.

Holding the trash before me like a shield, I peer over the bag. The young man at the far door is pale faced and blond, with round black glasses that circle his eyes.

My mind flashes back to a program about raccoons on the Nature Channel.

I shake my head and look away, wishing the trash chute were closer to the south end of the building. Unfortunately, it is just beyond the stairs at the north end, only a few feet from Mr. Williamson's door.

The man doesn't answer, but I hear the jingle of keys.

He is minding his own business, then. Good. In a moment he'll be inside, so I can begin to walk down the hall, trusting he'll be gone by the time I reach the chute.

I flinch when he turns and speaks again.

"I'm sorry to bother you," he says, his attention focused on something in his hand, "but the super gave me this set of keys and none of them seems to fit any of these locks. Is there a trick to this? Something I'm missing?"

I glance over my shoulder, hoping Aunt Clara will appear to rescue me, but I am the only other human in the hallway.

I pause, trash bag in hand. I'm about to suggest that he call Mr. Williamson, then my gaze falls upon the keys—they are old and dark, the elongated keys to the apartment's original locks. The modern lockset in Mr. Williamson's door is polished brass.

"He changed the locks." Without stepping even an inch in the stranger's direction, I point to the door. "About two years ago, I think. George has to have another set of keys somewhere. We're required to leave a set with him."

"That makes sense." The man's face brightens, then he walks toward me, his free hand extended. "I'm Philip Cannon. If that's your place"—he points to my apartment—"then I'm your new neighbor."

My limbs stiffen. When did this happen? My world is not large, but I thought I knew nearly everything about our neighbors.

Somehow I find my tongue. "What happened to Mr. Williamson?"

"Retired to Florida, I think. Fort Lauderdale, the super said."

I make a mental note to ask Clara when Mr. Williamson decided to move. She'll know what prompted such a permanent change; she may even know something about the young man standing here. She knows everything about the people on this floor; sometimes I think she knows something about everyone at the Westbury Arms. She has lived here as long as my mother, the two of them nesting like eagles on the top floor.

The man clears his throat. He is looking at me, his arm still extended, and I suddenly realize I am not holding up my end of this social interaction.

I force myself to take his hand. "Sorry. I'm Aurora Norquest."

"Nice to meet you, Aurora." Despite the pallor of his complexion, his grip is firm and warm. He jerks his head toward my apartment. "Lived here long?"

He has moved too close; I take an involuntary half step back. "My mother lived here until this past Monday. I buried her today."

His smile vanishes. "I'm sorry. I had no idea."

"How would you know? Excuse me, please. I have to get back to cleaning up. Mother would hate it if I left the place looking a mess."

"I'm very sorry," he repeats. He slips the useless keys into his pockets, then gestures toward the elevator. "Do you need anything from the super? If you need boxes or bags, I could bring some up for you."

I stare at him, unable to make sense of his offer, then the answer hits me—like the few people at the wake who recognized me, he thinks I am only visiting. That I have a life somewhere else.

I wave toward my apartment door. "I live there—I mean, I lived with my mother. She was sick for a long time, so I nursed her. So I live there, I mean *here*, I live here. So yes, we are neighbors."

I look into his eyes, afraid I will see proof he thinks I am scattered and senseless, but his eyes are warm and filled with something that looks like pity.

I don't want pity.

"Forgive me." He slips his hands into his pockets. "Here I am, making silly small talk while you are smack in the middle of a major crisis." He backs toward the elevator. "I'll get out of your way, but please don't hesitate to knock if you need anything. I think neighbors should stick together, don't you?"

I resist the impulse to snort a laugh. I would have said the neighbors of the fifteenth floor have stuck together so long we are practically glued, but we must not be as close as I thought. I still can't believe I didn't hear about Mr. Williamson moving to Florida.

Leaving Philip Cannon to wait for the elevator, I heave the trash up to the stainless steel chute, then struggle to fit the bulky bag into the rectangular opening. Finally, the metal plate over the receptacle closes with a clang. I glance behind me as I turn, a little disturbed to see the newcomer still waiting for the elevator. While the man doesn't look suspicious—he's too slender and friendly to appear threatening—he is still a stranger on this floor.

From some compartment in my brain, my mother's voice chides me. He is a new neighbor; he is a nice man; I should invite him in for a cup of coffee. But Mother is not here, she is dead, and my meager reserve of hospitality has already been stretched beyond its limits.

I walk back to my own apartment, but I continue to feel the guy's presence in the hallway. I linger at my dark threshold, pretending to fumble with my key, convinced that opening the door will result in an invasion of my privacy. He might glimpse the interior; he might see my furniture, yet another stranger would enter my house, eroding its sanctity and safety.

Finally the elevator dings and I hear the bronze doors slide open. When they finally close, my shoulders slump. Only then do I realize how the encounter has tensed my nerves.

A newcomer on our floor—what will Clara think? I unlock the door, then step inside the early evening gloom of my mother's apartment—*my* apartment now. I will have to adjust my speech and my thinking. I may have to call George and have him come up with whatever paperwork is necessary to change the lease. For years our accountant has been handling the utility bills and maintenance fees, but in my mother's name. I'll have to call him and make adjustments.

This is my place now. Mine alone.

I switch on the lamp atop the foyer table, then stare into the living room, now wreathed in shadows. The air feels stale, as if it has been breathed too many times.

I push through the gloom, then sink onto the sofa and stare at the nearly empty étagère. The apartment is quiet, more silent than it has been in months, and for some reason I find myself thinking I should be the one interred at the Cathedral Church of St. John the Divine and Mother should be sitting in this room, bemoaning the loss of so many beloved *objets d'art*.

The harder I try to ignore the thought, the more it persists.

3

APARTMENT 15 B

This new place of mine would be a lot more appealing if it didn't smell like a combination of wet dog and liverwurst.

Because the apartment is in desperate need of airing out, I cross to the living room window and tug on the lower sash. The old glass rattles within the frame, but the window won't budge.

I lean in for a closer look—as I suspected, the sash has been painted shut. I could work it free with a screwdriver and hammer, but I have no idea where my tools are. Packed in a box somewhere and sitting either in my old place, in the gallery, or downstairs in the lobby.

I blow out my breath and glance at my watch. The doorman, a young guy named Thomas, promised to keep an eye on several of my boxes, but how much time does a twenty-dollar tip buy?

Running my hand through my hair, I turn to look around my new apartment. I agreed to buy the place with its furnishings, but I'd paid little attention to the furniture when the real-estate agent walked me through the place. I'd been far more impressed by the open space that serves as living room/kitchen/dining area, framed with a wall of nine-foot windows granting me a panoramic view of Central Park. The three bedrooms are small, like the bedrooms in most older apartments, and the tiled bathrooms are positively Spartan.

But the building is in the Upper West Side, convenient to NYU, and miles away from St. Louis. The location, combined with the open living area and those glorious windows, so wowed me that I nearly accepted the selling price without even attempting to negotiate.

Selling myself to the board of directors, however, had been another matter. Before I could purchase the apartment, I had to provide the Westbury Arms' managing board members with an application for membership to the homeowners' association, personal and business references, a letter of employment confirmation, verification of my bank accounts and brokerage statements, the last two years' tax returns, and a copy of my mortgage loan approval. After going through my paperwork, they called me in for an interview, bluntly asking why they should allow me to live at the Westbury Arms.

"Because I'm quiet," I'd said, feeling a bit like a criminal under interrogation. "I think I'll be a good neighbor. And current research indicates that quiet neighbors tend to inhabit safe neighborhoods, while safe neighborhoods tend to create higher property values."

After withdrawing for a private vote, the four board members stepped forward to welcome me to the Westbury Arms.

Now I can't help but wish I'd sent a cleaning crew ahead of me. I am staring at ugly vinyl and chrome furniture, smudged walls, and carpets that smell of cigars, cooking grease, and dog. I suppose I shouldn't be surprised to find the place in need of cosmetic work, but my high hopes made the place look a lot more appealing when I signed the purchase contract and handed over a check for the first year's maintenance fees.

I reach for a wall switch and flip it, hoping to activate the ceiling fan. Instead, a light glows in the long gallery that leads to the foyer.

At least the light works.

Sighing, I pull a six-pack of diet sodas from a box on the kitchen island, then walk to the avocado-colored refrigerator and open the door. Five cans go into the fridge, the sixth I pop open. I'd drink from the can, but I can't stand warm soda, so I search through several cupboards for a glass. Finally I find a New York Yankees mug in a forgotten corner. The bottom is filled with little black things—roach droppings or dirt?—so I rinse the mug beneath a stream of hot water.

While the mug drips on the counter, I open the freezer and hope for an icemaker. No such luck. But the former tenant left me an ice cube tray—silver, like the ones my parents used before they broke down and bought new kitchen appliances.

I wince at the snap and creak of snapping ice, then drop a couple of clouded cubes into the mug. After dumping the rest of the ice into a plastic container from one of my moving boxes, I refill it with water and slide it back in the freezer.

I slide onto a barstool and smile as I sip from the mug. This isn't exactly my finest moment, but it's memorable all the same. The Lindbergh High senior voted most likely to remain a geek has accomplished his first domestic act at the famous Westbury Arms without breaking or burning anything. If I can get my other boxes moved upstairs without tying up the elevator or stepping on some other tenant's foot, surely I'll remain on good terms with my neighbors . . .

I set my mug on the counter when I hear a knock at the door. The doorman? The super? For a split second I wonder if I'll find Aurora Norquest standing outside—I'd like to apologize again for intruding on her grief.

But the woman I spy through the peephole is a familiar-looking silver-haired lady in a black suit with a fur collar. When I open the door, the petite woman lifts a white bakery bag and smiles.

"Welcome to the Westbury Arms," she says, her voice a genteel murmur in the silence of the carpeted hallway. "It's wonderful to have you here, Mr. Cannon."

I struggle to place her face, then I remember—this woman was one of the four board members who vetted my membership application. One of the four formidable guardians of the Westbury Arms.

I open the door wider. "Thank you, Mrs.—I'm sorry, but I'm terrible with names."

Her thin mouth twitches with amusement. "I'm Clara Bellingham, and I didn't expect you to remember my name. I'm sure you've had a lot on your mind in the last few days." She leans slightly to peer over my shoulder. "I hope you don't mind that I picked up a few baked goods to welcome you to the fifteenth floor."

"Thank you." Taking the hint, I step aside. "Won't you come in? I'm sorry the place is a mess, but I've just begun to settle in. Most of my boxes are still in the lobby—"

"You don't have to explain. I know Horace Williamson had no taste. But I think you'll find this *is* a nice apartment. It has nice bones; it just needs a bit of sprucing up." She walks forward, her gaze sweeping from wall to wall and floor to ceiling, then pauses outside the first door off the main hallway. "How many bedrooms have you, Mr. Cannon?"

I'm sure she knows the answer, but I'll humor her. "Three." I lean against the wall and cross my arms. "I'll use this room as the master bedroom. The room right off the foyer would make a good guest room, I think."

She presses her lips together. "Excellent idea. I believe that was the arrangement the McConnells used—they lived here before Horace Williamson."

I acknowledge this information with a polite smile. "The other bedroom—the one next to the living room—will be my office. It has more closet space than the others, and I have lots of files to store."

"It'll be a good space for you—and it's close to the kitchen. By the way, what do you think of the view from your living room?"

"It's wonderful. The windows were what sold me on this place."

Nodding, she follows the gallery until it ends at the open space that serves as the main living area, then turns to face me. "I'm surprised the unit doesn't look worse than it does—Horace was never one to invest much energy in his home. It'll be interesting to see what you make of the place."

"I do plan to fix things up—in my spare time, that is."

"We're always fixing things up at the Westbury. I don't suppose you've heard the history of the building?"

"Not really—is it colorful?"

Her smile deepens into laughter. "We're not nearly as colorful as the Dakota on Seventy-second—they filmed *Rosemary's Baby* there, you know, and John Lennon was murdered on the sidewalk right outside that building. The Westbury was built in 1885, the year *after* the Dakota, and the architect must have been determined to outdo his competition. That's why we're fifteen stories; they're nine. We have forty-five apartments, the Dakota's original plans called for only thirty-six. There are more now, of course—people at the Dakota are always chopping those grand old spaces up into smaller units. While our apartments have been renovated, we haven't allowed any to be subdivided."

Amused by the competitive comparisons, I do my best to suppress a smile. "How long have you lived here, Mrs. Bellingham?"

Thought narrows her eyes and tightens the corners of her mouth. "A long time, Mr. Cannon. Perhaps too long." She sighs, then looks at me with a smile that seems forced. "It'll be nice to have another young person on the fifteenth floor."

I laugh. "I have a niece who thinks thirty-seven is positively ancient."

"Children—what do they know?" Mrs. Bellingham holds out the bakery bag and looks toward the boxes on the kitchen island. "I should leave this with you and let you get to your unpacking. I don't want to interrupt."

I take the bag from her. "Thank you, and you're not interrupting. I've left some boxes downstairs, but as long as the doorman doesn't mind keeping an eye on them—"

"Thomas won't mind. He's an agreeable young man."

"Then . . . would you like to sit down?"

"Why, thank you."

As she walks toward the horrid vinyl sofa, I set the white bag on the counter and struggle to keep a straight face. Apparently reading my financial records and reference letters wasn't enough. The woman wants to know if my bellybutton is an innie or an outie.

"Can I get you something to drink, Mrs. Bellingham? I could offer you a diet soda or water . . ."

"That won't be necessary." When she sits and crosses her legs, I notice that she has dressed in heels and stockings even for this casual visit. "Tell me all about yourself, Mr. Cannon. New neighbors are an unusual treat on this floor."

I sit in a creaky chair that has seen better days. "Call me Phil, please."

"You look more like a Philip." She tilts her head, and from this angle I can see a discreet hearing aid. "Are you a native New Yorker?"

"No, ma'am. Born and raised in St. Louis, Missouri. But after college I wrote a few papers and the next thing I knew, NYU offered me a part-time position on their faculty. I teach there now. I do consulting work when I'm not teaching."

She lifts a brow. "You must do very well."

"I make a decent living. It's nothing spectacular, but it keeps me in computers and video games."

Her answering smile is more a mechanical civility than an expression of pleasure, so I assume she doesn't share my enthusiasm for technology.

"So . . . you've lived in New York for some time?"

"Before moving here, I had an apartment in Brooklyn. But I didn't like the commute, so as soon as I could afford it, I began to look for a place in Manhattan. My real-estate agent was thrilled to find this apartment." *Thrilled by the commission*, I want to add, but hold my tongue.

Mrs. Bellingham brings the tips of her fingers together in a delicate gesture. "It's hard to believe such a promising young man hasn't married."

She's diplomatic; I'll give her that. "I was engaged to be married once, to a girl from back home. But she didn't want to leave St. Louis, and I've always thought of myself as more suited to urban living. So we broke up."

Mrs. Bellingham makes soft tsking noises. "A shame you couldn't compromise."

I shrug. "I've decided some men aren't meant to be married."

"But you're not . . . you know."

She waggles her brows and heat flows from my neck into my face when I catch her meaning. "No, I'm not gay."

Pressing a hand to her thin chest, she manages a choking chuckle. "One can never be certain these days, especially in *this* city. Every Sunday I pick up the *Times* and read about those 'same-sex commitment ceremonies'—well, I'm sure you can see why it's not safe to assume anything anymore. Especially when you meet someone who is . . . legally unattached."

"I'm not single because I'm gay," I answer, trying to keep my tone light. "I'm single because I'm an economist. I meet women; they ask what I do; I tell them. Most of them run for the exit within sixty seconds."

Mrs. Bellingham twitters. "I find that hard to believe; you're such a charming young man. I love self-deprecating humor."

"Really." Amazed that she is so easily entertained, I decide to offer one of my best riffs. "I assume you know the definition of an economist."

She looks at me, brows raised, and gives me a half-smile. "Why don't you enlighten me."

"All right—an economist is someone who finds something that works in practice . . . and wonders whether it would work in theory."

Nine of out ten women who hear that joke only stare at me, but Mrs. Bellingham chuckles. "What a delight to have you on the fifteenth floor with us, Philip. Especially now that Mary Elizabeth is gone."

"Was she Mr. Williamson's wife?"

"Oh, no. Mary Elizabeth was Aurora's mother."

I nod; names and faces are beginning to connect. "Aurora is the young woman next door? I met her earlier today, but I think I caught her at a bad time."

"That's probably true." Her brow arches. "Did she mention her mother?"

"She said she buried her mother today."

"The service was held this morning." A faint line appears between the woman's thin brows. "Mary Elizabeth was my dearest friend, and I love Aurora like a daughter. I suppose that's why I'm so worried about her."

Not certain I want to hear gossip about my neighbor, I stretch my arm along the back of the chair and look around for an excuse to escape. I'd like to finish with Mrs. Bellingham's quiz so I can go downstairs and pick up my boxes, but it'd be rude not to reply to her statement. "Aurora seemed well enough to me," I answer. "A bit distracted perhaps, but surely that's normal in her situation."

"Distracted? My, what an understatement." She shakes her head with that helplessness I've seen women adopt when they talk about troublesome children. "Aurora is a jewel, but not really capable of functioning in the real world, if you know what I mean."

Despite my good intentions, I can't resist the bait. "I don't quite follow."

"You didn't speak to her at length, did you?"

"Only briefly."

"Well"—Mrs. Bellingham leans forward—"have you ever met people who are too naive and timid to survive in the real world?

Aurora is like that. Even as a child, she lived in books and fantasy worlds. As a teenager she would rather read than date, and I don't think she had a single boyfriend through her entire adolescence. I didn't think she'd summon up the gumption to go away to college, but she surprised me by enrolling at some small girls' school in Virginia—Sweet Briar, I think—but after graduation she came home and planted herself right back in her mother's apartment. She was working at a bookstore at the time, then she went and surprised us all by falling in love with a young man who actually wanted to marry her—but by that time Mary Elizabeth had begun to slip. So that was the end of that."

"I don't understand. What was the end of what?"

"Why, the engagement, of course! Aurora's young man wanted to marry her right away, and Aurora refused to put her mother in an institution. The young man—I forget his name—wouldn't even consider moving into the apartment with M.E. and Aurora, so they had a big argument and we never saw him again." Mrs. Bellingham flicks her hands in a dismissive gesture. "Afterward, of course, I told Aurora she was better off without him. He didn't seem to like Mary Elizabeth at all, and everyone knows you can't come between a girl and her mother."

"So . . . Aurora and her mother were really close?"

"Truly. Mary Elizabeth was thirty-five when she had Aurora, so she was a mature first-time mother and extremely devoted. When Mary Elizabeth's mind began to wander, Aurora quit her job and stayed home to help. I suppose you could say she's lived as her mother's shadow for the last ten years. She might have nursed her mother for another ten if Mary Elizabeth's heart hadn't given out. Now Aurora's rambling around in that big apartment all by herself. I'm worried to death about her."

Not knowing what to say, I prop my chin in my hand and regard my guest with what I hope is a compassionate look. Mrs. Bellingham seems sincere, but she has to be exaggerating. The woman I met in the hallway was no helpless ingénue. She stuffed that bulky trash bag down the chute with considerable determination.

"Well . . . I think it's admirable that she wanted to take care of her mother. I'm sure she'll find a way to make a new life for herself. Maybe she'll even look up that old boyfriend."

Mrs. Bellingham straightens and holds me in a level gaze. "I'm afraid that's quite impossible."

"Why not? Stranger things have happened."

"Aurora would never speak to that young man again. And all those years of being alone up here . . . well, I'm afraid they've broken her spirit."

"I've heard that care giving is extremely stressful—"

"Of course it is, but that's not what I'm talking about. But before I can explain her problem, you have to understand her background." Mrs. Bellingham lowers her voice to a conspiratorial tone. "Haven't you put it together? Aurora *Norquest*? Of Manhattan?"

I rake my hand through my hair, frustrated that I am failing a quiz on material I didn't know I was supposed to study. I am not a Manhattan blue blood, I have no idea what families are listed in the social register or if such a thing still exists, and I couldn't care less that the Westbury Arms is six stories taller than the Dakota—

From a sea of swirling thoughts, one possible answer leaps up at me. "The only Norquest I know is the horror novelist."

Mrs. Bellingham applauds, her face a mask of pleased surprise. "You *are* quick, young man."

My jaw drops. "Get out. Theodore Norquest lives *here*?"

"*Lived* here—until he abandoned his pregnant wife and ran off to Europe to raise another family. Aurora is his daughter."

I don't know anything about the writer's marital history, but probably three-quarters of the civilized world has heard of Theodore Norquest's spectacularly successful horror novels. Several of his books have been reworked as screenplays, and an A-list of Hollywood's finest have made his stories familiar even to the nonreading public.

I let my head fall back to the cracked vinyl and grin at the silent ceiling fan. "Theodore Norquest's daughter lives next door. How wild is that?"

"Several celebrities have lived in the building from time to time. Just like the Dakota."

I lift my head. "Anyone famous living here now?"

Her smile diminishes slightly. "Not at the moment."

My thoughts veer to my collection of first-edition Norquest novels, any one of which would become infinitely more valuable if autographed. "Does Norquest ever visit?"

"Sadly, no. Mary Elizabeth and her husband did *not* part amicably, and after the split M.E. couldn't say his name without hissing. Ted lives in Europe, and he's never met his daughter. I doubt he ever thinks of her."

I am too surprised to respond with more than a nod, then a dart of sympathetic pain makes me wince. I can't imagine being estranged from my parents. Even though I haven't lived at home in years, we still keep in touch.

But I don't want to discuss my family—and Mrs. Bellingham is obviously eager to talk about my neighbor's.

"Norquest must be ancient by now," I say, thinking aloud. "I remember reading his books when I was a teenager."

Mrs. Bellingham chuckles. "Careful, young man—Ted Norquest is my age. M.E. and Ted went everywhere with me and my husband, Charley, when we were younger. We used to go out for dinner and dancing two or three nights a week. When the Norquest marriage broke up, Ted moved to London. Shortly after that, Aurora was born. My Charley, God rest him, is the closest thing to a father the girl has ever known. She wept for days when he passed."

I look toward the long gallery that stretches to my door and the outer wall of Aurora Norquest's apartment. "Did Norquest never even *try* to see his daughter?"

"Not to my knowledge—and I daresay I know everything that's happened in that girl's life. I'm 'Auntie Clara' to her, and now that her mother is gone, I'm probably the only living soul who loves her." The woman's lined mouth quirks in a melancholy smile. "Sad, isn't it?"

"Extremely."

"So you can see why I'm glad you've come to live here. Aurora needs the company of someone her own age. She's had far too few male friends."

Uh-oh. A cold knot forms in my stomach when I look up and see the determination in her eyes. The *last* thing I need in my life is a matchmaker.

I lift my hand to cover an anxious cough. "I'm afraid I won't be much help in that department, Mrs. Bellingham. I think I'm certifiably undateable."

Her laugh ripples through the air. "That's the point, Philip—so is Aurora."

"Pardon?"

"She doesn't go out—she *won't* go out. She wouldn't even go to her mother's funeral."

I shift in the chair as my mind races. Once again I have the feeling she's testing me on material she's only allowed me to glimpse.

"All those years of nursing have turned her into a sort of recluse," Mrs. Bellingham says, a tinge of sadness in her eyes. "She has no interest in anything outside that apartment. Oh, she reads and watches television, and she's as bright as they come. But just try to get her out of the house—it's impossible."

"She doesn't go out at *all*?"

Mrs. Bellingham gave a tense shake of her head. "Not anymore. It's a tragedy, really. She's never been much of a social creature, and after she quit her bookstore job, she squirreled herself away in the apartment with Mary Elizabeth. She used to go out in the beginning—I'd sit with M.E. so Aurora could go to the drugstore or grocery—but while she was out, she couldn't stop worrying about her mother. Eventually she decided it was simpler to stay home and arrange for deliveries. Some of her friends used to come around and try to pry her out, but after a while, they stopped coming. Now I'm afraid I'm the only friend she has left."

Not certain what she wants from me, I shift my gaze to the cracked veneer on an end table.

"Please don't think I'm trying to arrange anything between you two," she says. "I'm not urging you to *marry* Aurora—she's proven she can take care of herself. But she could use a friend."

I look up, struck by the note of wistfulness in the woman's voice.

"Heavens, look at the time." Mrs. Bellingham taps her watch. "I have to run. I have to get to the library to pick up a few books for Aurora, then I have to run to a dinner appointment. But it's been lovely to visit with you."

I stand to walk her to the door, but Mrs. Bellingham is halfway down the gallery by the time I extricate myself from the uncomfortable chair.

She smiles as I reach out to open the door. "I hope you enjoy living here, Philip Cannon. If you need anything at all, don't hesitate to knock." She twiddles her manicured fingers in a quick wave, then sails away, moving down the hallway at a surprisingly quick pace.

I linger in the hall until she is safely inside, then I glance toward the Norquest apartment. No light seeps from beneath that closed door; no signs indicate anyone lives behind it. Hard to believe I'm living next to the daughter of one of the world's most successful writers . . . and harder still to believe my elderly neighbor wants to fix me up with a recluse.

At this point, I have more mundane things on my mind. I have to unpack, set up my computer, and decide which pieces of Mr.

Williamson's odious furniture can remain and which must be replaced. Once my apartment is set up, I need to analyze the data for my latest consulting project and grade a stack of papers from my students. Relationships, even friendships, require time, and I have never had trouble filling the hours of a day.

Now, though, I have boxes waiting in the lobby. I pat my pockets to be sure I have my keys, then close the door behind me. I press the elevator call button, then step back to study the layout of the hallway. Two elevators serve this floor—one beside my door, the other at the end of the hallway, next to Mrs. Bellingham's apartment and across from Aurora Norquest's. Three tall windows flood the public area with light and offer a lovely view of the building's center courtyard. Across from the windows, a flight of wooden stairs leads up to a single gray door marked with a "No Admittance" sign.

The stairway to the roof, apparently. Sometime after I am settled I might go up there and have a look around. Ought to be quite a view.

4

APARTMENT 15A

I smooth a wrinkle from my mother's best linen tablecloth, replace the silver candelabra and the floral arrangements, then step back to evaluate my efforts. Finally. This room, at least, would now merit Mother's approval.

I pull up my hair, fan the back of my neck, then hurry toward the kitchen, the next room on my mental list. The caterers brought food in long foil trays, which are now stacked by the sink and waiting to be tossed out. I could slip them into garbage bags and carry them to the chute, but the thought of meeting Philip Cannon again stops me. If the man is in the process of moving, he will be in and out of the hallway throughout the day and night.

I don't want to talk to him again.

Not today.

I run water in the sink until it burns my fingers, then plug the drain with the rubber stopper. After adding a squirt of dishwashing liquid, I drop my mother's sterling silver flatware into the basin. Should I count the pieces? Some of my mother's friends might have taken forks and spoons as souvenirs of happy dinners at her table . . . but I don't care. What do I need with twelve matching forks?

As the silverware soaks, I grab a dishtowel and wipe the counter, then reposition the salt and pepper shakers that have wandered away from the stovetop. The kitchen is small but efficient, and I am at home here. I am making progress, getting things done.

I open the pantry to return a box of plastic wrap, then pause, my gaze sliding over cans of soup, canisters of oatmeal, and jars of apple-sauce—all the easy-to-swallow foods Mother required. Awareness seeps around the edges of my concentration. Though Mother was the invalid, I adopted her limitations. But now I can have pizza if I want it. I can eat steak without guilt. I can scarcely remember what either tastes like, but I will enjoy them soon enough.

I close the pantry door on a wave of giddy relief.

A stack of assorted papers litters one end of the counter—a pile that didn't exist this morning. I pick up the stack and flip through its contents—sympathy cards, the program from the funeral, a copy of the caterer's invoice, a bulging manila envelope. Clara must have gathered these odds and ends for me.

I slide onto a barstool and read the cards. Several are from people whose faces I remember from the wake; many are from acquaintances I haven't seen in years. The memorial program is as Mother wanted it—short and simple—and the caterer's bill is merely a formality. The original will be sent to my accountant, who will write out a check without bothering me for approval.

The bulky envelope gives me pause—it bears the logo of the mortuary, and inside I find a white book, its cover stamped with gold foil: *In honor of your loved one, from Whitman's Funeral Home.*

It's a Holy Bible. I hold it flat against my palm, faintly amused by its presence. Clara brings me half a dozen library books each week, but she has never brought me a Bible—unless you count the time she brought *The Complete Bible of Eldercare: Learning to Live with a Difficult Older Parent.*

Curious, I open the leather cover and peer at the printing inside. The pages are thin, almost like tissue paper, and the writing dense and dark. The text is arranged in two columns on each page, and some of the pages have words printed in red ink—whatever for? After a few minutes of skimming the text, I have my answer—the red ink indicates the words of Jesus.

"Why not highlight them in yellow?" I ask the air. "Yellow over black text would be easier to read."

The sound of my voice warms the room, making me feel a little less alone. Clara would think I'd lost my mind if she heard me talking to myself, but months ago I realized that Mother rested more easily if she heard voices in the apartment. So I developed the habit of thinking aloud. When I didn't feel like talking, I turned on the radio or television to fill the apartment with sounds of life.

That's going to be a hard habit to break. I've grown used to background noise. And I have been my mother's keeper for so long I can't imagine myself playing any other role.

I tuck the Bible under my arm and move across the foyer and into the living room. I toss the cards onto the desktop and suddenly wish I hadn't given Gloria permission to take Mother's glass paperweight. I don't correspond with anyone regularly, but this week I will have to write a special letter to Aunt Clara, a message to the minister who performed the service, and thank-you notes to those who sent flowers. I would have enjoyed holding the smooth glass in my hand as I scratched out messages on Mother's linen stationery.

I sink into the desk chair and stare moodily at the stack of sympathy cards. So many ends to tie up after a death. Mother handled most of the details, but she couldn't do everything. She couldn't prepare me for the crushing emptiness I would feel or for the guilt that hunkers at the back of my mind.

I crouch in the desk chair, feeling myself compressed into an ever-shrinking space between the weight of loneliness and overwhelming relief.

My mother is gone—I loved her; I cared for her; I suffered with her. I wasn't a perfect daughter, but my weaknesses bound me to her. She forgave me for being the daughter of a man whose name she could scarcely stand to pronounce; every day I forgave her for countless rebukes and hurtful comments spoken in the throes of dementia.

Now . . . I am free. I can eat whatever I like; I can clean out this cluttered apartment; I can sleep through the night with my door closed. My life is my own . . . but what am I to do with it?

No one has asked that question, but I feel it hanging over my head like the sword of Damocles. Clara will be gentle, but she will certainly ask what I plan to do next. My accountant will ask. Mother's lawyer will ask when he calls to discuss the estate. When one of the doormen delivers a package to my door, he will casually ask: *And what, Miss Norquest, are you going to do now?*

The question is a hallway with a dozen shadowy doors, each of them opening to unknown terrors. I have no idea what to do next . . . because I have no idea where I fit in the world outside these walls.

If I could backtrack, perhaps I could find my footing.

When I graduated from college, I thought I might become a writer or an English professor. The one consistent passion of my life is a love of literature. Though I have been imprisoned by my mother's illness and my own anxieties, I have never minded my solitary state. Through the pages of books I have traveled the world and met people even bolder and brasher than Mother's friends. I have examined thoughts and measured philosophies far beyond my confined existence.

I would love to teach . . . but I'd have to take education classes and then I'd have to *go* to my students. Trouble is, I can't go anywhere.

The memory of my last excursion sets my teeth on edge. The day after Christmas 1998, Nadine Casper, my roommate from college, knocked on my door and begged me to join her in a Fifth Avenue shopping spree. What could I do? I tried to explain that my mother was ill, but Clara volunteered to sit with Mother all day. And Nadine had taken the train from Washington to surprise me and snatch up a few postholiday bargains . . .

Not wanting to disappoint one of the few friends who still kept in touch, I swallowed my anxiety, pulled on my coat, and left a list of instructions with Clara. I knew I shouldn't worry—Clara adored

Mother and would be an excellent sitter—but by the time Nadine and I reached the elevator, an ugly swarm of fearful thoughts had fogged my brain and clouded my vision. I couldn't conceal my nervousness; my hands trembled and my teeth chattered, but Nadine didn't seem to notice as we stepped into the elevator.

I should have turned back, I *wanted* to turn back, but going forward seemed easier than making halfhearted explanations that made no sense even to me. And so I faced the elevator doors and closed my eyes. Nadine rattled on about the stores she wanted to visit and her children's Christmas gifts, but I could barely hear her above the thudding of my heart and the raspy sound of my own breath. The thudding increased in volume and tempo as the car descended; my breathing quickened into short, abrasive gasps. When the doors finally opened, revealing a small knot of winter-clad neighbors, I . . . lost it.

Even now the memory has the power to sear my cheeks. I don't recall much about those moments—I remember screaming and running to the back of the elevator car, huddling on the floor while Booker, the doorman, knelt beside me, cradling my gloved hand in his. Someone called, "Get a doctor," but someone else said, "Get her upstairs," and even through my tears and crying I knew yes, yes, *home* was the answer.

They half-carried me back to the apartment and put me to bed, and Clara fussed over me the rest of the day, declaring that I'd caught some kind of virus. Nadine came into my room and apologized for convincing me to go out when I was obviously not feeling well. Before she left, she promised to come back when I was feeling better.

She never returned. I can't blame her, because I know she leads a busy life. If she thinks of me at all, she probably feels guilty, but I don't blame her for anything.

And I never got better—about leaving the apartment, that is. Now I know that I am like a conch, perfectly at home in my shell and completely vulnerable outside it. Clara seems to understand this, too, because after that day she stopped harping about my need for a social life.

So . . . I can't become a teacher. I could write, but what would I write about? Poets and novelists draw from their life experiences, and I have no experiences worth sharing.

Maybe I could be like Aunt Clara. She doesn't work; like me, she has money and time to spare. She serves on several boards, including the board of directors for the Westbury Arms and the Metropolitan Museum. I could follow her example and involve myself in volunteer work . . . but that might eventually require leaving the apartment and trying to negotiate a world I left so many years ago—

An icy quiver ascends to the back of my neck. I can't do that. Not now, not this month. I am too tightly wrapped up in this apartment, in all I know as home.

My thoughts skitter toward a word I have never spoken aloud, not even to Clara: *agoraphobia*, a condition that often results in panic whenever a sufferer attempts to leave home. I don't want to believe I have developed a mental disorder, but hours of reading about the topic have convinced me that mentally healthy people do not break down in tears and trembling after entering an elevator designed to carry them away from the fifteenth floor.

I prefer to think I am simply most comfortable here, in the home my mother created. I haven't had a panic attack in years, though I do occasionally become anxious during spells of bad weather. My affliction, if that's what it is, is under control. Like a compulsive overeater who has learned to avoid stressful situations that would trigger overeating, I avoid the elevator. I stay home. I'm fine.

But if I am going to change my life, I might have to step out.

I can't.

Well, maybe I could.

Perhaps I can take baby steps.

I can't help but smile as the image of Bill Murray flits into my mind. One of our local stations airs the movie *What About Bob?* at least once a month, yet I never grow tired of watching the phobic Bob/Bill Murray cling obsessively to his psychiatrist, a self-centered shrink who invents a therapy called "baby steps."

If Bob can find healing by taking baby steps, maybe I can, too. I can't deny that the hunger for change is gnawing at my heart.

My gaze drifts over the furniture in the living room—the upholstered sofa my mother adored, the high-backed wing chairs, the gleaming oak tables. A modern designer would probably consider this space a delightful example of traditional decorating, but I am yearning for something fresh. And now that Mother has no need for the security of familiar surroundings . . .

I'll redecorate. Room by room, on a careful and calculated timetable. I'll begin in here and work slowly through the apartment. That awful falcon wallpaper will disappear from the foyer, replaced by something soft and soothing. I'll ditch my mother's beiges and blues and grays and choose something brighter—yellow?—but I'll be cautious. Nothing too drastic, nothing that would send Clara screaming for her interior designer. I'll watch some of those home improvement shows and try to get a sense of what's stylish in furnishings these days.

I'll be happy.

I close my eyes, half-afraid I might burst from a sudden swell of exhilaration. Like those adoptive parents putting new clothes on their little ones, I will redecorate *my* apartment. I'll choose projects I can manage without too much difficulty. Surely I can learn to paint and wallpaper and sew draperies and pillows. If I work slowly, tackling no more than one room per month, my home improvement project will fill my days and nights for—I pause to count rooms on my fingers—at least nine months. Almost a year.

Suddenly energized, I shove the stack of sympathy cards to the side of the desk, but in my enthusiasm I overemphasize the gesture.

The Bible slides across the desk and falls, landing upside down and open on the carpet amid a cluster of cards.

I lift my gaze to the ceiling, hoping the God of the red ink won't consider my unfortunate shove some sort of sacrilege. When lightning doesn't rip through the plaster, I pick the Bible up and turn it over. A poem on the wrinkled page leaps up at me:

> Do not remember the former things,
> Nor consider the things of old.
> Behold, I will do a new thing,
> Now it shall spring forth;
> Shall you not know it?

I am pleasantly surprised. I've never read the Bible, and the few snippets I've heard quoted rumbled with thees and thous and dire threatenings.

But I like this. *A new thing?* Never has a line of poetry pleased me more.

I close the Bible and hold it to my chest, grateful that Clara set it aside for me. I'm ready for a new thing. I am ready to embark on a new adventure, and I like the flutter of independence rippling through my veins. I may be nearly alone in the world, but I can take baby steps.

Someday I will find the courage to leave the Westbury Arms . . . but first I have to attack the walls of this apartment. For years they kept my mother safely confined, but for too long I have let them imprison me as well.

I am curled up in the library, my feet tucked beneath me on the velveteen love seat, a chenille throw wrapped around my shoulders. A single lamp burns on the library table, casting a golden glow over the bookcase lined with leather-bound classics. Our largest TV (a whopping seventeen inches) nestles amid the books on a shelf. Because Mother always thought it the height of bad taste to place a television in the living room, our largest set has been banished to this former servant's chamber, an arrangement that suits me. The library is cozier than the living room, and I have always felt at home among books.

I press the button on the remote, then frown as the screen fills with the image of O. J. Simpson seated at a table with a man in a suit. I *know* this scene; virtually everyone in America watched portions of Simpson's murder trial. I squint at the TV, trying to remember who served as Simpson's lawyer. At the instant the name occurs to me—Johnnie Cochran—my mother drifts into the room.

My stomach drops. The empty place in my middle fills with a terrifying hollowness as Mother stares at the television, one hand plucking at her short summer nightgown, the other quavering as she points to the screen.

"I know that man," she says, her eyes focused on the TV. "He came to one of our dinner parties last year."

My hands are slick with sweat, yet my mind has gone cold and sharp, focused on what *cannot* be happening. My mother is dead; I don't believe in ghosts, so this *must* be a dream.

But it feels real.

"No, Mother." I answer in the flat, high-pitched voice of fear. "That's Johnnie Cochran. He's never been to our home."

"I'm sure he has." The voice that used to dominate Manhattan's finest living rooms and dining tables is velvet edged with steel. "You don't remember, Aurora, because your nose is always stuck in a book."

Trembling, I pick up the remote and press the power off. Years of living with a dementia patient have taught me not to argue.

When the screen goes dark, she looks at me. "I must speak with you."

Dream or not, I can't resist the force of her personality. Under the pressure of her burning gaze, I lower my feet from the furniture. "Is there a problem?"

"You threw out my eyeglasses."

"I haven't seen your glasses, Mother."

"You're always throwing them out. I always leave them on the desk in the living room, but they're not there."

"I would never throw anything of yours away. You've misplaced them, that's all."

"I am not stupid." She lifts one eyebrow, suggesting in maternal shorthand that I have committed a major transgression. "I suggest you get off my love seat and get busy finding my glasses."

"I will get up, Mother," I say, standing, "and I will help you find your glasses."

The thin line of her mouth clamps tight, then the soft flesh at her throat ripples as she swallows. "You hate me." Tears well within her blue eyes. "You want me dead."

"No, Mother, I don't."

"You love your pig of a father more than me!"

"Mother—"

"You are trying to kill me!"

"That's enough, Mother."

I take her arm, amazed at how solid she feels in my grip. Now I can be firm with her, unlike the early days when I suffered from the mistaken belief that I could allow her to remain in control. "Come, Mother, let me take you back to your room."

"No!" Her expression twists, the dignified veneer peeling away to reveal unreasoning terror underneath. I am still holding her arm, so she whirls toward me, slapping at my shoulders, my head, my cheeks . . .

"Mother!"

She is screaming now, cursing as expertly as a football coach. I bring one hand up to shield my face and tug at her with the other, but she resists, slapping and spewing invectives while she leans in the opposite direction. Her bare feet will not slide over the wooden floors, so when I pull her forward, she loses her balance, one frightened cry escaping her lips before she upsets a painting and hits her head on the edge of a table in the gallery—

The force of her fall yanks her arm from my grip. I turn in time to see her eyes close, her mouth go slack, and her feet slide out from under her.

"Mother?"

She is silent, lying on the floor, one arm extended toward me, the other curled beneath her cheek. I kneel beside her, fear blowing down the back of my neck as I slip my hand beneath her head. "Mother?"

Her eyes move beneath her paper-thin lids, then grow still as a small gasp escapes her lips. When I pull my hand free, a red smear adorns my palm.

Fear and anger have knotted inside me. "Mom?"

Her eyelids lift; she looks at me with triumph in her gaze. Her hand, bony and sharp, rises to snap around my wrist like a manacle. While I struggle to escape her grip, her thin frame wrinkles and shrivels and contracts in upon itself. Her face, which retained a measure of loveliness even in her long illness, goes the color of gray thunderclouds, while her lustrous hair stiffens to the texture of straw. But her eyes stay focused on me, hot and bright, until they finally cloud over, empty, and pop like crystalline eggshells.

I back away, my hands over my mouth, as her body disintegrates and a voice inside my head repeats, *This is a dream, not real, only a dream*, but I was touching her, hearing her, she was *here*—

I close my eyes to escape the horror, and when I open them again, I am alone in the library, an old episode of *Friends* is playing on the television, and the comforting hiss of the radiator beneath the window reminds me that it is autumn, not summer. I inhale deeply, and as the air rushes through my airways, I can taste autumn and wool and the lemon Pledge I used to dust the shelves a few hours ago.

I swing my feet to the floor, lean forward, and hesitate in my bent position. I've been dreaming, that's all. My subconscious has been overloaded with emotions and memories that couldn't help but spill out when I fell asleep.

I stand and look in the small mirror on the wall above the library table. My eyes are bloodshot, my hair frazzled. I should go to bed. Tomorrow, as Clara often says, will take care of itself.

I switch off the lamp, then turn to shut the door behind me. I don't know why I keep closing the interior doors—probably because Mother insisted on tidy habits. In the hallway, I notice that Mother's prized Jonathan Green painting has tilted. I reach out and touch the edge, nudging it forward, then frown when my fingers glide over the gallery table and dampness.

I bring my hand into the glow of the gallery chandelier, and the muscles of my throat move in a convulsive swallow.

My fingertips are wet with blood.

5

APARTMENT 15B

An unexpected sound tears me from my dream. I had been teaching, writing on the dry erase board, when an unseen student posed a question about statistics and probability. I had just begun to turn toward the class when a sudden blare of music jerked me from one world and thrust me into another—

I sit up, trying to orient myself, and remember I am no longer in Brooklyn. I'm in my new apartment, sleeping in the previous tenant's lumpy bed, and the Bangles are blaring through the wall.

Walk like an Egyptian . . .

What in the world?

I fling off the covers and move toward the door, then yell as my big toe slams into an unyielding object. Nursing my injured digit, I hop to the bedside table, fumble with the switch on the lamp, and glance at the clock.

Three a.m. A completely inappropriate hour for any civilized adult to be rockin' to the oldies.

I glance at the ceiling, half expecting to see the suspended fan vibrating in time to the music, but it continues to spin in a steady creaking whirl. Besides, this is the building's top floor, so I doubt a rock band would choose to rehearse on the roof.

I hiss softly as I draw breath through my teeth and massage my throbbing toe. The sound has to be coming from Aurora Norquest's

apartment. I'd never have expected a timid recluse to be a troublesome neighbor, but sometimes you can't tell about a person until
you've lived next to them for a while.

Groaning, I fall back upon the bed and close my eyes. Maybe I can
sleep despite the music . . . no, I can't. It's too loud, too rhythmic,
and too familiar. Part of my brain—the section charged with storing
adolescent memories—wants to sing along, and I'd like to pursue my
adult dreams without a guest appearance from the Bangles.

I sit up, yank my robe from a chair, and shrug my way into it.
Hobbling to favor my injured toe, I move to the doorway, then turn
and stare at the wall dividing my apartment from Aurora Norquest's.

What am I supposed to do? This would be easier if we were
friends. I could knock on her door, offer a sheepish smile, and say
something like, "Hey, Aurora, do you mind turning it down a
notch? I've got a busy day tomorrow."

If we were friends, she'd grin, apologize, and lower the volume.

But we're not friends. We're acquaintances, at best. I'm friendlier
with Mrs. Bellingham than Aurora, so maybe she could say something.

No. The older woman wears a hearing aid, lives on the other side
of the building, and probably doesn't even know Aurora likes to
boogie in the early morning hours. She's probably sleeping like an
infant while Aurora jams and that funky old Bangles video plays on
the backs of my eyelids.

I could call Aurora's apartment . . . if I had her number. The odds
of finding it in the phone book are slim, and I can't risk waking
strangers at this ungodly hour. I could call downstairs and ask the
doorman to ring Aurora's place, but she might resent being scolded
by a third party. Despite my annoyance, I don't want to make a bad
impression on my new neighbor . . . especially not on my first night
in the building.

And she's Theodore Norquest's daughter.

I walk back to the bed and press my fingertips to the wall behind the headboard. The plaster thrums faintly with the beat of the music, then stills.

Silence.

I remove my hand and hold it aloft, half-expecting the music to begin again, but a heavy after-hours quiet descends upon the room. After a moment, I sink to the bed and consider my options.

I have no idea how the apartment next door is arranged. The space behind this wall might be Aurora's bedroom, a library, or an exercise room. On my tour of the building, the super explained the original apartments had been renovated and modernized through the years; almost anything could lie behind this wall. And if my bedroom happens to lie next to Aurora Norquest's stereo, I might have to reconsider my sleeping arrangements.

I listen, hearing nothing but the clank of the radiator and the heavy sound of my own breathing. Perhaps it was an accident—an unattended CD player/alarm clock mistakenly set to the wrong time. Sure, it must have been a fluke. Nothing else makes sense.

I turn out the lamp and slide between the covers. Lying in the dark, I stare at the shadowed ceiling and listen intently, but no other noises break the quiet of the night.

After a long moment, I laugh, the sound muffled against my pillow as I turn onto my side. "Walk like an Egyptian?" I ask the darkness. "The *Bangles?*"

If my toe weren't throbbing, I might believe I dreamed the entire episode. And perhaps Aurora Norquest is blameless in this—some kid on the fifth floor might have his radio sitting next to a vent that snakes its way to the roof through the wall behind my bed. Old buildings are capricious, the real-estate agent had said, and they can be mischievous.

Still, for the sake of sociability, I ought to stop by and spend a little time with Aurora Norquest. If she's as reclusive as Clara Bellingham says, she might not welcome my visit, but I've found that people can be nice and neighborly even in New York. If I express an interest in the architecture of this old building, she might give me a quick tour of her place.

If she does, and if I discover her stereo behind this wall, I might need to move my things into the guest room.

6

APARTMENT 15A

The only window in my bedroom faces north, but sunlight spangles my walls when I open my eyes the morning after my mother's funeral. I slip my cold toes into my worn puppy slippers, then pull my robe from a hook on the back of the door and belt myself in.

Only one thing has changed since I went to bed, a small shift I can't help but notice as I glance at my nightstand. The CD player/alarm clock stands open; my favorite *Hits of the '80s* disc waits to be played again. After dreaming of blood and my mother last night, I had awakened in such terror that I'd turned on the lights and cranked up my music, then cowered beneath the covers for the length of my favorite Bangles song. By the time the last Egyptian had walked across the desert sands, the real world had closed around me once again.

Humming the Bangles tune, I open my door and brace myself to face the rest of the apartment.

The long gallery is dark, shut off to the sun by a series of closed doors, but I am hungering for brightness. Beginning with my mother's room, I move through the hallway and fling doors open, allowing the midmorning sun's reflected glory to seep over the carpets and warm the walls. I pause outside the library to check the gallery table and the Jonathan Green painting—everything is as it should be. No pictures are askew, no decaying bodies lie on the rug, the edge of the table is not smeared with blood.

Even my fingertips are clean.

I dreamed . . . everything.

I click my tongue against my teeth, chiding myself for my skittishness. I've been through a lot in the last week—anyone would agree with *that*—so maybe a crazy dream-within-a-dream isn't crazy at all.

A garbage bag, neatly tied, squats beside the front door—a reminder I set out last night before going to bed. The stainless steel door over the garbage chute—the chute directly across from Philip Cannon's apartment—closes with a clang, so I decided not to take out the trash at 1 a.m.

But surely my new neighbor is up and out by now.

I move through the foyer, my puppy slippers making soft shushing noises on the tiles, then release the three latches. After cinching my robe tighter around my waist, I pick up the trash bag, open the door, and step out into the hall . . . and discover I am not alone. Like security guards with nothing to do, Clara and Philip Cannon stand between me and my destination. Clara is wearing a suit, apparently headed out, but our new neighbor is wearing jeans, a flannel shirt, and . . . socks.

Staring at his feet, I realize he's not going anywhere.

I hesitate, wondering if I can slip back inside without being noticed, but Clara knows the sound of my door. "Good morning, Aurora," she calls, lowering her chin to peer at me through the top of her bifocals. "Sleeping late today, are you?"

I shrug to hide my embarrassment. "Excuse me—I gotta run back inside. I forgot something."

Suddenly grateful for the concealing bulkiness of my hair, I turn toward my door and wince when our new neighbor speaks, too.

"Wait, Aurora. Is that garbage? Let me get that for you."

My cheeks flush against the cool air of the hallway. I'm tempted to dash back into my apartment, but he'd probably think that strange.

I turn to face them. "That's okay, I can manage," I call in a loud voice, hoping to keep Philip Cannon at a distance. "As you can see, I'm not really prepared to greet anyone. I haven't had time to take a shower or . . . anything." Avoiding his eyes, I lower my chin, circle the neck of the trash bag with both hands, and waddle toward the chute . . . and my new neighbor.

The Boy Scout will not be dissuaded. "Don't worry; I've seen women in their bathrobes." His voice brims with humor as he moves to intercept me. "Back home, my mom fetches the newspaper and waters her garden in her pajamas every morning."

Despite my annoyance, I can't resist looking at Clara, who is watching with an amused smile.

Cannon draws closer; I hand off the garbage and step behind Clara's petite frame. I am suddenly aware that my flannel robe is faded, my slippers shoddy, my hair frowzy. I haven't even looked in a mirror yet, so for all I know I have gunk in the corners of my eyes, drool on my chin, and yesterday's mascara entrenched in the bags beneath my lower lashes. But maybe he won't notice my appearance.

"Nice slippers." Chuckling, he glances over his shoulder as he hauls the trash toward the chute. I am so convinced he's about to begin a bona fide conversation that I whirl on the ball of my foot and hurry toward my apartment as if the hounds of hell were giving chase.

Though I call a hoarse "thanks" for this unexpected act of gallantry, I know Clara will apologize for my appalling manners. She has become my surrogate mother, and any mother who discovers an available, reasonably attractive man lingering in the hallway would invite said gentleman in for tea and a shot at the unmarried thirty-five-year-old daughter no matter how unattractive his glasses.

I close my door and lean against it, but three or four minutes pass before my pulse slows to a more normal rate. I hear murmured voices from the hallway, but I don't need to eavesdrop. Philip Cannon is undoubtedly talking about his mother back in Hicksville; Clara will respond by saying I'm more well-bred than my manners would suggest.

My head clunks against the door as a sudden thought occurs— Clara, who has never approved of my mostly nonexistent love life, not even when I became engaged to Josh, stopped trying to fix me up only when Mother became ill. Now that Mother is gone, Clara is likely to resume her matchmaking efforts . . . beginning with Philip Cannon.

Poor man.

I tuck the thought away and lower my chin, regarding the foyer with bleary eyes. I need a cup of coffee. That and a hot shower will clear my head.

The kitchen, at least, is sunny and bright—a single window nestles between the cupboards, flooding the space with much-needed light. As I fill the coffee decanter, I tell myself not to think about the chores waiting at the end of the gallery. The three doors at the north end of the hall lead to my bedroom, a shared bathroom, and Mother's bedroom. I can't look inside the latter space without seeing a dozen things I need to handle, but I can't summon the willingness to begin.

Though my room is not as large as Mother's, I have always loved it. As a teenager I decorated the solid east wall with posters of Lionel Richie, Cyndi Lauper, Olivia Newton-John, and the cast of *Cheers*.

My mother took over when I went away to college. When I came home, intending to stay only a few months while I looked for work, my posters had been replaced by sedate art prints. I didn't care— within a few weeks I had taken a job at a downtown bookstore and fallen headlong into my one and only love affair.

Before Josh and I could set a date, I observed that Mother's short-term memory had begun to slip. Her friends didn't notice because Mother's social skills didn't deteriorate until much later, but I'll never forget the afternoon she told me the same story three times within an hour.

I sank slowly into a chair as my mother babbled on, repeating the same lines with the same inflections. When I realized I was experiencing something more than déjà vu, I called the doctor. He sent Mother to the hospital for tests, the results confirmed his diagnosis of progressive dementia, and Mother stoically accepted the reality of her condition.

I have never admired her more than on the day she learned her fate. She had always been resolute, but I expected tears and distress. Instead she looked at the doctor and said, "I have always lived for the moment, and I shall continue to do so for as long as I am able."

Then she looked at me. "If I have only one life to live, let me live it in New York, as a blond—"

"And in designer furs," I finished with her.

She stared at me a moment. "I trust you'll help me do that . . . and you'll have the good sense to know when it's time for me to withdraw from public view." She tried to laugh, but the brittle result sounded more like a cry of despair.

"Thank you, Doctor," she said, standing. "Call on me as often as you think best. And you will see that Aurora gets the help she needs, won't you?"

I left Dr. Helgrin's office with a stack of books about caring for dementia patients. As the months progressed, I began to recognize the symptoms the doctor had predicted—confusion, increasing memory loss, increasing clumsiness, an absence of any sense of time—and I resigned my job at the bookstore. Josh kept pushing for a wedding date; I told him I could not abandon my mother.

One night he kissed me good-bye and walked out of the apartment. As the door clicked behind him, I knew he'd never come back. But that was okay—wasn't love supposed to contain an element of self-sacrifice? If Josh couldn't sacrifice his comfort and move in with me and Mother, then what he felt for me wasn't real. I, on the other hand, adored my mother. Almost everyone did.

Instead of becoming a wife, I became my mother's security, her nurse and guardian. By the end, our roles had completely reversed. Mary Elizabeth became the child and I the parent . . .

So what am I now?

When water flows from the coffee decanter onto my hand, I turn off the tap and close my eyes. I've been through this already. Yesterday I'd been mostly conscious of cessation, an emptiness that wasn't even loneliness, but today I feel a yawning need. I need a goal. Yesterday I decided to redecorate this apartment, but what will happen after that? I need a long-term purpose.

I need something to *be*.

I stare at the slanting rays of the morning and realize I am a cipher—a big, empty nothing. I could disappear from the face of the earth and few people would even notice.

My mother died after ten years of virtual seclusion, but she still left a mark on the world. She married a famous man; she raised a daughter; she influenced countless people through her committees and society work. Even my father, pig that he is, has influenced thousands, maybe millions of people. Everyone knows his name. When he dies, the story will make front-page news.

My gaze drifts toward the gallery that leads to Mother's room. I need to clean out that space—call someone to remove the hospital bed, the bedpans, the boxes of leftover medical supplies. I could spend the better part of a morning scraping up the reflective tape I put down to mark the path to the toilet. That room needs airing out, emptying, painting.

But I can't wipe Mother out of this place, not yet. To remove her now would leave the apartment as empty as my existence.

I pour the water into the top of the coffee maker, then set the decanter on the heating plate. When the machine begins to hiss and gurgle, I lean against the counter and look through the pantry and into the dining room beyond. I am not ready to eliminate Mother from the apartment, but she did a thorough job of eradicating any trace of my father. He lived here fifteen years, but like a water spot on the ceiling, his influence has been neutralized and painted over.

I could never speak of him in Mother's presence—the mention

of his name was enough to drive her into a fury or a migraine. Sometimes, though, if Clara was feeling talkative and relaxed, she'd tell me about my father.

She once told me that the mahogany dining room set was a wedding present from my father to my mother, but I can't find a single hint of the man in the stately chairs and polished table. The furniture is traditional and elegant—am I to assume he possesses those qualities, or was his choice guided by my mother's tastes? Clara says at dinner parties he usually sat in the chair nearest the French doors because he liked to be in the center of things; from her whispered confidences and wide-eyed looks, I deduce he had been a charming host and a horrible husband.

I don't know why I'm thinking of him now—he had utterly vanished by the time I arrived, leaving nothing behind but the dining room set.

That realization answers my question—the furniture had to be Mother's taste, not his, or she would have donated it to the nearest charity shop and disdained the tax deduction.

I frown as someone buzzes at the door. I'm not expecting anyone, and Clara looked to be on her way out when I met her in the hallway.

My heart pounds as I move to the foyer and peer through the peephole. Clara stands outside, her blue eyes magnified by the telescoping lens.

Sighing, I undo the locks and open the door.

Clara's tense expression dissolves into a wavering smile. "How are you this morning, dear heart?"

"I'm fine." I lean against the edge of the door, halfheartedly blocking the opening. "I was just about to have a cup of coffee and head for the shower."

"You poor dear—you must be positively exhausted. You get some rest today. I'm on my way out, but before I go, I want to ask you a question."

She is looking at me with a pleased and secretive expression, but

61

I'm not in the mood for guessing games. When I don't respond, she presses on: "I wondered if you could come over tomorrow for a bite of lunch—perhaps around noon? I've invited our new neighbor so you two can have an opportunity to meet properly. I'd like him to see you in something other than funeral black and that ratty old robe."

I glance down the hall. Fortunately, the man under discussion is nowhere in sight. "Where is Dudley Do-Right?"

Her brows jut downward in a frown. "I would imagine he's working. Did I mention that he teaches at NYU? He also does consulting work for private clients. Apparently he does very well for himself, so you might consider adjusting your attitude—"

"Thanks for the update, Auntie, but I'm not in a very social mood. I've still got to go through Mother's things—"

"What's your hurry? That can wait."

I stare at her, unable to come up with another excuse.

"Didn't that woman from hospice warn you that going through your mother's things might be painful?"

The nurse who had begun to visit us once a week suggested that I begin to clean out closets even before Mother died.

I couldn't do it.

"Sorry," I murmur. "I just don't feel like going out."

"My apartment is not 'out,' Aurora, and you know it. I know you're upset, but don't you think I miss her, too? For those of us left behind, life must go on. "

Unable to explain my lethargy, I shrug.

"What about dessert, then? It'll give you the day to yourself and yet something for us to look forward to in the evening."

It's her use of *us* that sways me. Clara needs this. But tomorrow? Too soon.

I force a smile. "I really appreciate the invitation, but I can't come empty-handed. I'll have to choose a recipe and make out a grocery list and call the delivery service and find the energy to bake something—"

Teasing laughter spills from Clara's throat. "You don't have to bring anything, dear heart. But so you won't feel obligated, let's keep it light—plan on coming tomorrow night for coffee and dessert, and I'll provide both. So . . . can I count on you?"

I decide to level with her. "Clara, I know what you're up to."

Her eyes widen. "What do you mean?"

"You're trying to hook us up. But it's not going to work. Good grief, my mother just died and I have a thousand things to think about."

"Aurora Rose Norquest." Her nostrils flare as she stares at me. "I am not trying to do any such thing. I'm only trying to be sociable. I barely know the man, so I'm not about to meddle in his love life—or yours."

The corner of my mouth twists as my eyes meet hers. I love the woman dearly, but Clara can be as obstinate as a toddler. Anyone else would accept my refusal and go, but I am her only remaining "family."

And lately I've become painfully aware that when you have no blood relatives left in the world, you can't help feeling as though you're beginning to disappear.

"All right." I push at a hank of hair that keeps falling into my eyes. "What time?"

"After dinner tomorrow night—around eight? Don't bring anything but yourself. Dress casually, but do wear something nicer than sweatpants. Philip will probably spend the day unpacking, so I don't expect he'll go to much trouble for us."

I bring my hand to the edge of the door. "Thanks, Clara."

A smile gathers up the faint wrinkles by her pink mouth. "Get some rest, love."

I lock up before Clara can fabricate another situation designed to bring me and Philip Cannon together. The day stretches before me—Friday, if I am remembering correctly—and before I go back to bed, I have thirteen or fourteen hours to fill as I please.

Right now I have coffee to drink. And a shower to take.

Armed with a sense of purpose, I head toward the kitchen.

7

APARTMENT 15A

As the grandfather clock in the gallery strikes midnight, I yawn and put down the novel I've been reading. I glance at the windows, thinking I will see the lights from the building across the way, but instead I see a thirty-something-year-old woman in socks and pajamas reflected in the light from the library lamp. She is sitting sideways on the love seat, her feet partially tucked beneath a sofa cushion, her back against a mountain of pillows. She looks . . . tired.

I close my book. I had thought I'd enjoy an evening with no responsibilities and no one to look after, but free time chafes heavily on my nerves. I find it difficult to concentrate on the book in my hands—even though I know I am alone, my nerves keep tensing, my ears strain to listen for sounds from the sickroom.

Once I thought I heard static from the baby monitor. Without thinking, I dropped my book and walked halfway across the library before I realized I had to be hearing things—I turned the monitor off and placed it in a drawer a few days ago.

I am completely alone.

I set my book on the coffee table, then let my head fall back to pillows that smell faintly of age and decay. I ought to look into getting a new sofa for this room—this love seat has occupied this space for well over fifteen years. On one of Mother's more lucid days, I mentioned replacing it, but she lifted her hands in horror. "Aurora, that love seat is from Bernhardt! Barring a fire or other natural disaster, it will outlast both of us."

I have never been able to prevail against Mother's innate barometer of quality. Mary Elizabeth Norquest could differentiate between treasure and trash with one glance at a sample of furniture, clothing, or humanity.

"Aurora?"

My eyes fly open. The summons has come from the gallery, which leads to Mother's bedroom. A chill crinkles the skin between my shoulder blades, then slithers down my spine.

"Aurora Rose!"

I close my eyes and squeeze them tight. I have to be hearing things. Yesterday they laid my mother to rest. I received papers, copies of bills, and reluctantly served as hostess at a wake. Now I am regrouping, attempting to recover from years of nonstop nursing—

"Aurora Rose, I need you!"

As a shiver grips my bones, I curl into the softness of the love seat and clap my hands over my ears. This is a trick of my exhausted imagination, nothing more. I've been reading a confusing story; I am bone-tired; my nerves are frayed. Clara told me to relax; the hospice nurse warned that the days following a death could be difficult. Perhaps those two knew something like this might happen.

"Where are you, Auroraaaaa?"

I pull one of the pillows over my head as the voice breaks in a horrible, rattling gurgle. Is this a dream? Surely not. I can feel the ribbed texture of the pillow beneath my nails; I can smell the sofa; I can see the blue cover of the novel on the table beside me. I sat down to read after eating a frozen dinner of chicken breast and green peas, and the slightly chemical aftertaste of the sauce still lingers on my tongue.

I lift my head in a quiet so thick the only sound is the gentle *tick-tock* of the grandfather clock in the hallway. Still clutching the pillow in my arms, I creep to the library doorway and stare down the dark gallery toward my mother's room. Her door stands ajar—did I close it earlier? Perhaps not. But now it trembles slightly, as if moved by passing currents I can neither see nor feel.

A sludge of nausea stirs in my gut as I study the entrance to my mother's room. I can think of no practical reason why I should not stroll down and close the door, banishing my fears and relegating my imagination to its proper place. I know that room like I knew my mother's face. I am intimately acquainted with the stains on the carpet, the patch of peeling wallpaper beneath the light switch, the bars I screwed into the wall to help Mother negotiate her way to the bathroom. I know how many elastic-waisted slacks are in the top drawer; how many front-snap shirts are stacked beside the pull-on pants.

Nothing in that room can frighten me. Nothing fills it but reminders of my final responsibilities. I still need to sort through the remnants of my mother's life and decide what is to be kept and what tossed out.

Perhaps that's why I'm hearing this summons in my mother's querulous voice. I am being nagged by responsibilities left undone because I selfishly decided to take some time for myself.

Well . . . if my subconscious can nag me, it can obey me, too.

"You can wait." My answer echoes with a solidity my mother's voice did not possess. Dust motes dance in the light above my head; my voice has moved the air currents and changed, however incrementally, the elements of the atmosphere.

I know the ghostly voice is not real. It has no power to harm me.

But my legs are trembling when I step from the library into the gallery and I hurry toward my own room with a quicker step than usual. Once inside, I turn on the light and take a quick glance around, then relax in the reassuring normalcy of my surroundings. But before I leap into bed, I place one hand on my door and turn the skeleton key in the lock.

Feeling simultaneously relieved and ridiculous, I spin toward my dresser. I seem to remember Clara giving me a CD for Christmas last year . . . some goofy song collection that never appealed till now. That silly CD might be just the thing I need to insulate my mind from the memories that haunt this apartment.

I open the top drawer, shove aside stacks of cotton panties and a jumble of bras, then move to the drawer filled with flannel gowns and pajamas.

In the third drawer, I find the CD—*Alvin and the Chipmunks Sing Television Theme Songs*—amid playbills and ticket stubs and other souvenirs of a life once lived in public places. I grit my teeth as I struggle to tear the cellophane from the case, then spy a pair of safety scissors amid the odds and ends.

Finally the silver disc falls into my lap. I set it into my CD player on the nightstand, then lie back on my bed and smile as Alvin and his buddies warble out the lyrics to "Rawhide."

As sound pours from the stereo speakers, I close my eyes and drink in the comforting nonsense. A chorus of dead voices could call from my mother's sickroom tonight, but I won't hear anything but Alvin and his pals.

I crawl beneath my comforter and nestle the plastic CD case next to my chest. For some reason I don't understand, tears come easily now, hot spurts of fear and exhaustion. I press my hand against my face and weep.

8

APARTMENT 15C

The teacup Mrs. Bellingham offers feels entirely too delicate for my hands, but I accept it again and carefully take a sip of my third cup of Earl Gray, wondering if I'm supposed to extend my pinkie in the process. After a few swallows and a couple of harmless observations about the lobby décor, I glance at my watch. My smiling hostess keeps plying me with offers of cinnamon spice cake, but her fluttering hands betray her anxiety.

"I'm afraid your other guest isn't going to make it." I look pointedly at the clock on the wall. "Are you sure Aurora caught the correct time?"

"I told her eight," Mrs. Bellingham answers, her shoulders slumping in apparent relief that I've broached the subject of our missing party. "I'm *sure* I told her eight. And she's the most responsible person; it's not like her to forget something once she's made a promise."

"Maybe"—I lower the china cup—"she's just not up to facing people after the funeral. After all, if she's uncomfortable anytime she's away from home—"

"She's never been uncomfortable over here." Mrs. Bellingham's hand strokes the arm of her chair in a restless motion. "Aurora's always felt perfectly at home anywhere on this floor."

"Well"—I prop my ankle on my knee—"perhaps one of us should knock on her door. I'd hate to think something's wrong over there."

Mrs. Bellingham's eyes widen. "You think something could be wrong?"

"I certainly hope not," I answer, surprised by the woman's susceptibility to suggestion, "but it might be a good idea to make sure."

Mrs. Bellingham rises from her seat, one hand worrying the diamond brooch at her neck. "She won't be upset if I knock. She probably got caught up in a book or something."

I stand with my hostess. "I'll go, Mrs. B. You don't have to trouble yourself."

"It's no trouble, and yet now I am beginning to worry—"

I put my hand on her arm. "Thank you for the cake and tea; I've had a great time. I'll knock on Aurora's door on my way back— surely she won't mind a quick hello."

"I hope not." A frown lingers on the woman's brow as she walks me to the door. "Aurora seems to be having a hard time with her mother's passing. I can't really blame her, poor girl. Mary Elizabeth was the center of her universe for so long. M.E. was everything to both of us."

"I won't intrude on her privacy." I give Mrs. Bellingham a parting nod, then reach for the doorknob. "I'll tell her you were concerned and we hope to see her some other time. How's that?"

My hostess gives me a thin smile. "That's good, I think. I've never been confident around people in mourning. Even with people I love, I always seem to say the wrong thing at the wrong time. I knew Aurora didn't want to come over tonight, but I was sure she'd show up once she promised. But now I'm worried."

"If you don't hear from me again"—I open the door—"you can go to bed without worrying. If Aurora doesn't answer right away, I'll make a pest of myself until she does. If she gets upset, I'll take the blame. After all, I'm the new guy on the block."

Mrs. Bellingham laughs. "You're a nice young fellow, Philip. I'm glad you're here."

"Thanks, Mrs. B."

I wait in the hallway until I hear the clicks of her deadbolts sliding into place, then I cross the corridor. Something about Mrs. Bellingham reminds me of my mother, and I honestly enjoy the older woman's company. Aurora Norquest, on the other hand, seems about as friendly as a bear with a toothache.

But that's not fair. I'm not certain how I'd react if I had just lost my mother; it's a sure bet I wouldn't be serving as captain of the Welcome Wagon.

The entrance to Clara Bellingham's apartment lies catty-corner to Aurora's place, but I take a moment to gather my thoughts before approaching the door. I'm reasonably sure my neighbor won't be happy to see me. She's practically run from me on the two other occasions we've met, and she won't want to be reminded that she forgot—or purposely ignored—the invitation to Mrs. Bellingham's apartment.

Bracing myself to face a deluge of disapproval, I draw a deep breath and knock, then wait a full sixty seconds before rapping again. I am about to press the buzzer when I hear the reluctant sound of heavy deadbolts.

Aurora stands in the gap of the half-opened door, her eyes wide and wary. She is wearing navy slacks and a white blouse, a vast improvement over that flannel robe. Her dark hair billows about her head like a silk cloud.

"Miss Norquest?" I attempt a smile. "Mrs. B. and I wanted to check on you since you didn't make it over for tea and cinnamon spice cake."

"Mrs. B.?"

"Clara." I jerk my thumb toward the older woman's apartment. "Sorry, but I just can't call her by her first name. It's the Missouri boy in me."

Aurora frowns at me a moment, then lowers her gaze and blows out her cheeks. "I'll have to call her and apologize."

So . . . she isn't going to barbecue an unwelcome visitor. This is good, a move toward real conversation.

I squint to study her face through the narrow opening. "I know you have a lot on your mind. Anyone could understand that you forgot."

She lifts her head. "I didn't forget. I was watching a decorating show on TV and . . . I think I dozed off."

Is she joking? I search her face, looking for some trace of humor in her inky eyes, but I can see nothing but exhaustion.

"Well, if you're all right, then."

"I'm fine."

"I'll be saying good night."

"Good night."

She lowers her head, ready to bolt the door, but I suddenly remember the question that struck me two nights ago.

"One more thing—something I meant to ask you. Is your apartment laid out like mine?"

A line appears between her brows. "Pardon?"

"The floor plan—are our units similar? The super told me these apartments have been modified through the years, and I was curious about your layout." I offer a small smile to assure her I have no malicious motives. "You'll have to excuse my curiosity, but I'm always looking for ideas about how to improve things. I thought I might get some ideas from your place."

She shakes her head as if she's confused, but she doesn't close the door. In fact, she opens it wider, allowing me to glimpse a table, a bench, and books—stacks and stacks tucked beneath each piece of furniture in the foyer.

"My parents," she says, pressing her hand to her temple as if she has a headache, "made a few changes before they bought the place—the original apartments featured lots of small rooms for servants, you know. Mr. Williamson made his own changes to your place—I think you have fewer rooms than I do, but your rooms are bigger and more open."

"I see." I slip my hand into my pocket. How can I ask about the late-night noise without getting too personal? "Maybe you can give me a tour sometime. I'll show you my place, but you'll have to wait until I've finished unpacking a few more boxes."

She takes a half step forward and presses her hand to the door. "I've got to go."

As the door begins to close, I catch what could be the shimmer of tears in her eyes. "Wait—are you sure you're all right?"

She nods, then closes the door.

I linger in the hallway as three deadbolts shoot home in a rhythmic progression. So she is still upset. And I have been stupid to question her while she is mourning her mother.

I turn and walk back down the hall, but when I reach my door, I hear a quiet rustle behind me. I turn, half expecting to see Aurora, but Mrs. Bellingham is coming my way.

"Is she okay?"

I pull my keys from my pocket. "She said she was watching TV and fell asleep. I think she's going to call you and explain."

Mrs. Bellingham brings her fingertips to her lips. "Did she sound okay to you?"

How should I answer? Because while Aurora Norquest had been perfectly polite, she had seemed anything but okay.

"She'll call you." I insert my key in the lock. "Good night, Mrs. B. Thanks again for the tea and cake."

I am drifting on a tide of soothing sleep when an electric guitar riff jerks me upright. Clutching a loose puddle of sheet to my chest, I stare into the darkness but see nothing remarkable in the dim glow of the November moon.

The guitar, however, continues to wail from behind my bedroom wall, and this sound is too immediate to originate in one of the lower floors. If through some miracle of physics it is *not* coming from Aurora's apartment, she has to be hearing the same music.

I will act this time—no man can be expected to sleep through rock music at 3 a.m. Chivalry demands that I be polite to my neighbor, but my body demands uninterrupted sleep. Though this is a weekend, I have to work on my consulting project tomorrow afternoon. I'll need a clear head, but how can I think with sleep-deprived brain cells?

I pull my robe from the hook in the closet, shake out the wrinkles, and pull it over my bare shoulders. After fumbling for my keys amid the odds and ends on the bureau, I drop the keys into my pocket and hurry into the hallway. The music is not as loud here and it fades as I stride by the tall windows, but my hand is still fisted when I pound on Aurora's door.

"Miss Norquest! Please open up!"

When no one answers, I press the buzzer. The distant guitar fades into silence. So—she turned off the music. But if she cowers behind this closed door without answering my knock . . .

The silence in the hallway suddenly splinters into the tinny strains of Whitney Houston singing "Didn't We Almost Have It All?"

Biting back an oath, I pound again, then the locks tumble and the door opens.

I recognize one of Aurora's brown eyes as it peers at me above the door chain.

"Miss Norquest." I take a deep breath and force myself to calm down. "We have to talk about the music. I know you have a right to listen to whatever you like whenever you please, but I'm pretty sure your stereo is right behind my bedroom wall."

Her head lowers; her eyes disappear behind a curtain of bangs. "I'm sorry."

"Sorry's not going to help me get any sleep. I know tomorrow's probably just another day to you, but I have to work."

A flush mantles her cheeks. "I'll turn the music off."

"Thank you." I try to gentle my tone. "I know it's none of my business, but can I ask why you need to play such loud music at this hour?"

"I've . . . been having bad dreams." Her chin quivers. "Nightmares—ever since Mother died. I'm sorry to wake you. I've been waking myself, so I know how frustrating it is, but I can't seem to stop dreaming about terrible things. The old songs help me feel . . . grounded again."

I can't believe it, but her explanation makes sense. I'd probably do the same thing if I were in her shoes, except I'd be playing "Every Breath You Take" by the Police.

"Listen, have you tried headphones? You could listen all you want and not bother anybody."

"Yeah? Okay, I'll think about it." Her lips tilt in an expression that barely qualifies as a smile, then she holds up a finger. "By the way—did I wake you last night with Alvin?"

"Who?"

"Alvin and the Chipmunks. Did you hear me playing anything that sounded like chipmunks?"

"No—no, I can't say I did."

"Oh." She looks away, shifting the focus of her gaze to some interior field of vision. "Well, that explains it, then."

I blink in dazed exasperation. "I'm sorry—what explains what?"

"Why I couldn't find the Chipmunks CD when I woke up. I think I dreamed it, too."

Her lower lip trembles with this odd confession and my irritation melts away. My fingers itch to reach out and give her some sort of reassuring touch, but the door stands between us.

"Listen," I say, wishing she would look up so I can see her eyes. "I'm sorry for coming on so strong. Would it help to talk about it?"

9

APARTMENT 15A

Talk about it? Here, *now*?

I glance at the clock on the foyer table. It's after 3 a.m. and Philip has already made it clear that all good college professors ought to be asleep at this hour. Besides, I couldn't let a man into the apartment in the middle of the night—especially a man wearing pajama bottoms and a flannel bathrobe. The very idea would give Clara a stroke.

I draw a breath to tell him it's impossible, but when I look up, he's smiling . . . and without those round glasses, he looks better than I remembered. "Hey, I'm awake," he says, shrugging, "and I'm a good listener."

"I'm sure you are." I offer him a tidy smile. "And I'm really sorry for waking you, but I don't want to keep you up."

"You think I can sleep now?" He gives me a look of mock surprise. "You might want to tell me about your nightmares. Sometimes the act of talking sort of chases the bad vibes away."

"Thank you, Dr. Freud. But I'll let you get your rest."

He shrugs and turns away, mumbling a "g'night."

Abandoning him to the hallway, I close the door and methodically twist the locks. I rub my eyes as I walk into the kitchen. Apparently since Mother died I've been cursed not only with nightmares, but with a neighbor who is both a light sleeper and independent of hearing aids. I could have invited Metallica to jam in my bedroom when Horace Williamson lived next door; he wouldn't have heard a thing.

I pull a glass from the cabinet and fill it with cold water from the fridge. I drink it down in a series of deep gulps, then lower the glass to the counter, picturing myself as a lush at a downtown bar. If this were a movie, I'd lean toward the bartender, flash my cleavage, and murmur, "Hit me again," in a husky voice.

But this isn't a movie and I'm not Mae West. This is my life, what little there is of it, and my nightmares have to be the result of something physical—maybe exhaustion combined with dehydration. I read somewhere that a lack of water can result in a corresponding lack of brainpower, so maybe that's been my problem these last few days.

Shivering from the coldness of the water, I head back to my bedroom and tumble into bed. But no sooner does my head touch the pillowcase than the awful images of my nightmare spring back to life, grinning at me from wherever they'd gone when I tried to banish them with music. I turn over and pound the pillow, hoping a change of position will send the dreadful cast of characters scurrying back into the dark, but they are still with me, leering from the shadows as they wait for me to surrender to sleep.

I won't be able to get any rest here. I sit up, groggy and irritable, and pull the blanket from the bed as I stump down the gallery toward the living room. That sofa is virgin territory, free from evil associations and ghostly gremlins. If by chance some macabre vision does arise from my subconscious, at least I'll be able to turn on the radio without fear of waking Philip Cannon.

I pull one of the pillows from the back of the sofa and prop it against the armrest, then lean back and stretch out. The old couch is comfortable, but now I don't feel the least bit sleepy. The *tick-tock* of the schoolhouse clock is loud in my ears; the hiss of the radiator echoes like a giant lizard on loan from some Japanese creature feature. In the distance, a siren screams in the night.

I cross my arms over my chest and stare at the ceiling. As a girl, I used to talk myself to sleep by pretending I had been gripped by some terrible disease. As I lay on my make-believe deathbed, I would visualize the faces of my loved ones and rehearse my final farewells. Eventually, at the climax of my pretend play, I fell asleep.

My brain feels too wired to shut down, but my tired body is more than willing to cooperate. My arms are already folded in the traditional pose of the dead, so I command my legs to become insentient. When my limbs are heavy, I open my eyes and imagine my mother standing over me . . . and there she is, as real as death.

I'm sorry, Mother. I don't have to speak aloud; she can read my thoughts. *I have not behaved in a manner appropriate for your daughter.*

"It's all right, Aurora, darling." She sinks down next to me, her silk skirt spilling over her knees and onto the floor as her hands caress my unfeeling arms. A smile nudges itself into a corner of her mouth, pushes across her lips and up over her cheeks. It's an indulgent smile, a look of affection and wisdom, and my eyes sting at the sight of it. I haven't seen my mother smile like that in years.

"You know," she speaks in the gentle voice people tend to use with children and old folks, "I'm actually proud of the way you've handled everything in the last few days. Keep Clara close, dear heart, and know that you'll always be safe as long as you remain at home. Nothing can harm you here, nothing at all."

I want to ask if she knows of some danger lurking beyond the building, but I can't seem to move my mouth.

"You're dreaming, darling." Her graceful hand floats up from the blanket and caresses my face with compassion.

I've been having nightmares.

"Of course you have." Her voice is fainter than air, but I catch every word. "You've been processing information, making decisions, considering choices. But the nightmares will pass. In time, everything passes."

She places her hands on my shoulders and bends to kiss my cheek. I close my eyes, savoring the moment.

When I look up again, a shadow has fallen over us. Mother is glaring at someone or something behind me, an entity I can't see. Her face hardens in an expression of remarkable malignity. "What are *you* doing here?"

"She is my daughter." A man speaks, underlining the word *daughter* with a deliberate ferocity.

My mother shows her teeth in an expression that is not a smile. Despite her anger, I would give anything to see the man who remains out of sight. I try to turn my head, but it is as immobile as my arms and legs.

"She is not yours." Mother spits the words like stones. "You *never* loved her."

"I have always loved her . . . even as I loved you. But you wanted nothing to do with my love, Mary Elizabeth, because you wanted nothing to do with fidelity."

I grit my teeth, struggling to turn, but I cannot conquer the paralysis of this pseudosleep.

Mother rises, baring her teeth like a wild animal. "You have always been demanding, but you can't command me now. You turned your back on us. You destroy people; you cast them away. You say you love, but you are cruel and pitiless—"

"I have always loved my daughter. Would you have me remain where I am not wanted? With your own words and choices you alienated yourself, but I will not let you keep Aurora from me, too."

No matter how hard I struggle, I cannot overcome the stupor that grips me. I feel the patter of impending panic in my chest, but I resist by trying to turn my thoughts toward the outsider. If Mother can hear my silent speech, perhaps he can, too.

Dad?

"Aurora." He speaks in a low rumble that is both powerful and gentle. I still can't see him, but by the look of revulsion on Mother's face, I know he is bending closer. In a moment he will step around the corner of the sofa and I will see the father I have secretly yearned to know . . .

"I won't let you have her. Don't look at him, Aurora!"

My mother throws herself on me, her chin digging into the flesh above my collarbone, her hands clawing at my shoulders until our bones grate together, skeleton against skeleton. The river of her hair covers my eyes like a silken blindfold, while a fierce wind rises from behind me, a hot current of air with the dryness of the desert in its breath. Now the sofa is sliding across the wooden floor, its legs screeching in protest as my mother pushes herself up, her mane blowing back to reveal an empty-eyed skull from which a few blond tufts sprout above yellowed teeth that grin in celebration of some demonic victory . . .

"No!" Summoning all my strength, I open my eyes and cry out to ward her off . . . and find myself in bed, my lamp burning on the nightstand, my sheets crumpled in fists that cannot, even now, relax.

Restless and unable to sleep, I pace in the hallway and wish I'd learned how to smoke. Smoking might send me to the grave before I've lived a full life, but at the moment I don't care much about living. Smoking would at least give me something to do with my hands, something to focus my frazzled attention.

But there are no cigarettes in the apartment, not even in the silver case Mother kept for guests. I can't even find a stray stick of gum in the desk. I pull out several drawers, rummaging through items I ransacked yesterday when I looked for the Alvin and the Chipmunks CD, but the only useful instrument I find is a crochet hook, size H. I could sit on the sofa and crochet as I have on so many other sleepless nights with Mother, but I used up the last of the yarn a few months ago.

I pause in the foyer and rest my hand on the front door, taking the pulse of the sleeping building. I could walk over to Clara's, but without her hearing aid she'd never hear my knock. I'd have better luck raising my mother from the—

No. Mustn't think that thought, mustn't let myself drift toward melancholy and things that go bump in the night. Because I don't believe in the supernatural, the visions I've been experiencing have to be dreams rooted in my subconscious and sprouted from my overgrown fears. I've been falling in and out of sleep at odd moments, but that's only because I've been exhausted for ten long years . . .

"It's all right." I run my hands up and down the sleeves of my robe as I pace in the gallery. "Grief hits different people in different ways. You've come through a terrible situation, you're relieved the ordeal is over, and you feel guilty because you're relieved. You've been unable to go through a normal mourning process, and all those latent emotions are bubbling up in bizarre dreams."

I catch my reflection in the glass over the grandfather clock's round face. *Now* who's playing Dr. Freud? My problems stem from reading too many books and watching too many talk shows. If I had a life outside this apartment, maybe I could focus on something other than my pathetic little miseries.

Without warning, anxiety crests inside me like a wave, breaks, and sends streamers of terror in every direction. The walls of the gallery bend and bow as the sound of my own quickened heartbeat fills my ears. The apartment is alive; the walls are closing in on me; the air is disappearing. I struggle to draw a breath; I hear a death rattle in my throat; I feel my lungs labor to expand. My ears fill with a dull roar while darkness hovers at the edge of my eyes.

I slip to the floor, feel the polished wood under my knees and my perspiring palms. In a moment I will pass out, I will die, and no one will even notice that something is dreadfully wrong. This can't be happening. In years past I have experienced panic attacks in the lobby, on the street, and in the elevator, but never have I felt threatened in my own apartment! Yet the gallery walls are alive, shimmering and slick, pulsing with every ragged breath I take. These walls have betrayed me, they have broadcast the existence of my sleepless nights even to the neighbor next door, and they have imprisoned me for years.

What am I to do? The easiest thing would be to curl into a ball, but I can't let Clara find me dead on the floor. So I inhale as deeply as I can, steady my knees, and run to my room. Once inside, I slam the door and leap onto the bed, then wrestle with the comforter until I can pull it over my head.

I curl up in the heavy darkness and wait for this terror to either strangle me or subside. My breathing gradually slows. After a few moments in the moist darkness, I am able to draw a deep breath.

I gulp back a sob, not knowing what to do next. This panic attack is fading, but what's to stop another one from ambushing me here? I've always felt safe at home, but now I can see I will never be safe from fear.

I huddle beneath the bedcovers and press my wet hands together. What to do? I want to stay in bed, but fear still clings to me and I can't allow it to inhabit my last refuge. I fling off the heavy comforter, shiver in the cool air, and move to the door. After crossing the threshold of my room, I totter down the gallery like a drunken woman, pausing at the midway point to steady my breathing.

My home is no longer a safe place. Lingering here in this condition will taint these walls with the shadows and stains of anxiety. I have to leave, but where can I go?

Driven forward by unreasoning terror, I hurry through the gallery, cross the foyer, unbolt the locks, and stumble into the hallway.

While I stagger in a circle, one hand pressed to my forehead, the other groping for some support, a rational voice whispers in my brain: *What am I doing? Where could I possibly go from here?* If desperation drives me downstairs, the night watchman will call the police or a mental health counselor. The other floors offer no sanctuary—they are nearly identical to this one, long corridors with black windows and faceless doors.

My hand finds the wooden banister; I cling to it. At the foot of the old staircase, I bend and clasp my knees. My heart is a wild thing, raging in its cage of ribs; my mind has regressed to a state where emotions and fears overpower words and thoughts.

My mother, were she alive and in possession of her faculties, would laugh at my weakness. What had she advised in my dream? She told me to remain close to home. She meant I should not only keep my feet from wandering, but I should be content with ordinary dreams. I am not my mother; I could never hope to ascend to her level of prominence. Too much of *him* lives in me, the faceless betrayer who gave me life and abandoned me to live it alone.

As I hunch in the dim glow of a security light, my gaze flicks automatically to the nearest elevator, registers the bronze doors, then glides over the faded carpet on the staircase. Upstairs, the gray door marked NO ADMITTANCE gleams faintly, glowing with significance.

I know my imagination has been stretched beyond its limits, yet that door beckons like land to a sailor who's been too long at sea. If I can make it up those steps, I'll know I'm not crazy, not bound by my mother's memories, history, dreams . . . or my own fear.

I grip the banister, convinced no one has climbed these stairs in months. I've lived most of my life in this building, and I don't think I've ever used these steps for more than a place to sit while I waited for Mother or Clara.

My mind vibrates with a thousand thoughts. Did Mother ever climb this staircase? Perhaps she drifted over these bowed steps when her spirit left her body. While I washed dishes and tried to follow the shifting storyline of an *ER* rerun, my mother's soul slipped through the gallery and drifted up these stairs on her way to eternity.

A half smile quirks the corner of my mouth as I grip the carved wooden rail and begin to climb. I count eight steps up, then catch my breath and count eight steps more. When I reach the door at the top of the stairs, I turn the knob, expecting to find it locked, but apparently the super is not terribly concerned about residents visiting the rooftop.

The heavy door requires extra effort. Marshaling my strength, I shove it open, shiver in a blast of frigid wind, then spy a cinder block a few inches from the threshold. Some still-functioning part of my brain decides it would be prudent to make certain the door doesn't lock behind me, so I bend and drag the cinder block into the space between the door and its frame. Then I straighten and inhale a deep breath, filling my lungs with air so fresh and cold it stings my throat.

Above me, a frosted light on a rusty pole illuminates the rooftop and reveals a matted green bath towel, a weather-beaten chaise longue, a pair of clay pots. Brown twigs occupy both planters—the trees are either long dead or they have entered winter hibernation. Beside a protruding vent pipe, two pigeons huddle on a thin nest of twigs and dryer lint.

I step forward on the barren surface, surprised to see that some-one has spent time up here—sunbathing, by the look of things, and gardening. But no one has been up here in months, if not years. The tattered towel has suffered through storms and sun while the wrought-iron chaise longue would probably qualify as an antique.

Beyond this litter, the rest of the rooftop spreads to my left and right like unexplored territory. At the center, which is open to the courtyard below, a brick wall and iron railing prevent trespassers from stumbling over the edge.

My worn slippers carry me away from the doorway and over an expanse of graveled roof. Ghost spiders scurry along the backs of my knees, but I no longer care. In coming here, I have come to the end of myself. New territory—either the end or the beginning of me.

The view beyond the boundary of this rooftop is the stuff of nightmares—endless open space, intense darkness, stone towers that stare down with glassy eyes. I lift my chin, daring these surroundings to ignite my fears, and what I see steals my breath more effectively than panic ever could.

After so many years, how could I not know I was living on the edge of a glittering fairyland?

I take another deep breath, inhaling the shades of night as the constraints of the building fall away. The buffeting wind erases the staleness of my memories, my suffocating panic, the dull ache of loneliness. I raise my arms and tilt my head back to gaze at the wonder of it all.

If this is the last sight I ever see, I will be content.

I am standing atop one roof among dozens, marveling at sights never glimpsed from the ground. I've heard people say the Westbury Arms has fallen from her former glory, but they haven't glimpsed the treasures she offers from this lofty perspective.

Beneath a concentrated black sky, the towers of Manhattan stretch upward, their windows glittering in hues of white and gold. The moon hides her face behind a veil of clouds, but the other celestial bodies have been overwhelmed by the lights gleaming from myriad glass windows.

I lift my hand and hold it before my face, smiling as the spaces between my fingers fill with sparkling orbs. I am an astronaut, walking the surface of an unexplored planet and ready to follow the stairway of stars . . .

Now that I no longer care about living, I find myself in a strangely buoyant mood. I move about the roof, careful not to step so heavily that I might wake a sleeper below, and peer out at sights I haven't seen in years.

To the east I can see the darkness of Central Park, where thick stands of trees strive to compete with graceful stone towers. I catch a quick silver glimmer amid the trees—the lake, reflecting the shy moon.

I cross my arms in a delicious shiver and set out for the southern boundary. I smile when I realize I am treading the tarpaper above Clara's bedroom. What would she say if she knew where I was? The question makes me laugh aloud.

At the southeast corner of the building, I lean into the curve over Clara's bay window and study the building across the street. A penthouse occupies the uppermost space, an unusual structure with a sloping glass roof and transparent walls. I hunch forward, staring into the apartment. In the gleam of decorator lighting, I see a white piano surrounded by greenery, cream-colored carpet, a curving white sofa before a stone fireplace. Another room connects to this space, a bedroom, because in the dim glow of a bedside lamp. I see a bed occupied by a single sleeping form.

Embarrassed, I avert my eyes. I came up here to escape, not to become a Peeping Tom. Yet what sort of person lives in an apartment with glass walls and a transparent roof? Surely he or she doesn't care if the odd observer happens to see into the house. Such a person must crave attention.

Moreover, how can someone with the courage to sleep beneath the stars require a night-light?

When a gust of wind rocks me, I look down and grip the railing, startled by my new position. As long as I looked up and out, I didn't have to consider the distance *down*. Now, though . . .

I cling to the metal rail, which has been mounted atop a brick skirting as high as my waist. Why am I feeling queasy? I came up here to escape my life of fear. My choice is to either start pushing back on my encroaching borders or straddle the wall, enjoy the view for a moment, and then push off, ending my dilemma . . . no one will care if I follow Mother up the stairway of stars. A quick exit now would be far less complicated than trying to battle the world that is mine. Clara might miss me, and Philip Cannon will probably beat himself up for not forcing himself into my apartment for a serious heart-to-heart chat. But other than those two, no one else will care.

I pause to knit the raveled strands of my courage. The bricks are rough against my knees; I can feel their scrape even through my robe and gown. The wind tosses my hair as I stare out at the city and consider the winding length of thirty-five years.

Will no one regret my death? I can't remember any college professors who thought I possessed a unique gift. No high-school teachers gave me special encouragement. No neighbors are close to me except Clara. My high-school classmates are long gone; my college friends no longer take the trouble to send Christmas cards. Josh hasn't looked back. My mother's friends are dead or fading. If I jump, no one would do anything more than sigh and praise my devotion to my mother. "Poor thing took her life right after Mary Elizabeth died," they'll say. "She simply couldn't find her footing once her mother passed."

I wipe my watering eyes on the sleeve of my robe. *She couldn't find her footing—that's why she fell from a building.* Ha! Perhaps that should be my epitaph. People who collect odd gravestone humor will appreciate my final witty contribution to the human adventure I could never seem to enter.

Have I expected too much? I never thought I would cure cancer or save mankind from a terrorist attack; still, it would be nice to create something that outlived me. A simple purpose for living could be useful—some task to call me out of bed and prod me toward the coffeepot each morning. I'd like to have some small item on my to-do list that will count for something more significant than repainting the walls of my apartment.

The memory of a professor's voice comes back to me in the whoosh of the wind: *According to Newton's law, every object will persist in its state of rest or uniform motion unless it is compelled to change that state by forces imposed on it.*

My mother's death was certainly an imposing force—but instead of propelling me forward, it has weighted me with soul-numbing weariness. I have come to a crossroad, but at this point it would be easier to climb over this railing and lean forward into space than to go downstairs and try to construct the semblance of a meaningful life.

I tilt my head, searching for another interesting thought, and in that instant the wind ceases. Silence flows around me, covering the rooftop, swirling around my perch, filling my ears as completely as cotton. Then a commanding voice rips away the silence.

I have always loved you.

The sound startles the indignant pigeons into flight and sends a tremor of mingled fear and anticipation shooting through me. It is the male voice from my dream, and again it comes from behind me. I want to turn and see who is speaking, but I'm terrified I'll see Mother standing on the graveled rooftop, a grim look on her face.

Could I be dreaming now? No, this cold wind is whipping my hair, pressing against my robe, and tugging at my slippers. I can feel the crust of this rusted railing beneath my palms. This is no nightmare, so the voice must have been real . . .

I must be losing my mind. Crazy people hear voices all the time; delusions are completely real to the people who suffer from them. I think I am sane, I *ought* to be sane, but the pressure has wounded me. Perhaps I do have a genuine case of agoraphobia, but I'm not crazy.

On the other hand, do mentally healthy people perch on rooftop railings at 4 a.m.? Do they hear voices? Do they experience dreams within dreams?

Anxiety rises like a balloon in my chest, swelling until my lungs are too crowded to breathe. My fingers tighten around the railing as I stare out into a sea of black night. Lights twinkle from windows around me, but no one is watching at this hour. No one, except whoever spoke in my ear.

The one who said he loves me.

My father.

Suddenly I don't care if he *is* only a figment of my imagination. The thought that my father might love me drops like a rock into the shallow pool of my heart, sending ripples of warmth in all directions. I pause a moment, letting those waves lap against me, again and again.

Why not try welcoming this illusionary night visitor? I've lived under my father's indifference and disdain for so long that living in his love might prove . . . refreshing.

"My dad, Theodore Norquest." I speak the words aloud for the sheer joy of it. I never dared speak his name in the apartment. Even in the merciless grip of senility, Mother never failed to react with anger when Clara slipped and alluded to his existence.

Now that Mother is gone, I could enjoy the freedom to speak of my father. It's only a baby step, but it's something I can try before I decide to quit trying.

The wind gusts for a moment, then the night floats around me, quiet and still once again. I realize I am smiling.

Why not choose life . . . for a few more days or weeks? While I'm entertaining the fantasy that I have a father who loves me, I will adjust my surroundings. I'll toss out the old sofa, find new wallpaper for the kitchen, maybe paint the walls a sunny yellow instead of my mother's boring beige. I'll ask Clara to bring some decorating books from the library . . . maybe even a Theodore Norquest novel.

I bite my lip, thrilled by the prospect of trying something, anything different. Who knows? If I can make little changes in my world, perhaps I'll be able to find the courage to leave the fifteenth floor. Agoraphobia is a real condition, but I've read about people who beat it. I could lick this thing.

I've been sequestered for too long, and I've never been much of a social creature, but I'm willing to think about rejoining the world. I have no conversational ability; my looks are mediocre; it's been years since I've seen a dentist or a professional hairdresser.

I'm not equipped for a social life. But I'm not ready to die.

As I wrap my arms around myself and hurry back to the rooftop door, I know I cannot remain a hermit. Even if I never return here to end it all, something inside me will die if I do not find a reason to live. And though I will have redecorated the apartment, read scores of new books, and watched every TV show with even a whiff of originality, I will still lack a meaningful life.

I close my eyes as the black sky whirls above me. Aunt Clara's life is filled with meetings, volunteer activities, charity fund-raisers. She stepped into the shoes Mother vacated years ago, and her life brims with busyness. But she is a social person.

Perhaps I don't have to become a social butterfly. After all, Philip Cannon seems happy and successful, and he's far from fashionable. He also works from a home office.

I could work from the apartment . . . once I train myself to do something useful. I could even educate myself from home; I've seen several TV commercials for distance learning programs. An advertisement for NYU's online degree program airs every morning before my favorite talk show.

I could get a master's degree and learn to do something with my life . . . all from the security of my redesigned apartment.

All I need is a computer.

And someone to teach me how to use it.

And a fantasy father to applaud my efforts when I'm finished.

For an instant I am overcome by the familiar burden of inertia— I have heaped too much on my plate; I cannot handle so many things at once.

But in my dreams at least, my father loves me. Here, in the star-spangled world between heaven and my home, he told me so. That assurance will give me the courage to take baby steps.

An incoming tide of ideas and possibilities carries me to the door, where I leave the wind-whipped rooftop and descend the stairs.

10

APARTMENT 15A

I wake in my own bedroom . . . and for a sickening moment I am afraid that I have dreamed another dream with textures and sound effects. Then I lift my palms to the light and see flecks of rust from the rooftop railing.

I didn't dream my climb up the stairs . . . and I didn't dream that masculine voice in the darkness.

I roll out of bed and walk to the kitchen with a quick step, then turn on the small countertop TV. I punch at the remote, searching for my favorite news program, then realize today is Sunday.

Why not begin my new life on the first day of the week?

I click through a half-dozen infomercials, then discover a decorating show on The Learning Channel. A perky brunette is in the midst of explaining how a single coat of paint can change a room from boring to bold.

Perfect.

I move to the pantry and pull out a box of Shredded Wheat. Mother always liked this cereal, but I soaked it overnight so the little rectangles would be soft enough for her to chew.

I set the coffee to brewing, pour myself a glass of orange juice, and perch on a barstool as the brunette describes the different personalities of color. "Green is soothing," she tells me. "That's why so many operating rooms are painted green. Red is invigorating, a good choice for kitchens and bathrooms. Blue is serene, a nice selection for bedrooms, while yellow is lively and bright. It's almost impossible to feel depressed in a yellow room."

Bingo. I flash the brunette a thumbs-up, then reach for the cereal. The little squares of Shredded Wheat are pinging against the bowl as someone buzzes at the door.

Despite my annoyance at the interruption, I stride forward with more energy than I've felt in weeks. The peephole reveals Clara, her face painted and her neck framed by fur. She's dressed for church.

I undo the deadbolts and open the door. "Good morning, Auntie."

"Well!" She gives me an approving smile as she crosses the threshold. "I'm glad to see you're up and about."

I lead her back to the kitchen. "Would you like some coffee? I just put a pot on—"

"No, thank you, dear, I'm on my way to church with Arthur. But I have to walk right by the library, so I could drop a few books in the depository if you have a stack you've already read."

"I do have some to return," I say, crossing to the counter where I have piled last week's assorted novels. "But if you'd rather wait until tomorrow to take them, that'd be fine. In fact, I'd love some decorating books, if you have the time to search for them. I'm going to redo the apartment."

Disbelief struggles with humor on her fine-boned face as she looks at me. "Redo the apartment? Whatever for?"

"Because this place is in need of a face-lift." I keep my voice light as I embrace the stack of novels. "How long has it been since Mother last updated anything—twelve, fifteen years? Times change, Clara. Styles, too. I want something to reflect my taste."

She waves away my words. "You're too young to know what your tastes are. Take my advice and hire a decorator. Then you'll know you're getting quality and not trendy mishmash."

I think she has just insulted me, but long ago I learned to overlook Clara's unintentional digs.

"All the same, I want to improve a few things." I drop the books on the counter in front of her. "And I want to do a lot of the work myself. What else do I have to do with my time? The work will be good for me. And while I'm working, I can do some evaluating."

"What in the world do you want to evaluate?"

"I don't know. Life in general, I suppose."

"You've all the time in the world to evaluate life, Aurora. What you need to be thinking about is marriage. You need to find yourself a husband—and in your situation, that may be easier said than done."

I'm not sure what she means, but I can guess. She could be referring to any of the various strikes against me—my embarrassing panic attacks, my age, my social backwardness, my estrangement from my celebrity father. Still—

"I'm rich," I blurt out. "That's something in my favor."

Amusement flickers in Clara's eyes. "Money attracts flies more readily than gentlemen, my dear. I *do* want you to find a husband, but he should be someone of quality, someone with a fortune of his own."

I feel heat creep into my cheeks when I realize how easily I fell into her trap. "Wait a minute. I don't want to talk about marriage. First I need to create a life for myself."

Laughter floats up from Clara's throat. "Darling, I have news for you—I was present at your birth; I know exactly when, where, and how you came into the world. You *have* a life; what you need to do is live it."

"Exactly." I tap the countertop for emphasis. "And that's what I intend to do—beginning with my rejuvenation of the living room."

Clara's blue eyes blaze into mine with the most extraordinary expression of alarm. "The living room? I can see why you might want to freshen the bedrooms and baths, but you can't be serious about redoing the living room!"

I am about to assure her I am, but she doesn't give me a chance to speak.

"Why—that room was your mother's favorite! She brought in that Fifth Avenue designer to select the furniture. The sofa is Henredon, for pity's sake!"

"It's fifteen-year-old Henredon."

"Your mother spent hours choosing the right wall color to coordinate with the sofa. And those tables are antiques! You don't dump antiques, Aurora. You have to let them *appreciate*. They're heirlooms."

I chew my thumbnail and consider debating the sense of holding on to antiques I despise versus ordering modern furniture I like, but enthusiasm is dribbling out of me like helium from a balloon. If we get into an argument, I'll be defeated.

Better to switch tactics than die on this battlefield.

"Did I say the living room? I should have said the north rooms, Auntie—the two bedrooms. Beginning with my room. Mother never cared a whit for it, so I want to paint it and get new carpet and drapes, maybe some new artwork for that long wall."

She lifts a brow and studies me intently, then her gaze thaws. "Of course you can do as you like, dear. I think refurbishing is a grand idea. But when I told you to make a fresh start, I was thinking you'd add a few new art pieces, not turn into one of those rabid DIY fanatics."

I shrug. "I don't know. Do-it-yourself must be a lot of fun, or so many people wouldn't be doing it."

She closes her eyes and pinches the bridge of her nose, then opens her eyes and smiles. "Would you like some bedroom books, then? I can't get into the library today, but I'll return those books tomorrow and stop in to have a look around."

"And maybe some books on color? I'm thinking yellow would be nice. My bedroom gets so little direct sunlight; I'd love to find a way to perk it up."

"Of course, dear." As she reaches up to pat my cheek, I catch the sweet scent of her lilac perfume. "Is there anything else you need while I'm out?"

I glance back at the television. The enthusiastic homeowners on the screen are slapping paint on their walls. Before the day is over, they'll have done something to improve their world.

I may not make great changes today . . . but I'm going to take a baby step and insist on getting those library books.

I give Clara a deliberate smile. "Thanks, but if you bring me those decorating books tomorrow, I won't need anything else for a long time."

11

APARTMENT 15B

Distracted by the sound of voices in the hallway, I leave my coffee mug on a stack of boxes and lean toward the door. A quick look through the peephole reveals Mrs. Bellingham calling to someone, undoubtedly Aurora, as she summons the elevator.

I chuckle and turn away, amused by the women's close relationship. Mrs. Bellingham is undeniably a busybody, happiest when inserting herself into other people's affairs, but Aurora doesn't seem to mind the woman's frequent visits. Most of the young women I know are proud of their independence and determined to maintain it. In New York, anyway.

I return to my moving boxes, take one last sip of my rapidly cooling coffee, then head toward the kitchen. I'd hoped to unpack a few boxes before I have to leave, but time has slipped away. I still need to run a comb through my hair and find a tie before I can go downstairs and hail a cab. I've found a small community church in midtown that feels like home, and the worship service begins in half an hour.

I dump my cold coffee in the sink, leave the mug on the counter, and am halfway to my bedroom when someone knocks on the door. My irritation vanishes when I discover Aurora Norquest in the hallway. Two bright spots of color mark her cheeks—what on earth?

"I'm really sorry to disturb you," she says, glancing at her hands when I open the door, "but I wanted to apologize again for waking you last night. From now on, I'll try to keep my music turned down."

She looks half-frozen, a deer ready to bolt. Who *is* this woman? Why is she so skittish?

"It's okay." I lean against the doorframe, then gesture over my shoulder. "Want to come in? I was getting ready for church, but if you want to talk—"

"I don't want to hold you up." She half-turns, then crinkles her nose. "Is . . . is that popcorn?"

I laugh, caught off guard by the wonder in her voice. "I had some last night while I watched a movie. You like popcorn?"

"I . . . I used to. I had to stop buying it when Mother started to choke on the kernels. I couldn't eat anything she couldn't eat because she always wanted whatever she saw me eating and we'd get into these huge arguments . . ."

Her voice trails away. I nod, suddenly fighting an inexplicable urge to pop her a bowl full of popcorn, slathered with butter, salt, cinnamon, anything she wants—but she shrugs and takes a half step back. "Well, that's all I wanted to say. I'm sorry about the noise."

"Hey—that reminds me." I straighten and open the door wider. "I won't keep you, but after talking to you last night, I remembered I have a book you might find interesting—it's about dreams."

She tilts her head and gives me a small smile. "You're interested in dreams?"

"A little—economists need a basic understanding of human nature, so I've done some reading on psychological subjects. Let me get that book for you, okay? I'll be back in a sec."

Not wanting to spook her, I leave the door open and cross to a cardboard box outside my bedroom. "Sorry about the mess," I call over my shoulder, "but I haven't had time to unpack everything. But this box says 'nonfiction,' so if my system holds up, the book we want should be right here . . ."

"You have a packing system?"

I glance back at her. "Don't you?"

"I don't know." She shrugs. "I've never had to move."

I flip through the contents of the box, shuffling through outdated texts on economics and societal trends, then I pull a gray and white paperback from the stack.

"Here it is." I wipe dust from the upper edge, then hurry back to the doorway. "The author gives the interpretation of several common dreams and nightmares. I'm not sure any of this will pertain to you, but it might."

Her eyes narrow, but she takes the book. "*Dream Diagnosis*," she reads, "*How to Understand Common Images God Plants within Visions*."

She snorts with the half-choked mirth of a woman who rarely laughs. "I was expecting something more . . . psychological."

I slip my hand into my pocket. "I think you'll find there's plenty of psychology between those pages."

"But this looks like a religious book."

"Are you not religious?"

"Not really. Mother stopped going to church shortly after I was christened. Clara attends St. Pat's every week, but I think it's more of a social obligation than anything else."

I'm sure she's going to hand the book back, but after a moment she shrugs and lowers it to her side. "I've gotta go."

"Lots of plans for the day, huh?"

"Something like that."

I tilt my head, trying to figure out what's different about her. She's combed her hair and put some color on her lips, but it's more than makeup. Her eyes now look like they're lit by sunshine.

I nod. "See you later, then."

"I'll bring the book back tomorrow or the next day. I'm a fast reader."

"No rush. Keep it as long as you want."

She laughs again. "I'm not sure I want it at all."

12

APARTMENT 15A

After a lunch of Doritos and a tuna sandwich, I sink onto the living room sofa and purposely prop my feet on the antique coffee table. I close my eyes with this little act of rebellion, almost expecting to hear my mother's horrified gasp, but the silence remains unbroken.

I am quite alone. And the book in my hand proves I didn't dream my encounter with Philip Cannon.

I can't quite believe I gathered up enough nerve to go over and knock on his door. That was a *huge* baby step, my second brave act of the day, so now I intend to take it easy.

I hold the book in both hands and read the subtitle aloud: "*How to Understand Common Images God Plants within Visions.*"

I had no idea God would be interested in keeping anyone from a good night's sleep, but . . .

I flip open the cover, thumb through the introductory material, then settle into the first chapter. Dreams, the author tells me, are but one way God has of speaking to his human creations. He speaks through the Bible, through preachers and prophets, and through the nudges of conscience. But when people prove hard of hearing, sometimes he speaks through dreams.

I snort softly. The only prophets I know are the astrologers and pet psychics, and none of them has said anything profound lately.

Sighing, I focus again on the printed page. Famous dreamers have included Joseph, who saved thousands by interpreting Pharaoh's dream of a worldwide famine; Jacob, who dreamed of a ladder stretching from earth to heaven; and Joseph the husband of Mary, who kept the infant Jesus safe because God used dreams to warn him of threats against the child's life. "Not all inspired dreams are comforting," the author writes. "Some must have been absolutely terrifying. Ezekiel once had a vision of a valley filled with skeletons. While he watched, tissue and sinew and arteries and flesh clothed the bones in a display that modern moviemakers might have trouble reproducing."

I read a few more pages, then close the book. I'm not dreaming of famines or ladders, so I see no reason why God might be involved in my dreams. Even if he were trying to speak to me, I don't have the power to affect anything. I can't even change my life except in miniscule baby steps.

I am dreaming of my mother, who is completely beyond my reach, and my father, who might as well be.

Still . . . I'm intrigued by the thought that God might be interested in my little life. What would he say if he spoke to me? Unless he wants to warn me of an earthquake or a jet destined to shear off the top floors of the Westbury Arms, I don't think God and I have any outstanding business to discuss.

I'm not a bad person. A weak person, maybe, but not an evil one. Some people think I'm almost a saint. As I wandered through the apartment at the wake, I kept overhearing phrases like "what a sacrifice" and "what a dear girl," all with my name attached.

So it's not like I've harmed anyone or done anything to merit a divine reprimand. God and I aren't exactly tight, but if he's feeling the need to reach out and talk, I'm sure I'm at the bottom of his list. If he's got to communicate with people through dreams, why isn't he talking to the serial killer currently terrorizing Los Angeles? Why isn't he keeping the president up nights? I'm sure he needs to whisper in the pope's ear occasionally, and maybe he speaks to TV preachers who claim they're receiving messages about people with liver cancer and blood clots and bad bunions.

God has nothing to say to me.

I toss the book onto the coffee table, then stretch out on the sofa, my head pillowed by the upholstered armrest. I'd like to take a nap, but a phrase from that book keeps whirling in my brain: *Not all inspired dreams are comforting. Some must have been absolutely terrifying.*

That statement makes no sense at all. Everybody knows God is supposed to be goodness and light, and Jesus is the gentle shepherd. I never figured that God was into horror flicks, and my dreams have been terrifying, even gruesome. In every movie I've ever seen, the scary supernatural stuff always comes from the devil. God is peace and light; his adversary deals in terror and shadows.

I blow out my cheeks and turn onto my side, trying to get more comfortable. What do I know about dreams? Mine are probably perfectly normal for a woman in my stressed-out condition. It's no big deal to add one more item to the list of my mental weaknesses—if I were alphabetizing, *delusional* fits perfectly between *agoraphobic* and *paranoid.*

I roll onto my back and stare at the ceiling. Am I going crazy? Maybe a little. On several occasions in the last few months I caught the hospice nurse looking at me with concern. She said that I needed to get out occasionally—ha!—because I needed a break. She said that the strain of caring for a terminal patient could crack even the strongest personality, and you couldn't shift from an independent lifestyle to being a full-time caretaker without experiencing major stress.

What she didn't know is that caretaking came naturally to me. I'm finding it hard to suddenly move from caretaking to independence.

I don't think I've ever been truly independent. Even at college I wasn't really self-reliant—my mother called every couple of days and flew me home at least once a month.

And I didn't mind. I only made a few friends at Sweet Briar, and since it's a women's college, higher education did nothing for my love life. While I enjoyed sitting in the classrooms and riding horseback through the forested hills of central Virginia, I only got close to my roommate and a couple of other girls from my dorm. They're all scattered now, with husbands and children and careers. I've scared away the one who ever dared to try to keep in touch.

I yawn at the ceiling—the warm coziness of the living room has made my eyes heavy. But maybe I shouldn't take a nap. If I sleep now, I won't sleep deeply tonight, and tonight I want to be too tired to dream.

With an effort, I roll out of the sofa cushions and head toward the kitchen. I fill a glass with ice, then pull a diet soda from the fridge and pop the top. As the can exhales its excess carbonation, I pick up the TV remote and power on the small set beneath the counter.

Manhattanites get an extra-hearty helping of television—all the major networks, the movie channels, and more specialty channels than I have time to watch. When Mother reached the point where she couldn't be unsupervised for more than a few minutes, television became my best friend. When I couldn't sleep because *she* wouldn't sleep, I'd sit by her bed watching the exploits of the pet police, various home designers, and an assortment of emergency room docs.

Now I surf through several stations, stop to watch a home remodeling show until they cut to a commercial, then click to the next channel. A petite woman with overblown red hair is standing before a lectern, but her words give me pause: "Make no mistake, God is calling you," she says. "He is calling *you* because he *loves* you. You will hear his voice if you take the time to listen."

My thumb hits the channel selector almost reflexively. God may be calling hordes of big-haired ladies down South, but I think he's lost touch with Manhattan.

I dream.

I am standing upon a luminous floor in some sort of room where gravity exerts no effect, for the area before me is filled with gleaming puzzle pieces. Whirling through space, the jigsawed planes dance in slanting beams of bright light, connecting and separating, swirling on the breath of a gentle and silent wind. The beauty of their ballet distracts me from my fear, and after a moment I reach out and stir the currents with my open hand.

The pieces twirl away, then gravitate back to me, shyly spinning in a golden light. I catch the corner of one piece, momentarily halting its movement, then release it to frolic with the others. The air is filled with a crystalline tinkling that reminds me of the wind chimes Clara once hung in Mother's window.

Curious, I turn to look for the source of the light. It lies somewhere behind me, but my eyes can't handle such radiance. My lids clamp down in self-defense, and though I lift my hand and try to shield my eyes, I cannot open them in the face of this brilliance.

Somehow, through intuition or instinct or awareness, I know this is *living* light and its power is responsible for the gravity-defying puzzle pieces that seem to live and move and exist only to reflect these pure of brightness.

I don't understand any of these thoughts, but I'm unspeakably grateful that this vision does not include monsters or darkness or death. I catch another piece and hold it on my hand. I brush my palm against its iridescent surface, where bronze and gold and silver blend in a metallic rainbow. I am surprised to discover initials inscribed in the metal: T.N. The piece is as large as my hand, and as I flip it from one palm to the other, I see other initials on the opposite side: A.N.

Like a child pouring sand from one hand to the other, I flip the piece back and forth, enjoying the variations in its metallic gleam.

T.N.

A.N.

What in the world does it mean?

Like a startled bird, the puzzle piece flies from my hand. Sudden tears sting my eyes, but another piece settles onto my palm as calmly as one of the placid pigeons from the rooftop.

This piece gleams with brilliant blues, greens, and golds.

T.N., one side says.

A.N., says the other.

Again I flip the piece from hand to hand, but this piece is more eager to fly than the last, zipping off before I can consider it further.

A flock of other pieces arrives, a half-dozen enameled in black and white. I catch a few and verify that these are engraved like the others, then release them and stand back to watch them pinwheel in that glorious light.

T.N.—Tennessee? Ted Nugent? No . . . Theodore Norquest.

So A.N. must represent Aurora Norquest. Simple.

But what does it mean? That we're flip sides of the same coin? That we'll always be connected but never see each other face to face? That we are destined to remain apart?

What in the world is my subconscious trying to tell me?

I wake myself with wondering, but find no answers in the silence of my room.

13

APARTMENT 15A

On Monday morning, I decide to tackle the day's baby step right after my first cup of coffee: I will empty the small room between the front bath and the library. When I have cleaned it out, I will transfer my mother's antique writing desk from the living room to the storage room and this space will become my den.

Coffee cup in hand, I open the door to the storage area and frown at the collection of boxes stacked inside. This space was originally intended to be a maid's bedroom, but Mother never used it for anything but storage. The back window has been completely blocked from view, and I can't even tell what color the walls are painted.

But none of that matters. I'm going to go through these boxes with ruthless efficiency. Anything I don't absolutely have to keep will be dragged into the hallway. Later I'll call the super and pay him to haul the stuff to the Dumpster.

After surveying my challenge, I go to my bedroom, corral my hair with a kerchief, and stride back down the gallery with a felt-tipped marker, ready to begin.

The first few boxes are filled with Christmas decorations—silver tinsel and plastic wreaths and smashed velveteen ribbons that have begun to flake and fray. I hold up a wreath sprinkled with stems, all the holly berries long since devoured by roaches. Since I haven't celebrated Christmas in years, all of these containers are marked for the hallway.

Farther into the room, I discover boxes of yesteryear's fashions—pillbox hats, yellowed gloves, worn pumps. Each succeeding carton represents a different decade of my mother's life—lace shawls, white patent leather boots, belts as wide as my hand. I'm pretty sure all of this stuff would be welcomed at some of the vintage shops in Greenwich Village, but I'm not about to haul it down there. The Dumpster can have all of it.

I find a carton of old albums—maybe even antique—but as I lift out the first book, a roach skitters across the surface and I recoil, nearly breaking my leg as I stumble backward. I make a face as the insect disappears into the shadows of the box—now I'm not sure I want to investigate that box at all. I don't mind spiders, I don't think I'd even mind seeing a mouse, but roaches have always made my skin crawl.

I would throw the box away, but on some slim chance that the albums belonged to my father, I go to the kitchen and pull a can of roach spray from under the sink. I spray the offending box, and after ten minutes, I gingerly lift out the top album and open the cover. The photos inside are sepia-toned and stiff; the black pages loose and crumbling at the edges. I stare at pictures of somber-eyed men and women standing beside Model Ts, but I haven't a clue who these people are. Finally, on the back of one picture, I see names: Eula, Lela, Horace. Old friends of my parents? Grandparents? There is no one left to tell. I scrawl "dump" on the outside of the box and haul it—and its offensive insect cargo—outside.

I find a carton of clothing I wore in high school, a box of winter woolens the moths have destroyed, and a bag crammed with souvenir programs from charity events, Broadway shows, and ballets. I toss the bag into the gallery, then stand and press my hand to the small of my back—I'd forgotten what a pack rat Mother was.

From that point, I give myself five minutes to root through each container; if I haven't found some indispensable treasure by then, I shove the box and its contents into the gallery. When the gallery fills up, I pull on my sneakers and slide the boxes through the foyer and out the door. As trash piles up in the public hallway, I realize I had better warn George about the mess—he may want to make several trips to help me get rid of this stuff.

The old grandfather clock is striking ten when I pull the last carton from the far corner of the room. My back aches from a steady effort of lifting and pushing; my fingers are coated in the fine grime that has collected on every surface in this room. But I have uncovered the window on the west wall, and dust motes are dancing in the sunlight that warms this liberated space.

I sink onto the worn carpet and stretch my legs, then lift the folded flaps of the last box. The first item is a black felt hat—and as I lift it, I feel a curious tingling shock. This is a man's hat, an old hat, and it has to be my father's.

I hesitate, the felt warm in my hand. Didn't Clara once tell me that Mother got rid of all my father's stuff when she kicked him out? I can't imagine her keeping anything—she was nothing if not resolute—but perhaps he placed this box in this room before their breakup. Mother may not have known about it.

With the care of an archeologist who has just stumbled across the find of a lifetime, I set the hat on the floor, then rise to my knees. The next item in the stack is a wool sweater patterned with clipper ships. I lift it out, hold it up—the moths have been at work here, too, but they have left me more than enough to get a sense of my father's size. Broad through the shoulders, trim at the waist, a man who might have liked to sail.

I drop the sweater and return to the box. I find other sweaters beneath the first, all cashmere or wool, all of fine quality. They are all winter garments, which convinces me that my father might have tucked this box of seasonal garments away before Mother purged every trace of him from the apartment.

At the bottom of the box I find a cream-colored wool scarf so fine and soft it feels like a cloud against my cheek. I drape it around my neck, imagining it under the lapels of my father's tuxedo, and as I stroke its softness I breathe in the lingering scent of cedar from some long-forgotten storage chest.

I'm not sure how long I sit there, but eventually I put the clothing back into the box and cover the sweaters with the hat. I decide to keep the scarf—I might actually use it one day—but when I pick up the marker, I find I'm not able to consign the entire carton to the dump. These things are all I have of the man whose genes I carry. The man living in Europe may be a louse, but the father of my dreams has always loved me . . .

If I say it often enough, maybe I'll come to believe it.

Leaving the scarf around my neck, I shove the box back into the corner, then cover it with an old tablecloth from the linen closet. I'll put a lamp, some books, and a box of tissues on it so Clara won't notice anything odd.

My mother's wide desk, the antique with curved legs and a delicate hutch along the back, is finally positioned in the former storage room. It has taken me over an hour to push and pull the heavy piece through the living room, foyer, and gallery, but George was nice enough to give me a hand when he came up to survey my Dumpster donations.

I gave him fifty dollars, told him he could do anything he liked with the boxes in the hallway, and thanked him for his help.

The desk fits beautifully along the south wall. The window stands at the edge of the desk, which means I'll be able to swivel my chair and look out at the neighboring buildings while I work.

I am wiping sweat from my forehead when someone buzzes at the door. I swipe my hands on a bathroom towel, tuck a stray hank of hair back into my kerchief, then hurry to the foyer. Clara is standing in the hall, her arms laden with library books.

I greet her with a smile. "You didn't have to get so many!"

"Oh, I found all sorts of lovely things." She walks past me into the foyer, then turns left and enters the living room. "Books on color, on bedroom design, on the latest trends—"

She stops and stares at the empty wall. "Don't tell me you got rid of your mother's desk. I saw the boxes, but I never dreamed you'd—"

"I didn't get rid of it." I slide my hands into my pockets. "I moved it into the storage room."

"Whatever for?"

"Because I'm going to get a computer. That room will be my . . . well, I guess you could call it my office."

She turns and blinks at me. "Why in the world would you need an office?"

"Because I'm trying to figure out what I'm supposed to do with the rest of my life." I step forward to accept the load of books. "I need a computer because I'm thinking about getting my master's degree. With a computer, I can take classes online."

She slides the books into my arms, then touches the tips of two fingers to her brow bone. "I thought you were going to redecorate the apartment."

"Yes—that, too. But I can't spend the rest of my life redecorating."

She sinks into a wing chair. "Sometimes I don't understand what goes on in your head, Aurora."

"You sound like Mother."

"Well, it's the truth. Dear heart, do you realize how many people would give their right arms to be in your position? You have a lovely home; you have money; you can live a life of leisure—"

"I need something more." I slide the books onto the coffee

table, then reach for her hand. "Come here, I want to show you something."

I lead Clara to the storage room, where the white walls are in desperate need of paint and the carpet is begging for a quick burial. Mother's desk and chair, however, look perfectly at home beside the window. "When I'm working on my master's, I'll have all this space to spread out my books." I gesture toward the desktop and the hutch. "I can order other bookshelves to line these other walls—you know how you're always saying I have too many books. It'll be quiet in here, so I can think. If I have guests and don't want them to see the mess, I can simply close the door."

She stares at me as if I have just announced I'm flying to the moon. I'm not sure which part of my comment surprised her most—the part about getting my master's degree or the part about having guests.

Finally, she sighs heavily and crosses her arms. "After all you've been through, you deserve a rest. Why on earth do you want to go back to school?"

"Because someday I might get a job. I'd like to be of use to somebody."

"Darling, your job was taking care of your mother; don't you realize how important that was? Now it's time to relax a little and enjoy yourself. Your mother wouldn't want you to work. She wouldn't want you to put yourself through anything you might find difficult—"

"No . . . she only wanted to chain me to her side." A surge of anger catches me unaware, like a white-hot bolt of lightning through my chest. "You don't know everything, Clara—you weren't with her twenty-four hours a day."

"Darling, I was right here with you both."

"You could leave! But I couldn't, not even if I'd wanted to. Even before she got sick, Mother couldn't stand to be alone—couldn't stand to think I might want a life of my own. But I do, Clara. I've either got to start living or . . . I'll die."

I feel myself trembling all over and recognize the heat in my chest and belly as pure rage. I'm not sure where this anger has come from and I don't want to cry, but water is overflowing my eyes . . .

Clara says nothing, but holds out her hands. And as I enter her embrace, I feel her cool palm against the back of my neck.

"You're wrong about your mother, darling girl; more than anything she wanted you to be happy. You have a wonderful life and you have me. You can do anything you like with the apartment and I'll help, but you must promise that you won't push yourself too far. What will you do if you attempt something and it all goes wrong? Who will you call if I'm not around to help? Stay close to me, darling, and you'll stay safe."

We cling to each other for a long moment, then she pats my cheek with her hand. I step back and turn to tug a tissue from the box on the makeshift table while she bends to open one of the lower desk drawers. The drawer obeys with a protesting screech, revealing bulging manila folders and the yellowed edges of countless papers.

Clara clucks in dismay as I blow my nose. "I was afraid of this. Your mother was completely disorganized when it came to her papers. I suppose that's why she wanted me to go through her things after the funeral."

I shrug. "She had everything important sent to her accountant or her lawyer. Don't worry about that mess; I'll clean the drawers out."

Her powdered cheek curves in a smile. "I'm going to help you. While you plan and decorate and whatever else you want to do, I'll go through your mother's files."

"Honestly, you don't have to—"

"Nonsense, dear. I'm sure I'll know what's important and what's not. If I'm not sure, I'll ask you before tossing anything that might be significant."

She is rolling up her sleeves, preparing for work, and I am helpless to intervene. How can I stop her? She is trying to make amends for her earlier lack of enthusiasm.

I blow out my cheeks and push the hair off my forehead. "Okay—have at it. I'll get a big trash bag."

Clara doesn't answer because she has already slid into the desk chair and pulled a yellowed folder onto her lap.

14

APARTMENT 15B

I'm on a roll; economic brilliance is practically flashing from my fingertips, but an unexpected sound causes me to pause at the keyboard. Was that a knock? I ought to ignore the interruption and keep writing—this project is not coming together as quickly as it should, and I owe my client a preliminary draft by Friday—but the pull of procrastination is too powerful.

I open the door and find Aurora in the hall. "Hi," she says, the corner of her mouth twitching in an uncertain smile.

"Hi, yourself." I step out and glance around the corner. "Is the buzzer broken? I thought I heard a knock."

"I did knock. If you were real busy, I didn't want to interrupt you."

I lean against the doorframe, surprised and charmed by the sight of my neighbor in jeans and a T-shirt. A smudge of gray dust outlines her cheek. And she's daring to meet my gaze—oops, no, now she's looking at the floor. *Put her at ease, Cannon. Make her smile.*

"Hey, I know that look—you've been unpacking."

"Something like that." A nervous expression replaces her fleeting grin. "Listen, I hate to bother you—"

"No bother. I'm always looking for a reason to get out of my chair."

"Okay . . . well. The thing is, I need to buy a computer and I know absolutely nothing about them. I thought maybe you could give me some pointers."

I straighten, grateful that at last she has broached a subject where I can be of real help. A woman who wants to learn about computers? This could be love. "Nothing I'd like better. Do you know what you'll be using the computer for?"

"Um . . . not exactly." She grimaces. "I want to take some online classes—I was thinking of getting my master's degree."

"So you'll want Internet access."

"Yes. Probably. I mean, if you say so."

Grinning, I look into her eyes. Currents are stirring in those dark depths, determination and desires I've never noticed. Unlike most of the women I meet, there's a lot unspoken about Aurora Norquest.

"If you'd like to come in"—I open the door wider—"I could show you my setup and make a few suggestions."

"I don't want to be a pain in the neck."

"You're not, trust me. Most people who work at home have refined their procrastination skills to an art form. Why work at noon, we figure, when you can work at midnight?"

She looks at me and blinks hard, then moves past me into the gallery. She takes two steps past the first bedroom door, then backtracks. "This," she points inside, "is where you sleep?"

"Yeah."

"Then I really do apologize for the noise. My bedroom is *exactly* behind this wall."

I nod. "Okay. Well, the next time you have a bad dream, try sending me a message in Morse code."

"Do you, um, *speak* Morse code?"

"No. But trying to figure out how to send the message will take your mind completely off your nightmare, I promise. "

She looks at me as if she's not sure I'm joking . . . and for an instant I wish I'd been blessed with something stronger than dry humor. She needs distraction, serious distraction. This visit is obviously testing the boundaries of her comfort zone.

"The computer's in the old master bedroom." I jerk my head toward the end of the hall. "It was the biggest and brightest space, and since I spend most of my time at my desk . . ."

She nods. "I understand."

I lead her past a stack of taped boxes, then turn into the office. Though everything around the desk is still in a state of chaos, my machine is humming, ready to go.

"This is a typical setup." I point to my work station. "Keyboard, monitor, mouse, CPU. The four basic building blocks. You will probably also want a printer, maybe a scanner and a digital camera. But you can always pick those things up later. I have a pocket PC and an extra hard drive hooked into my system, but you may not want those—at least, not for a while."

She pushes at a ribbon of hair that keeps falling into her eyes. "It seems so complicated."

"It's really pretty simple." I reach down and tap the black box on the floor. "This is the CPU, or central processing unit—the brain of your computer. The keyboard and mouse are how you tell the machine what to do, and the monitor displays your results. They make nice flat monitors now, a big improvement over the boxy models that take up half your desk space."

"But how do you get on the Internet?"

"I use a cable modem—a little box that sits on top of the computer. You won't have to buy that, though—just call the cable company. They'll come out and provide everything you need."

Remaining a good three feet from the computer, she crosses her arms and nods.

Remembering my manners, I pull out the chair. "Why don't you sit down and take it for a test drive?"

She slides two steps back. "I'd probably break something."

"You can't break anything—well, not usually. Come on, sit down. Have you ever used a computer before?"

Looking as nervous as a clipped canary in cat country, she sits on the edge of the chair and wipes her palms on her jeans. "I used to use the machines at college. But I'm sure things have changed a lot since then."

"You bet they have—most things are a lot simpler. Look at this." Propping one hand on the back of the chair, I lean over her and grab the mouse, then click to minimize the word processor displaying my project in progress. With another click I open a window for Internet Explorer. "Have you ever googled anyone?"

She arches an eyebrow. "I'm not sure that's something a woman should admit."

I laugh. "It's innocent, I promise. One of the best search engines currently on the Internet is found at www.google.com, and with it you can find out almost anything about anyone. All you have to do is type in their name—"

"Okay, I want one." She swivels in the chair and grins up at me, determination flashing in her eyes. "Can you recommend a company I can call?"

"Good grief, you're an easy sale. But let's get the lingo right— you don't have to *call* anyone; you can do everything online." Crouching next to her, I click to the Web page of an online computer supplier. "These folks can custom build you a computer and ship it out within twenty-four hours. Tell me what you want, and we can order it online."

"Now?"

"Sure."

"You trust these people?"

"Absolutely. I've ordered several computers from them and haven't had a single major problem."

I shift my gaze to meet hers. "Do you trust me to put a system together for you?"

She looks at the ceiling for a moment, then smiles. "You seem to know what you're doing. Sure, I trust you."

"Then the first thing I need to know is your budget. How much do you want to spend?"

She stares at the multiple images of computers on the screen. "Just pick whatever you think is best for me. I'll put it on my credit card."

For someone who is reportedly estranged from her millionaire father, the woman seems supremely confident about her finances. Okay, then. I'll build her a bleeding-edge system that ought to run anything the software developers put out for at least two years.

"Not often I get carte blanche. Just a minute." I walk to the kitchen, grab an extra chair from the table, and carry it into the office. After taking over the keyboard and mouse, I assemble a system with the fastest microprocessor available, a flat monitor, extra room on the hard drive, loads of memory, a wireless keyboard and mouse, and an inkjet printer.

"That comes to"—I wait while the Web page calculates the total—"$2,654.13."

She doesn't even blink. "Fine. Place the order."

I drop my hand into my lap. "We'll need your credit card number. I can wait if you want to go get it, then I can let you type it in—"

"I have it memorized." She looks at me. "I could never leave my mother alone, you see, so I had to order everything by phone . . . and after a while I learned how to streamline the process." A faint blush colors her cheeks as her smile deepens. "I'll tell you my account number—and if unusual charges show up on my statement, I'll know where to find you."

Gotta hand it to her, she's more trusting than most New Yorkers.

"Okay, then." I navigate to the order page; she recites her card number; I type it in.

"What kind of delivery service do you want?"

"Depends . . . what are my options?"

"Standard—that's cheapest and slowest. They have a priority service, and they have an insured and guaranteed person-to-person service for deliveries in Manhattan. That's the safest."

"Fine, I'll take that."

I click the box, watch as a new total appears, then glance at my pensive neighbor. "That's it. You ready?"

"Ready."

I click the "place order" button, then lean back and creak my chair as a new page comes up.

Aurora raises one bemused brow and cocks a smile in my direction. "Wow. Just like that, it's done?"

"Just like that."

"Your order has been accepted," she reads, leaning toward the screen with her chin in her hand. "Your new computer will be arriving within seventy-two hours. If you have any questions, visit our customer care center."

Her eyes are wide and glowing when she looks at me again. "I think I can handle this"—she lowers her hand—"but if I get stuck—"

"You come get me." I nod at her. "Most computers are plug and play, but every once in a while you can run into a glitch. So don't hesitate to pound on the wall and send an SOS if you need help."

"Am I still making too much noise? I know the walls are thin, but—"

"I'm kidding, Aurora. In the last twenty-four hours I wasn't even aware I had a neighbor."

"Okay . . . good." She stands and looks back at the computer. "You know, this is the single most exciting thing I've done in years."

Watching her, I feel a stir of compassion for my reclusive neighbor. I don't know why she limits her world to the upper floor of this apartment building, but if a computer can help her reconnect with others, I'll do all I can to help her.

After all, I've spent most of my life feeling like an outsider . . . and I know how it hurts.

15

APARTMENT 15B

The phone is ringing when I return to the apartment. Clara picks up the kitchen extension as I come through the doorway, and as I toss my keys on the foyer table, I hear her say, "Just a moment, please—she's right here."

A secretary is on the phone—will I hold for Bert Shields? Since he is my mother's lawyer—and now mine—I agree.

A moment later Mr. Shields's resonant voice vibrates over the line. "Good morning, Aurora. How are you?"

I haven't seen Mr. Shields since the wake. Because I'm supposed to be in mourning, I try to match his sedate tone, but I'm still feeling slightly giddy from the excitement of my computer purchase. "I'm fine, Mr. Shields, thanks for asking."

"Glad to hear it. Listen, Aurora, we need to get together soon. As executor of your mother's estate, there are some things I need to discuss with you. This is largely a routine matter because you are the primary beneficiary, of course, but you might have a few questions about a couple of provisions in your mother's will. Can you come down to my office sometime this week?"

I stand in silence, blank, amazed, and shaken. It's an innocent request; it's not like he's asking me to travel out of the city, and I no longer have to worry about leaving Mother.

But the thought of exiting this building fills me with atavistic and inexplicable terror.

I glance toward the storage room, where Clara has gone back to weeding through Mother's desk drawers. If Mr. Shields were here, she would quietly cover for me, but she can't help me now.

I bite my lip. Nothing to do, then, but try to hide my humiliation. "I hate to make trouble for you, Mr. Shields"—is that a tremor in my voice?—"but could you possibly come to the apartment? I'm in the midst of a redecorating project, and it's going to be hard to get away. I'd really appreciate it if you would come here."

I close my eyes, bracing myself for a refusal. Any man who has his secretary place his calls obviously considers his time valuable, and I've just asked for an unexpected chunk of it. Then again, my mother's estate is large, and she did consider Bert Shields a personal friend.

The lawyer clears his throat, then coughs. "Well . . . I suppose that'd be acceptable. How's Wednesday, sometime around noon? I have a meeting downtown at one, so the Westbury Arms will be on my way."

My eyes flutter open in relief. "Thank you. I'll see you Wednesday."

I replace the old phone in its cradle, cling to it a moment in relief, then move into the storage room. A stack of folders clutters the desktop, a blizzard of papers lies around the trash bag, and Clara's lap is covered in yellowed documents.

"Bert Shields," she says, proving that she was listening to at least my half of the phone conversation. "Is it time for the reading of M.E.'s will?"

I lean against the wall and fold my arms. "He's coming Wednesday."

"That's good." She looks at me, thought working in her eyes. "Are you going to be able to handle that? Sometimes these rituals can be a little . . . disconcerting."

"I don't see why I should have any problem. Mr. Shields said everything will be largely routine. He's only coming because he thought I might have a couple of questions."

"Would you like me to be here with you?"

The question strikes me as odd until I look at Clara's face. Her blue eyes, which have watched me for so many years, are shining with compassion and concern. "I know all about your mother's will," she says, giving me a slow, sad smile. "When she realized she could not escape her condition, she updated her old will and had me witness it. So you don't have to worry about protecting me from what may or may not be in it. I'd be happy to be with you if you want some emotional support."

I'm not sure why the reading of Mother's will should require emotional support, but Clara is always welcome here.

"Thank you." I pull myself upright. "If you want to stop by, he'll be here at noon."

I reach for the garbage bag, intending to fill it with some of the papers strewn about, but Clara grabs my arm. "Leave it, dear. I'm still sorting through things."

"But these are all rejects, right? I can clear some of this stuff away—"

"Don't trouble yourself. Let me do this while you prop up your feet and look through those library books. I found some really nice ones with lots of clever ideas."

I am about to protest that I *want* to help her, but I've learned to carefully choose my arguments with Clara.

So I leave her at my mother's desk, sorting through papers in which she insists I would not be interested.

My heart thumps almost painfully in my chest as I approach Philip Cannon's apartment for the second time in a single day. I'm not exactly sure why I've been drawn back here—maybe I'm bored, or maybe I'm infatuated with the thought of my new computer.

All I know is I can't sit in my apartment doing nothing for another minute.

Clara finished emptying Mother's desk at three and left, taking the bulging trash bag with her. By four I had skimmed all the decorating books she brought from the library; by four fifteen I had decided to paint my bedroom and den in a yellow shade called "buttercup buff." I called a local paint store and ordered two gallons of a national brand; the store promised to deliver the paint and supplies within twenty-four hours.

At four thirty I did something I hadn't done in years: I walked to the yawning emptiness beneath the staircase and descended halfway to the fourteenth floor. I turned around and ran back up the staircase two steps at a time, but I didn't faint or fall apart.

Amazed at the baby steps I squeezed into a single day, at four forty-five I sat down to catch my breath and sorted through the mail. A home decorator's catalog caught my attention. Within ten minutes I had found a wonderful bedspread and coordinating carpet, and best of all, I saw that I could order them online.

I could order them today . . . if I had a computer. Or if Philip Cannon will let me use his.

I am embarrassed to go over and beg for Internet access, but I do still have his book, so at five o'clock I find myself outside Philip's door. I knock lightly, reasoning that he won't hear me if he's deep in concentration, but suddenly the door opens and his eyes are smiling at me through round glasses.

"Don't tell me—now you want to order a Hummer."

My mind goes blanker than a slab of granite, then I remember—Hummers are huge, boxy, military-type vehicles favored by athletes and movie stars. You can order them online?

"I don't drive," I tell him. "But I've seen them on TV."

His smile diminishes a degree. "I was kidding."

"Oh." I bump up my own smile to assure him that I do have a sense of humor. "Listen, I don't want to bother you, but I *did* promise to return your book—" I wave the book at him, but he is stepping back, silently inviting me to enter.

"I've just quit work." He holds the door as I pass by. "I work for as long as my brain cells will fire, but when I start typing typos, I know I'm done for the day. Right now nothing would please me more than a little conversation. Come on in."

I walk through the long gallery and lower my head, painfully aware that I'm blushing. It's been so long since I made casual conversation with a man that I'm not sure how to respond. Is he flirting? Or just being nice?

Once inside his apartment, I hold up his book again. "Thanks for letting me look at this. It was . . . interesting."

He leans forward and crosses his arms on the large kitchen island. "You didn't read it, did you?"

"I did—well, I read most of the first chapter. But I told you, I'm not religious. I don't think God speaks to people in dreams."

"Don't you think he can?"

"Well . . . if God exists, I suppose he can do anything. But just because he *can* doesn't mean he *does.*"

"I thought it might be helpful."

"I'm not sure there's any help for me—apart from time, that is. I've been through some rough spots, but I've been thinking a lot lately and I'm sure I'm going to be fine. I've been making some small changes, trying to figure out what to do next—"

"Like buying a computer?"

"Exactly. And redecorating the apartment. I'm ready for a fresh outlook on life."

I half expect Philip to frown, but he just reaches out for the book. "Thanks for bringing it back so quickly. You can't believe how many books I've loaned out and never seen again. You must be a thoughtful and responsible person, Aurora Norquest."

"I don't know about that." I look away as heat burns the back of my neck. I shouldn't be talking about myself. A good conversationalist always turns the dialogue toward the other person, so I gesture toward the computer in the next room.

"So, neighbor—what, exactly, do you do all day?"

"Not much." He straightens and slips his hands into his pockets. "When I'm not teaching at NYU, I write and research reports about economics. I know that sounds about as exciting as watching trees grow, but it's fairly lucrative and sometimes it can be interesting."

"For you and who else? I mean, who hires you?"

"Various companies." He moves toward his office and beckons for me to follow. I wait until he slumps into a rolling chair before I slide into the empty seat next to the desk.

"People hire me to study markets and extrapolate data to help them forecast trends in industry and business. For instance, last year I did a study for a homeowner's association and proved that real-estate agents who represent their own properties tend to sell for more profit than their average client." He chuckles. "That one didn't go over well with the realty companies."

"Because . . . you discovered that Realtors are cheating their clients?"

"They're not cheating—but they do tend to move their clients' sales along to make a quick buck. A lot of Realtors tell their clients to jump at a contract when it's highly likely a better offer will come along if they'll only wait awhile. Realtors know this; their clients don't. And statistics demonstrate that Realtors profit from their knowledge."

"Wow." I have never purchased a piece of real estate, but I can see how Philip Cannon's work might be valuable. "What else have you learned?"

"Well"—he grins—"a study I did for the mayor's office proved that crime isn't all it's cracked up to be. We tend to think of the typical drug lord as living in a luxury apartment and riding in limos, but most urban drug dealers live with their mothers." He lifts a brow. "So what do those facts tell us about crime and its wages?"

"That crime doesn't pay?"

He winks at me. "You got it, sister."

I chuckle, but I can't help wondering if he thinks it odd that his thirty-something neighbor was living with her mother until last week.

"So how do you do this work?" I ask, eager to change the subject. "Do you go out and canvas drug dealers, or what?"

Philip folds his hands. "I notice things."

"What kinds of things?"

"Little things—telling things. Okay, here's an example. A few months ago I had to go out of town. I was stopped at a traffic light in this little city upstate and noticed an attractive woman by the side of the road. She was getting out of a new SUV."

I lower my gaze as my cheeks heat again. The man notices attractive women—has he noticed me in that way?

"I watch her for a minute, trying to see if she needs help. I'm not much good with cars, but I thought I could at least call her a tow truck if her car was dying. She was nicely dressed—pleated shorts, a leather belt, the sort of shirt women wear to play golf. But she doesn't go to the hood of the car—she goes to the back, opens it up, and takes a brown paper bag from a cooler."

"She was eating lunch?"

He laughs. "I was curious, too. Plus, by then my internal alarm systems were on full alert because this scraggly looking bum on crutches starts walking toward her from the street. I had barely noticed him before—he had been panhandling at the intersection—and all of a sudden I realize he's going to approach this woman. He draws closer as she's closing the back of the SUV. Just when I'm about to blow my horn to warn her, she sees the guy, smiles, and hands him the brown paper bag."

"What was in it? Alcohol? Food?"

Philip blows out his cheeks. "His *lunch*. She was his wife, so I deduced the guy wasn't broke. According to the obvious economic markers—the woman's clothes, the new car—he was doing about as well as I am."

I shake my head. "I don't know if you can safely make those kinds of assumptions. What if she was a friend? Or a volunteer from some social agency?"

"She kissed him good-bye—and trust me, it was more than a friendly kiss. But to be sure, I gave the guy a good look as I drove away. He had a Walkman in his pocket and an expensive pair of Sony headphones dangling from his neck—not the kind of thing you buy when you're on a tight budget."

"Who hired you to do research on *that*?"

"No one." Now *he's* blushing. "I just . . . notice things. After a while you learn to see everything in the light of economic theory."

I look toward the window and reconsider my goal of ordering my bedroom furnishings from his computer. Philip will notice what I order, he'll see the price, he'll guess my taste, and he'll probably figure out my entire pitiful life history within an hour.

I'm not sure I'm ready for him to know my history. I like him, I'm excited about having a new friend after all these years, but there's only so many baby steps a girl can take in one day.

So . . . how can I make a tactful exit after barging in like this?

"Your work sounds interesting," I say, "but I really stopped by to let you know I'll be doing some renovation next door. Nothing major—I'm not tearing out walls or anything—but I will be painting and maybe scraping off some old wallpaper. I hope the commotion won't bother you."

"Not at all. But I thought you dropped by to return the book."

He grins as heat creeps up my cheeks again.

"Yes. That too."

"By the way"—his eyes narrow slightly—"how did you sleep last night?"

Aside from that mystifying dream about the flying puzzle pieces, I'd slept like a baby.

I try to smile naturally, pretending his intimate question doesn't fluster me, though my pulse rate would tell him otherwise. "I think I'm going to be sleeping very well. I'm going to keep busy from now on. I'm redecorating, I'm going to check out some online courses, and I have lots of reading to do. Busy, busy, busy."

"That's good—if you like to keep busy." He props one ankle on his knee, then points at me. "Hey, do you want to stay for dinner? I have some frozen chicken breasts I was about to toss into a salad. I only need to shred some cheese, tear the lettuce, and nuke the chicken."

I open my mouth to protest, but he springs up and moves toward the kitchen. "I really shouldn't stay," I call after him. "I've come barging in without an invitation—"

"I'm inviting you now. Please stay and be my first dinner guest."

I press my hand to my chest, half-afraid the unexpectedness of this invitation will prod me into panic mode, but my heartbeat remains strong and steady. Still fast, but strong. Somehow it is easier to say yes than no.

Ten minutes later I am sitting at the kitchen counter, running a block of Parmesan cheese over a grater while Philip slides two chicken breasts into the microwave.

"Tell me about Clara Bellingham." He closes the oven door. "You two seem close."

"We are." It's been years since I've shredded anything and my fingers feel uncoordinated. "Clara was my mother's best friend and the only person who came around after Mother got sick. You've probably noticed that she's still keeping an eye on me." I frown at the miniscule mound of cheese. "Sometimes I think she keeps *too* close an eye on me."

"She's obviously fond of you."

I laugh. "She likes you, too. And Clara doesn't like everybody. She wasn't terribly fond of Mr. Williamson. She's opinionated, but that's to be expected, I suppose. Uncle Charley, her late husband, died years ago, so she and Mother had to learn to get on as single women. They had to be strong."

"Clara has no children?"

"None."

"And you're an only, like me."

"An only . . . oh, an only child?"

"Right. I used to beg my parents for a brother, but they told me one was enough. My dad said the only way I'd ever have a sibling was if I'd been born second, not first. I guess I wore them out."

I lift the grater and again check the miniature mountain of cheese beneath it. I think it's enough for two. "Do you get along with your parents now?"

"Oh, sure. They're not wild about me living in New York, and they're not thrilled that I haven't given them any grandchildren. But I tell them the only way they'll have grandchildren is if I'd been born"—something that looks almost like bitterness enters his face—"a sports star instead of a geek."

"You're not a geek." The words spring to my lips before I know what I'm saying.

A reluctant grin tugs at his mouth as he tears at a head of lettuce. "You don't get out much, do you, Aurora? Don't feel bad; I don't mean that as a slap. But if you did get out, you'd realize I'm a far cry from a metrosexual or a dude or whatever they're calling the hot guys these days."

Awareness thickens between us. He's braver than I am, quick to acknowledge his reality as well as mine, but I'm not yet ready to admit defeat.

"I don't like to go out. While other people are out in the rat race, I'm at home . . . reading, mostly. But I'm not completely cut off from the world."

I slide the plate of cheese over the counter. "I hope this is enough." *And I hope that's the end of this conversation.*

"I suppose I'm happy to be who I am." He tips his chin downward, forcing his glasses to the end of his nose, and peers at me over the tops of his specs. "Do you know why God created economists?"

"No. Why?"

"To make weather forecasters look good."

Groaning, I bring up my hand to cover my eyes. "Is that your idea of before-dinner entertainment?" I feel like a character on one of those reality shows, trying to make up witty repartee before an unblinking television camera.

"Afraid so. Mrs. B. laughs at my jokes. You should laugh more, Aurora. Despite what you see on the news, the world isn't such a terrible place. If you stepped outside every once in a while, you might find that it's pretty wonderful."

I draw a quick breath. Maybe I should leave. He seems intent on probing at my sore spots, and nobody enjoys being probed, not even when the probing is gentle . . .

But it'd be rude to leave after accepting his invitation. And maybe he doesn't realize what he's doing, so if I can change the subject . . .

The microwave beeps for his attention. While he turns to grab the chicken, I pick up a framed photo on the island.

"This your family?"

He glances over his shoulder. "Yes. That's Mom and Pop Cannon. My folks."

"Do they ever visit?"

He reaches for a knife from a drawer. "Sometimes I think they'd rather visit Sodom and Gomorrah than New York. They're real down-to-earth people."

"You're lucky to have them." I run my fingertip over the image of the tall man in the photo. "I've never known my father."

Blade in hand, Philip looks up. "Your father is Theodore Norquest."

"Right."

"You don't know him at all?"

I shake my head.

He slices the cooked chicken with steady, deliberate motions. "That's what Clara told me. I guess I was hoping she had exaggerated the story."

I shrug. "Unfortunately, my father is a jerk. By the time I was born, Mother despised him. I've never even spoken to him."

Philip tilts his head. "That's hard to believe."

"You think I'd make up a story like that?"

"No, that's not what I'm saying. But when a person is famous, you want to believe they deserve that kind of fame, you know? It galls me to think the man is a jerk. I've always loved his books."

Despite everything, my interest flickers. "You read his stuff?"

"Every Norquest book I can get my hands on. When I was a kid, my folks used to get me the latest Theodore Norquest novel every year for Christmas. I'd thank them and sit down to Christmas breakfast, but the entire time I was dying to get away and start reading. My mother used to say I was the only kid she knew who could go into his room on Christmas Day and not come out for twenty-four hours."

For some inexplicable reason, this information thrills me. "Were his books really that good?"

"They're still that good. Though he's not publishing at the same pace he used to, I scarf up his stories whenever he puts out a new release. He's grown better as he's grown older . . . but his last few books have made me feel sad, and his stuff never affected me that way before." He shrugs. "Maybe it's me. Maybe I'm sad because I know he won't be around forever."

I can't respond—I'm not sure I ought to respond. We are discussing the man who created me, but we might as well be discussing Al Capone. I think my mother would be more likely to forgive the infamous gangster than my father.

I press my hand to the countertop and study the tips of my fingernails. A hundred questions about Theodore Norquest have risen in the back of my throat, but for years the mere mention of his name sent tremors of revulsion through my household. To ask about him feels disloyal somehow, especially with Mother barely gone . . .

"Did you never read him?"

Philip's question jars me out of my silence. "Are you kidding? Mother would have fainted if she'd seen one of his books in our apartment. For years she wouldn't even go into a bookstore because she was bound to glimpse one of his novels on a table."

Philip gives me a sidelong look of utter disbelief. "Would you *like* to read him? I have a few of his books packed away, and I think I could find them without too much trouble. I'd be happy to lend you as many as you like."

My mouth goes dry. I feel like Pandora hesitating before that beautiful fatal box, enticed by curiosity and completely certain that unless I lift the lid I will never know happiness or contentment.

But what might that contentment cost me?

"I'll have to hide the book from Clara," I whisper, thinking aloud. "She might have a coronary if she sees one of his books in the apartment."

"I won't tell," Philip promises. "Not a word."

I bite my lip. My questions will never be answered unless I am able to judge my father for myself. So what if he is a cruel and callous man? He is also a literary genius. Surely I can enjoy the genius without endorsing the monster.

"If I were to take one of the books—I'm not saying I want one, but if I did—which would you recommend?"

Philip rolls his eyes toward the ceiling. "That's hard to say— some of them are very different. Norquest went through a dark phase a few years back . . . but some of his most memorable work came out of that time. One book scared the willies out of me when I read it, so I suppose it's my favorite. I try to read it at least once a year."

"Why on earth would you want to reread something that scared you?"

He dumps the sliced chicken into the salad bowl. "I think it helps me face my fears. I'm always at a different place when I read it, so the story resonates in a different way every time."

I hesitate, not certain I ought to ask the question that leaps into my mind. "What are you afraid of?"

"That's a personal question, Ms. Norquest. Are you sure our friendship has advanced to that level?"

Despite the twinkle in his eye, I'm ill at ease. I've gone too far. "Maybe not . . ." I force myself to keep my rear on the counter stool, but my leg twitches like it wants to bolt for home.

He laughs lightly and sprinkles the shredded cheese over the salad bowl. "I'm afraid of the usual stuff, Aurora—change, the future, loneliness. All the uncertain elements of the human condition. I'm afraid that some night I'll be sitting in bed and choke on a ham sandwich with no one around to administer the Heimlich. Plus spiders. I don't like spiders at all. And I seem to recall that Norquest novel as being liberally peppered with spiders."

Spiders are an awful lot like cockroaches . . . a shiver runs down my back, but I ignore it and raise my chin. I will not be dissuaded.

I rap my knuckles on the countertop. "Okay, I'll take one book. Not that scariest one—I don't need any more fodder for nightmares. But another of your favorites. The least frightening one."

He grins. "It'll take me a while to dig through the novels, but I'll find a good one for you. The man writes horror, remember, but there are some . . . well, you'll just have to read it for yourself to see what I mean."

"Thanks—but if I read it and hate it, will you be mad if I say so?"

"Honesty is always the best policy between friends, don't you think?"

He sets a pair of salad tongs beside the bowl, then slides an empty plate toward me. And again I am reduced to blushing when I realize we have become something other than mere acquaintances.

By the time Jay Leno signs off, I can no longer stay awake. My visit to Philip's apartment reminded me that nothing but a thin wall separates us at night. If I so much as whimper in a bad dream, he's likely to hear me . . . and ask me about it the next morning.

Last night I was lucky—my dream was puzzling, but innocuous—but something tells me my luck won't hold. My visit with Philip chased some of the shadows from my heart, but the moment I crossed my threshold, they came back, slinking and sliding into their accustomed places. They are with me now, smelling of Mother; they are in her room, hiding under her hospital bed and lurking in her closet.

Repressing a shudder, I step into the bathroom and brush my teeth. I keep my gaze lowered, afraid to look in the mirror, terrified of what I might see standing behind me. This feels real, this *is* real, but my nightmares are expert pretenders, counterfeiting the senses of touch and taste and smell to wreak their havoc.

After rinsing my mouth, I reach upward, feel the rim of the cup I use to hold my toothbrush, and drop the brush in. To avoid looking in the mirror, I grab the edge of the medicine chest and swing it open. Instead of staring at a ghost, I find myself studying glass shelves lined with amber-colored medicine bottles, souvenirs of Mother's latter months.

One bottle, nestled between my razor and a container of dental floss, catches my eye. It's Halcion, a drug the doctor prescribed for nights when Mother couldn't—or wouldn't—sleep. "I always hesitate to do this," Dr. Helgrin had said, "but we must face facts—you need your sleep, Aurora, if you're going to care for your mother, and you can't sleep unless she does. So I want you to give her these, but only occasionally, only as a last resort."

I take the bottle out of the cabinet and twist the lid—at least a dozen pills remain. Mother had done well on the Halcion, waking the next morning with no apparent ill effects. Most important, she had slept deeply, and on those nights I hadn't had to worry about her getting out of bed and wandering around in the dark.

If I take one of these, perhaps I will sleep below the level where dreams stir and nightmares make mischief.

Without further thought, I pop one of the pills into my mouth, then splash up a handful of water and swallow.

Nervous flutterings invade my stomach as I close the medicine cabinet and confront my reflection in the mirror. Mother is not standing behind me, hollow-eyed and accusing.

I am alone.

16

Wednesday afternoon I am standing on a stepladder, painter's tape in hand—relishing my morning's success of eyeballing the thirteenth floor in the stairwell—when the buzzer sounds. Clara, who popped over about ten minutes ago, is in the kitchen, so I call out to her. "Can you get that, Clara?"

I hope it's the cable guy—Philip told me to have the cable company put a jack and modem in the den. I have no idea what those things are, but since the computer's coming tomorrow, I want to have everything ready.

Which is why I am desperate to finish taping the line between the wall and the ceiling in my bedroom. I've already painted two walls, and if I keep pushing, I'll have the entire room done by dinnertime. I painted the computer room yesterday and am terrifically pleased with the results.

Clara doesn't answer, but I hear the click of her shoes across the tiled foyer. She leans into my bedroom a moment later. "Did you forget your mother's lawyer was coming by today?"

"Aw, shoot." I press another three inches of tape to the ceiling, then rip the piece free of the roll. "Yes, I forgot. But I'm coming. Just give me a minute."

Clara's face remains locked in neutral, though I'm sure she disapproves of me meeting Bert Shields in my paint-spattered jeans and

T-shirt. The thought doesn't bother me—after all, Mr. Shields said it was a routine matter.

I climb down from the ladder, wipe my hands on a wet rag, and bend to peer into the mirror I've set on the bed. The downward view distorts my face, but it assures me I'm not wearing buttercup buff as eye shadow.

When I'm sure my hands are clean, I lift my chin and hurry down the gallery and into the living room. Mr. Shields is sitting on the sofa across from Clara, but he rises when he sees me.

"Good afternoon, Miss Norquest."

"Thank you for coming, Mr. Shields. And please forgive my appearance—I've been doing a bit of painting."

"You're a brave woman." His smile gathers up his sagging cheeks like curtains. "Last time I set out to paint a room, I ended up wearing half a can of harvest gold. The wife hasn't let me near a paintbrush again."

"I guess I was ready enough for a change that I was willing to risk the same encounter with buttercup buff."

When I gesture toward the sofa, he sits again and sets his briefcase on the coffee table. "This won't take long, but I need to make certain you are familiar with the details of your mother's will. According to the terms of the trust she established in 1994, the estate transferred automatically to you. There are, however, a few provisions we need to discuss."

I try to catch Clara's eye, but she is staring at the papers in the lawyer's hand.

I sink to the sofa next to Mr. Shields and accept the document he hands me.

"As you can see"—he runs the tip of his pen over the typed lines of his copy—"the opening language is standard: the estate, including your mother's personal property and interests, transfers to you upon your mother's death." He glances over at me. "These holdings, combined with the trust fund established by your father, have made you a wealthy young woman."

The news slams a punch to the center of my chest. "T-trust fund?" I stammer. "My *father* established a trust fund for me?"

Mr. Shields's face draws in upon itself, a knot of apprehension. "Surely you haven't forgotten."

I turn to Clara, who is glaring at the lawyer with barely disguised distaste. "Auntie? Did you know about this?"

"Subsequent to the divorce proceedings," Mr. Shields says, speaking more rapidly, "your father established a trust fund for you with an initial contribution of one million dollars—an amount which has now multiplied to nearly thirty-three million." He reaches up and tweaks the end of his mustache. "I'm sorry, but I was certain you knew about this. The file contains a sworn affidavit with your signature."

As he lowers his head and peers into his briefcase, my thoughts skip back to Clara's gentle insistence that she go through the papers in my mother's files. Did she throw away evidence of my father's provision for me? Why would she do such a thing?

I wave my hand before her frozen gaze. When she finally looks at me, I ask again: "Did you know about this?"

Her eyes have gone icy blue. "Your mother wanted nothing to do with that man. Yes, he established a trust, but I'm sure he did it only to keep people from thinking of him as a complete rogue. You don't need his money. Your mother was determined that you should never need anything from him."

Clara's face is pale, with deep red patches over her pronounced cheekbones. "I blame him for your mother's unhappiness in her final years. I know about dementia; I know how it makes people regress to their younger days. That's why your mother was so difficult and angry—she was reliving all those bad times with *him*."

Mr. Shields and I look at each other. I don't know how much he knows about my parents' relationship, but Clara's outburst is bound to make him uncomfortable.

The lawyer tugs at his collar, then pulls a bound document from a folder. "Here it is." He hands the folder to me. "On the second page you'll see an affidavit dated February 15, 1990, and signed with your name."

I flip to the second page and study the letter, signed the day after my twenty-first birthday. The slanted signature is a good forgery, but it is a forgery nonetheless. I can still remember spending my twenty-first birthday alone in my dormitory at Sweet Briar. I was nowhere near Manhattan.

My mother forged my signature. I know it; Clara knows it. Mr. Shields now knows it, and he's probably sweating bullets to think I might sue his firm for being remiss in their fiduciary duties.

But what good would it do to sully Mother's name?

I force a smile and lower the document to my lap. "I'm sorry, Mr. Shields, that my memory is so spotty. I have forgotten all about this."

"I can assure you, Ms. Norquest, that the fund has been well-managed. You have earned an average of 10.5 percent over the years, and your portfolio should continue to do well. Anytime you need to withdraw funds, all you have to do is ask and we will set the wheels in motion." A flash of humor crosses his face. "So you see, if you want to hire a professional painter, you can certainly afford to do so."

I acknowledge his comment with a weak smile, then skim over the remaining pages in the document. Theodore Norquest established the trust fund in April 1969 as a direct gift to his legal daughter, Aurora Rose Norquest. The trust remained under the authority of the directors of Shields, Wilt, and Stock until February 14, 1990, at which time legal authority transferred to Aurora Rose Norquest. In lieu of Aurora Rose Norquest's personal involvement, the financial directors of Shields, Wilt, and Stock were to continue to manage the trust fund.

One caveat catches my eye: Before any of the monies can be withdrawn, Aurora Norquest must agree to meet personally with Theodore Norquest or one of his heirs.

"What's this paragraph?" I jab at the paper with my index finger. "Before I can withdraw any money, I have to visit Theodore Norquest? What kind of stipulation is that?"

"An unusual one." Mr. Shields presses his hands together. "Your mother and father did not have an amicable parting. Apparently your father was afraid your mother would prejudice you against him, so before the money can be disbursed, you must arrange a personal visit with Mr. Norquest or, if he is deceased, one of his other children."

I shake my head. "I've never heard of such a thing."

"It sounds like him." Clara's mouth is a thin line of disapproval. "That man looked for any opportunity to hurt you and your mother. Look what he's doing even now."

"I don't know that asking a daughter to meet her father is hurtful." Daring her disapproval, Mr. Shields lifts a bushy brow and transfers his gaze to me. "But unless you're planning on buying a professional sports team or real estate, you don't need your father's money. Your mother's estate is valued at nearly fifteen million in mostly liquid assets. In other words"—his lips twist into a cynical smile—"you don't need to run to your father for an allowance."

I accept this news in stunned silence. I knew Mother had come from money, but I had no idea her estate was still worth so much.

I manage a hollow laugh. "Sort of makes my plans to get a job seem silly, doesn't it?"

Clara laughs too, but Mr. Shields only twiddles his mustache.

"Quite the contrary, Ms. Norquest. You are a fortunate young woman in that you've been given an opportunity to be useful to mankind. With the kind of money your parents have provided, you could establish a business, fund cancer research, endow any number of worthy philanthropies. You're still a young woman with a lifetime ahead of you. I'm hoping you'll take this opportunity to meet your father . . . for other than financial reasons."

I lower my gaze, feeling the pressure of Clara's eyes upon me. If she weren't here, I'd ask Mr. Shields if he knew how I could contact my father, but Clara would recoil in horror if I even mouthed the words. I had hoped that Mother's passing would temper Clara's aversion to my father; oddly enough, she seems more determined than ever to despise him.

"Your father's trust contained another interesting provision." The lawyer flips to another page. "In addition to the fund he established, he has also bequeathed the copyrights of his first thirty books to you. After his death, royalties from those books will be paid into the trust. Given the rate his older novels are selling, that amount could be quite substantial."

Clara sinks back, her hand going to her chest. Apparently this news caught her by surprise.

"And now there is this." Mr. Shields picks up the copy of Mother's will, then flips to the back. "If you'll look on page 10, you'll find that Mary Elizabeth was making an annual disbursement. She wished to continue this disbursement after her death, but she did give you the power to stop disbursing funds if you choose."

"What was it, an investment?"

"It was a gift. To a friend."

I read the terms of the bequest: *On January 1 the estate of Mary Elizabeth Wentworth Norquest shall pay an annual sum of $350,000 to Mrs. Clara Bellingham, a gift that shall continue until the recipient's death or until Aurora Rose Norquest chooses to invoke her authority and cease disbursement. Any revision by Aurora Rose Norquest must be offered in writing and copies delivered to Clara Bellingham and the offices of Shields, Wilt, and Stock at least ten days before the payment due date . . .*

I turn wide eyes upon Clara.

"We were *friends*," she whispers, looking small against the wide back of Mother's wing chair. "My husband—your Uncle Charley— did not provide for me as well as he should have. He had a gambling problem, you see, and . . . well, when he finally died, he left me nothing but debts. But your mother, bless her, stepped in and made this . . . arrangement. She didn't want me to suffer for Charley's terrible decisions. Mary Elizabeth's gift has enabled me to keep the apartment and maintain appearances . . . and that's just one reason why your mother meant the world to me."

She looks so frail, so frightened, that all I can feel is pity for her. This is why she wanted to be here today—and this is probably why she didn't want me rummaging through my mother's papers. Perhaps she had hoped to find a way to broach the subject beforehand but failed. Like Mother, she is a proud woman.

I stand and go to her. "Don't worry, Auntie," I murmur, wrapping my arms around her shoulders. "Why should anything change? Everything's going to be fine."

She is patting my arm, sniffling awkwardly in my embrace, when Mr. Shields clears his throat.

"If at any time"—he shuffles papers in his briefcase—"you wish to change the status of any of the items we have discussed, you have only to call my office. If you wish to avail yourself of your father's trust fund, be sure that I will immediately make all the necessary arrangements." He picks up his briefcase and leans forward as if to stand, but hesitates. "I should remind you"—he catches my eye— "that your father is an elderly man. If you want to see him, you should act soon."

What can I say? My mother's best friend is blubbering in my arms, weighting me down with the past. And I've just promised her that nothing will change.

"There's no need," I say, patting Clara's arm. I release her, then stand and face the lawyer. "Thank you for coming, Mr. Shields.

My mother trusted you implicitly, and I'd like to continue our association."

He extends his hand. "Your father trusted me, too."

I shake his hand and thank him again, then walk him through the foyer. Clara slips by us, murmuring something about getting something from the kitchen, but I know she is going to the bathroom to splash water on her tear-streaked cheeks.

I wish Mr. Shields a good day, then close the door behind him. I can hear water running in the bathroom—Clara will remain in there until the last trace of blotchiness has left her face.

I sink onto the bench beside the foyer table, my mind reeling with revelation. In the last half-hour I've discovered that both my parents had reservoirs of generosity I never expected to find.

17

APARTMENT 15A

By Thursday morning, my bedroom is shimmering with two coats of buttercup buff. I finished the second coat late last night, and I've dedicated the morning to clearing away the last of the painter's tape, the newspapers, and the rags I used to swipe paint from the baseboards and crown molding.

The phone rings a couple of times while I'm working, but I ignore it. I refuse to answer calls from telephone solicitors this morning because I'd like to get the bedroom furniture back in place before lunch. I am expecting delivery of my new computer today, and I am as excited as a kid at Christmas.

I am shoving my bureau into position along the wall when the door buzzes. Feeling suddenly guilty because I might have ignored a call from Clara, I hurry to the door and find old Booker in the hall.

"Booker!" I glance down the hall. "Should you be away from your post?"

"I rang you a couple of times, Miss Aurora," he says, a beatific smile curving his mustache. "When you didn't answer, I figured I'd better get up here and check to be sure you were okay."

"Thanks, Booker, but I'm fine."

I am about to close the door, but he lifts a warning finger. "The reason I rang you, ma'am, is because there's a courier downstairs with packages for you. The fellow keeps insisting that you come down and personally sign for them."

An icy finger touches the base of my spine. "Can't you sign for them, Booker?"

"Not this one, ma'am," he says, backing away. "It's some private company and they said you signed up for person to person. The man says it's gotta be you or they won't leave the boxes. And they won't wait much longer."

"Can't he bring them up?"

Booker shakes his head. "No, ma'am, he won't bring them up until after you've accepted delivery. I already asked him."

This isn't fair! I glance toward Clara's apartment, but I know she's gone out for lunch and won't be back for at least a couple of hours. Philip might be home, but what'll I do if this is his morning to teach at NYU? I'll look like a fool in front of old Booker, one more person who'll think I'm positively deranged.

"If you'll excuse me, Miss Aurora, I need to get back to my desk."

As Booker moves to the elevator and presses the button, I linger in the doorway, torn between retreating to my safe place and going to get my computer—

He looks at me. "You comin', ma'am?"

Well . . . why not? If I can take the stairs to the thirteenth floor, surely I can take a quick trip in the elevator.

"Just a minute. Let me get my key."

I dart inside and grab my key from the foyer table, then stuff it in my pocket and hurry to the elevator. The bronze doors slide open as I approach; Booker steps inside and holds the door for me.

I gulp a deep breath and sidle through the double doors. As the elevator descends, I press my right shoulder against the wall and stare at the panel of buttons by the doors. Booker folds his hands and whistles under his breath. His isn't a pure whistle, but the kind of scraping sound people make by pushing air through their teeth. After a while, that sound could really grate upon a person's nerves.

He glances over his shoulder at me. "Nice day outside."

"Is it? I hadn't noticed."

"Oh, yeah. Supposed to be in the seventies by this afternoon. Weatherman says we'd better get out and enjoy the sunshine while we can."

"I suppose he's right."

Prickles of unease nip at the back of my arms when the elevator lurches to a halt on the tenth floor. I lower my gaze as the doors open, then lift my head enough to see an elderly woman step aboard, her arms filled with her bichon frise. She nods at Booker, then smiles at me. The fluff ball squirms in her grasp, but she scolds him: "Mind your manners, Matthew."

Don't stare at the freak.

I squinch my eyes shut and huddle in the corner, breathing only when the elevator begins to move again.

It'll be worth it, I remind myself. *In only a few minutes, you'll have your computer. Down and back. How hard could it be?*

"Nice day outside," the woman says, speaking to the doorman. "Have you been able to enjoy it at all?"

"Walked to work this mornin'," he answers, a smile in his voice. "Might walk home this afternoon, if the weather holds."

"It can get rather chilly when the sun goes down."

"Right chilly. That's why I'm glad I get off at one. My grandson comes on at one—have you met Thomas?"

"Indeed I have. Lovely boy. You should be proud of him, Booker."

"Yes, ma'am, I am. Right proud."

For no reason I can name, their inane conversation raises the hair at the back of my neck. My right shoulder is jammed against the wall for support, but it's not enough, so I press my hands to the smooth surface, clinging to solidity. I have no reason to panic. This is an elevator, not a spaceship; I'm going to the lobby, not to hell. Clara and Philip and Booker and dozens of other people walk through the lobby every day; no dangers lurk there. And Booker would protect me if something went wrong, wouldn't he? Helping tenants is part of his job, and if ever a tenant needed help, I do.

I'm not sure how many times we stop—I refuse to count after the third time I feel the soft bounce of the car upon its cable. The elevator has filled with people; I can hear and smell them. The elderly woman has fallen silent, but a couple near the front of the car whisper in low tones while Booker continues his tuneless whistling. Somewhere near my left elbow, the old woman's bichon is panting in time with my racing heart.

I hear a ding, then the rush of the sliding doors. My shoulders slump when the elevator begins to empty.

I look up to find the doorman watching me with concern in his eyes. "Everything all right, Miss Aurora?"

A bead of perspiration traces a cold path from my hairline to my neck. "Everything's fine, Booker."

I step out on legs that feel as insubstantial as marshmallows. My companions are sailing toward mailboxes and the glass revolving door, through which I glimpse the street and cars and buses and cabs and crowds—

"Aurora Norquest?"

I want to weep with relief when a man in a gray uniform calls my name. "That's me."

He holds out an electronic clipboard. "Sign here, please."

Feeling faint, I scribble my signature across a dark screen. He nods, then grabs the handle of a dolly laden with boxes. "These are for you." He shoots a pointed glance at the doorman. "Can you give us a hand?"

"For Miss Aurora, anything." Booker takes the dolly and wheels it into the elevator. I follow, drawing a deep breath as I step back into the enclosed car. As frightening as the elevator is, the lobby is worse.

"Thanks," I whisper to the courier. I close my eyes against a tide of nausea. If I say more, I'll throw up.

Apparently intuiting my discomfort, Booker says nothing on the ride back to the fifteenth floor. When the elevator doors open, I rush ahead of him, ostensibly to open the door.

The moment my feet cross the threshold, my pulse begins to steady. I wait there, my arms and chest soaked with perspiration, as Booker whistles his load through the doorway.

When my boxes and I have been safely delivered to the apartment, I take a minute to grab a glass of water from the kitchen, then hang my head over the sink until my pulse slows and my vision clears. Soon I am ready to attack the packages, but a feeling of dread overwhelms me as I stare into the first box. A large sheet with color illustrations lies on top of the contents, but I'm terrified I will make a mistake. Even more terrifying is the realization that I am on my own . . . well, not quite. Philip has offered to help. I intend to take him up on his offer, but before he comes over, I want him to see that I've at least made an attempt to begin.

I slide the boxes into the freshly painted den, then tug them into position beside the desk. The drawers have been emptied, the desktop polished.

The medium-sized box contains the monitor, a thin model of black plastic. I set it toward the back of the desk and leave the cords dangling.

The largest carton contains the big metal box Philip called the "brains" of the computer. I know it should go on the floor, so I pull it free of its foam packaging and push it inside the desk's kneehole. I lean back and wonder if it can breathe in a confined space. I'm pretty sure there's a motor inside, and everything with a motor gets hot and needs cooling, doesn't it? That's a question for Philip.

Tucked away in the large box are the keyboard, mouse, speakers, and what looks like enough cables to wire the entire fifteenth floor. Fortunately, these are color-coded—one end of the green cable goes into a green hole at the back of the computer while the other end slides into a speaker. The heavy three-pronged black cords are for the monitor and printer and CPU.

I'm feeling pretty confident by the time I have most of the cables attached to something. I sit in the chair, hold my breath, and press the power button on the black box. I hear whirring sounds, I see lights flicker inside the black box . . . but nothing else. The monitor is not bringing me the Internet, e-mail, or any of the secrets of the universe.

Perhaps it requires a firmer touch. I jab the power button again, then bite my lip as the flickering lights die out.

I think I may have killed it.

Staring at the mound of packing materials at my feet, I consider my options. I could sit here and fumble through this mess for hours, hoping to strike upon the right solution . . . or I could go for help.

I stand and stride to Philip's apartment.

Thankfully, he's home . . . but he's wearing a white shirt, tan slacks, and a navy tie. I've never seen him in a tie.

"Hey." He grins when he sees me. "What's up?"

"The computer," I tell him. "It's here."

His eyes brighten, then his fingers tug at the knot of his tie. "Let me get out of this noose and I'll be right over."

He arrives at my door a couple of minutes later. "Are you excited?" he asks as I lead him toward the den.

"I will be—as soon as the thing starts to work." I point to the lifeless machine. "There it is."

He kneels on the floor and checks my connections, then presses the power button. "The CPU seems to be working," he says, rising to sit in the chair. He touches the lower right corner of the monitor, and I hear a zip of static. Almost instantly, the screen fills with the Microsoft logo.

"You have to turn the monitor on, too." He winks at me. "Not every peripheral has its own power button, but most of them do.

I'd advise you to leave them all on and plugged into a power strip. That way they'll power on and off when you hit the computer switch."

I'm too mesmerized to reply. WELCOME, the screen says. To what?

Philip grins at my bewildered expression. "Need some help setting things up from here?"

"You mean there's more?" I sink cross-legged to the floor. "Please, do whatever you like."

"Okay." He faces the desk; his fingers tap-dance over the keyboard. He moves through several screens of information, then swivels to look at me.

"Did you plug the cable modem into the computer and the wall outlet?"

I nod—this is one thing I'm sure I did right. The cable guy brought a modem and installed the extra line yesterday.

"Good." When Philip clicks on a little picture on the screen, a registration form appears. "You'll need to create a name for your e-mail address," he says. "You can be creative or straightforward, whatever you like."

"You mean—" I try to remember some of the e-mail jargon I've heard on TV. "Like eBay.com?"

He laughs. "Your Internet service provider is Manhattan Road Runner, so the ending of your e-mail addy will be manhattan.rr.com. You create the first part of the address."

I nod, mentally adding several new words to my expanding technical vocabulary. "Okay—so let's make my addy Aurora Rose."

He smiles as he types. "Is that your real name?"

"It's the only name I have."

"Aurora Rose." He murmurs my name absent-mindedly, then sends me a grin. "Anyone ever call you Rosie?"

"Not in this lifetime."

I'm about to tell him no one in the world could possibly think of me as a *Rosie*, but a message flashes across the screen—success! I am now accessible through AuroraRose@manhattan.rr.com.

"Do I have to type it like that? With a capital R?"

Philip shakes his head. "Lowercase shouldn't make a difference. Don't add a space, though, or your e-mail won't get through."

I cross my arms, content to watch him fly through procedures that would take me hours to figure out. "You'll want to create folders here," he says, pointing to the left side of the screen. "When you visit a useful Web page, mark it as a favorite, then you can find it again in a second."

"So you're on the Internet now?"

"Sure am. Surfing the World Wide Web. You can find anything here."

He moves through Web pages for shopping, research, entertainment, and gossip, explaining things in a casual voice that floats right through my head. I feel like Rip Van Winkle, waking in a world that has progressed far beyond my imagining.

"You seem to be sleeping better," he says.

The abrupt conversational shift startles me. "What? Oh . . . well. I haven't had any nightmares in a while."

It's not quite the truth, but I don't want to share the secret that has been helping me sleep. I haven't even told Clara about the pills I found in the medicine cabinet. For all I know, I could be having nightmares, but the pills make me sleep so soundly I don't wake up . . . and I don't remember.

"Maybe you're under less stress . . . since you've had a little time to adjust to your mother's being gone."

I nod. "I'm sure you're right."

He swivels to face me. "At least I haven't heard you rocking out at 2 a.m."

His grinning approval pleases me more than I can say. I feel my cheeks begin to heat and am grateful when someone buzzes at the door. Leaving him at the computer, I get up and hurry to the foyer, tapping my flaming cheeks on the way.

Clara stands at my threshold, a canvas bag on her shoulder. Seeing me, her eyes narrow to mascaraed slits. "What's wrong, dear? You look feverish."

I stifle a sudden urge to laugh. "I'm fine, Auntie. I'm excited about my new computer."

She makes a face as she drops her bag onto the foyer table. "I don't trust those things."

"Come on back and you'll see how useful it is. The Internet is fascinating. Philip says you can find out almost anything about anybody."

Her expression remains serious, but one corner of her mouth twists. "Philip Cannon is here?"

"He's getting my computer set up—and yes, he's been here awhile."

"That's interesting."

I don't ask what she means by that comment, but I assume she's hoping Philip and I will make some sort of match. I shouldn't have to worry about her dropping broad hints in front of him, though— she's too refined for that sort of behavior.

Clara arches a brow when she sees the computer on my mother's antique desk, but she refrains from comment as Philip greets her.

"I've added the Google search page to your favorites folder," he says, turning to me, and I'm thrilled to realize I understand what he means.

"So anytime I want to look something up, I just click on the little picture?"

"The icon. Exactly. Like this." He demonstrates with a click of the mouse, and a millisecond later we are looking at the Google search page.

Philip grins. "I've got an idea—why don't we Google Mrs. B.?"

"I'm not sure I like the sound of that," Clara answers, but she leans closer while Philip types her name into the rectangular box. He hits the enter key, then sits back as the screen fills with a list of entries.

"Oh, my." Clara's hand rises to her throat. "How does that computer know about me?"

"It's not the computer, Clara." I lean toward the screen again and point. "What are those, Philip?"

He is skimming the listings. "Most of these are references to newspaper articles . . . and here's a page from the Met. Looks like a roster of board members."

Clara stiffens. "Well, of course, I've been on the board fifteen years. But not everybody in the world needs to know that."

Philip gives her a reassuring look. "Not everybody in the world will look you up, Mrs. B. And these are perfectly innocent references. Nearly every organization you can name these days has a Web page, so sooner or later everyone will show up on the Web. The more active you are, the more often your name will show up."

"Really?" Clara's tone is distant, but she takes a step closer, touching my sleeve as she peers at the monitor. "How many times did my name . . . turn up?"

Philip consults the bottom of the screen. "Looks like there are at least five pages of entries. You're quite the celebrity."

"Ridiculous." She shakes her head, but when one corner of her mouth lifts, I know Philip's comment has pleased her.

Clara turns away and walks to the door, then glances over her shoulder. "I still don't trust those things—how can anyone enjoy a measure of privacy with computers in every home?"

"Privacy is not something you can take for granted anymore," Philip answers. "But we're a long way from Big Brother watching us."

Afraid I've somehow offended her, I follow Clara to the door. She taps her fingers on the foyer table in a meditative rhythm, then picks up her bag. "He's a nice young man, Aurora, but be careful."

"I know he's nice—and I'm probably *too* careful."

"You can't be too careful, especially not with young men. He is not one of us."

I hesitate, blinking with bafflement. "What do you mean?"

Clara takes a deep breath. "I mean he's not from around here. I've never heard of his people, and he seems a bit—I don't know, a bit rough around the edges. Furthermore, I don't trust these computers. I hear about young girls meeting strange men on that Internet; dangerous perverts who hang out in talk rooms and convince innocent women to meet them in strange places—"

"They're called chat rooms, Auntie, and I'm not about to meet anyone anywhere. I don't even know how to get into one."

She snaps her fingers. "That reminds me—there was an odd package in your mailbox today."

"Probably some new kind of junk mail."

"I don't think so—it felt heavy, like a book. But it's from some place I've never heard of, though I think it had something to do with the Internet . . ."

She pulls a cardboard box from her bag, and I read the return address: "Amazon.com?"

Clara crosses her arms. "See what I mean? These people are all in cahoots with each other. How could you order something if you didn't even have a computer until today?"

"It's a gift." Philip's voice cuts into our conversation, and my face flushes when I turn and see him leaning against the gallery wall. His eyes flick at the package, then look back to me. "It's something I think you'll enjoy."

I nearly choke on a lump of guilt. Without being told, I know it's one of my father's books . . . a gift Clara would never approve.

She settles her bag on her shoulder. "The last thing Aurora needs is another book. You're living next to one of the best-read women in Manhattan, Philip."

I am suddenly eager to send Clara on her way. "Thanks, Auntie, for bringing the mail."

"If you need me to pick up anything else, I'll be going by the library tomorrow. I could return those decorating books you have out—"

"Thanks, but I'm not quite finished with them. As you can see"—I flap my hand toward the gallery—"I'm not done with decorating."

"Well." She takes a step toward the door, then lifts her head. "If you need anything, dear heart, you know who to call."

I give her a quick hug and send her on her way, but the guarded note in her voice makes me wonder if she resents my new friendship.

After an hour at the keyboard, Philip has given me a crash course in computer basics. I can now open a document in Word, track my bank accounts in Money, and send an e-mail.

"And here"—he clicks on an icon that looks like a little man—"is how you can reach me anytime I'm at the keyboard. This is Messenger, and if we're both online, you can use it to send me an instant message. So if you ever need a quick answer, you can think of that cartoon guy as your friendly geek next door."

I grin at him, disarmed by his self-deprecating humor. "I don't know where I'd be right now without you."

"Aw, you'd have probably gotten a book from the library and figured it out."

He stands, then grabs one of the rectangular foam packing pieces and spins it in the air. The movement startles me, reminding me of the dancing puzzle pieces of my dream.

T.N.

A.N.

A father and daughter destined to remain apart.

"Aurora? Where'd you go?"

I blink, brought back to the present by Philip's question. "I'm sorry, what?"

"I asked if you were in the mood for a pizza."

"Oh. Maybe." I pick up the box Clara brought. "But I think I'd like to open this first—do you mind?"

"Why should I mind? Like I said, it's a gift."

I struggle for a minute to open the corrugated container, then pull out a hardcover volume wrapped in a dust jacket. As I suspected, it's a novel by Theodore Norquest. The title, *Shadowed Sanctuary*, is spelled in gold letters below his name.

"I couldn't find the book I was telling you about," Philip says, "so I thought I'd have his latest sent to you. They say it's his best work to date."

"Do you think so?"

"I haven't read it yet."

"You shouldn't have gone through the trouble." The words spring to my lips from habit, but something in me is very glad he did.

"Maybe we can read it together and compare notes."

I look up from the stunning black and gold cover. "You want to borrow my book?"

"I ordered my own copy—it's probably downstairs in today's mail."

I run my fingertips over the matte finish of the jacket. "It's beautiful, isn't it?"

I close my eyes, silently grateful to share this moment with someone. Lately I have been living in a state of anticipation—of redoing the apartment, getting the computer, going back to school, finding something to do with my life. But the thing I have been anticipating the most is learning about my father . . . even if I only learn about him through his books. I'd give anything if Clara would share this adventure, but she is so set against anything affiliated with Theodore Norquest that it's a miracle she tolerates me.

I hug the book and smile at my friend. "Thank you. You have no idea how much this means."

He's about to answer, but the cell phone in his pocket warbles. He pulls it out, glances at the number, then gives me a disappointed smile. "I'll have to take a rain check on the pizza. This is my client, and I owe him a progress report on our current project."

"Go ahead." Cradling the book against my chest, I stand and step toward the door. "I'll catch up with you later."

He winks, then presses the receive button and holds the phone to his ear. I let him out, then lock the door and go into the library where I can relish this forbidden pleasure in privacy.

After sinking into the love seat, I open the novel and wonder what sort of story Theodore Norquest has laid out for his readers . . . and for me.

I read until well after midnight. And even though my eyelids are heavy and my limbs numb with exhaustion, dread has snaked down my spine and coiled in my stomach. Now I know why I have never read horror. This is the least scary of his novels?

Shadowed Sanctuary is the story of a woman who's trying to protect her child from the ghost—or memory, I can't tell which—of a former lover. When I finally put the book down for the night, a murky mist of fear is churning across the sea of my soul.

And just behind it is a crushing disappointment that I may not be able to understand my father through his novels. Why'd he have to write horror, of all things?

The room is warm, yet I shiver. Every lamp in the library is blazing, yet I sense shadows in the gallery and the bedrooms beyond.

I cross my arms and force a laugh that sounds hollow in my ears.

Tomorrow I will have to tell Philip I can't handle Theodore Norquest. Yes, he's good; sure, he tells a gripping story, but lately I've been jumping at shadows. How can I read books *designed* to scare people silly?

I hug my knees to my chest, then leap up from the love seat—careful not to let my feet land where a phantom beneath the dust ruffle could grab my ankles—and hurry to the kitchen. I pour a glass of Diet Coke and bend to watch the amber bubbles streak past the ice cubes to pop on the surface.

I've poured the drink in preparation for taking my sleeping pill. I want to curl into the soft darkness of my bed and close my eyes, wishing all of this away, but my brain feels too wired for sleep.

What in the world is wrong with me?

I sink onto a barstool and sip my soda. I've been making good progress, I think, since Mother died. I've been taking baby steps, working on the apartment, learning about my computer, letting Philip into my safe little world, pushing myself to go down the stairs—I even managed the elevator. Sure, I had a hard time, but I didn't have a full-blown panic attack.

But the experience of reading my father's book has frightened me to a point that feels like regression. If I take that pill—if I curl up and fall into a drugged sleep—tomorrow I will busy myself with everything *but* reading. I'll surf the Internet, browse through catalogs, consider a new wallpaper for the kitchen. I'll invite Clara over for lunch; I'll watch *Oprah* and *Jeopardy;* I'll come up with a thousand things to do.

But I won't pick up my father's book. And one of the things that kept me from jumping off the roof the other night was the realization that I am finally free to learn about my father. I still can't picture myself going to England, but if I can at least read his books, perhaps I can discover that he is not abhorrent, but admirable.

God knows I need to admire him.

But tonight my father's book has frightened me half out of my wits. So unless I can do something or *confront* something that frightens me even more, I will never pick up that book again.

Before the logical part of my brain can argue the point, I slip into a sweater and put the apartment key in my pocket. I walk quietly through the hallway and climb the stairway to the roof.

The wind hoots a welcome as I brace the door with the concrete block. My elevator companions were right—the weather is cool, but warmer than a typical November night. In the distance, toward the east, bright veins of lightning pulse in the sky, followed by a low throb of thunder.

That explains the unseasonable warmth. Mother always said unseasonably warm and muggy weather preceded a thunderstorm.

With my pulse pounding, I slip my hands in my pockets and walk around the rooftop, reversing my course this time. Across the street, I see the bearded man's rooftop garden, bare except for an evergreen bush he keeps in a ceramic pot.

As the ambient light of New York City lights my way, I step carefully over the rooftop, skirting vents and odd pipes and pieces of flapping tarpaper. I don't have to tread softly here—the apartment below is mine, and currently inhabited only by bad memories. I reach the southern edge and lean into the bow of my dining room's bay window. Not much to see from here—and not much I haven't seen from my own apartment.

I walk across the southern edge and cross the halfway point— now I'm tramping across Clara's ceiling, but there's not much chance of her hearing anything once she's gone to bed.

I move to the railing above her dining room window and stare at the glass penthouse across the street. Brilliantly lit from within, the place gleams like a diamond. The resident of this glass palace—a woman—is sitting before her dressing table. She is wearing a black cocktail dress and her blond hair has been swept up in tousled curls.

She pulls a tendril free from the cluster in a gesture that swims up through the years . . . my mother used to do the same thing.

My eyes fill with tears at the memory of Mother preening at her vanity. As a little girl, I used to lie on her bed, my chin propped in my stubby hands as I watched her apply perfume and powder, blush and eye shadow. If I was quiet and good, sometimes she would take her little brush and paint lipstick on my mouth. Then she would make a smacking sound in the vicinity of my forehead (even then I knew that she couldn't kiss me without mussing her makeup) and tell me to run along to bed.

I squint into the light, trying to see if the penthouse woman has a daughter, but I can't see anyone else in the apartment.

The woman pauses before the mirror in her bedroom, checks her reflection one last time, then stands and moves gracefully through the living room toward someone or something I can't see.

I cling to the railing as memories flit past my face like moth wings. I have never been graceful. I don't think I've ever been described as beautiful. Mother was always the center of attention; any attempt to compete with her would have been a waste of time. And now . . . it's too late. Whatever beauty I may have cultivated in my younger days is long gone.

Abruptly the wind rises, swirling across the rooftop, chillier than before. I shiver and rub my hands over my arms. What am I doing here? That's right—steeling my nerves against true terror. The rooftop is not a safe place; it is dangerous territory. I will stay out here as long as my thumping heart can handle the strain, then I will go downstairs and know that nothing in my father's novel could hurt me.

The woman from the penthouse crosses back into my field of vision, interrupting my musings. She is no longer alone—someone follows her, a bald man in a dark suit. He reaches out to embrace her, but she flits away, her head tilting as if to tease him.

He pulls out his wallet and drops money on the table behind the sofa. She melts into his arms; they kiss. And as she leads him along the transparent wall linking a public room to a private space, I feel the truth like an electric tingle along my spine.

My knees buckle beneath me. I sit down, hard, on the rooftop while one hand clings to the iron railing now above my head. I am suddenly back in the sickroom, listening as my beautiful Mother curses me with language she never should have known.

How foolish of me to imagine that beauty and goodness are inevitably linked. I never saw ugliness in Mother until the disease took control, but now I know Tolstoy was right—what a strange illusion it is to suppose that beauty is goodness.

I lift my head to see the moon distantly glowing in a sky as black as airless space. When I look at the penthouse again, I see that the woman who keeps a night-light burning when she sleeps alone has extinguished the lights for now.

18

APARTMENT 15A

After waking from a hard, drug-induced sleep, I sit at the kitchen counter and write out my to-do list for the new day: go online to order my new bed linens and carpet; ask Aunt Clara about art prints to match whatever bedding I select.

It's the twelfth of November, so I also need to do an online search for a master's program. I've been thinking a lot about what I'd like to study, and I'm feeling good about a graduate degree in English literature. If I never find the courage to step out of my building's lobby, at least I'll enjoy the two years of study.

I'm feeling pretty confident on the Internet, and Google is my new best friend. I love the way Philip uses the word as a verb, and when I sit down at the computer, fully intending to search for bed linens, I find myself googling another name: Theodore Norquest.

Last night I slept with *Shadowed Sanctuary* on the nightstand, and no ghosts rose from those pages to torment my dreams. My trip to the rooftop did more than take my mind off the haunting story—it focused the cold light of reality on the scene I observed across the street. I've been trying not to think about the woman in the penthouse, but I keep seeing her in that man's arms. She is Beauty and the Beast, both personalities encased in a slim, golden-haired package.

Any woman who can do what she does for a living has to be a

calculating actress. How can a person look so delicate and be so manipulative?

After chasing that thought around and never coming up with an answer, googling my father's name seems an innocent diversion.

I type his name into the box and click enter, then sit back in stunned amazement when Google returns hundreds of entries—"hits," Philip calls them. Each of my father's books is listed on myriad pages of online booksellers; I also see dozens of fan forums devoted to his work. He is on the recommended reading lists of scores of libraries; teenagers cite him as their favorite author on their "all about me" pages.

I find a photograph of my father on another site—a black-and-white photo that appears to be more recent than the shot featured on the back of *Shadowed Sanctuary*. In the Web site photo he is wearing a dark coat over a light turtleneck sweater, the garb of a professor. He has a white beard, salt-and-pepper hair, and dark eyes that seem shadowed . . . either that, or this is an expression the photographer urged him to exhibit. He *looks* like a brooding horror writer . . . and something in me desperately wants to find a smiling picture to balance this melancholy image.

Before I can look further, the buzzer sounds. I groan, then hurry to the door and find Clara wearing an apologetic smile.

"You're going to think I've taken leave of my senses," she says, keeping her head low, "but my bridge club is coming over tomorrow and I want to make a chocolate chess pie."

I stare at her, unable to understand why I should be alarmed.

"Trouble is"—she folds her hands—"I don't have the recipe, and Beverly Piper absolutely refuses to share hers—she says it's a family secret. So I went to the library and spoke to the woman at the reference desk, who assured me I could find it on the Internet much more easily than digging through cookbooks. She pointed me toward a computer."

It's all I can do to keep from laughing. I know Clara would never admit that she doesn't know how to type or use a computer, but still, I have to ask: "So? Did you look it up?"

"In a public place?" Clara's hand clutches the lace at her throat. "Of course not. But then I remembered you have a computer and the Internet, so if you could look it up for me . . ."

A warm glow flows through me—vindication, however small, is sweet. "I'm sure we could find something." I step aside to let her in, then lead the way to the computer room. She follows, babbling about Beverly Piper's culinary snobbery, but when I touch the mouse to deactivate the screen saver, the flow of her words sputters and halts as if someone has turned a spigot in her throat.

My father's face fills the screen. The air in the room thickens with the sound of silence.

I put my hand on the mouse, but I'm nervous and I can't remember what to click to make the photo go away.

"Aurora," Clara whispers, her voice ragged with pain. "How could you?"

I click the green arrow next to the back button, which removes the picture but takes me to the Google page. My father's name occupies the search box, bearing mute testimony to my disloyalty.

"Your mother would be crushed if she knew."

Why? I want to scream. *Why should curiosity about my father equal disloyalty to my mother?*

I clear my throat as questions push and jostle in my throat, but she lifts a hand to silence my protests.

"That man cares nothing for you. He cared nothing for your mother. You are nothing to him—why can't you leave the hurts of the past alone? Move on with your life, Aurora. Forget about him, because I'm sure he's forgotten about you."

I exhale in exasperation and highlight that traitorous name. With a jab of the delete key, it disappears.

I can't look at Clara.

"What was it you wanted?" I ask, my voice clipped. "Chocolate pie?"

"He hates you," she says. "Oh, I know it looks like he was being generous when he set up that trust fund, but he only did it so he wouldn't look like a heel to his public. You've never met a man more concerned about his image than Theodore Norquest."

I grit my teeth. *What* public image? I have been reading versions of his biography for the past half-hour, and I've read nothing about the man's personality, philanthropy, or family life. Apparently he guards his privacy.

But to say more would only invite trouble. "Was that chocolate pie?"

"Chocolate *chess* pie."

I type the words into the search box and click enter; the screen fills with a list of links. Clara leans over my shoulder and peers at them through her glasses until one suits her fancy: "That one looks promising."

I click the link and give her a moment to skim the ingredients. When she nods, I hit the print key and send the recipe to the printer, where it appears on two crisp sheets of paper. As Aunt Clara pulls the pages from the tray, I know this diversion will not hold. In a minute she will launch another attack on my father.

"If you are planning to run to the grocery," I say, standing and moving toward the kitchen, "would you mind picking up a dozen eggs for me?"

She follows, a question in her blue eyes when I glance back at her.

"I thought it'd be nice to make a bowl of egg salad. Philip's been helping me with the computer, and I'd like to have something ready so I can offer him a sandwich."

She pauses outside the kitchen doorway. "I *do* like that young man, you know."

"But you told me to be careful around him."

"You should always be careful, Aurora, because the heart is a fickle thing. But while some men make good husbands, others are best kept as friends." She smiles as she meets my eye. "And if you disagree with what I've said about your father, ask Philip what he thinks about a man who ignores his flesh and blood for thirty-five years. I'm sure he'll agree that sort of person is *not* a parent worthy of a daughter's attentions."

I don't argue but walk through the foyer and open the front door. She would have a fit if she knew my neighbor has been encouraging my quest for information . . . but what she doesn't know won't hurt her.

When she is gone, I return to the computer and defiantly retype my father's name in the Google search box. On a Web page sponsored by his longtime publisher, I find an article that sparks my attention:

> *Born at the foot of the Catskills, horror novelist Theodore Norquest lived the early part of his life in New York City. At the age of thirty-six, however, he moved to London, where he began writing novels of far greater intensity.*
>
> *"Despair sent me to London," he once told a reporter. "And there I found the faith to hope for complete healing. I consider my writing before that time an apprenticeship of sorts—a man in search of what life and love are all about. And if a novelist improves with age—as all writers should—then I hope to produce my most meaningful work in my latter years."*

Swallowing hard, I wrap my arms about myself. So he found his life in London . . . and that's where he discovered what love was. Which means that while he lived here with Mother, he did not love, he did not live.

Jealousy wells within me, hot and black. I want to be part of his present family, born when he knew how to love, born to a woman he could cherish and support.

What am I doing? Despite the warnings of a woman I have always known and trusted, I am yearning for a relationship with a man I do not know. It's illogical. It's crazy.

But I have never claimed to be mentally robust.

I press my hand to my mouth and look away from the computer monitor. It's not fair. But Mother always said most things in life were either miserable or horrible . . . survivors learned to make silk purses out of sow's ears.

After a moment, I look back to the computer, braced for whatever terrible things I might read, but the rest of the material is an advertisement for Norquest novels. One bulleted note, however, catches my eye. The quote from Theodore Norquest, it says, was taken from an interview that appeared in *Ten Top Authors Talk about What Makes Them Tick*, published by Writer's Marketplace Books.

Without hesitation, I click on the link, then smile in satisfaction when it takes me to a Web page with the actual article. The interview's been done in the Q&A style, and one series of questions practically leaps off the screen:

Q: *You have four sons—*

A: *Actually, I prefer not to talk about my family in print. My children have not chosen public careers and I respect their choices.*

Q: *All right then—shall we talk about your books?*

A: *By all means.*

Q: *Some have said there's a common theme to your work—a "missing piece." You seem to feature characters who need something to make their lives complete.*

A: *Isn't that the way life is? We all have a particular empty spot in our souls, and few of us find the proper way to fill it. My characters, like people in real life, experiment with all the things you'd expect. In the end, however, they find what they're seeking.*

Q: Have you found what you're seeking, Mr. Norquest?

A: As a creative being, yes. As a husband, certainly. As a father—well, children are never quite finished turning out, are they? Like all parents, I pray that my children will make good decisions . . . and I wait for them to complete their course. As long as we are living, none of us is finished.

I sit back and exhale a deep breath. So—my father never mentions his children in interviews. He doesn't need to, for apparently his life is complete and satisfying without me.

Wincing, I click away from the page. I don't need to think about the aloof man in Britain—I have a fantasy father who loves me completely. I will make silk purses out of this sow's ear.

I will also continue to read Theodore Norquest's novels. Despite my initial dislike of horror, I finished *Shadowed Sanctuary* between breakfast and lunch. By the time I closed the book, good had firmly triumphed over evil, equipping the protagonist to face the future with a sense of hope . . . a quality I yearn for myself.

After finishing the book, I went to the computer and ordered several other Norquest novels—so many the UPS man may develop a hernia from lugging so many packages to my apartment.

I hope he delivers when Aunt Clara is away from the building.

That thought reminds me that I need to find a place to hide my collection of Norquest novels. Carpentry is more than I want to tackle in my renovation project, but perhaps I can find a carpenter . . .

I reach for the yellow pages to begin my search, then laugh when I remember that the yellow pages are on the Internet. With a few clicks of the mouse, I find a carpenter who works the Upper West Side, and within seconds I am dialing his number.

As the phone rings, I look around my sunny office space. I'll have bookcases built—with closet doors. I'll keep all my Norquest novels in this room, my personal retreat, and the closed doors will protect them from the decaying effects of dust, light, and Clara's opinion.

The carpenter doesn't answer, so I leave a message on his machine. I have no sooner lowered the phone to the desk when it rings again. I pick up, thinking that somehow I've managed to call myself, but Clara's teary voice fills my ear: "Aurora, darling, I can't stop thinking about what I saw on that computer of yours. If your mother were living, she'd be crushed, heartbroken by your ingratitude. In the face of all she's provided, I can't believe you could still be interested in that man. Is it his money that's driving you? I never thought you were the avaricious type, but if it's his fortune you're after—"

"I'm not after anyone's money." I cut her off, my voice hoarse with frustration. "Can't you understand that I'm only curious?"

"Curiosity can kill, dear; don't you know that? You don't have to put your hand in a fire to know it can scar you for life. And you don't have to know Theodore Norquest to know he can hurt you. Whatever you've been doing, Aurora, please stop."

I draw a deep breath and lift my gaze to the ceiling. "The man is my father, Clara. I've never had a chance to learn about him."

"Because your mother wouldn't approve, you mean. Well, I'm the closest thing you have to a living relative, and I don't approve, either. I love you, Aurora. I don't want to see you hurt, and if you persist in this, well, I—"

Her words are cut off by a choking cry, and I don't have to see the tears to know she's weeping. Part of me wants to be irritated with her; another part of me wants to beg her forgiveness for even mentioning my father's name.

After ten minutes of assurances, I manage to convince her that I'm not going to do anything foolish or run off to England. I'm not sure she believes my promises, but she hangs up.

I lower the phone and look at the computer, but my attention has drifted away on a tide of fatigue. Weary of the room and the apartment, I head toward the stairs.

19

APARTMENT 15A

Like a scolded child, I leave my apartment and run to the rooftop. It's not yet noon, but dark clouds have moved in to blanket the city. The wind is rowdy today—my sweater ripples around me, and the legs of my jeans snap like sails in a gale. Lights glimmer from dark windows as my neighbors resist the premature gloom.

With my hands in my pockets, I walk around the roof and survey the city. The neighborhood looks vastly different in daylight— the buildings are not black and gray, but shades of beige and cream and white.

It feels good to stretch my legs and walk, though I can't quite believe I've chosen to come up here. I draw a deep breath and press my hand to my heart, then smile when I find it beating in a regular rhythm. I quicken my pace, exulting in this small but satisfying victory. Somehow I have enlarged the boundaries of my safe place, and that is one heck of a baby step.

A flock of geese cuts through the clouds, heading southward in a perfect V. It's been so long since I've observed anything other than insect life that I stop walking and stare, moved beyond words by their grace and beauty. They fly in perfect rhythm, gliding and stroking to music only they can hear.

Something in me wants to shed my flesh and join them, like the doomed brothers of Hans Christian Andersen's *The Wild Swans*. If I could fly away from this place . . . surely things would be easier.

My gaze lowers to the concrete and glass towers around me. My life is not a fairy tale, nor is it as extraordinary as the heroine's in my father's novel. Mine is a simple life, hemmed in by fear and the good intentions of those who love me.

I am growing weary of Clara's interference, but what if she's right about my father not wanting to see me? Why am I so curious about a man who has never written me a single letter? While Mother lived, I hardly ever thought of him. Uncle Charley was always pleased to serve as my escort when I needed a father figure. After he died, Mother was always able to convince a friend's son to step in on those rare social occasions when I needed to promenade on someone's arm. Truthfully, I don't suppose I've ever missed having a father, because I never knew what a father was supposed to do.

Still . . . something in me yearns to know the man whose image I bear. I have studied his photograph on the cover of *Shadowed Sanctuary*, and I think I can see his eyes in mine. And despite what Clara said, I don't think a man would part with a million dollars unless motivated by some sort of honest feeling. And he named me as an heir to so many of his copyrights—an act that could mean more than his monetary endowment. I'm no expert about copyright law, but I know he is entrusting me with the fruits of his creativity, allowing me to control and reap benefits from his work. With that responsibility comes the power to prevent his works from ever being published again . . . or ensure that they are published throughout the world.

I lower my head into my hands as all my loneliness and confusion meld together in one upsurge of insatiable yearning. Can't Clara understand why I want to know him? I may have been dreaming, but I think I've heard his voice . . . and I need to believe he loves me. Nothing Clara can say will ever shake me from that need.

Theodore Norquest is my father. And I've been obsessed with learning about him because time is growing short and an ocean stands between us.

And life is uncertain.

The wind tugs at my hair. I look up to see the bruised and swollen sky bulging with saturated clouds. Soon it will rain, and I will have to go inside without . . . what?

Why have I come up here? Because I need a place to entertain thoughts I could never consider in my mother's apartment. I need the freedom to admit that I want to learn about my father. I'm not sure I'm ready to meet him, and I'm not planning a trip to Europe—

Or am I?

A series of possibilities opens before me like the pages of a book. I could contact him . . . on the pretext of claiming my trust fund. He set the stipulations; he probably expects me to reach out. He may think I'm desperate for money, so if I write him, I'll tell him I intend to donate my trust fund to a charity. I'll let him know that Mother, who did her best to meet my emotional needs, has also met my financial needs. I can live a perfectly content life without him.

Yet I can't deny how desperately I want to know him. Though I've never experienced the pain of unrequited love, I've read about it in books and I have to be feeling something similar. I feel empty, almost nauseous with unsatisfied hunger, and nothing but knowledge of my father can fill the empty place in my heart . . .

My wandering gaze slides across the penthouse atop the building across the street. Lights illuminate the glass house, and I am startled to see movement—the woman walking before the bedroom window. Though it is nearly noon, a robe of purple silk shimmers beneath the cascade of her long hair. She sinks to the edge of her wide bed, sets a stemmed goblet upon the nightstand, then folds her hands and lowers her head.

Is she *praying*?

I can't tear my eyes away from the tableau. An inner voice tells me I shouldn't watch—I am invading this woman's privacy—but another voice whispers that people who value their privacy shouldn't live behind transparent walls and ceilings.

She lifts her head and swipes at her cheek with the back of her hand—she is not praying, then, but weeping. I take a wincing breath as the silent movie I am watching shifts from drama to tragedy. Perhaps she is merely gathering her thoughts—no, her head falls again and her shoulders slump in the universal body language of sorrow. I stare, hearing only the sound of my own quickened breaths, until she lifts her head and plucks a tissue from a box to dab at the hollows beneath her eyes.

Her motions are deliberate and careful, probably to protect her makeup. Why? Can she be expecting a client?

I shiver and rub my hands over my arms as the penthouse princess moves to the dressing table, where she pats powder on her nose. Then she brushes her hair and tosses what looks like a practice smile at the mirror. She lowers her hairbrush and hesitates for a moment, then rises and moves to the living room.

She's going to answer the door. She's going to continue in the lifestyle that makes her miserable.

I close my eyes as a blush burns my cheek. What am I doing? Am I so desperate for experience that I must siphon it from strangers?

When I open my eyes again, I restrain my gaze to the rooftop. I turn and walk across the pebble-sprinkled tarpaper, taking note of the pots with their skeletal trees, the weathered and rusty chaise longue, the empty paint cans. A pair of pigeons squat near the dilapidated chair while a flock of sparrows fly overhead, their shadows dotting the rooftop at my feet.

I know she weeps.

The voice comes from out of nowhere, startling me with its clarity. It is the voice I heard in my dream, the voice that spoke to me here a few nights ago. The voice has presence enough to startle the pigeons and the sparrows overhead. The flock splinters apart and flutters downward, falling from the sky like shards of a shattered vase. I whirl around and look toward the door, almost certain the building superintendent has crept up behind me, but I am alone on the roof.

I look around, my frustration rising. The first time I heard the voice, I was convinced I was hearing my father. In the deep darkness of my despair, it was easy to believe he had found a way to reach across time and space to assure me of his love.

But this is daylight; this is *real.* Traffic jounces through the streets below; crowds of pedestrians clog the sidewalks. So what I've just heard has to be broadcast noise coming from an open window somewhere in the building.

I listen, half expecting to catch other voices, but I hear nothing but the wind's whistle and the soft flutter of pigeon wings as the roosting pair flap their way back to their nest.

Despite the cold, a single drop of sweat trickles down my spine and runs to the hollow of my back. I rub my hands over my arms and walk toward the street, hoping to glimpse an open window across the way, perhaps some apartment with an overzealous heating system.

I see the woman in the penthouse. She is standing alone at her window, her eyes wide and expressionless as she stares at . . . nothing. Her guest, if she had one, has gone.

I know she weeps—could the voice have been referring to *her*? If by some miracle someone did intend to speak to me, how am I supposed to help a weeping woman I don't even know? I can't help her. I can't go to her apartment. She lives across the street, but she might as well live in Europe . . . or London.

I shiver in the thickening darkness, then shake my head. I must have been hearing things. After I saw the woman crying, through some combination of exhaustion, nerves, and the Halcion still in my system, my subconscious concocted another voice. If Clara or Philip had been standing here, they wouldn't have heard anything.

But the birds heard. Even the sparrows fifty feet away.

No. Something else spooked the sparrows, some movement or sound I didn't notice. The pigeons startled because I flinched.

I must be more on edge than I realize.

One rock of truth is visible in this sea of confusion, and I grip it with both hands: I must stop taking my mother's pills.

20

APARTMENT 15B

As the soundtrack for *Star Wars* streams from the CD player, I glance at my notes, then close my eyes and type:

> New York City's falling crime rate, while undoubtedly influenced by the mayor's efforts to bolster the municipal police force and enforce even trivial laws, is more likely the economic result of lower mortgage interest rates.

I pause to skim the copy. It's bulky, but it makes my point: More affordable housing has led to wider home ownership, and wider home ownership has pulled thousands of people away from urban population centers. Fewer people per square mile equals less crime.

I am about to continue when a *gluddle-lunk* emanates from the computer speakers. Aurora is sending an instant message.

AuroraRose: You busy?

I click on the box, then answer:

Phil627: Not too. Whassup?
AuroraRose: I think I'm dreaming again—this time in broad daylight.

I prop my chin in my hand and study the message. Aurora doesn't like to discuss her dreams unless it's 2 a.m. . . . so she's either finding it easier to talk about them through the detached medium of e-mail or something is really creeping her out.

Phil627: Maybe you should give me details.

I wait a full thirty seconds before the computer tells me she is typing a reply.

AuroraRose: I was up on the roof, and I could have sworn I heard a voice. It's happened twice now.

Phil627: Wait a minute—you were on the ROOF?

AuroraRose: Yeah. I went up there for some fresh air.

I find myself grinning at the monitor. Aurora Norquest is finally beginning to spread her wings. This is progress. I know she's dared the lobby to retrieve her computer equipment . . .

Phil627: That's cool. Where'd the voice come from?

AuroraRose: I'm not sure. I thought I was hearing things, but the noise startled some birds on the roof—at least I think it did.

Phil627: Maybe you heard someone's TV.

AuroraRose: I don't think so. I would have heard more than just one phrase.

Phil627: Someone could have been setting a radio station.

AuroraRose: Nobody else was around.

Phil627: Well—what'd the voice say?

AuroraRose: It said, "I know she weeps." How crazy is that?

Phil627: Reminds me of that movie Field of Dreams. *Did you see that one?*

AuroraRose: If you build it, he will come. I saw it. But nobody's telling me to build a baseball field.

Phil627: Okay—so what is the voice telling you to do?

AuroraRose: If I knew that, I wouldn't be asking your opinion.

Phil627: Let's back up a minute. That was a movie. You're talking about real life, right?

AuroraRose: Right. And I shouldn't be hearing voices. But I swear I did.

Phil627: Then somebody had to be talking.

AuroraRose: Right. I say nobody else was around, but I did see the woman who lives in the glass penthouse across from Clara's place. But there's no way I could hear anything from that apartment. One thing was odd, though—I saw her crying right before I heard the voice. Weird, huh?

I cock a brow. My internal alarms are clanging, and Aurora is definitely venturing into the twilight zone. She's a nice woman, smart and sweet, and she could be really attractive if she wanted to be . . .

But she's carrying some heavy baggage, and it sounds like she could use more help than I can give. She might even need a psychiatrist—a good one.

So . . . how do I handle her question? I can't encourage her fantasy, but I can't tell her she's nuts, either. And I do want to be her friend, because in some ways, she's a lot like me.

I rest my fingertips on the keyboard.

Phil627: Definitely weird territory, kiddo. Maybe you're the empathetic type. Maybe you've heard that phrase somewhere and when you saw the woman crying, it popped into your brain.

AuroraRose: I don't know where I would have heard it—does that phrase mean anything to you?

I search my memory. The phrase does seem memorable, but almost any phrase could be memorable given the right circumstances.

Phil627: Sorry, I can't place it. I think it may be an Aurora original.

AuroraRose: I hope not. I don't want to walk around hearing things. But thanks for the input. Sorry to bother you.

Phil627: No bother. You can IM me anytime.

I click the X that will close the program, then wait, half expecting her to send one more note. But Messenger remains silent.

Thoroughly distracted from thoughts of my project, I cross my arms and rub my chin. Aurora is charming and self-sacrificing, attributes I have always admired in friends. And she could be attractive if she gave her looks and clothing half a thought, but she's plagued by more than the usual fears of single urbanites. That business about her father would keep any self-respecting shrink occupied for two or three years, plus she's also dealing with nightmares and what looks like agoraphobia . . .

"Face it," I mutter, clicking back to my word processing program. "The woman is a mess."

Most of the guys I know would run from Aurora without a second thought. The Manhattan dating scene is tough enough without adding genuine psychological problems into the mix. Then again, last year I had a couple of dates that left me wondering if everyone in Manhattan was slightly out of touch with what passed for reality in St. Louis. *Swinging* is too conservative a word for the sex-saturated atmosphere of the clubs where my dates wanted to meet me. Nearly everyone in the place was drunk or getting there, and the moment I walked through the door, I felt the pressure of prying eyes on every inch of my nothing-special body—

No wonder I prefer to stay home on weekends.

I had pretty much given up on dating and the hope of ever having a girlfriend until I moved into the Westbury Arms. Then I met Aurora . . . and I couldn't help liking her. I was beginning to think God had decided to bless me with hope for the future, but now I'm wondering if God has anything to do with this budding friendship.

No doubt about it, life would be simpler if I didn't become involved with Aurora Rose Norquest. No sense in inviting trouble while I live in this building—after all, I want to stay here a few years, so I'll need to remain on good terms with all my neighbors, especially those on this floor. So I should be friendly to Aurora and Clara, but that's all. If I allow my relationship with Aurora to grow deeper, I'll become entangled, and nothing hurts more than cutting your way out of a tangled relationship.

From another compartment in my head, a memory surfaces: Mandi Norton, the beautiful girl I worshiped in school. I used to follow her through the halls of Lindbergh High like a starving puppy, and she could have easily turned and annihilated me with one sharp comment.

But she didn't. Even though her friends teased her—I heard them—and her boyfriend stomped around looking as though he wanted to launch any guy within ten feet of Mandi into next week, one day she caught me alone in the school parking lot. "You're a nice guy, Phil Cannon," she'd said, smiling as she wrapped a strand of her blond hair around her index finger. "But I don't think I'm ever going to be able to keep up with you. You're going to do great things one day."

She smiled and walked away, but I stood rooted to the spot, wrapped in a cocoon of euphoria. She *believed* in me! And her belief thrilled me even more than a kiss would have. Her gift buoyed my confidence and carried me through the dog days of high school and my first few semesters of college. Many's the night I thanked God for Mandi Norton's kindness.

But who believes in Aurora Rose Norquest? Clara Bellingham hovers like a shadow, but Clara would never help Aurora conquer her demons. Theodore Norquest has remained out of the picture for thirty-five years, so he isn't likely to show up. Aurora has no job, no social support, no apparent friends . . . except me.

The words of a proverb float back to me on a ripple of memory: *Never abandon a friend . . . in your time of need, it is better to go to a neighbor than to a relative who lives far away.*

Though I can count my New York friends on one hand, compared to Aurora, I am wealthy with friendship. If I were to gather around the water cooler at NYU and ask my peers what they would do in this situation, I know they'd tell me to run from Aurora as fast as humanly possible.

But I've been brought up with different standards . . . and in St. Louis, neighbors reach out to help one another. Is what I'm feeling fatal attraction . . . or destiny?

After saving my work, I push away from the desk and head toward the door.

Aurora's on the phone when I buzz. She lets me in with a smile and a slight lift of her brows, then mutters, "Uh-huh," into the phone. I realize she isn't surprised by my arrival, which is probably a good thing.

"No, Clara," she says, shaking her head. "I'm not overstressed. And no, I haven't finished the painting, but I'm not calling in a professional. I like doing the work myself, and I have yet to fall off a ladder."

Smiling, she leads me into the living room and gestures toward the sofa. I take a seat, then feel something jabbing me in the back. I reach for the object and pull a book from behind a pillow: *Seventeenth-Century Poetry*. Aurora has eclectic tastes.

"I'm fine," she assures Clara as she sinks into the wing chair. "And I've got to go, 'cause Philip just came in. Okay. Talk to you later."

She disconnects the call with her thumb, then slides the phone between two stacks of books on the coffee table. "I don't know why I was hoping Clara could shed some light on what I heard. She's convinced I'm losing my mind." She presses her hands over her face, then peers at me from between splayed fingers. "You think so, too, huh?"

"No," I say, "but I am concerned about you."

She smiles, another good thing. I'm thinking we might make real progress toward getting her some help, but the buzzer rattles again.

Aurora rolls her eyes. "That'll be Clara."

"Maybe it's a delivery?"

"No, it's Clara."

She gets up and goes into the foyer. A moment later she returns, followed by Clara, who is continuing her telephone tirade. "Something's not right with you, Aurora. Grown women don't hear voices coming from out of the blue."

The older woman faces the younger, whose arms are clamped around her middle. Clara glances at me, but my presence doesn't seem to register—either that, or she doesn't care that I'm here. "Either you tell me what's going on"—she turns back to Aurora—"or I'm having Dr. Morgan come up here to examine you."

Aurora closes her eyes and exhales through pursed lips. "Philip's here, Auntie. Maybe we should talk about this later?"

"Some things can't wait until later—besides, I've a hunch you've already told him about this. Am I right?"

An accusatory note underlines her voice, and as Aurora's gaze catches mine, I understand. Clara may be concerned about Aurora's mental health, but she's also concerned—maybe even threatened—because Aurora has confided in me.

A weight settles upon my shoulders—the heft of responsibility. And in that moment I realize I have a choice—I can stand, excuse myself, and leave this apartment . . . or I can remain here and accept the responsibility inherent in this friendship.

Leaving would be the easiest option. Clara would be relieved and Aurora probably wouldn't hate me. We could still be cordial, still exchange pleasantries when we happened to meet in the hall. I could concentrate on my work without the distractions of a troubled neighbor; life would continue in a smooth, untroubled rhythm.

But what sort of a man walks away from a friend in need? My life has been centered on a creed that champions unquestioning faith, limitless perseverance, and sacrificial love.

I prop my arm on the sofa's armrest and decide to stick.

Like an awkward teenager, Aurora stands with one arm down, the other blocking her body. "I don't need a psychologist, Auntie."

"Convince me."

"I'm fine. I'm just a little stressed . . . and I've been taking some pills to help me sleep. I think maybe they were too much, so I've already decided to stop taking them."

Clara blinks, her features hardening in a disapproving stare. "You're using *drugs?*"

"Just Halcion—to help me sleep." Aurora drops into the wing chair as if she is suddenly too exhausted to stand. "I was having nightmares, so I took some of Mother's pills. I didn't intend to take them forever—only for a couple of nights. They made me sleep so soundly I didn't wake up."

Clara scowls furiously at Aurora, her fine brows knitting together, then she turns the heat of that scowl upon me.

"Did you know about this?"

I flinch, overcome by a sudden feeling of guilt. "About the sleeping pills, no."

"But you knew about the nightmares?"

"Well . . . yes."

The tight bud of irritation blossoms to anger in her thin face. "And you didn't tell me about this?"

I glance at Aurora, but she's staring at her hands. "I didn't think it my place to tell you," I say, meeting Clara's hot eyes. "Aurora is fully capable of taking care of herself."

Clara's gaze travels from me to Aurora as if she can't decide who is most deserving of her anger. Finally, she points a bony finger at Aurora. "You are to flush every last one of those pills down the toilet. And if you hear any other voices, you are to tell me at once so I can call Dr. Morgan. And you"—she whirls on me in a flash of fury—"you will tell me about anything that threatens this girl. Aurora is as dear to me as my own flesh and blood. If she's having problems, I want to know immediately."

I am at the point of automatically agreeing with her when an unexpected dose of courage dribbles from some inner reservoir. "I think, Mrs. B., that Aurora is capable of deciding whether or not she needs—or wants—help. And she's confessed to using the sleeping pills—a justifiable need after all she's been through—and confession is hardly the habit of drug abusers. Somebody has to give this woman permission to take responsibility for herself."

I haul my gaze from Clara's tight face and return my attention to my hostess. "Aurora." I soften my voice. "Would you like to speak to this Dr. Morgan? Or do you think you're getting a handle on things?"

Her gaze drops like a stone to the floor, and for a moment I hear nothing but the sound of a LaGuardia-bound jet shuddering overhead.

"I think"—Aurora lifts her head and meets my eye—"I am going to be fine. I'm not taking the pills anymore, and I'm making lots of good changes. I think I'm better than I've ever been in my life."

Inwardly, I cheer her courage. If she can stand up to Clara, she just might make it.

The older woman lifts her hands in a gesture of surrender. "But you're hearing *voices*. If that's what you call fine—"

"Don't worry, Mrs. B.," I say. "I've been keeping an eye on her."

The line of Clara's mouth tightens a fraction more. "Both of you have given me a major headache. Aurora, take a nap; you need to rest. Philip, go back to your own apartment and let her be. The girl has been through major trauma. She needs time to adjust."

I choke on a sudden surge of laughter. Aurora Norquest has waited thirty-five years to begin her life. When is she going to be allowed to live it?

I cross my arms, fully intending to remain on the couch until Clara leaves, but Aurora stands and plucks at my sleeve. "Thanks for stopping by, Philip, but maybe you had better go. A nap sounds like a good idea—I think I'll stretch out and try to get some rest."

I search her eyes for some hidden message, but apparently she means exactly what she's saying.

"Okay." I stand, but tap her shoulder before moving into the foyer. "If you need anything, call *me*."

She nods, but I'm not sure she understands my real meaning.

21

APARTMENT 15A

Relieved to be alone, I go into my bedroom and turn on my little television, then lie down. The old comforter is soft beneath me; my pillows exude the faintly medicinal scents I will always associate with the sickroom. I used these pillows to support my back when I had to sit up with Mother.

"Poor pillows," I murmur, caressing the yellowed linen as a home shopping club hostess chirps in the background. "Been on active duty far too long."

My thoughts drift lazily along a current of memory, then focus on a distant shore. My arms and legs grow heavy, as if I've been swimming for miles, then I blink and find myself in a dark tunnel. A metallic screech rattles my nerves as a shaft of light appears at the end of the long cylinder around me.

Is this the proverbial light at the end of the tunnel? Some kind of near-death experience? This stupor doesn't feel like death.

I extend my hands and in the light I see that my hand is no longer adult. My nails are soft and short, my fingers pudgy. I move forward on legs that feel stumpy, then lose my balance and fall, landing on my knees and elbows. The tunnel is smooth, almost like plaster, and sand clings to my damp palms. I move forward again, then realize that this tunnel isn't the portal between life and death—it's a concrete pipe, one of several at the old playground that used to occupy the corner of Seventy-fourth and Central Park West.

As I totter toward the light, the world broadens and comes into focus. Beyond the edge of the sand, my mother is sitting on a green bench. Her face is young and unlined, her hair long and soft and straight. A man is sitting next to her, his arm on the back of the bench, his fingers teasing Mother's shoulder. He is young, too, and my heart skips a beat. Is this my father?

"Cut it out, Charles," Mother says, and I understand. This isn't my father; this is Clara's husband, Uncle Charley. He's younger and thinner than I remember, but as I draw closer, there's no mistaking his hooked nose.

Half-hidden by the pipe, I wait in the safety of its circle. Though Uncle Charley's lips are curved in a smile, his eyes are angry and his fingers keep touching Mother's shoulder even though she swats his hand away.

"I said, cut it *out!*"

The smile vanishes from his face. "Why should I? You can't speak to me like some nobody."

"You have no right to treat me like some broad you'd pick up at Grand Central Station. Mind your manners."

"I always mind my manners. That's why you find me so charming."

"I found you charming once. Now I tolerate you for Clara's sake."

"That's not true and you know it. The real question"—he strokes Mother's shoulder with a single finger—"is why you tolerate Clara."

"She's my friend."

"Ah, yes, and M.E. must have her friends. What would you do, Mary Elizabeth, without someone to adore you?"

"Shut up, Charles."

Uncle Charley opens his mouth to reply, but this time no sound emerges. Instead his eyes widen and one hand flies to his chest. He sits there, one hand clawing at his breast pocket, while he slaps at Mother's shoulder with the other, desperately trying to get her attention.

She will not look at him. She has pulled her purse onto her lap and is sorting through its contents. "Where are my cigarettes?" she mutters, dropping a brush, a compact, and a cigarette lighter into her lap.

When Uncle Charley makes a strangled sound, her eyes dart toward him. Surprise blossoms on her face, then the corner of her mouth twists.

"Having trouble, Charles?"

He pounds his chest and makes a helpless wheezing sound.

Mother looks up and spies me in the concrete pipe. "Aurora, darling." She extends her hand. "Come, dearest. We have to go."

I look at Uncle Charley, who has slumped onto the back of the bench. One hand is clutching at the ruffled handkerchief in his breast pocket; the other is straining for Mother's skirt.

She slaps at his hand as if he were an annoying mosquito.

"For God's sake, Mary—" he says, wheezing. "H-help me."

Mother looks around. We are alone in the park—no other children have come out on this gray day; no watchful eyes are visible in the apartment windows above. In a city of millions, no one will help.

"Come, Aurora." She bends to smile at me. "It's time for your nap."

I can't look away from Uncle Charley. His eyes are bulging, distended with disbelief and pain. His lips move, faint drops of spittle marking the corners. A rattling sound comes from his throat, and now he is lying on the bench, his back pressed against the wooden slats, his brown wingtips kicking at the ground.

I stare at the dots in those wingtips and wonder how Auntie Clara will clean them.

"Aurora! Come with me now!"

Impelled by my mother's anger, I hurry out of the pipe and take her hand. She sets a quick pace, faster than I can manage, so she swings me onto her hip and carries me from the park.

I cling to her shoulder and lift my eyes. Behind us, Uncle Charley has fallen to the ground, where one leg twitches in the sand.

❧

I sit up into the trilling of the telephone. For a disconcerting moment I can't remember where I am, then I realize I've been dreaming . . . again.

Images of sand and wingtips hover at the edge of my mind as I reach for the phone. Clara is on the line, wanting to know if I want a slice of chocolate chess pie. "I doubled the recipe," she says, and I know this offer is her way of making sure there are no hard feelings between us.

I hesitate, hearing the nervous click of her pearls as she runs her thumbnail over the strand at her neck.

"Sounds good," I finally say. "By the way, Auntie—how did Uncle Charley die?"

She coughs. "Good grief, Aurora, don't you remember?"

"I thought I did—but I'm not sure I trust my memory."

She heaves a sigh over the phone line. "He died in . . . let's see, it must have been '82. Heart attack."

"Eighty-two?" I was thirteen years old. Not a child by any means, and far too old to be carried on my mother's hip.

"Did he have a history of heart problems?"

"Goodness, yes. He'd had a bypass a few years before. The doctors kept telling him to watch his diet and exercise, but the man had a stubborn streak the size of the Tiffany's showroom."

"When did he . . . I mean, when did you first know about his heart condition?"

"Let's see." I can almost hear her thoughts shuffling as she sifts through memories. "He had his first heart attack in '71—no, '72. He wasn't feeling well, so he left work early. He was on his way home when he collapsed on the street. I was horrified, of course, when the police called to tell me they'd found him. That was our first sign of trouble."

"Where did he collapse?"

She laughs. "Honestly, Aurora, does it matter?"

"Just curious, Auntie."

"Well . . . I think it was a corner a few blocks from here. There used to be a little playground on that spot."

I close my eyes. Charley didn't collapse on the street, I want to tell her. He had the heart attack in the park, on a bench, where he'd met my mother. Whoever found him must have assumed he'd wandered in from the sidewalk.

"I'll never forget that day." Clara's voice has gone wistful. "I was so frightened by the experience that I threw out all the clothes he was wearing—I couldn't help but believe he would tempt fate by wearing them again. It's silly, I know, but I couldn't stand the sight of that suit, that tie, even those silly wingtips—"

"I think I understand," I whisper. My mind has darkened, and thoughts I dare not speak aloud are welling up, a nasty swarm of them.

"Aurora . . . are you sure you're okay? You sound a little off."

"I'm fine, Auntie." I brush hair from my eyes and stare at my beautiful buttercup walls. "Thanks for the offer of the pie. I'll come over later, okay? I was napping, and I'm still a little drowsy."

"And you need your rest." She is maternal again, all urgency and compassion. "Take care, dear."

"You, too," I whisper.

I don't go back to sleep after hanging up the phone. I do lie back down, but remnants of my dream are clinging to my pillow. When I close my eyes and feel myself falling back into the bottomless reservoir of memory, I open my eyes, get up, and walk to the computer room.

When the machine whirs to life, I click on the Internet Explorer icon, then blink when an error page fills the screen:

PAGE NOT FOUND. Check your connection and try again.

I click again. Zilch. I power down the computer, then flip the power switch again—according to Philip, this action is a first step toward curing almost any computer problem. But the Internet still doesn't connect.

Finally, I get on my hands and knees and crawl beneath the desk, running my hand along the heavy white cable that runs from the modem to the wall.

And therein lies my problem. Somehow—probably with an absent-minded kick—I have managed to pull on the cord and loosen the wire from the connector.

I grab a small flashlight from the desk drawer and crouch in the narrow kneehole, then use my thumbnail to pry the connector out of the wall jack.

After backing out from beneath the desk (and grateful no one is around to watch this distinctively ungraceful maneuver), I hold up the decapitated cord for a closer examination.

I have no idea how to join the cord and its connector, but Philip would know how to solve the problem. I almost reach up to send him an instant message, but with no Internet . . .

With cord and connector in hand, I walk over to his apartment. He grins when I show him the broken connection. "How'd you manage that?"

I shrug and follow him through the foyer. "Just clumsy, I guess. Are we looking at major surgery?"

"No way. Strictly an outpatient procedure. But first, we must prepare for the operation."

He leads me, not to his office, but to the kitchen, where he pushes his glasses up on his nose, then opens a cupboard door and pulls out a box of microwave popcorn. "Manna from heaven," he whispers with a waggle of his brow.

"You always eat before surgery?"

"Can't operate on an empty stomach."

He slides a package of popcorn into the microwave, presses a touch pad, then turns to pull tools from a drawer. While he snips and twists and fusses over my wires, I sink onto his sofa and inhale the heavenly scent of butter and popcorn. As the *rat-a-tat* of the popping kernels fills my ears, a realization hits me—he's making popcorn because the other day I mentioned that I haven't had it in years.

He's making popcorn for *me*.

Inexplicable tears burn my eyes. Blinking them away, I stare at a stack of financial magazines on his coffee table.

"I've been dreaming again," I say, trying my best to speak in a steady voice. He's so intent upon my cord I'm not sure he's even listening, but I need to fill the silence between us.

"I took a nap after you and Clara left. And this was one of those weird dreams that feels real—more like a memory than a dream. I was with my mother and Uncle Charley—"

"Clara's Charley?"

So he *was* listening. "That's the one. Anyway, Charley starts having a heart attack in this little park, and my mother just takes my hand and leaves him there. I can't believe what she's doing, but I'm really little and she drags me off while he's clutching at his heart and gasping on the ground."

"Sounds uncomfortably realistic," Philip murmurs.

"That's not the worst part. The phone rings—in real life, I mean—and wakes me up. It's Clara, so I ask her about Charley. I knew I was a teenager when he died, but then she tells me he had his first heart attack when I was three. He had it right in the spot where I dreamed he had it."

I turn on the sofa to look at him. He has already repaired the broken connection, but now he's studying the end I popped out of the cable modem. "Don't tell me that thingamajig is loose, too."

He glances over at me. "A little. But I can fix it."

I turn back to the magazines and pick up a copy of *Fortune*. "Want to know the weirdest thing about my dream? Before Charley started gasping, he and my mother were arguing about something. And their relationship was odd—nothing like I remember it. Do you think their relationship was really odd, or was my subconscious improvising details?"

When Philip doesn't answer, I look over my shoulder. He is using a pair of needle-nose pliers to push the connector over the wire, then he shakes the cable, testing the connection.

Satisfied, he holds it up like a prize. "I told you, a minor procedure. And two connections for the price of one."

"Thanks." I rise to reach for the cable, but he holds up his hand.

"Wait—popcorn first, then testing."

While I walk to the kitchen island, he pulls the steaming bag from the microwave, then expertly rips it open and dumps the contents into a big mixing bowl. "Here"—he hands the bowl to me—"you take charge of the popcorn while I check the connection. No sense in you getting back and discovering one of the wires isn't making contact."

I cradle the bowl in my arms and follow him to his office, then linger in the doorway while he connects the cable far more efficiently than I would have. I toss a few steaming kernels in my mouth and close my eyes, repressing a groan. Popcorn may not actually be manna from heaven, but at this moment, I'm a believer.

When I open my eyes, Philip's computer is blazing through his favorite Web pages.

"Works fine," he says, navigating to Google.

"Hey." I move toward him as a sudden thought strikes me. "You can Google anything, right?"

"Sure."

"How about a phrase?"

He peers at me over the top of his glasses, then reaches for a handful of popcorn. "What'd you have in mind?"

"I know she weeps."

He gives me a look of curiosity, pops back a couple of kernels, then types the phrase in quotation marks and clicks the enter key.

Before I can blink, the screen has filled with lines of text. "What's all that? Does it mean something?"

Philip leans toward the monitor. "Wow. Looks like half of these are blogs."

"What?"

"Web logs—online diaries. People write online for the creative thrill and other people read what they've written. But a lot of these aren't blogs—they're references to a book."

A chill creeps over my bones. "What sort of book?"

"That's the title, *I Know She Weeps*. According to this listing, it's a novel by Andrew Noble."

I make a face. "Never heard of him."

"We could look it up on Amazon."

"Go for it."

He makes a few clicks. A moment later we are staring at an Amazon page featuring a black and silver paperback.

"*I Know She Weeps*," Philip reads, "by Andrew Noble, published in 1987 and now out of print. Looks like it was well received, though—forty-eight customer reviewers gave the book five stars."

I'm staring at the cover. Could there be any connection between this book and the voice I heard on the rooftop?

I close my eyes. "This is crazy. I feel like an old hippie reliving some acid experience—"

"You weren't tripping," Philip says. "I'm not sure what happened up on the roof, but I don't think you were tripping."

I blow out my cheeks. "It doesn't matter. The book's out of print, so it's gone."

Philip rests his chin on his hand, an amused smile on his lips. "Don't you know old books never die? There are a dozen used copies for sale right here. You can get one for a penny from Books Bazillion. Shipping will cost you, but you'll be getting the book for practically nothing."

"Thanks, Philip. I read almost everything, so I might as well read this one."

I'm walking toward the door, on my way to order the book from my own computer, when his laughter stops me.

"Wait," he calls, his voice muffled. I walk back and see him under his desk, his rear jutting up in the air. "You'll need your cable, right?"

Sighing, I cross my arms and wait.

22

The next week passes in a pleasant blur. I grow more familiar with the computer, becoming confident enough to find and apply to a university with an online program through which I can earn a master's degree in English. While I wait for their response, I order wallpaper for the kitchen from a seller on eBay and ask the local hardware store to deliver glossy paint for my bathroom in a luscious shade of periwinkle blue.

I do not hear the voice again. I don't venture up to the roof again, either, and Clara's guarded expression relaxes. She drops by every morning to have a cup of coffee and see if I need anything, then she heads out to keep her appointments with Arthur and various women friends.

Philip—who now seems more like a "Phil" in my eyes—stops by every day, too, but he's more useful than Clara. He tackles any project I set before him, and though he's built more like a willow than an oak, he proves surprisingly strong.

One evening he helps me in the bathroom, volunteering to tackle the neck-breaking job of painting the ceiling. When we run out of painter's tape, he volunteers to go out for another roll. If he hadn't, I'd have had to phone in the order, which might have taken a day or two to be delivered.

Like Clara, Phil has accepted my homebound state, but unlike Clara, he's not above tossing me a challenge now and then. When he slips on his jacket to go for the tape, he looks at me with a twinkle in his eye. "The hardware store is only a couple of blocks," he says. "A nice walk, if you're up for it."

I am about to shake my head, then I pause. "I have been taking walks." I lift my chin. "On the stairs. I've made it to the thirteenth floor."

"Really." His eyes gleam with what looks like honest pleasure. "Well . . . the lobby is only a few feet past the thirteenth floor, and the hardware store is only a few feet past the lobby."

This time I shake my head and mean it. "I can't go out on the street. Not yet. But maybe I can walk as far as the twelfth floor with you, and you can take the elevator from there."

"Why not come with me to the lobby? Make it a real red-letter day?"

I bite my lip, but the challenge I see in his eyes is mingled with friendliness. He's not judging me; he's offering help. And he's not asking so much—after all, I made it to the lobby when I had to sign for my computer.

How can I say no to a guy who makes me popcorn?

"Okay." I nod slowly. "I'll go with you to the lobby."

"Will you wait for me?"

"Of course. I can't paint until you get back with the tape."

"Wait for me in the lobby, I mean. So we can come back up together."

I wince. My mind had already filled with the image of me waving good-bye as he leaves the elevator and heads out; now he's asking me to step out of the elevator, sit on a sofa in a public place, and wait there for who knows how long . . .

I rub my hand over my watch. "I'll wait five minutes."

"I don't know if I can be back that quick. The store might be crowded. Besides, if you get worried, you can always talk to the doorman."

I am about to refuse, but he reaches out and touches my hand. "You can do it, Aurora Rose. I know you can."

He is right—somehow I pull it off. I can barely breathe by the time we return to the apartment, but when Philip takes the roll of painter's tape from the bag, I realize no trophy has ever required more effort.

Phil knows this, too; I can see it in his eyes. "Whaddya think?" He sets the roll of tape on a shelf. "Shall we have it mounted?"

I punch his arm. "Don't make fun."

"I'm not making fun." His gaze moves into mine as his voice lowers. "I think this roll of tape is precious . . . nearly as precious as you."

And so my victory becomes *our* victory. I'm not sure how much I want to share with Phil Cannon, but I do know this—for the first time in a very long time, my heart is stirring with . . . hope. Surely that's a good thing.

My baby steps proceed on other fronts, too. The carpenter returns my call and stops by to measure the space where I want bookshelves. He won't be able to begin work until after Christmas, he says, but I give him a deposit and sign an agreement.

On Friday, I get an e-mail from Unisa Online, the organization offering a master's degree in English by dissertation. I have been accepted into the program, and after a period of three years I am to produce a written study concentrating on gender studies, women's writing, medieval history, romantic verse, Victorian literature, science fiction, or American novels.

I print out the e-mail and set it on my desk. I can't wait to show Clara and Phil.

I am distracted, however, when Clara comes up with the mail—among the assorted catalogs are two packages. The first contains my wallpaper order (red and black roosters on a beige background), and the second padded envelope holds *I Know She Weeps*.

"What is that?" Clara asks as I pull the novel free of its packaging.

I hold the volume up for her inspection. "A book."

"Andrew Noble? Never heard of him."

"Me, neither. But I think this book will be good."

She crinkles her nose. "I could have brought that from the library. You don't have to waste money on books I could pick up for you—"

"It's okay, Clara; I may want to keep this book. Besides, it's probably not in the library. It's out of print."

When she leaves, I go to my bedroom and move my latest Theodore Norquest novel from the nightstand to the shelf beneath it. Well aware that Clara doesn't want me reading my father's work, Phil has joined me in a quiet conspiracy. My favorite online bookstore usually ships books via UPS, so every afternoon Phil checks at the lobby desk to see if I have any packages. He saves the doorman a trip upstairs, I get my Norquest novels, and Clara remains blissfully ignorant of my new reading choices.

Phil has brought me four boxes of books so far, and I think I'm slowly growing used to my father's style. Plot lines that first struck me as horrifying now seem merely unusual; my father deals more with supernatural themes than with blood and gore. Now that I've learned to accept his fictive premises—*okay, suppose we live in a world where this scenario could happen*—his stories flow more logically for me.

I haven't set out to read *I Know She Weeps* in one sitting, but the minutes slip by. I stop long enough to grab a sandwich in the kitchen, then perch on a barstool and eat, flipping the pages in between bites.

Phil phones at eight—he wants to know if I want to come over and watch a DVD. I tell him no thanks; I'm into a book I honestly can't put down.

"Which one is it?"

"*I Know She Weeps.*"

"Ah." He pauses and I know he's remembering why this book is significant. "So? Whaddya think?"

I glance at the open volume on my lap. "The tone is different from the Norquest books I've been reading—primarily because it's a medieval adventure, not a contemporary horror story—but like Norquest, Andrew What's-His-Name has an interesting vocabulary and an engaging style."

He laughs. "You ought to be a professional reviewer."

"That'd take all the fun out of reading. I'll take a rain check on the movie—and I'll let you know more about the book when I'm done."

I lower the phone and return to my reading, finally finishing the story at 2 a.m. on Saturday morning. When I close the cover and set the book down, I feel as though I have run a marathon.

I go into the computer room and send Phil an instant message. If he's asleep, he won't hear the quiet *gluddle-lunk* that announces my message. If he's at the computer, though—

He is.

Phil627: Hey. You still up?

AuroraRose: Yes. Just finished I KNOW SHE WEEPS.

Phil627: And the verdict is—

AuroraRose: I've never read anything like it. I'm wiped.

Phil627: Is that good?

AuroraRose: Definitely. A great story.

Phil627: What's it about?

I hesitate, not sure if he's asking out of politeness or genuine curiosity. Probably curiosity, or he'd have accepted my review and moved on to something else.

AuroraRose: It's set in medieval times, the story of an earl
married to an unfaithful woman. Before he discovers the
extent of her philandering, she gets pregnant. He loves the
idea of having a child and, despite everything, he loves his

wife. But when he finds out that she's been unfaithful—-think Guinevere and Lancelot—he doesn't cast her off, he only insists that she change her behavior. But she's too set on having her own way, so she threatens to destroy him with lies.

Phil627: Sounds like a soap opera from the Dark Ages.

AuroraRose: LOL. It is, sort of. The earl goes off to the Crusades when the wicked wife stops speaking to him, but he can't get the coming child out of his mind. So he keeps sending gifts which, of course, the wife rejects. She won't honor his messengers or accept his letters, and she even has one of her guards kill her husband's manservant. Anyway, the baby is born—a girl—and the kid grows up thinking her father is the most malicious man in the world.

Phil627: Sounds like a case for King Arthur and his knights.

AuroraRose: I think you're in the wrong century. I don't know— I suppose this all sounds melodramatic, but it was a rollicking read. I think you'd like it.

Phil627: Not unless there's a handsome economist in the story— you know, sort of a cross between Ben Affleck and Tom Cruise. Sir Knows-His-Books?

I chuckle as I read his message. He's having such a good time that he's missing the obvious. The story resonated with me because it could almost be *my* story. I, too, have a father I've never seen. My mother was Lady Bountiful compared to the witch in the story, but I could identify with the daughter. Part of me yearns to love my father, and the other part can't break the habit of hating him.

AuroraRose: I think it's time to say good night, Phil.
Phil627: G'night, Phil.

AuroraRose: Talk to you tomorrow.

Phil627: Wait—what do you get when you cross the Godfather with an economist?

AuroraRose: Do I have to play?

Phil627: Of course.

AuroraRose: Okay, what?

Phil627: An offer you can't understand. LOL. I crack myself up.

AuroraRose: Good night, Phil.

Phil627: Night, Rosie.

I close the Messenger program, then cross my arms and stare at the computer screen. *Rosie.* No one has ever called me Rosie, but Phil has become a good friend—aside from Clara, my *only* good friend. This relationship may be going somewhere, but I'm not sure I'm ready to get closer to Phil or anyone else. When you get close to people, you have to trust them, and when you trust them, they expect you to do things you don't want to do and go places you don't want to go.

Phil's already nudging me. He's not pressuring me, but if we grow much closer, he might.

I click the appropriate buttons to power down the computer, then watch as the screen goes black.

23

APARTMENT 15A

Two days later, I'm still thinking about Andrew Noble's novel. Though I wouldn't say Noble is a better writer than my father, something in his prose sticks with me. I can almost *see* that medieval lord yearning for his daughter . . . probably because since Mother died my thoughts keep returning to my own father. In my fantasies he waits for me with open arms, but then I open my eyes and look around the apartment he vacated so many years ago—

He never came back. Unlike the lord in Noble's story, my father never even sent a letter.

Is that kind of devoted love and longing still possible in this day and age? I doubt it. The Middle Ages may have been dark, but this age is saturated with cynicism and despair.

I'm still pondering the story when Phil pops over after lunch. "Surprise," he says when I open the door. As I gape at him, he holds up a plastic gadget with two dangling cords.

"One of my clients is overstocked with these things, so I thought you might like one. It's nothing fancy, but you might like to try it for fun."

"What is that thing?"

"A digital camera. You snap the picture, load the image into the computer, then you can e-mail it anywhere. You can even set the camera up as a Web cam so people can see you working."

I can't think of anything I'd hate more than letting the world peek at me, but Phil has already crossed the foyer and is heading to the computer room, trailing cords behind him. By the time I catch up, he is inserting a CD into my computer tray.

"Um, about this camera—I don't have to use it, do I?"

"Of course not. But you'll have it if you need it. You never know when you might want to unload something on eBay, and a picture always helps."

I perch on the edge of a spare kitchen chair and point to the CD. "What's that?"

"The software—nothing runs without software, Rosie."

I stiffen, momentarily embarrassed. He's called me that a couple of times now, but never to my face. This time it feels . . . intimate.

When I look up, Phil is examining my face with considerable concentration. "You okay?"

"Yeah—the name just caught me off guard, that's all. I don't think of myself as a Rosie."

"If you'd rather I didn't—"

"It's okay."

He glances up at the screen, which has filled with some sort of program, then clicks through it. "Rosie fits you," he says, not looking at me. "Aurora seems a little—"

"Stuffy?"

He grins. "You said it; I didn't."

"That's okay." I draw a deep breath. "I call you Phil; I guess you can call me Rosie."

Another baby step. We've moved to another level in a relationship that could be either a blessing or a burden . . .

Phil picks up the camera and turns it toward me. Before I can lift my hand to block the shot, he snaps my picture.

"Don't you need film in that thing?"

"No film required." He sets the camera on a little plastic base, then clicks a square on the screen. "Watch this."

The computer whirs, a light glows atop the camera, and suddenly I am staring at my wide eyes and pale complexion on the monitor. It's a horrible picture, nothing I would ever want anyone to see, but Phil highlights it, rattles the keyboard for a moment, then clicks on the picture again.

"There." He swivels and leans toward me, elbows propped on his knees. "I just e-mailed a copy of the picture to my computer. The next time you send me an instant message, your face will pop up next to the text box—it'll almost be like talking right to you."

"It'd be easier for you to walk twenty feet and come over," I grumble, but though I'm horrified he'll see that terrible picture, I'm more surprised he'd *want* to see it.

He leans forward, about to stand, but I catch his arm. "I'm actually glad you're here," I say, pulling a yellow legal pad from beneath a book on the desk. "I had a couple of things I wanted to run by you."

"Yeah?" His eyes glow with interest. "What's up?"

"First, there's this." I pull out a copy of the e-mail from Unisa and offer it to him. "I've been accepted in the master's degree program. I'm really going to do it."

He takes the letter with a smile that lingers on me, more warming than the feeble sun at the window. "Wow. That's great, Rosie. Absolutely great."

I clasp my hands and lean toward him, a blush heating my cheeks. "See all my choices? I haven't decided which field I should concentrate on—there are so many options. But I'll have three years to research materials for my dissertation."

His smile fades. "The Department of English," he reads, "from . . . the University of *South Africa?*"

His face has gone blank, so I hasten to reassure him. "The program is completely legitimate. I checked it out. And if I enjoy that study, once I've earned the master's degree I can go on to apply for admission as a doctoral student."

The paper slips from his hand and falls to the floor. "You could have checked into a master's program at NYU," he says, his voice curiously flat.

I shrug. "I did a Google search; it didn't come up."

"How hard did you look? There are dozens of universities around here; you could have applied to any of them."

I cross my arms. "Why do I have to work with a university near New York? I liked this program, I can do it all online, and I like the options of study—"

"You like it"—irritation roughens his voice—"because the school is on the other side of the planet!"

My mind whirls at his response. "Who cares where it is? You're always telling me the world is shrinking because the Internet brings us all together—"

"You like it"—his words are clipped—"because there's not a chance in a million you'll have to leave this apartment and go to the school for a class, a symposium, or God knows what else. If you had applied at an American university, there's a pretty good chance someone might ask you to leave your ivory tower, if only for the graduation ceremony."

"That's not true!"

"Yes, it is! I've been watching you, Aurora, and I've noticed you're an expert at keeping people at arm's length. You're refurbishing this huge old apartment so you won't have to go out and look for something more suited to your situation. You're getting another degree so you won't have to get a job. You're taking classes from South Africa so you won't have to go to school. You'll probably major in medieval women or some obscure subject because that degree won't equip you for anything but further study."

His words pile up inside my brain, slamming against a door I cannot open. "I don't know why you're so upset," I tell him. "This is my home. Why should I leave it? I need a degree and I love to study. I don't have to work, so what's the rush?"

"Denial," he says, his brow arching over the round rim of his glasses, "is *not* a river in Egypt."

I stare at him, faltering in the silence that engulfs us, then I explode in laughter. "If that's economist humor," I say, shards of hysteria piercing my voice, "I don't think I want to hear any more."

"Oh, Rosie." He catches my hands and holds them as he lowers his head to mine. "I don't want to hurt you, but it's time you opened your eyes and saw things as they really are. You're taking baby steps, but if you want to see a real difference in your life, you need to start thinking about some giant steps."

"I've been doing pretty well, considering—"

"You've made some good progress, kiddo, but you've got a ways to go. I respect Clara and appreciate all she does for you, but she's not doing you any good. She's nothing but an enabler—"

I tug at my hands, trying to get free. "Clara is almost like my mother!"

"That's the problem." His hands open, releasing me. "I don't know what bound Clara and your mother, but she's not doing you any favors by making life easy for you up here. She treats you like a child, and until she stops, I'm afraid that's all you're ever going to be."

My mouth opens, but no words come. I want to be angry, but Phil's eyes are shining with softness and concern . . . and at some place deep inside, I know he's right. I suppose I've always enjoyed having Clara fuss over me; after giving so much of myself in nursing Mother, it was nice to have someone care about me for a change. But Mother's gone now, and I don't need a nurse.

I need a friend . . . one who won't coddle me. One who will push me, even if it hurts.

Phil.

I lower my head, avoiding his eyes. Silence rolls over us, broken only by the background murmur of the television in the kitchen.

We've come too far, too fast. Even if we just end up as friends, this intensity threatens to stifle me.

"If you're finished scolding me," I manage to say, "there is one other thing I wanted to show you."

Instantly, he releases his grip. My hands tingle beneath a rush of cool air, and something in me misses the warmth of his touch.

But I've effectively changed the subject.

Blank faced, he leans back in the computer chair, folding his hands at his waist. "What?"

I pull the legal pad from my lap and point to the first hand-written page. "I started to write a letter, but I need to run it by someone before I send it. Clara wouldn't understand, so you're nominated."

A flicker of interest crosses his face. "As long as you're not writing the management to complain about my loud parties."

"I was writing—*trying* to write—my father."

Phil sucks at the inside of his cheek a minute, his brows working. "Good girl. That is a giant step. So—what made you decide to take the plunge?"

"I can't get that medieval story out of my mind—the father and his daughter, you know. So if it's even remotely possible my father wouldn't mind hearing from me, maybe I should write."

"Aurora." He underlines my name with reproach. "I'd bet my last dollar he wants to hear from you. What father wouldn't?"

"A father who hasn't called or written in thirty-five years," I remind him. "A father who abandoned his wife and daughter for another family."

"You told me he established a trust fund for you."

"A trust fund with strings attached—but I'm not writing about that. I don't need his money; I don't want it. I'm only wondering if he hates me as much as he hated my mother."

Phil grimaces at the word *hate*. "I think you've been listening to too many of Clara's stories. Forget what she said. Look at what your father provided for you. You've got to know he doesn't hate you."

He crosses his arms, waiting for me to read, and I settle the legal pad on my knees. But before I can read more than "Dear Mr. Norquest," my eyes fill with tears, blurring the words on the page.

I look up and blink the wetness away. "Maybe I'm fooling myself. Maybe I'm only doing this because Mother is gone and I feel like I've been orphaned—"

"Or maybe she disliked your father so much that only now can you feel free to discover things every kid ought to know." Lines of concentration deepen along Phil's brows and under his eyes. "I don't mean any disrespect to your mother, but I think every girl has the right to love her father. Your mom was wrong to deny you that opportunity."

I shake my head. "She didn't want me to be hurt. She told me, you see, that he had married someone else and had another family. He had sons, she said, and no man could ever love a daughter as much as he loved his sons."

Phil snorts softly. "I don't think that's true."

"Mother said it was. And everybody else seems to think so, too— well, except Andrew Noble. The father in his book certainly loved his daughter. But he didn't have any sons to compete with her."

Phil leans his elbows on his knees again, then nods at my legal pad. "Are you going to read the letter?"

Fueled now by a measure of resentment, I force myself to concentrate on the penciled page.

"'Dear Mr. Norquest'—do you think that's too formal? I thought about writing 'Dear Father,' but that sounded strange. After all, he's never acted like my father." My throat tightens as I look at Phil through a sudden swell of tears. "How am I supposed to do this? I don't even know how to address him!"

"It'll be all right. You'll find the words." Phil reaches out, squeezing my blue-jeaned knee. His touch is so reassuring that fresh tears spring to my eyes.

Betrayed by my weakness, I let the legal pad drop to the floor as I lean back and pull away from Phil's comforting grasp. "Forget it. I can't do this."

"You've made a start, Aurora. That's something."

"A start of *what*? I don't even know what I want to say. 'Hello, I'm your daughter and I thought I'd send you a note to say hello.' How's he supposed to respond to that?"

"How do you want him to respond?"

The question cuts deep, and for an instant my heart empties of everything but a rush of pure yearning.

What do I want? I want . . . love. I don't want promises or fame or money. I don't want to be named in his will; I don't even want the trust fund reserved in my name.

I want to know my father loves me like the steadfast father in Andrew Noble's novel. A fiction.

A fairy tale.

I hang my head in the silence. "You probably think I'm being stupid."

"I think your feelings are pretty normal."

"It's a bad idea." I wipe my cheeks with the back of my hand, then turn and look at the camera on my desk. "So—I just point and click if I want to take a picture?"

Phil gestures to my new toy. "Take the camera off its stand, take as many as a dozen shots, put it back in its cradle. The connection is automatic—almost foolproof."

I force a laugh. "I'm sure I'll find a way to mess it up. But thanks, Phil. I appreciate the thought."

"No problem."

Correctly interpreting my abrupt change of subject as dismissal, he stands and squeezes my shoulder, then heads toward the foyer. I follow, wondering if in the last half-hour I've managed to injure the fragile growth of something precious.

"I'll see you later," he tells me at the door, "but I'd better get back to work."

"Okay," I answer, injecting a falsely cheerful note in my voice. And as I latch the door, I'm afraid I've poisoned whatever might have been budding between us.

The first man to ever call me Rosie may never call me again.

24

Frustration, some sage once wrote, is the wet nurse of violence. Which probably explains why I'm currently resisting the urge to strangle Aurora Norquest.

Good grief, what am I supposed to do? Last week my pastor said that love was a conscious decision to make someone else become precious to you. Well, I've decided that Aurora *could* be precious to me—I love the woman I see cautiously emerging—yet at the same time I am constantly frustrated by her slow pace and the way she clings to unhealthy habits. How can she get better if she doesn't make choices that will help heal the wounds of the past?

Baby steps, she keeps telling me; she's taking baby steps. I can't deny that she is. She's working hard on that apartment, she's enrolled in a master's program (even if the school *is* in South Africa), and she's learned how to use the computer. She's gone up to the roof and down to the lobby; she even managed to endure fifteen excruciating minutes of waiting in a place she views as threatening.

I had hoped the Internet would broaden her circle of friendships, but apparently I'm the only person she e-mails.

I let myself into my apartment and stand in the hallway for a long moment, my hands clenched in my pockets. I ought to get to work, but Aurora has my brain tied in knots.

What is it about the woman that drives me to distraction? I like her. I think she likes me. She's intelligent and refined and well read, which automatically lifts her above 98 percent of the women I meet.

And she needs me. Not only as a computer geek, but as a friend. Unlike all the other women who've invited me over just to fix a hang-up in their operating system, Aurora needs me to help her through these rough patches.

It's wonderful to feel needed.

I go into the kitchen and pull a diet soda from the fridge, then pop the top and take a sip. As my eyes drift toward the wide windows along the wall, I find myself wondering if need bound Clara and Mary Elizabeth. From what little I know of her, Aurora's mother was definitely an alpha personality. Clara must have been content to be a beta.

Maybe that's why I enjoy being with Aurora. I've been a beta my entire life—water boy to the football players in high school, tutor to the frat guys in college. Even now, I'm only a part-time professor at NYU, and I convinced the Westbury board of directors to approve me not because I was accomplished, but because I was *quiet*.

Aurora, however, respects me. With her, perhaps I can escape my second-string life.

On an impulse, I pick up the phone and punch in my parents' number.

Mom answers on the second ring. "Hello?"

"Hi, Mom." I carry the phone into the living room and sink into the repugnant vinyl chair. "How's everything?"

"Phil? What's wrong, son?"

Good grief, the woman can read my mood in two words. "I'm fine; I just wanted to check in. Haven't talked to you in a while."

She's silent for a few seconds, and I can almost see a worry line forming in the center of her forehead. "Are you sick?" she finally asks.

"Never healthier."

"Oh, no. You lost your job."

"I can't lose my job; I'm self-employed, remember? Work is steady. And the university needs their part-timers. Saves money."

"Everything going all right in that new place of yours?"

"The apartment's fine, Mom. Still needs a little work, but I've got time. You and Dad ought to come up here and have a look. I have a guest room now, you know."

As usual, she dismisses my invitation with a laugh. "Oh, your father and I would be as helpless as kittens up a tree in New York City. We'll see you the next time you come home."

I sigh. "Okay."

"What's on your mind, son?"

Looking out at my spectacular view of Central Park, I begin to search for words. "I met a woman, Mom."

"Really?" Her voice rises to a higher pitch. "Is she nice?"

"Of course. And she's bright. Pretty, too, but not in a fussy way."

"Did you meet her at church?"

"She's my neighbor. Next-door neighbor, in fact."

Silence rolls over the line. My mother is waiting for me to say more, but I'm not sure I want to. If this thing with Aurora doesn't pan out, I don't want her to be stuck with a mother-of-the-groom dress.

"Mom, when you first started seeing Dad, was it easy? I mean, did things fall into place, or did it take some time for you to figure out that you were supposed to be together?"

She laughs, and the warm sound makes me glad I've called. "Oh, son, nothing ever falls into place right away. Your father and I dated a few months and he never told me anything about his feelings. So one night I pinned him down and asked him where he thought our relationship was going. You could have knocked me over with an eyelash when he said he didn't know."

"He said that?"

"Yessir, he did. I thought he was ready to declare that he was as in love with me as I was with him, but truth is, he hadn't decided how he felt. So I had a choice—I could give him more time, or I could move on to someone else. But your father . . . well, he was worth waiting for. I chose to hang in there, and I've never regretted it."

I quote a verse from a plaque that hangs above Mom's kitchen sink. "Love is patient, love is kind."

"That's right. You can't rush people when it comes to matters of the heart." She hesitates a moment, then asks: "Do you love this woman?"

"I'm not sure, Mom. I think I could . . . if she'll let me." *If she'll take bigger steps. If she'll let God heal her heart.*

"Well, then. I'll be praying for you. I'll ask the Lord to light your path so you'll know what to do."

"Thanks, Mom. Appreciate it."

I ask about Dad and their dog, then I tell her good-bye. And as I sit in the chair with the phone resting on my chest, I remember the rest of the words on that kitchen plaque:

Love is patient, love is kind.

Love never gives up or loses faith.

Love is always hopeful and endures through every trial.

If the Lord wants me to love Aurora, I'd better buckle my seat belt.

25

APARTMENT 15A

I am crouched behind the sofa in a child-sized body, my knees pressed to the carpet, my hands warm against my chilly cheeks. Before me, shimmering like a green miracle in the living room, is the tallest Christmas tree I have ever seen.

The tree glimmers with multicolored lights and fancy glass balls. Clara suggests that we string popcorn for a garland, but Mother says we can't use anything that smacks of homemade—the tree has to be perfectly elegant for her bridge game tonight.

Without being told, I know I'm not allowed to touch the tree. So I remain tucked behind the sofa, inhaling the fragrance of pine and Christmas. I lift my head long enough to see Mother tug a stray piece of tinsel into place, then she takes Clara by the arm and leads her into the dining room.

I rise to my knees and rest my arms on the back of the sofa. For this moment the tree is magical, mysterious, and all mine.

A soft knock at our door interrupts my thoughts. Neither Mother nor Clara nor Charley moves to answer it, so I stand and walk into the foyer. The peephole is far above my head, but I grab the arm of the bench and drag it to the door, then hop up to peek at our unexpected caller.

The man in the peephole is Booker, the doorman, and he's peering at me from behind a huge cardboard box. I like Booker. He always has a kind word for me.

I scramble down and pull the bench out of the way.

"Hello, young missy," he says when I open the door. "Would you mind opening that door a little wider so I can set this inside?"

I remain where I am, rooted to the spot by sheer amazement. "What is *that*?"

"Now, how could I be knowing what it is? But I can tell you one thing—this box has come an awful long way, according to these stickers. Somebody across the pond thinks a great deal of you, Miss Aurora."

Overcome by a feeling of dangerous excitement, I step aside and let Booker in, too amazed by mystery to worry about allowing the doorman into the apartment without Mother's approval. He heaves the huge box across the threshold and slides it into the foyer, then his dark face creases in a smile.

"You see here?" One black finger taps a red-bordered address label. "This package came all the way from London just for you. That's your name, right here."

A thrill shivers through my senses. I know I will soon get presents from Mother and Aunt Clara and Uncle Charley, but no one from across the ocean has ever sent me anything.

"Is your Christmas tree in there?" He peers into the living room. "I should probably put this right by that big old branch with the shiny gold balls."

He lifts the box, pretending to stagger under its weight, and I can't help clapping as Booker straddle-steps toward the tree—

"What in the world are you doing?"

Booker straightens as Mother steps out of the dining room, her eyes as sharp as her tone.

I shrink back against the wall, more than willing to let the doorman fend for himself.

With grave dignity, Booker lowers the box to the floor, then taps it with his fingertips. "Excuse me, Mrs. Norquest, but this package came for your young miss."

"You are not authorized to bring packages up here without my permission—especially packages from that devil. I thought I had made my wishes clear."

I don't know much about devils, but I can see Mother is upset. She wipes her hands on her apron with particular vehemence, then looks at me. Anger flickers in her eyes like heat lightning, softening only when Clara approaches and touches her sleeve.

"There's no harm done, M.E.," Clara says, offering me a smile. "Just ask Booker to take the package away."

Mother drops the edge of her apron, then smooths it over her dark skirt. "Fine. Take that cursed box away, Booker; we don't want it."

The doorman gives me a brief, distracted glance and tries to smile. "Yes, ma'am. But where do you want me to take it?"

When Mother lifts her gaze to the ceiling, Clara steps in. "You can carry it to my apartment, Booker. We'll take care of it."

I don't understand what Booker and I have done to deserve my mother's displeasure, but at least Clara doesn't seem upset. She smooths the sleeve of Booker's red uniform and smiles. "I'm sure there's been a mistake," she says, winking at him. "After all, it's not yet time for Santa."

The doorman looks at me, his face lighting with comprehension. "Yes, ma'am, I see what you mean. I'd be happy to tote it over to your place."

"Thank you, Booker. You can be sure I'll remember this kindness at Christmas."

Like a good soldier, Booker lifts the box and follows Clara through the foyer. Because Mother has disappeared into the dining room, I follow them, where I linger with one eye pressed to the crack in the door. I watch as Clara leads Booker to her apartment, where she fumbles with her keys while Booker shifts his weight beneath the bulky box.

"So it's a gift, then, from the little girl's daddy?" he asks. "Perhaps one of those fancy English dolls?"

Clara unlocks her door, then pushes it open. "I don't care what it is, but if it's come from London, it's not welcome in that apartment. I thought you were aware of the situation."

"Yes, ma'am, I was, but I thought maybe time had changed things. Especially come Christmas."

Clara sighed. "Nothing's changed, Booker. Nothing at all."

Booker mumbles a response, but I can't hear it from this distance.

The click of the latch is loud in my ears as I close the door. I turn, pressing my spine against the wood, and wonder why the devil would want to send me a package. Maybe it wasn't the devil, but the wicked witch of the west from *The Wizard of Oz*. I am standing there, thinking of Dorothy and the scarecrow, when my mother steps into the foyer. Her blue eyes, narrow with fury, bore into mine, and suddenly I am sliding down the wood like spittle as my bones turn to jelly beneath my skin. The falcons on the foyer wallpaper swarm before my eyes, dark and dagger clawed and dangerous, and as I lift my gaze to the line where the wall meets the plastered ceiling, the fierce birds swoop from the paper and cover me, weighting my arms and legs and covering my eyes and ears and mouth until I cannot breathe or scream.

I sit up in darkness, my sweaty hands clutching the sheet at my waist. I am in my bedroom, safe in my bed, and I've had another nightmare.

Only a dream. The foyer, were I to get out of bed and go check, would be fine, the falcon wallpaper still in place. And I haven't seen Booker the doorman in days, so it's not likely he has paid me a visit in the last half-hour.

I widen my eyes, assigning names to the gloom-shrouded objects as I adjust to wakefulness. Through the dim glow of the night-light in the bathroom, I see my bureau, my book-burdened nightstand, my robe across the foot of the bed.

Awareness hits me like a punch in the stomach.

Eight feet away, sitting in a faint rectangle of light, is the box from my dream, complete with international stickers and a red-bordered address label. Against a backdrop of soft gloom it is all angles and sharp edges except for the uppermost line, which curves slightly . . . because the top of the box is rising and falling with a slow shudder, the exhalation of a living thing.

Terror lodges in my throat, making it impossible to swallow. I stare at the box and search my childhood memories, desperately trying to recall if I ever saw Booker's box again—did Clara and Charley deliver my father's gift, or did they toss it out?

The question hangs in the still air. The box waits for an answer, its lid rising and falling in a steady rhythm, but I can't move. My mother's words have imbued the diabolical container with power, and at this moment I'm convinced it has come from beyond the gates of hell.

"I don't know what happened," I whisper in a strangled voice, "and I'm not getting out of bed, so you can wait all night if you want to."

The air around me is heavy, cold, and still, filled with a hushed malevolence that paints my fear with frustration. Why won't the thing leave?

As if the entity inside has read my thoughts, the lid rises more sharply, pushing at the packing tape that seals its edges. I hear the slight pop of breaking plastic; I see the lid fall. My ears fill with the sound of moving air, as if the thing inside is catching a breath to marshal its strength, then the lid strains upward again, pushing until the tape breaks free at one edge. Now all that separates me from the demon inside is a narrow bit of cellophane across the opening of the box.

Another inhalation, another whoosh, and the malevolent force labors to break the remaining tape. Again I hear a pop, followed by a steady ripping sound. As one of the cardboard flaps rises, shivers trace the length of my spine like spits of sleet sliding down a windowpane.

My ears fill with the querulous sound of my mother's voice as it was before she entered that mindless fog where I did not exist: "Auroraaaaa . . ."

I bury my head in my sheet, close my eyes, and scream.

26

APARTMENT 15B

I wake as if slapped from sleep by an invisible hand. For an instant my mind reels with confusion, then I realize someone is screaming—someone nearby.

Aurora.

I throw on my robe and head out. A moment later I am pounding on my neighbor's door, my blood swimming in adrenaline. "Aurora? Can you open up?"

I'm not sure how long I wait, but when the door finally opens, I'm glad I came. Aurora's eyes are red and swollen; her hand trembles on the doorknob.

"What is it?" I study her face, pale above her flannel robe. "Are you all right?"

She hiccups the answer. "A nightmare—two of them. More real than anything I've dreamed before."

I catch her cold hand and rub it between my palms. Her fingers are like marble. "Let's go into the living room. We'll sit and you can tell me about it."

She moves like a sleepwalker, but I manage to guide her onto the sofa. I pull a velveteen throw from the arm of a chair and drape it over her shoulders.

"Comfortable?"

She nods.

"Warm enough?"

"Yes."

"Good." I sit beside her and catch her hand, leaning forward so I can watch her face. "Tell me about it."

She looks at our interlocked fingers as if she's never seen clasped hands before. "The first dream wasn't so bad—in the beginning. I dreamed old Booker brought me a package for Christmas. I'm sure it was a gift from my father. But Mother said it was from the devil, so she had Clara take it away."

"Was that really a dream—or could it have been a memory?"

"I don't know." Her hoarse voice holds a note halfway between disbelief and pleading. "I think . . . maybe it really happened. Or maybe I *want* it to have really happened, I don't know. My father never sent me anything for Christmas, so maybe I want to believe he did."

"Or maybe he did . . . and you never received it."

I feel a shiver run through her, but she doesn't answer.

"What about the other dream? The worst one?"

The muscles of her forearm harden beneath my hand. "The box came back."

"Which box?"

"The box from the first dream—the package from my father . . . or the devil." Her face clouds with uneasiness. "I know I was dreaming the first time because I was little, but then the box came back. But that time I was awake, sitting up in bed, touching my sheets, looking at my furniture, and yet I saw the package! It was inside the doorway and it was moving and breathing while something inside was trying to get out. For the longest time I watched it struggling to get free, but when it broke through the tape and was about to climb out—well, that's when I closed my eyes and screamed."

"And you woke up?"

Her dark eyes move into mine. "If you say so. But when I opened my eyes again, I was still sitting in the same position. Everything was exactly the same, but the box was gone and you were beating on the door." Her face twists, and her eyes screw tight to trap the sudden rush of tears.

"Shh." I slip my arm around her shoulder and pull her to my side. She melts into me, dropping her head to my chest while I stroke her arm. For a long time she weeps, then her tears stop, but her trembling breaths tell me she is still terrified.

When her breathing slows to a steadier rate, I turn to look down at her. "Aurora," I say, "I know Clara's mentioned this before, but have you thought about seeing some kind of counselor? You've been through a lot in the last few weeks. A professional might be able to help you sort through some of these confusing emotions."

She pulls her head from my shoulder and releases a hollow laugh. "So now *you* think I should see a shrink?"

"Maybe it's a good thought."

She wrinkles her nose. "I've had these nightmares before—when I was thirteen, right after Uncle Charley died. When I started having dreams within dreams, Mother took me to a psychologist, Dr. Morgan. We had a standing weekly appointment for an entire year."

"So . . . he must have helped."

She shrugs. "Maybe he did; maybe I got better on my own. Now I think those dreams were my way of adjusting to Uncle Charley's death . . . like I'm adjusting to Mother's passing now. These dreams are terrible, but I don't think I need Dr. Morgan to tell me I've been under stress."

I nod without speaking. Aurora probably needs to see a psychologist for more than grief counseling, but she'll never see anyone if it means having to leave the apartment. I squeeze her hand. "What if I went with you?"

Her eyes widen. "I can't ask you to do that."

"Why not? Sometimes I need a break from my work. I like taking long walks in the city. Fresh air is good for you."

"I hate to tell you this, but the air in this city isn't exactly fresh.

You're probably polluting your lungs walking around next to all those cars and buses—"

"It may not be fresh, but it's the only air we have. If you'll come down with me sometime, maybe we can walk over to the park—"

"I can get fresh air if I want it." She raises her chin. "I can go up to the roof."

I scratch my head. "Yes . . . but you hear voices up there."

Something flares in her eyes. "I'm not crazy, if that's what you think."

"I didn't say you—"

"And I haven't heard the voice since I stopped taking those sleeping pills."

"That's good." I smile, grateful she has moved from fear to irritation. "Now—are you ready to talk about your dream? Maybe we can analyze it."

"I've never been able to figure out any of my dreams. The first dream could be a memory, but does it really matter? I got lots of presents at Christmas every year, from Mother and Charley and Clara. It's not like I was underprivileged."

I nod. "You might have gotten gifts from your father, too, if Charley and Clara didn't throw those packages out. What if they gave you those gifts and took credit for them themselves?"

Aurora's jaw drops. "Do you think a woman like Clara could actually *do* that?"

"Why not?"

"It just seems . . . tacky. It's one thing to refuse a gift; it's another to take credit for someone else's."

"But the gift isn't what matters. The important thing is knowing your father remembered you. If your brain is conjuring up memories instead of dreams, maybe he thought of you every year but your mother prevented you from receiving his gifts."

A shadow settles on Aurora's brow. "Let's say you're right and my father did send a package or two. Then why would I be so terrified of the box that showed up in the second dream?"

"Maybe . . . the thing you're most afraid of is the truth. Your mother and Clara have always said your father cared nothing for you, but your subconscious could be trying to set the record straight."

"That makes no sense."

"Maybe it makes all the sense in the world. Your mother was a formidable woman who demanded all your time and attention, especially in her last years. Now that she's gone, you're finally able to think about things you've repressed your entire life."

Tilting her head, she looks at me from beneath her lashes. "What makes you such an expert on this stuff?"

I manage a laugh. "Psych 101. Required for all economics majors."

"You may be right, but what does it matter? What's done is done. I can't undo the past."

"But you can change the future. Earlier today you talked about writing him. Maybe it's time you followed through."

"I could finish that letter, I suppose. It might take me a week to fig-ure out what to say, then it'll take another week to get to England—"

"Forget the U.S. mail. That'll take too long."

"Why should I hurry?"

"Because we both need to sleep through the night. I'm pretty sure you can reach your father in hours, not days."

Her brow wrinkles. "I assume you're talking about the computer, but I'm not following you."

"E-mail is a wonderful thing, Rosie." I stand and extend my hand. "Want to bet I can find Theodore Norquest's e-mail address within five minutes?"

"Are you serious?"

"Absolutely. If I can't find his address, I'm sure we can look up his publisher and they'll forward the e-mail to him. Why should you wait a week when you could have a response in hours?"

She looks down, her long lashes hiding her eyes. "Do you really think I should do this?"

"Only thing quicker is a telephone. Your lawyer would have his number—"

"No, there's no way I'm ready for that. I wouldn't know what to say."

"Then write an e-mail, send it to his publisher, and ask them to forward it. Nearly everybody has e-mail these days."

"I didn't."

"Then you're to be congratulated, because I think you were the last person in the Upper West Side to hook into the Internet. But if by some chance your father is among the holdouts, his publisher can print out the letter and fax it. He will get the message, I promise. Especially when you say you are his long-lost daughter."

Her eyes are as wide and blank as mirrors when she meets my gaze. "Show me."

A few minutes later I have taken a seat at her computer and navigated to the home page for Bleak House, publisher of sixty-five Theodore Norquest novels. I click on a link and smile as an e-mail form appears. "Right here," I say, tapping the screen. Aurora is sitting beside me, her half-finished letter in her lap. "You can either type a note to your father or ask the publicist to contact you. Either way, your message will be on its way."

Frowning, she looks at the screen, then touches it with her fingertip. "Wait—what's that?"

I lean closer to read the tiny print. "Um . . . a link to sign up for the publisher's newsletter. It's probably designed to let readers know when the next Theodore Norquest novel is coming out."

"Click that, will you?"

I do. A subscription box appears, and Aurora's face relaxes as she drops her hand to the back of my chair. "Sign me up. For now, that's all I want to do."

"But Theodore Norquest may never look at this subscription list. Those things usually come from a publicist's office—"

"Baby steps, Phil. I can only take baby steps."

I look at her narrowed eyes, then sigh and type her e-mail address into the sign-up form. With a click of the enter key, the form disappears. Theodore Norquest's reluctant daughter is now one of thousands of readers who receive his newsletter.

Still, she moved forward. Took a baby step.

"You may not hear anything for months." I turn to face her. "I've a feeling they only publish a newsletter when he has a new release. How often is that—twice a year?"

She straightens her shoulders, unspoken pain alive and glowing in her eyes. "While I'm waiting, maybe I can think of a better way to approach him. I still don't know what to say."

I bend to pick up her legal pad, which has fallen to the floor. "Then you'll need this. Might as well keep going."

"I suppose so." She takes the tablet, then yawns dramatically and taps her fingers over her mouth. "Oh! Excuse me."

Taking the hint, I stand. "It's late—and we both need to get some sleep." I walk to the foyer, aware of her soft footsteps behind me. She catches my arm as I open the door.

"Phil?"

"Yeah?"

"Thanks for coming. I don't know what I'd have done if you hadn't come."

As I walk back to my own apartment, the worn carpet slick under my bare feet, I remember the pounding Bangles music and how I was nearly tempted to move my bed into another room.

Now I can't imagine sleeping anywhere else. My life has become intertwined with Aurora's, a woman who has every quality I need—and a mountain to climb in baby steps.

Love is patient . . .

27

I am standing in my bedroom, my hand pressed to my pounding forehead, when the door buzzes. My morning visitor has to be Clara—Phil wouldn't be over this early, not after dispensing psychological diagnoses at 2 a.m. I am barely awake myself, having been distracted from my desire for coffee by the throbbing behind my eyeballs.

I stagger to the door and let Clara in, then leave her standing in the foyer as I trudge to the kitchen.

"Aurora Rose!" she calls, shock in her voice. "You look like something the cat dragged in. What's happened?"

"I had a late night."

I reach for the plug to the coffeepot and accidentally send a glass clattering over the counter before it drops into the sink. I brace myself for the sound of breakage, but the tumbler is cheap and thick.

From the library, I hear the clink of empty mugs and the rustle of an empty potato chip bag. Clara is cleaning up after me, an old habit she hasn't yet seen the need to break. At least she'll stay busy while I get something to drink. I need caffeine before I can face an interrogation.

I don't think I'll have time for coffee, so I open the fridge, pull a can of Diet Coke from the shelf, then pop the lid. I tip my head back and guzzle like a newborn seeking the breast.

The bubbles tickle my nose, assuring me that at least some part of my body is awake. "Do you want coffee, Clara?" I call down the gallery, but she doesn't answer. She's pouting, then. She's probably wandering around and checking on the state of my housekeeping, which means she's undoubtedly disappointed that I'm not keeping the place up to Mother's lofty standards. I'm pretty sure I left a wadded-up napkin on the love seat in the library, and I can't remember the last time I scrubbed out the tub in my bathroom. The computer room is a complete mess, with catalogs scattered all over the desktop and a half-empty can of Diet Coke on the window sill.

Clara will join me in a moment, but she won't be cruel. She'll put her arm around me and gently suggest it's time I phoned Mildred or found someone else to help me with the housekeeping.

Maybe Phil is right about Clara treating me like a child.

"I'm putting some coffee on for you," I call. I splash enough coffee for a couple of cups into a filter, then pop the filter into the coffee maker. Fully aware of the silence emanating from the gallery like a cold wind, I run water into the decanter, then pour it into the machine.

I cross my arms and lean against the counter as the Mr. Coffee begins to hiss and rumble. If she's pouting, well . . . let her pout. If she tries to coddle me this morning, I may say something we'll both regret. I'm too tired to put up with intrusive comments, and I'm not in the mood to hear that my mother was the perfect woman. I love Clara, I loved my mother, but if my dreams contain even a shred of truth, the two of them have been unfair to me and my father.

As the coffee finishes brewing, I turn off the power and pull a clean mug from the cabinet. As the coffee maker cools, so does my temper. Maybe Clara's not upset with me—maybe she's been distracted by a memory . . . or maybe she's found my Theodore Norquest novels on the nightstand.

I forgot about those.

I hurry and splash coffee into two mugs, then add a heaping teaspoon of sugar to each. By the time I've colored Clara's coffee with a dash of cream, I've braced myself for anything she might say.

Increasingly perturbed by the silence, I lift the mugs and walk down the gallery, peering into rooms as I pass. I find Clara sitting on the love seat in the library. The skeletal remains of a sandwich lie on a plate next to a pair of empty juice glasses.

My first thought is relief—she hasn't found my Norquest novels; she's upset about the mess on the coffee table.

But I don't think poor housekeeping has the power to make her face fade to the color of old newsprint. She is staring not at the mess, but at my yellow legal pad . . . and the page where I began a letter to my father.

At my approach she drops the tablet to her lap and folds her hands. She does not look up at me. Wordlessly, I set a mug on the coffee table, then sink onto the love seat and steel myself for the storm.

I am expecting shouts and tears. What I get is a broken whisper.

"I can't believe," she says, her chin quivering, "you could even *think* of writing that monster."

I want to tell her she shouldn't be snooping, because I'm a grown woman who can take care of myself. But the thought shrivels when I see the pain on her face. I have opened my life to her, so I can't blame her for looking into its cracks and crevices.

"He's my father, Clara." I am thinking of Phil's comments, but I try a softer approach. "Surely a grown woman ought to be able to write her father."

Clara lifts her chin and looks toward the window. "There are things I have never told you about Theodore Norquest. Things I never wanted to think about, much less speak about. Things I hoped we could leave unsaid."

Something in me crumbles as I look at her woebegone face.

"Theodore Norquest is the devil himself," she says, finally meeting my eyes. "Have you never asked yourself *why* your parents divorced?"

She bends her head toward me, her face alive with troubled question, and I can't answer. For years I've lived with my parents' divorce as ancient history. Though Mother never explained anything, rumors of my father's "London woman" occasionally drifted through our door. Those rumors have solidified and become fact in my mind, but something in Clara's eyes tell me I have not heard the entire truth.

"I heard he was unfaithful," I tell her. "I thought that was the reason."

She closes her eyes and draws a reluctant breath. "There was a lot more to the story. It was all kept quiet, of course. No one outside the family ever knew what was going on, but Charley and I knew everything—walls are thin up here on the fifteenth floor. Your mother never wanted you to know about the abuse, the beatings, the *awful* things he did to her. M.E. had good reasons for sending him away, Aurora. It took her a long time to find the courage, but finally she did."

My mind spins with bewilderment. "He *abused* her? And what do you mean, she sent him away? I thought he left her when he found out she was pregnant with me."

Aunt Clara closes her eyes and pinches the bridge of her nose. "A woman will say many things to protect her loved ones. She never wanted you to blame her for sending your father away—so you must forgive her for bending the truth. But you're old enough to hear it, Aurora, and you should know that Theodore Norquest was a cruel, jealous, bitter man. During the years they were married, he abused your mother in the foulest ways imaginable."

"I don't believe it." The words slip from me before I can stop them. I don't know why I'm defending him—I've never heard him described in anything but uncomplimentary terms, but I can't imagine Mother tolerating even a minute of verbal or physical abuse.

She lifts a silver brow. "You should believe it. You know what they say about writers—they are moody, temperamental people, given to drink and long periods of morose silence. Your father fit the stereotype exactly. When his books didn't sell fast enough or when he had an argument with his editor, he took his frustrations out on your mother.

She was horrified, of course—imagine her, a Wentworth, having to endure the sort of abuse that's more common to lower-class households. She put up with his drunken tantrums as long as she could, but when she found out she was pregnant, she gathered her friends around her and locked him out. She didn't want you to suffer, too."

Clara looks toward the window, her face arranged in lines of deep concentration. "I'll never forget that day. Your father had gone to London on a business trip, so M.E. called me and Charley to help gather his things. Booker, the old doorman, carted everything downstairs. When Ted came home, he found his clothing and possessions waiting in the lobby. We were terrified he'd make a scene, but he took charge of his belongings and went right back to London. Later we learned he had a woman there."

Clara leans back and waves a limp hand at me. "The rest of the story is public record. He didn't contest the divorce, he married his English mistress, and he raised another family overseas. He never saw Mary Elizabeth again."

I can't speak. My mind is sifting through Clara's story, comparing it to snatches of information I've gleaned through the years. My mother certainly despised my father—that much of the tale rings true—but I have never heard anyone characterize him as abusive or alcoholic. And they were married fifteen years—how could a woman like Mother stand abuse for that long?

But maybe that's why she was so strong by the time I came along. Maybe those difficult years forged her iron will and strengthened her backbone.

On the other hand, my father's books are wonderful stories of love and longing and family. Though they take place in surreal settings with mystical rules, every novel I've read is underlined with themes of compassion and faithfulness. A thread of love runs through every story, every page.

How could such an inspiring writer be an obnoxious human being?

Reluctantly, I meet Clara's gaze. "This is hard to believe."

"It's the truth."

Those three words prick at the deepest part of my soul. I don't want to believe Theodore Norquest is a devil because half of what I am springs from him.

Please, God, don't let him be evil.

I close my eyes and imagine the scene that unfolded so long ago in the lobby downstairs—my father coming home, pausing in the lobby to see boxes and suitcases piled in a corner. Booker would have been standing nearby, his hands folded at his waist, his expression nervous and forlorn. That poor man—how could he explain what Mother had done?

The image of Booker lingers in my mind's eye—faint at first, then as vivid as a photograph emerging in a developer's tray. He was full time in those days, so it's likely he helped my father move his things out of the building . . . and last night he appeared in my dream.

"Clara, did my father ever send me Christmas presents?"

The spidery lashes shadowing her cheeks fly upward. "What a notion! Why would you think such a thing?"

"I seem to remember packages arriving . . . from England. I think Booker brought them up to the apartment."

Clara releases a sharp laugh. "Charley and I used to order gifts from Harrods. That's probably what you remember."

"Why would you order from Harrods when Macy's and Bloomingdales are right here in New York?"

"Darling, everyone shops at Macy's and Bloomies. Charley and I wanted our gifts to be unique."

Of course she'd have an answer. I look away and sigh as my hopes collide like bits of glass in a kaleidoscope. I longed for a father worthy of my love. Since learning of the trust fund, I had been hoping Mother was wrong, that somehow, for some reason, Father loved me.

But if he is the sort of man who could abuse and despise my mother, surely he feels nothing but contempt for me. If I were to approach him, he'd probably refuse to acknowledge me. That clause in the trust fund agreement is nothing but a ruse—if I were to visit him, he'd take that opportunity to officially cast me off. Surely he has no intention of giving me anything. I am more loathsome than a squashed insect under his shoe, a disagreeable remnant of a life he cast aside.

Perhaps Clara is right; he only established the trust fund to preserve what little of his reputation remained.

I reach across the love seat and clasp Aunt Clara's hand. "I'm sorry, Auntie, for making you dredge all that up. I understand why you didn't want to talk about it."

"Aurora." Her eyes soften as she says my name. "You are so naive in many ways. Your mother and I never wanted you to know about the seamier side of your father's life."

"It's okay, Clara. I'm a grown woman; I can handle it."

"I'll try to remember that." She smiles at me, but the customary expression of good humor is missing from the curve of her mouth and the depths of her eyes.

I nudge the coffee cup toward her. "I made this for you."

"Thank you, dear." She takes the cup and lifts it, then smiles at me across the rim. "I'm glad the truth is finally out in the open. I've carried that nasty little secret far too long."

After Clara leaves, I gather our mugs, the trash, the empty juice glasses, and carry everything to the kitchen. After setting the dirty dishes in the sink, I stride back into the library, plump the pillows on the love seat, then spy the legal pad on the table. Without a second thought I rip the letter to my father from the pad, then shred the page into tiny pieces. As the fragments snowflake from my hands into the trash can, I resolve to clean the apartment from north to south. I will mop and organize and dust and scrub.

When I have cleaned up, I will tackle my mother's room. I will call the medical supply company from whom we rented the hospital bed; they can pick it up and haul it away. I will fill boxes with medical supplies and clothing; I will set everything in the hall for George. I will ditch the old recliner, donate the antique dresser and mirror to a thrift store. I'll strip the old wallpaper and check the condition of the plaster beneath it. I will be ruthless with that space, and when it is empty, I will find a new use for the room.

Because as long as I am consumed with projects at home, I won't have time to think about reaching out to a father who never cared a whit for me.

I bend to straighten a stack of books at the far edge of the love seat, then hesitate. *The Merchant of Menace*, by Theodore Norquest, sits beneath a copy of *Cry, the Beloved Country*, and suddenly I am convinced that merely touching the Norquest book will burn my skin.

I pull a pillow from the love seat and cover the spine so I won't have to look at it. Thank goodness Clara didn't see it.

Back in the kitchen, I stack the dirty dishes in the dishwasher. My thoughts drift back to Clara's story, and I keep struggling to see my mother as an abused woman. I knew her better than anyone, and I never saw her as anything but proud and strong. She had such inherent strength . . . but perhaps that quality attracted my father to her. For all I know, he wanted to find a strong woman to defeat, a proud woman he could humble.

I give myself a stern mental shake. For memories of my mother's married years, I have to trust Clara. Mother had healed by the time I matured; she had put the past behind her. She had developed strength to survive. I've seen enough abused women on television talk shows to know it takes tremendous courage to leave an abuser— most women are so trapped in the cycle of mistreatment that they are imprisoned by their own insecurity. Battered women who accept the lie of their unworthiness often find that their refusal to resist results in their own destruction.

But Mary Elizabeth Wentworth Norquest conquered her fears in a time when abused women were society's secret. I can understand why she would choose to hide the real reasons for her divorce . . . and why Aunt Clara would circle the wagons and protect me from the truth.

I shake my head, still finding it hard to believe the genial man in the black-and-white author photographs could be cruel and abusive. Despite his frightening fiction, my father looks as gentle as Santa Claus. But what do I know of men? I can count the men I know and trust on one hand: Uncle Charley, Mr. Williamson, old Booker, George the super, and . . . Phil Cannon.

The thought of my neighbor makes me smile. Something tells me he's not the typical single woman's idea of a dream date, but he came running to my aid last night. And men don't come running unless they feel *something*.

Grateful that Phil hasn't given up on me, I put the last of the dishes into the dishwasher, then close the door and move into the computer room. The machine is humming softly, so I nudge the mouse to wake it and check for e-mail messages: none yet. After our late night, Phil may be sleeping.

I am organizing my mountain of computer manuals when my gaze falls upon *I Know She Weeps*. This book draws me, and my hand lingers on the cover as I pick it up—that book touched a secret part of me, but why? Did it affect me because an unworldly voice told me to read it . . . or did a subconscious voice tell me to read it because somehow I knew it would touch me?

My father's mysticism must be affecting me. I wouldn't be thinking this way if I hadn't been reading his novels.

Intrigued by the question, I sit and mentally shuffle through all the television programs I've watched in the last month. Oprah hasn't picked the title for her on-again, off-again book club, I'm sure. Nor has it been featured on *Live with Regis and Kelly* or the *Today Show*'s book club. My subconscious brain could have absorbed the title while I was taking care of Mother and half-listening to a television program, but the book is so old it's hard to believe anyone would have been promoting it recently.

I open the cover and run my hand over the title page, unable to keep a smile from my lips. I loved this story, but most of all, I loved these characters. And I don't need Phil to explain why.

Tucking one foot beneath me, I flip to the last page and reread the ending.

And Lord John, who had traveled from one end of his territory to the other searching for the child of his heart, dismounted and drew the frightened girl into his arms. For a long while neither spoke, their hearts merging into one contented rhythm.

At last he lifted his head to look upon his daughter's face. "I have yearned for you," he said, smoothing her dark hair, "since the day I first learned you would be born. I have searched for you without ceasing. The blood of my dear messenger has been shed on your behalf, but I would have given the last of my treasures to win your heart."

"Papa," she whispered, the word musical on her tongue, "I am so glad to have come home."

And while the wind whistled outside the castle walls, while the demons of Aragon howled in protest, the father and his daughter crossed over the drawbridge and went inside the fortress to acquaint each other with the lives they had spent apart. Before the shades of night had fallen, each promised they would never be parted again until they were welcomed at the throne of the eternal Father and God of all those who seek heaven as their forever home.

And it is said that whenever a citizen of that realm wished to know what love looked like, all he need do was look to the lord of the castle, who embodied love through his decrees, his deeds, and even the intents of his heart.

For he had loved his child completely and had willingly sacrificed all he could to bring his daughter home.

I close the book, momentarily wishing my mother had been attracted to Andrew Noble, medieval storyteller, instead of horror writer Theodore Norquest. Another thought trails in the wake of that wish—has Andrew Noble written anything else?

I move the mouse, which wakes the sleeping monitor. One stroke of the keyboard sends me to Google; a swift clattering of keys and the search box fills with Andrew Noble's name.

I exhale as a short list appears on the screen. At least a dozen reviews of *I Know She Weeps* are referenced, as well as several pages where mostly female readers have cited the novel as their favorite book. After a bit of searching, I conclude that Andrew Noble must have been a one-shot wonder. Neither Amazon nor Barnes and Noble lists any other titles under his name.

How could he stop with one book?

I try www.andrewnoble.com and receive an error message. Typing www.iknowsheweeps.com gives me nothing.

But Phil has taught me to look for back doors on the Web. I check the book's copyright page—the novel was published by Waterman-Dale, Inc., so I enter the publisher's name in a search engine. Within minutes I have found the company's home page, and I'm amazed at the size of the conglomerate. Waterman-Dale features nearly a dozen smaller imprints—Little Fox Press publishes children's literature, Best Foods produces cookbooks, Waterman Faith specializes in inspirational titles, Dale and Stock prints textbooks, Waterdale designs coffee table books, Bleak House focuses on horror.

My heart contracts like a squeezed fist when I recognize my father's publisher. How could the people at this company publish scores of

Norquest novels and only one by Andrew Noble? My father is a great writer, but so is Andrew Noble. If his book didn't sell well enough to justify extending him another contract, they should have done more to promote the book; they should have told the world they had snared some kind of literary *genius.*

I bite hard on my lower lip. I want to write someone about Andrew Noble, but I've no idea how to address my letter. Finally I settle on the link for the publicist at Waterman-Dale. Phil says e-mail is easy to forward—fine. Let them forward my letter to someone with authority, because they have made a tremendous mistake. Andrew Noble should still be writing and publishing. If he's still alive, they should be encouraging his talent.

I flex my fingers and prepare to type the first fan letter of my life:

To Whom It May Concern:

I have just read I Know She Weeps, *published by your company in 1987. I know the book is out of print, but I have only recently become aware of this title.*

I read a lot—probably ten books per week—and while I may not be an expert literary critic, I do have a rudimentary knowledge of good storytelling. I Know She Weeps *is a wonderful book, a story that profoundly influenced me. I would love to read more books by the author, Andrew Noble, but I am unable to find any other titles under his name.*

I would love to know more about Mr. Noble. Is he still living? Is he still writing? Has your company done all it could to encourage his talent? I would hate to think I Know She Weeps *is Noble's first and last book.*

Any information you can send me would be most appreciated.

Sincerely,
Aurora Rose Norquest
AuroraRose@manhattan.rr.com

I look at the e-mail and wonder if I should delete my last name. Norquest is not a common name, and my father is well-known in publishing circles, but it's not likely anyone knows about me. Besides—I can hear my mother nagging in my inner ear—it would be impolite to send a letter, even an e-mail, without a proper signature.

I check the text for spelling errors, then click send.

After the screen clears, I curl up in my chair and hug my knees, hoping Andrew Noble is alive and well and a wonderful human being. I won't even mind learning that he's eighty and bald with a wife and ten children.

I need to believe in someone.

28

APARTMENT 15B

Pleased that I am entering the Thanksgiving break without an arm-load of economics papers to grade, I step off the elevator, turn toward my door, and nearly step on Aurora. She's sitting on the floor beneath the trash chute, but the tense expression on her face tells me she's come out of her apartment for a more pressing reason than garbage.

"I'm glad you're back," she says simply.

"Hi." I shift my shopping bag to my left hand, then slip my key into the lock. "Sorry I wasn't here, but I had some errands to run after class." I give her a smile as I push the door open. "You should come out with me later. It's a really nice day."

I'm not surprised when she doesn't rise to the bait.

"I was hoping we could talk," she says, pushing herself up from the floor. "But if you have to work, I could come back later."

"Surely by now you know I'm always happy to procrastinate." I step over the threshold and hold the door for her. "Come on in. Want something to drink?"

She follows, rubbing her hands over her arms. "Diet soda, if you have it."

"No problem." I lead the way down the gallery, then turn into the kitchen and drop my bag on the counter. When I'm sure she has followed, I gesture toward the stools at the bar, then begin to unpack my shopping bag.

"I found this little bodega a few blocks from here—it's a nice walk, especially if the wind is brisk, but they have just about anything you could need for groceries." I toss two large oranges into the refrigerator crisper, then hold the door and search for soft drinks among the foam containers of leftover takeout dinners. "Hmm . . . Diet Coke okay for you?"

She nods as she slides onto one of the stools.

"You want it in a glass?"

"The can is okay, if it's cold."

I hand her a can, then pull a bag of apples from my bag and pour the fruit into the refrigerator drawer. Something is on Aurora's mind, something heavy. Thinking of my mother's advice, I wait for her to speak.

A silence settles over the kitchen, an absence of sound that has almost a physical density. Aurora is not the most outgoing person in the world, but I've never known her to be at a complete loss for words.

I close the fridge and lean on the kitchen island. She is studying her soda can. When I bend to meet her gaze, I see a look of unutterable distance in her eyes. "What's wrong, Rosie?"

A shadow crosses her face. "Clara came to see me this morning."

"And how is Mrs. B.?"

"She's been better. She caught me right after I'd crawled out of bed, so while I was making coffee, she started to tidy up the apartment."

"Being messy isn't a crime."

"No . . . but being ungrateful is."

"You'll have to explain that one."

A smile spooks over her lips. "She found the letter I'd been trying to write—to my father. I must have left it in the library, and she was as pale as chalk when I found her with it. That's when she sat me down and told me why my parents got a divorce."

The room swells with silence as I try to make sense of this news.

"Let me get this straight. Nobody ever told you why your parents weren't together?"

She wipes her eyes and grips the Coke can with both hands. "I knew he had a woman in England . . . and I knew he left after he found out Mother was pregnant with me. Mother always said my father was the devil. Not exactly what a kid wants to learn, but after hearing that, I couldn't ask for specifics. I didn't want to hurt her . . . and I didn't want to make her angry."

I step around the island and sit on the stool across from Aurora, not wanting to disturb the silence through which she is laboring to stitch words together.

"This morning, Clara said"—her voice breaks, but she pushes on—"that my father was abusive . . . and my mother suffered while they lived together. My mother's social circle—well, she moved in a hoity-toity crowd, if you know what I mean. Mother came from money. I imagine she could have had her pick of young men, but she married my father. So—to see all her dreams turn to ashes—that had to be hard. And life with an abusive husband must have been a nightmare. Clara says Mother finally found the courage to kick him out when she learned she was pregnant with me."

I stroke my chin as I study her. Aurora has obviously been shaken by this news, but why is Clara airing the family's dirty secrets now? Aurora has been making progress, taking real steps toward establishing a life of her own, so how is this news supposed to help her?

"Aurora"—I gentle my voice—"why did Clara tell you these things today?"

She blinks. "I . . . I don't know. Because she saw the letter, I suppose. You should have seen her face; she was dreadfully upset."

"Doesn't the timing seem strange to you? I mean, from what you've told me, neither Clara nor your mother ever had a nice thing to say about your father. So why did she want to make him look even worse today?"

Confusion and anger are warring in her eyes. "What do you mean?"

"You should be getting on with your life and putting the past behind you. Like me, you're at the midpoint of your life. This is the time we're supposed to make peace with the past so we can move into the future."

"How can I make peace with the past when it keeps coming back to haunt me?" Her voice, so flat a moment before, is suddenly vibrant with restrained fury. "You don't know what I'm going through, Phil. You aren't having nightmares every night. I read my father's books, I fall in love with his stories and his genius, then I learn he's nothing but a hypocrite! They told me he was awful, and now I know how awful he was!"

"What did Clara tell you, exactly?" I know I'm venturing into tender territory, but something drives me on. "Did he hit your mother? Mistreat her? Did he call her names, did he drink, did he cheat on her—"

"He drank." Aurora leaps on the word. "This morning, Clara said he drank."

I slap the table. "Okay, that's something. He drank. Was he an alcoholic? Did he have drunken rages? Don't you think it's odd you've never heard anything about this until now?"

The color has fled from Aurora's face. "I . . . they wanted to protect me, of course."

"But you are a grown woman! Surely at some point before this, Clara would have thought you were strong enough to hear the truth."

Aurora glares at me with burning, reproachful eyes. "Why are you defending him?"

"Why are you *attacking* him? I don't understand you, Rosie—you want to meet the man, you're desperate to talk to him, yet you shy away from every opportunity. You won't write him a letter, you won't e-mail his publisher, you won't even leave this building when the Bleak House offices are located right here in Manhattan—"

She stands so abruptly the stool scoots backward across the tiled floor. "That's not fair! You can't understand!"

I want to yell back, to fling words like weapons, *anything* to dispel her lethargy, but I can't hurt someone so vulnerable. I can't wound someone I want to love.

I draw a long, quavering breath, barely mastering the frustration boiling at my core. "Think about it, Rosie, please—wife beaters, even alcoholic ones, are predictable; they follow a pattern. Yet by all accounts, Theodore Norquest has been happily married to his present wife for something like thirty years. Not a breath of scandal has ever touched him. His other children praise him, his wife adores him, and his publisher thinks he's the best thing since sliced bread."

"You'd think he was great, too, if he was worth millions to your company."

"Lots of companies have million-dollar authors, but not all companies speak highly of them. Believe it or not, Aurora, not everyone in the world is comfy-cozy with everyone else. Yes, people disagree, sometimes passionately, and yes, the world is full of injustice and anger. But people get by. They find ways to get along. They risk safety and security, and do you know why? Because human beings thrive on challenges. Sometimes we win and sometimes we learn by losing. But you wouldn't know any of this because you've locked yourself away in your ancient apartment—"

"Stop!" She flings her hands over her ears and turns away, her slender body trembling.

I feel myself shiver as a cold lump of remorse settles in my chest. I've gone too far. I've said too much and she'll never forget or forgive me. After this she may never want to venture into my apartment again.

"Rosie." My blood runs thick with guilt. "Please, sit down so we can talk this out."

I stand and reach for her, but at the pressure of my fingers she winces as if I have nipped her flesh. "I have to go."

I hurry to block her path. "Come on, please sit down. I'm sorry, I didn't mean to climb all over you like that."

"Let me go."

I hesitate, then step aside and lift my hands in a gesture of surrender. She moves down the gallery with a determined step, but when she reaches the foyer, I know I can't let her go like this.

"Please think about it." I lengthen my stride to catch her. "Put your emotion aside and consider the situation logically. You are allowing one woman's testimony to determine your entire future—are you sure Clara deserves that kind of power?"

Aurora pauses at the door, her back to me. "She's all I have left." She turns her head until I can see her profile. "She's my only family."

"She's no more closely related to you than I am, Aurora, and I think she's doing you a disservice. You've come so far in the last couple of weeks—you've made so much progress. Don't allow Clara to stop you from pursuing something that might make you happy. You deserve to know your father, no matter what kind of man he is. You deserve to plan your own future based on what you learn about yourself. Don't let Clara's fears keep you locked away from your future."

She closes her eyes. For a moment I think my words have taken hold, but then she clenches her jaw and tugs on the door. Before I can catch her, she is moving through the hallway with a quick step.

I stand in the entry and hear her door slam, followed by the distinct snap of deadbolts shooting home.

Aurora Norquest is safely locked away.

Again.

29

Battered by conflicting emotions, I run to my bedroom and crawl beneath the covers. In the stuffy darkness of my safest sanctuary, I weep out of sheer frustration. What makes Phil think he knows Clara better than I do? What gives him the authority to give me advice? He has not lived in this building all his life; he has never suffered from paralyzing fears. He grew up in Middle America, the child of two contented parents. I can just see him as the brainy kid who made the dean's list and loved computers more than his peer group.

What does he know about my life? He didn't think twice about moving from St. Louis to New York—alone! He didn't hesitate to move from Brooklyn to Manhattan, and he took an apartment in the Westbury Arms without knowing a soul in the building.

I can't even *dream* of such courage. I would *die* if I had to move to another building. Clara would have a fit, too, at the thought of me moiling about in some strange place . . .

My thoughts come to an abrupt halt as something clicks in my mind. Clara *would* be terribly upset if I left the building—I know this as surely as I know the sun will rise tomorrow. But why should she mind? It's not like she depends on me for anything—she does far more for me than I do for her.

No, she would protest because I'm the daughter she never had . . .

but don't most mothers rejoice when their children mature and leave the nest? That's the way things are supposed to work.

So why would Clara mind if I left?

One of Phil's phrases floats to the surface of my mind: *I don't know what bound your mother and Clara.*

I reach up and pull the heavy comforter from my face. The cooler air of the apartment tingles my skin.

What *did* bind those two women? Friendship, certainly. Love. Clara loves me, but love isn't supposed to be confining. I've read enough books to know that real love liberates. If Clara loved me like a mother, she'd want me to overcome my fears; she'd encourage me to take my baby steps. But every time I mention one of my little changes, she objects.

The thought is disloyal, but it strikes me as true. I see Clara's resistance in other areas, too—she likes Phil, but only to a point. When I began to confide in him, she began to warn me away.

Why would Clara want me to remain locked inside my past? The question hammers at me. From deep within my subconscious, a new thought struggles to be born, but it won't emerge.

I roll onto my back and stare at the ceiling, where the shadows have shifted from west to east. Lunchtime has come and gone and I haven't taken the time to eat. Truthfully, I don't feel hungry. My stomach is tied in knots.

I curl onto my side and close my eyes, trying not to think about my argument with Phil. If he were here, he'd be quick to agree that Clara is unusually attached to me . . . would he be able to explain why? He has no problem telling me to ignore her, to doubt her, to think of her as some kind of compulsive liar. But he hasn't grown up with her; he doesn't know how many times she has preserved my sanity. When Mother was sick but still ambulatory, sometimes Clara would take Mother to her apartment so I could have a few minutes of solitude to clean, read, or sleep. Clara has acted as the buffer between me and the world, bringing my mail, running my errands, handling a hundred little things I can't even bring myself to contemplate.

She knows—like I know—that my fears are illogical, but she tolerates my limitations. She loves me and supports me completely because I am my mother's daughter and Clara adored Mary Elizabeth Wentworth Norquest.

How could I doubt a woman like that?

And yet . . . if I were to conquer my fears, I know she'd disapprove. Why? Have I depended on her so long that the idea of my independence threatens her self-image? Surely not. Clara enjoys a full social life apart from me and the Westbury Arms. She doesn't depend on me for fulfillment or meaning or even affection.

She doesn't depend on me for anything . . . but money.

I open my eyes as my thoughts crystallize into a startling realization—now that Mother is gone, I am Clara's sole support. The annual bequest pays Clara's bills and allows her to maintain her lifestyle. Clara needn't worry that I will exercise my power to cut her off, but she *might* worry if I moved away . . . or if I began to depend on someone else.

That admission springs from a place beyond logic and reason, and I am quick to silence the cynical inner voice. Clara would never do anything to hurt me. She is completely loyal, trustworthy, and loving. She wants the best for me; that's why she's protected me all these years.

And that's why she doesn't want me to change—she doesn't want me to suffer, that's all. She knows how I panic when I stumble into situations beyond my control. She's seen me hyperventilating; she knows that a panic attack leaves me trembling and feeling I'm about to die.

Who would wish that on someone they loved? No one. That's why she protects me. It's that simple.

⌒◈⌒

I'm not sure how I manage to sleep with so many thoughts running through my head, but somehow my grip on reality slackens and I tumble into a light doze. When I lift my head, it's after two o'clock—I've been asleep for more than an hour.

I sit up and drag my hands through my hair, trying to readjust to a world that seems strangely altered from the world I knew this morning. It's hard to believe my mind could ever suggest that Clara clings to me for financial reasons, but the silly thought has made a deep impression.

I'm tired, though, and when a body is tired, the brain doesn't function properly. I'll go have a cup of tea with Clara, and ten minutes of conversation will set things to rights. When the world looks the way it's supposed to, I'll come home and finish my cleaning. If I work quickly, I may have time to start on Mother's room.

Sighing heavily, I lower my feet to the floor, pat my cardigan pockets to be sure I still have my key, then stick my feet into the slippers I've kicked off beside the bed. I duck into the bathroom long enough to be sure I don't have melted mascara beneath my eyes, then practice a smile in the mirror.

I'm no beauty, but there's nothing in my appearance to rouse Clara's suspicions.

After I press the buzzer at Clara's apartment, I glance toward Phil's place—his door is closed, without even a sliver of light above the threshold. Either he's gone out or he's working in his office at the back of the building.

Clara still hasn't answered, so I lift my hand to knock. As my knuckles hit the door, it moves.

A sense of unease creeps into my mood like a wisp of smoke.

Clara never closes the door without engaging the deadbolts. We joke about it; she is as paranoid about personal safety as I am.

"Clara?"

I push at the door with my fingertips. It swings easily on its hinges, revealing the long, narrow gallery lined with photographs and art.

"Clara?" A lamp glows on the foyer table, but an odd stillness fills the apartment. "Auntie, are you home?"

Coldness settles in my belly, as if I've recently swallowed a huge chunk of ice. I've never felt threatened in Clara's apartment, but my heart is beating so heavily I can feel each separate thump like a blow to my chest.

Something is wrong. I ought to run back into my apartment, lock the door, and call for help, but what if there's no time? Clara might need me; she might be gasping out my name this very minute.

I catch my breath, lower my head, and charge through the gallery at a hellbent stagger, my eyes watering against the surge of panic rising in my chest. I glance in the first doorway on the left—no Clara; I peek into the living room on the right—Clara is not there. Gasping a fresh breath, I hurry through the kitchen, looking over the island, afraid I'll find her lying in a puddle of water she's spilled and slipped in, but Clara is not in the kitchen, the pantry, or the adjoining storage room.

Pausing in the doorway, I peer into the dining room, hoping to find her sitting at the table without her hearing aid, but the most striking thing in the space is the mammoth flower arrangement she has delivered every Monday morning.

I catch my breath. The gallery turns at a right angle, with four bedrooms and two baths lying off this second passageway. Clara might be in any of them, so I need to relax. She's an older woman; she might have forgotten to lock the front door. I'll probably find her taking a nap or soaking in the tub. She'll be embarrassed to discover that I was able to wander in, but tomorrow we'll laugh at her oversight.

"Auntie Clara?" I call in my brightest voice. "It's me. I don't want to startle you, but you left the front door unlocked."

The first bedroom, a guest room, is empty. The second bedroom was Charley's—the door squeaks when I turn the knob, but the counterpane is smooth and the curtains drawn over the bay window.

The guest bathroom is vacant, and Clara's room . . .

I peer through the doorway and exhale when I see the empty bed. I am about to turn and leave, assuming Clara went out and forgot to lock up, but an odd sight sends a ripple of apprehension through me.

A shoe beyond the edge of the bed is out of place. I take two steps before I realize the shoe is attached to Clara's foot. She is sitting on the carpet with the phone in her hands, muttering under her breath as she tries to insert the jack on the receiver into the body of the phone.

I know something is wrong when she doesn't look up at my approach. Her hair, usually smooth and neat, is loose about her shoulders; her jacket is unbuttoned. She is sitting in the most un-dignified position I have ever seen her assume—one leg extended on the floor, the other tucked beneath her.

I can't imagine what has happened, but I kneel on the carpet and catch her busy hands in mine.

"Auntie? What's wrong with the phone, dear?"

She looks up. Her eyes widen for a moment, then they narrow as her brows rush together. "It's you," she says, no trace of welcome in her voice. She jerks her hands free of my grasp. "Why do you keep bothering me?"

Tides of goose flesh race up my arms and collide at the back of my neck. Something has happened—she's had a stroke, a break-down, *something*. I need to get the phone from her; I need to call 911. "Auntie," I whisper, adopting the tone I would use with a con-fused child, "may I have the telephone? I think I can fix it."

She clutches the phone to her chest as I reach out, so I grab her arm and hold tight. At my touch a shiver of revulsion—a spasm of hatred and disgust—rises from her core and radiates through her flesh.

"You were never worthy," she hisses, her eyes conveying the fury within her. "M.E. was a goddess; you are a spineless shadow of *him*."

"Clara, I need the phone." I'm trying to concentrate on the task at hand, but her words cut me to the quick. "You're not yourself, so let me have the telephone so I can call someone to help us—"

"I don't want your help." Like a possessive child, she twists her upper body, holding the phone out of my reach. "I've never wanted anything from you, but M.E. had to go and leave you in charge. I hated her for that. But I could never hate her as much as I hate *him*."

"Clara, please." Her words pelt me like stones, but I can't let them hurt me. She is not herself.

For a moment I consider getting up and going into another room to make the call, but none of the other phones will work as long as she has this extension off the hook.

"M.E. could have anything she wanted." She is concentrating again, trying to force the tiny plastic jack into the hole on the back of the telephone. "She even wanted my husband for a while, and you know what? I didn't care. We all adored her, and I knew she wouldn't keep Charley for long—he bored her to tears. She could have had the sun and the moon if she wanted them; she was the crème de la crème . . . but your father could never accept her for what she was. He wanted loyalty; he wanted faithfulness; he wanted her to love him alone. Ha! As if a goddess could ever be happy with the adoration of just one man."

"Clara." I am trying to speak firmly, but my voice breaks and I resist the impulse to clap my hands over my ears. I don't know if she's telling me the truth or if all this is coming from some deep well of paranoia, but her words, combined with the thunderclouds in her blue eyes, are more frightening than anything I've experienced outside my apartment.

"Clara, give me the phone now." I reach out and take hold of the base, which she surrenders, but when I grab for the handset, she pulls away and tries to hit me with it. I lean forward, trying to wrest it from her hand, but in our struggle she topples backward, striking her head on the edge of the nightstand before she slumps to the floor.

"Clara?" I am holding both sections of the phone, but I can think of nothing but the still form in front of me. "Auntie, wake up, okay?"

My adrenal glands kick into overdrive. I drop the phone and press my hand to her cheek. The flesh, flushed a moment ago, feels cool beneath my fingertips. "Clara, wake up!"

For an instant I am helpless—torn between assembling the phone and attempting to administer CPR—when I hear a faint rasp. I hope I'm hearing the ragged sounds of breath, so I crouch beside her and lower my ear to her mouth. "Auntie, can you hear me?"

The sound becomes a susurrous whisper, but when I lift my head to look for a flutter of eyelids or a trembling lip, I see a flood of cockroaches streaming from her mouth . . .

Vomit threatens the back of my throat, a revolting geyser I can barely restrain. Every neuron in my brain snaps, compelling me to recoil, but paralysis grips my limbs. I am frozen on my hands and knees, panic congealing my heart into a lump of terror, and as the roaches advance like a buzzing army toward my hands, my knees, I hear someone screaming, but only when I see chunks of white plaster raining from the ceiling do I realize that *my* shrieks are bringing the place down around me, *my* fears have finally proved my undoing, and now there is no one, not even Clara, left to help me.

Suddenly, without turning, I know I am not alone in the room.

Someone else is with me, a goatish, vile presence, and it is responsible for killing Clara. It will kill me, too, destroy me with its poison and hatred and falsehoods.

"Auroraaaaaa . . ."

The monster whispers in my ear, and this time I know I will not escape.

30

Apartment 15B

I lift my head as the heart-stopping scream pierces the wall, then instinctively glance at the window, still warmed by the afternoon sun. Could Aurora be having a nightmare *now?* Doubtful. But if she is not dreaming, she is in terrible trouble.

I bolt from the desk. A moment later I am pounding on her door. I pause, pressing my palms to the wood as I listen for a response. The screaming has stopped, but no one shrieks like that unless something has gone horribly wrong.

Waiting in the eerie silence, I take a deep breath and feel bands of tightness in my chest. I am about to pound again when I hear the clicks of deadbolts withdrawing.

Aurora opens the door. Her face is ashen and her hands tremble as she pushes her hair behind her ear. "Sorry," she says, her voice as thin as tissue paper. "I fell asleep. But I guess you knew that."

Exhaling, I brace myself on the doorframe. "Aurora," I say, irritated at her response and the adrenaline current roaring through me, "this has gone on long enough. What will it take to convince you that you can't go on like this?"

Fresh misery darkens her face. "I don't know." She wavers on her feet. When I reach out to steady her, a sob escapes her lips.

I pull her into the circle of my arms as she weeps. "It's all right. You're going to be fine, Aurora. You just need to get some help."

She clings to me; I can feel her uneven breathing on my neck. "This dream was worse than the others—it was *too* real. I went to visit Clara, but she was dead. And something else was in the room, some sort of monster—"

"A monster?" I lift my head to give her a smile. "Are you sure you didn't eat spicy foods for lunch?"

"It was real, I tell you." She looks at me through tear-clogged lashes. "It was like someone was trying to tell me something."

I struggle to control my own swirling emotions. I have come running every time she has needed help, but she insists on keeping me at a distance. What am I supposed to offer—comfort or confrontation? Hard to know what she needs, especially when she doesn't want my advice. Still—Clara has done nothing but coddle Aurora, and someone has to help this woman face reality.

"What do you think someone might be trying to tell you?"

"I don't know." Fresh tears rise in her eyes. "Something terrible is going to happen to someone I know—maybe me or Clara. Or it's already happened. We need to check on Clara."

I pull her arms from my neck, then hold up a warning finger. "Wait here."

Leaving Aurora in the doorway, I cross the hall and knock on Mrs. Bellingham's door. No one answers. After pressing the buzzer, I turn and shrug. "Nobody home. She must have gone out."

"I think she's in there." Aurora's brow creases with worry. "I think she's hurt. Please try again."

"I've tried twice," I insist. "Maybe she's napping, but if you have a key—"

"I used to, but she changed the locks and never got around to having a copy made for me. She had to give the spare to George, so will you *please* get the super?" Aurora is clinging to the doorframe, her knuckles white from the strain. "This is it. Clara's in trouble—I know it."

Something—either the look of helpless appeal in her eyes or the tremor in her voice—propels me toward the elevator.

Thomas, the afternoon doorman, doesn't know where the super is, but he uses his walkie-talkie to locate George Baltross.

"He's on the fifth floor, looking at a plumbing leak," the doorman tells me. "I can ask him to head up to your floor when he's done."

"How long will that take?"

The young man shrugs. "Dunno—maybe an hour, maybe longer. George isn't the fastest thing on two feet, if you know what I mean."

The image of Aurora's white knuckles flits before my eyes. "The thing is, Thomas, I think we have an emergency on our hands. Can't George come up now and deal with the plumbing later?"

Thomas picks up the walkie-talkie and murmurs into it. I prop my elbow on the counter as the radio hisses, then George's voice squawks through the speaker: "What kind of emergency they got up there?"

Thomas lifts a brow. "What seems to be the problem?"

"We think Mrs. Bellingham might be in trouble—unless you've seen her leave the building."

The doorman squints, then shakes his head. "She hasn't been downstairs since I came on."

"Then we need Mr. Baltross as soon as possible."

Thomas presses the button on the radio. "George, we think there's a problem in Mrs. Bellingham's place. Can you run up there right away?"

When George responds with a flurry of curses, Thomas discreetly turns down the volume. "He'll be right up."

I take the elevator to wait with Aurora; five minutes later we are joined by the super.

I glance at Aurora as George ambles toward us—her eyes are filled with infinite distress, but she manages to smile at the sight of the building superintendent.

The man grumbles under his breath as he sorts through the collection of keys on his ring, then he catches my eye. "What seems to be the problem up here?"

"Mrs. Bellingham doesn't answer her door."

"Maybe she's not in the mood for visitors."

"She doesn't answer her phone, either," Aurora adds. "And that's not like her."

"Maybe her hearing aid died."

I cross my arms. "Just open the door, please."

George hesitates, tapping a key on his callused palm. "You gonna take the heat if she's mad about this?"

My frustration spikes. "Let me put it this way, George—either you open the door or I'm pulling the fire alarm. You want to tell the residents why they've been forced to evacuate the building?"

The super slips the key into the lock, but not before glaring at me. "I'm only doing this because of her." George jerks his chin toward Aurora. "I know she's tight with the old lady."

He turns the key in two separate locks, then swings the door open. Grinning in mock gallantry, the super extends his hand toward the foyer. "You two better be right about this. And I'd be careful roundin' the corners. You're likely to get yourself plugged if she thinks you're breaking into the place."

"She doesn't own a gun," Aurora says.

I step through the doorway, but with the grace of a cat Aurora sidles past me, tiptoeing down the long gallery and glancing into doorways. After checking the living room on the right, she steps through a storage room on the left, then disappears into the kitchen.

"Oh, no," she says, her voice hoarse. "Clara?"

When I round the corner, I find Aurora kneeling beside Clara. The older woman is lying on the floor, one hand curled under her cheek, the other clutching a cordless phone.

Aurora's complexion has faded to the color of parchment, but she picks up the old woman's hand and presses two fingers to the thin wrist. "Call 911." She looks at me, not George. "Please."

While I take the phone and dial the number, George wanders in, curses softly, and wipes his face with his hand. "I hate when this happens." He looks at me for only a second, then breaks eye contact, his gaze moving off to safer territory. "The older ones sometimes drop in their tracks, you know."

I am about to ask why George wasn't quicker to respond to our call for help, but the 911 operator comes on the line. As I give information to the dispatcher, Aurora begins to cry.

Aurora, George, and I are standing in Clara's kitchen, eyes downcast, useless hands tucked away, as two emergency medical technicians wheel the gurney out of the apartment.

A third EMT lingers, standing by the kitchen table with somber eyes, a mournful expression, and sagging shoulders—the body language of respectful sorrow. "I'm not qualified to make an official diagnosis, but I suspect stroke," he says. "Her pulse is thready, but she may pull through." His gaze darts from Aurora to me. "I'm not sure who should handle the paperwork for her admission—"

"Have the hospital call me." Aurora's voice is a croak in the heavy silence. "I'm the closest thing to family she has."

The EMT nods. "If you'd like to come with us, I'm sure they'll want to get information directly from you—"

"I can't go," she whispers, the corners of her mouth tight with distress.

"If this isn't a good time, you could come later."

Aurora looks at me, her eyes filled with unspoken entreaty. She can make it to the lobby without suffering a panic attack, but all the way to the hospital? I resist the urge to step up to the plate. If I go to the hospital for her, I'll be just like Clara, stepping in whenever Aurora is too afraid to face her fears.

I wrap her hand in mine. "I'll go with you."

She closes her eyes, but even from this distance I can feel a subterranean quiver ripple through her. She's almost there, almost ready to take the biggest step to date—

"I'll call Dr. Helgrin." Aurora opens her eyes. "I'll have him meet you at the hospital."

Disappointment surges through me. I drop her hand and move away so I don't add to her burdens.

"Fine." The EMT jerks his head in a brief nod, then follows the gurney into the elevator.

When he has gone, Aurora collapses into a chair at Clara's kitchen table. "What am I supposed to do now?"

I look at George, who is still standing in the doorway, his eyes wide with a rubbernecker's curiosity. "Thanks, George."

I lift my hand in a gesture of dismissal, but the super takes another look around, then jerks his thumb toward the door. "I know you're close to her and all, Miss Norquest, but I gotta know if you'll be needing to get in here. If it looks like she won't be coming back, you'll let me know, right?"

From lowered lids, I shoot a commanding look at the insensitive superintendent. "It's too soon to discuss anything like that, George. We're hoping Mrs. Bellingham will make a full recovery."

"It's my fault." Aurora presses her fingertips to her temple. "She got so upset when she was in my apartment this morning."

I slip my hand under her arm and gently lift her to her feet. "Come on, Rosie, let's get you back to your own place."

George jingles his keys. "Want me to lock up?"

"Please," I call over my shoulder. "We'd appreciate that."

31

With surprising gentleness, Phil walks me back to my apartment. I dig for the phone book in the kitchen, then call Dr. Helgrin's office with news of Clara's condition.

After telling the nurse everything I know, I hang up and stumble to the sofa in the living room. I sit, then fall across the armrest and let my head drop to my elbow—I feel half-dead. I might as well *be* dead, because the burning rock of guilt in the pit of my stomach isn't going anywhere. Clara was in perfectly good health, but this morning I upset her terribly. My subconscious must have realized the extent of the damage I'd done, because I dreamed about her dying . . . and now she might. That EMT didn't seem to hold much hope for her survival . . . and if she's in the hospital, I won't be able to comfort her in her last days.

Phil has vanished into the kitchen, but I don't really care where he's gone. He could have made things easier for me back there—he could have offered to ride with the EMTs to the hospital. He owed Clara at least that much. If he has any real feeling for me, he should have stepped forward to deal with a situation I couldn't handle. But he wouldn't because he wants me to be something I'm not. He wants a woman who's not afraid of anything.

He doesn't want me.

It's so obvious to me now. I'm not and never will be the kind of woman he needs. This fledgling thing between us should stop before it gets out of hand. Right now we're good friends; perhaps we can take a couple of steps back. He can concentrate on his economics project; I'll go back to bed.

And stay there.

I close my eyes as footsteps echo on the wooden floor of the living room. Phil enters, a steaming mug in his hand.

"Here," he says, not unkindly. "I thought you could use some tea."

Utterly miserable, I turn away.

"Come on, Rosie. You need this."

"Don't call me that."

"Why not? It suits you."

"No, it doesn't. I thought it could, but I was wrong."

He presses the mug into my cold hand. "Drink this."

"I don't want it."

"Drink it or I'll hold your head and force-feed you." He's smiling, but a look in his eye makes me think it wouldn't be wise to test him.

I grip the mug and take a sip, but the mango tea I usually like now tastes like gall.

"Good?"

"Great," I lie. "Thanks."

I set the mug on the coffee table, intending to stand, but he steps in front of me and drops his hands to my shoulders, forcing me back to the sofa. "Where are you going?"

"If you must know"—I lift my chin—"I was going to see you to the door."

"And then?"

"Then I'm going back to bed. I'm exhausted, I didn't get enough sleep last night, and I can't seem to think straight."

"You're not going to bed because you're tired, Aurora. You want to go to bed because you're too afraid to go anywhere else."

I stare at him, my head swarming with words. "You . . . you don't know me as well as you think you do."

"I know you better than you think I do. I know that right now you want to lock yourself in your room and stay there forever—give up all your hard-won ground—but you know what? You can't do that. Because if you do, you'll be walking away from your *life*."

"I'm not walking away. I'm tired."

"You say you care about Clara. But when she needs you, what do you do? You go to bed."

"She'd understand," I counter. "She knows I can't go to the hospital."

"What happens if *you* need a hospital, Aurora? Because you're going to, you know. If you turn back now, soon you're going to crawl so far into your shell that you can't do anything for yourself. So someone else will have to do everything for you—make your decisions, tell you what and when to eat, cook your meals, clean your room—"

I clap my hands over my ears, not wanting to hear. Yet he continues, droning on and on—

"They lied," I interrupt, flinging the words at him. "Everybody says life goes on after someone dies. But it doesn't. It just stops, and you're left wondering how in the world you're supposed to fill twenty-four hours every day of the week."

A tremor passes over his face, and when he speaks again, his voice and his eyes are gentle. "You're supposed to *live*, Aurora. You're supposed to go out in the world and find a way to celebrate the unique life God gave you. You're supposed to care about your neighbors, the ones in your building as well as the ones in your city."

"I care about Clara—and I gave her a stroke."

A muscle flicks at his jaw. "Have you stopped to consider that I care about you? And you're driving me crazy!"

My lower lip trembles as I meet his eyes. "What gives you the right to care about me? You're no better off than I am. You hide behind the word *economist* like it's some kind of excuse for why you don't have a social life, a wife, and a family—"

He closes his eyes, opens his mouth—a silent signal that I have strained the limits of credulity.

"Maybe I do hide sometimes," he finally says, a weight of sadness on his thin face, "because I don't feel like I'm a perfect fit for the world out there. But at least I haven't been pushing love away with both hands."

I wait for him to explain, but he doesn't. He just looks at me, his eyes damp with pain, then he lifts his hands in the universal symbol of surrender. "Go to bed, Aurora. Lock yourself in your room, crawl under the covers, turn up your CD player to full volume. But you know what? One day you're not going to be able to get out of bed. Your fears will eat up every inch of this apartment until you're too afraid to lower your feet to the floor. Then one of the doormen will notice the mail piling up downstairs, and they'll call George to break into your apartment and take you away. By that time, if you don't want to get out of bed, you won't have to. You can spend the rest of your life under the covers in a nice, tidy institution."

My strength returns as my heart pumps fear and outrage through my veins. I am sky high with indignation, angry enough to draw back my hand and scrape my nails across his face—

He catches my arm in midflight and restrains me with surprising strength. "You are a lovely, charming woman," he says, his voice ragged. "I care for you a great deal. When we first met, I thought it'd be a neat trick just to make you smile every once in a while, but now I want more for you . . . and for us. People are waiting to love you, Rosie, but you're not giving us a chance."

"There is no *us*," I say, avoiding his eyes. "And I've been loved by lots of people. My mother loved me; Clara loved me; Uncle Charley loved me. I've never needed anyone else."

"You wouldn't know what love is if it bit you in the foot. Clara didn't love you. For some incomprehensible reason she *served* you."

"You don't know what you're talking about!"

"I think I do. And I think you're in major denial."

"There you go again with your pop psychology. I don't want to hear it."

His face flushes. "I don't remember much from my psychology professor, but I do remember this—anger and fear are reciprocal emotions. When one is in full bloom, the other is the root. You're terrified, Aurora—so beneath those fears, you're spitting angry about something. Maybe you should find out why."

Bitter gall burns the back of my throat even as I croak out a denial. What does this man know about my life? He knows nothing, nothing! He wasn't around when Mother was sick; he doesn't know that caring for her was an honor, not a burden. I'm not angry at anyone, not Mother, not Clara, not Charley or even my father—

From out of nowhere, like a swift arrow, comes the realization that Mother nursed an unrelenting hatred for my father. I was born into that hatred; I witnessed it; I grew up under its heavy hand. If what I've been seeing in my dreams is true, the fabric of my being has been woven and spun of furious threads . . .

Too weary for words, I lift my hand. "Leave me alone, please."

I can feel his gaze prying at my lowered eyelids. "Are you all right?"

I open my eyes, turn toward my bedroom, and take a tentative step. "Close the door tightly, please."

He hesitates—I hear him take a quick breath behind me—then the door clicks. Without bothering to fasten the deadbolts, I walk as far as the kitchen doorway, then stop, one hand on the doorframe, the other on my knee as I bend to clear the dizziness from my head.

How do other people do it? How can they go about their business as if they haven't a care in the world? I know people have problems— I see evidence of them every day on television—but those people must have either spines of iron or hearts of stone.

I have neither.

With one hand pressed to the wall, I make my way down the long gallery, then stumble into my room. The television on my dresser is on, but turning it off would require more energy than I have to spare.

Still wearing my slippers, I crawl beneath the covers, pull the comforter over my head, and close my eyes and ears to the voice droning from the TV. While I lie there, my thoughts whirling too fast for sleep, I hear Phil's voice, alternately accusing and challenging. He may be right about my fears—they *could* eat me up. I know my knees are gelatin while others' are bone and cartilage. Clara has always been my strength, but what will I do if she dies?

She's not a young woman. If I don't lose her today, I may lose her next month. And then I will have no one, for Phil has made it clear he will not do anything to help me.

My thoughts are whirling and bobbing like aimless pieces of flotsam when a name enters my stream of consciousness. "Theodore Norquest," a woman on television says, "is one of the world's best-loved authors and also one of the most private. The literary world was stunned yesterday to hear that Mr. Norquest has been taken to a London hospital, where doctors say he is suffering from pneumonia. Our thoughts are with his family."

I pull the comforter from my face and stare at the television on the bureau. A well-dressed woman with a compassionate smile is sitting in a wing chair before a fireplace; a portrait of my father stands on an easel behind her.

"In honor of Theodore Andrew Norquest," she continues, "we are rebroadcasting an interview recorded last year in France, where Norquest has a summer home. We're certain you'll enjoy this candid conversation with a fascinating, colorful character."

Transfixed, I push myself up and lean back against my pillows.

The opening credits are unfamiliar, but there's no denying the expressive face gazing into the camera. The man who would be my father smiles gently, then motions toward a path in front of him. "Shall we walk?"

The interviewer, who remains out of sight, agrees, and the camera follows my father through a vineyard. In a careful, well-modulated voice he talks of vines and horticulture, then he gestures to a table and chairs in the shade of a sprawling tree.

A moment later the camera focuses on his lined face. I lean forward, wrapping my arms about my legs, as the invisible interviewer casually tosses a question: "The public has long known of your fascination with scary stories—you have published more horror novels than any living writer. Why are you drawn to this genre?"

My father looks at his hands, then absently rubs one thumb with the other. "I think it's important for us to realize we are only mortal," he says, glancing up at the camera. "Many times we humans forget that we are limited in scope and reason. My stories aren't intended to frighten people—they are intended to bring us closer to the inexplicable and the supernatural. To God, if you will."

The interviewer laughs. "To God? Your books don't seem to be religious."

"I prefer to think of them as spiritual. I want to explore possibilities that exist beyond our finite world, places that could not exist and events that could not occur within the laws of nature and science. God is beyond us, and though we cannot hope to understand him, I believe he is pleased when we exercise our minds as fully as we are able."

"Do you think God wants to scare us to death?"

"To death?" He blinks, then a humorless smile gleams through his white beard. "To life, perhaps. We are frightened by things we do not understand, and no one is even remotely capable of understanding God. Many of his aspects are terrifying. Just as evil is horrifying, so is holiness. We would be frightened of him, fearful of ever approaching, if not for his love."

Silence sifts down like a snowfall. Though I can't see the interviewer, I can tell he's befuddled by the conversation. But like any good reporter, he has a list of questions.

"Did you ever flirt with any other genre?" he asks, changing the subject.

Norquest looks away and laughs, then rubs his hands together. "You may be surprised"—he drops his chin into his palm—"to learn I did toy with something different once, something very different."

"And it was?"

Teeth flash in his beard. "A historical adventure—a bit of a romance, actually, though not in the conventional sense. But it was definitely about love. The purest form of love."

The interviewer laughs. "Whatever possessed you to write a novel so far from your usual style? Was it just a lark?"

"It was far from a lark. It was—well, I was casting my bread upon the water, so to speak. I sent it out in the hope it would come back to me."

"Did it?"

My father looks into the camera, then lowers his gaze. "Not yet."

"You're seventy years old and a fabulous success. Will you ever retire, or are you planning another novel even now?"

"Faith never gives up." Norquest's faint smile holds a touch of sadness as he looks into the camera again. "I'll never give up as long as I have breath in my lungs."

The screen fades to black; the image of a new Honda sedan replaces my father's face. I sink back into my pillows, staring at the blank ceiling as my senses struggle to retain the images and sounds I've just absorbed.

I've just heard my father's voice, but it wasn't the first time. I've heard it before, in a dream and twice on the roof. I can't explain how it happened, but perhaps it's like he said—some things are beyond our comprehension.

I reach up and pull his wool scarf from the headboard where I draped it a few days ago. I bring it to my face and feel the softness against my cheek. It's odd—before today I'd seen his picture and held his clothes, but until this hour I'd never seen the way his eyes crinkle at the corners when he smiles or the way he rubs his hands when he's thinking. I've just met him, yet he seems so familiar—

Perhaps this is what comes from reading his books. I've read that a novelist's personality will seep through the edges of his story, so it's possible I know him better than I think I do.

Yet I didn't know he thought so much about God. That revelation surprises me, because Mother never indulged in God-talk. Clara has always gone to church, but God never seems to interfere in her daily routine. Phil talks more about God than anyone I know.

I smile at the sudden thought of Phil sitting down for coffee with Theodore Norquest. Those two have more in common than my father and I do.

I cross my arms atop my knees, then rest my chin on my wrist. My father's fixation with God reminds me of Al Hirschfeld, the *New York Times'* cartoonist who was still drawing when he died at age ninety-nine. Hirschfeld sketched everyone from Jerry Seinfeld to Ethel Merman, and in nearly all of his drawings he included his daughter's name. Her name was never obvious, but when you knew what to look for, you could usually find it hidden somewhere in the sloping black lines that defined texture or background. Every weekend as a kid, I poured over the *Times'* theater pages, scanning the Hirschfeld cartoon for NINA.

Now that I know what to look for, I think I could pick up a Norquest novel and find God sketched between the lines. My father's sympathetic characters are always flawed; they face impossible odds until they receive supernatural help.

Is that how he copes with fear?

I breathe deeply and feel a stab of memory, a phrase recalled from something I've read: *"Despair sent me to London,"* he once told a *reporter. "And there I found the faith to hope for complete healing."*

Why would a man eager to join his mistress feel despair? His comment doesn't fit with what Clara has told me, but it matches the man I saw on television.

I push the thought aside. Why does any of this matter? Theodore Norquest is in a hospital and seriously ill. He might recover—people recover from pneumonia all the time—but he's over seventy years old.

I close my eyes, revisiting the image of my father's bearded smile, while a commercial drones in the background. Beneath the window, the radiator clangs and hisses, filling the room with warmth.

I slide into sleep.

I am dreaming, surely, for there's no other way I could find myself here on this plain. I look behind me and recognize the Castle of Aragon, just as Andrew Noble described it.

I have dreamed my way into the book I loved.

I take a deep breath and relax down to my toes. I am safe here, for this realm is ruled by Lord John of Aragon Castle. The last time I checked, he and his daughter had been reunited and were happy together.

I inhale the crisp air and walk toward the castle, marveling as the long grass swishes beneath my slippers. Does anyone else dream in surround sound? I grin as I glance at my feet—I am wearing the stuffed animal slippers Phil found so laughable. What will the lord of the castle think of these?

I climb to the crest of a small knoll and look into the valley between the hill and the castle—there they are, Lord John on his horse and his daughter in the grass. The earl wears his battle armor, his daughter her simple gray dress—my heart does a double beat. Are they about to enact the last scene of the book? Perhaps I've entered a parallel story universe where characters live the story from page 1 to 400 in a continuous loop.

They are still a good thirty yards from me, but Lord John dismounts and advances toward his daughter, one arm outstretched. Hoping to catch his final words, I lengthen my stride. I see him open his arms; I see his daughter step into them. He embraces her, his hand smooths her dark hair, and I know he is about to utter the sentence that absolutely shredded my heart—

"Wait!" I lift my skirt (odd that I am wearing a medieval gown and puppy slippers) and jog to close the gap between us.

Lord John tucks his daughter beneath his arm and looks at me with patient amusement. When I finally draw near, winded and perspiring, he looks into my eyes and smiles. "I have yearned for you," he says, a gleam of unguarded tenderness shimmering in his eyes, "since the day I first learned you would be born. I have searched for you without ceasing. The blood of my dear messenger has been shed on your behalf, but I would have given the last of my treasures to win your heart."

As before, the words pierce me. My hand against my breast, I look to the daughter, ready for her response.

But the girl has vanished as completely as morning dew. Lord John and I are the only two people beneath the gilding warmth of this medieval sun. He is waiting . . . for me.

Somehow I have become the daughter. The realization unsettles me; I can't remember my line.

But Lord John has a gift for improvisation. "I have loved you," he says, not missing a beat, "with an everlasting love. With unfailing compassion I have drawn you out."

I release my heavy skirt and press my hand to my side, where I've developed a stitch in my ribs. As much as I'd like to participate in this scene, I'm breathless and confused and mystified by the turn of events.

I squint up at Lord John. "Are you talking about me?"

I know what's been scripted. He's supposed to take me by the hand and lead me into the castle while the wind whistles and demons howl in protest, but I'm afraid to move without hearing a direct cue. Like an automaton, Lord John turns, his extended hand empty, and walks toward the castle gate. I try to hurry and catch up, but my feet are mired in quicksand. I struggle against the pull of the muck, but I can't follow; I can't even move. I call out to Lord John, but he can't hear me above the whistling winds and howling demons. Emissaries from one of those enthusiastic unions—either the local winds or demons, I can't tell—are pressing against my shoulders with invisible hands, pushing me into the quicksand. I fight back, twisting my shoulders and slapping at invisible foes, but they are relentless and strong—

I wake in a gray fog. I blink and try to focus my eyes, and after a moment I think I can see the vague outline of shadowed walls. Unless I have slept for hours and darkness has fallen over the apartment, I have advanced into another dream. That thought brings relief, for the oily gloom surrounding me is so corporeal I can taste it.

"What time *is* it?" My voice sounds weak and timid in my own ears, but apparently it has the power to startle. Somewhere in the darkness, something skitters over the floor. I am not alone.

I stare into the dark and feel the *swoosh* of my blood rushing along veins and capillaries. For an instant the murk is preternaturally silent, then the shuffling creatures become conspiratorial, plotting together in incomprehensible chirps and clicks. In the far corner, a pair of unblinking red eyes meets mine. The sight batters my heart, evoking every terror I've ever known, so I close my eyes and direct my thoughts to the unseen father who's been speaking to me.

"If you really love me, if you've been searching for me, pull me from this place . . ."

Crystal-clear light sweeps over me in a blinding wave, one so powerful it drags me from the darkness. Caught in a riptide of realization, I flail against the uncertain feeling of falling, then I open my eyes and find myself in my bed, my pillow beneath my head, my slippers still on my feet.

After an instant of speechless wonder, I laugh. Why didn't I call out to him before this?

He is present and he loves me. I know this with pulse-pounding certainty. The events of the last few days fall into place like a puzzle—

Why, my dreams have revealed everything! My father and I are not destined to remain apart. The initials on the flying puzzle piece represent Theodore Norquest and *Andrew Noble*—they are the same person. *I Know She Weeps* was written for me.

It is a romance . . . about the love between a father and his child.

My father established a trust fund because he wanted me to know him. He wrote a medieval adventure because he wanted me to read it. The story resonated within me because it is *my* story. I am the lost daughter. He is the father. And my mother . . . has lied to me. For money, love, or vindictiveness, Clara has joined in her deceit.

I press my hand to my chest as my heart expands in an upsurge of emotion. Elation and sorrow battle within me, each emotion striving to claim my attention.

For the first time in recent memory, I decide to let joy have the upper hand.

32

My knees snap and crack as I kneel to pull my hidden collection of Norquest novels from my nightstand.

How could I have been so blind? My father's books—the ones I've read, at least—are the same story woven into scores of different fabrics. In *Live to Die*, the injured scientist who travels forward in time is trying to reach the daughter he's never known. In *Memory's Mayhem*, a blind mother struggles to find her amnesiac son who's been kidnapped by a vengeful ex-lover. *Pizutti's Pattern* is the tale of a young woman trapped in a virtual lab where reality is a web of computer-generated lies.

I flip open the cover of *Solstoy's Syllabus* and stare at the dedication:

For A.N.

If a shepherd has one hundred lambs, and one wanders away and is lost, what will he do? Won't he leave the ninety-nine others and go out into the hills to search for the lost one? And if he finds it, won't he rejoice more over it than over the ninety-nine that didn't wander away?

I have read this story of an Irish farmer whose greedy wife insists on genetically manipulating his flock. I have read this dedication, but I assumed the initials belonged to someone else. I thought the patter about sheep and shepherds was somehow linked to the story.

Now I understand—my father has a loving family in Europe, but I am the one-hundredth lamb! I am the one out of reach; I am A.N.

I am the missing piece in every Theodore Norquest novel.

And I am too late. My father is gravely ill, in the hospital, probably on his deathbed. Yet if I can't go downstairs without feeling like I'm about to die, how am I supposed to go to Europe?

My elation ebbs as I lift my gaze to the window, where a dusky twilight is sinking over the Upper West Side. Lights are coming on in apartments across the horizon. As darkness approaches, hundreds of people like me are locking themselves into safe places to await the coming night.

I breathe deeply as the brooding sorrow pressing on my shoulders spawns and spreads until it mingles with the million other sorrows emanating from these glass and concrete towers. This city is home to millions who barricade themselves behind security guards and triple deadbolt locks—who am I to think I'm special? How can I possibly defeat my demons when I'm surrounded by so many others who live in fear?

My thoughts drift toward the woman in the glass penthouse. She is lovelier than I am, younger, and more graceful. She has probably had zillions of opportunities I've never encountered, yet she has chosen to sell herself to high-paying weasels.

My mother possessed the beauty, strength, and courage of ten women, but now I see that none of those qualities brought her happiness or peace. She demanded loyalty and service from everyone in her circle, including me and Clara, but I'm not sure she ever felt satisfied. Not even the Wentworth fortune could sate her appetite for pleasure and power. If she couldn't find joy . . . how can I, her shoddy shadow, ever hope to claim it?

Holding my breath, I stand perfectly still and hear my heart break. It is a sharp, swift sound, like the cracking of a pencil, and after an instant of blinding pain, something within me gives way.

Life has become too painful. I surrender; I'm finished. If my father is on his deathbed, perhaps we can be united in the next life, if such a thing exists. He has faith—it shines through his stories. Perhaps his faith will bring us together.

Somehow I find the energy to stagger toward the door . . . and the stairs.

Wrapped in a cocoon of anguish, I hold the edges of my sweater together at my neck and cross the pebbled rooftop. The neighboring buildings loom over me, their rooftops rimmed with the first gray tatters of dusk. A full moon has moved into the eastern sky, vying with the light from apartment windows.

I've come to the roof before, but this time death is more than a distant possibility—now the Reaper is beckoning, promising peace. His lips move without sound, but I can hear his rasp in the wind: *Come. Be at rest.*

I'm almost ready to accept his invitation. There's a lot I still don't understand about my life—I don't know why my mother taught me to hate my father; I don't understand why Clara would remain a slave to Mother's dominance even after her death. I think I would have liked to know Theodore Norquest—if I'd been born a stronger person, I could have walked out of my apartment, hailed a cab for LaGuardia, and purchased a ticket to London; perhaps we could have established a relationship.

But someone once said that the tragedy of life lies in the difference between the person we are and the person we were meant to be. I never intended to be the woman I am. I didn't know I'd have to deal with Mother's dementia or my own agoraphobia. But sometimes life spins out of control, and when it does, maybe it's useless to resist.

With a quick step I move over the roof of my own apartment, then turn at the southwest corner and walk to Clara's bay window. Once I reach the familiar spot, I step up to the railing and grip it with both hands. The cold metal sends a shiver up my spine. The wind whistles, howling like the demons on the plain of Aragon, but now I know Lord John is not waiting to lead me into his castle. At least not in this life. Maybe in the next. Or maybe not at all.

I lift my eyes to the sky, now streaked with color. Against this tapestry of living light, the angles of the neighboring buildings look like jigsawed pieces of a puzzle. Random lights twinkle within those depths, and soon anyone looking out will not be able to see me through the encroaching darkness . . . so perhaps I should wait until sunset before beginning the awkward business of climbing over this rail and dropping to the pavement below.

Darkness would be a mercy to anyone who might be watching. I'd hate to be the cause of some innocent child's nightmares.

My heart thumps steadily; my mind is clear and settled. Somehow I manage a weak laugh. It's almost funny—every panic attack left me feeling like I was going to die. Now that I fully intend to take my life, I've been overpowered by the strange drug of calm.

My gaze slides over the building across the street, then rises to the penthouse apartment. The golden-haired princess is standing at the glass door leading to her terrace, arms crossed, lips pursed, eyes staring moodily ahead. What is she thinking? Is she dreading her next appointment, considering a career change, or trying to decide if she should color her hair?

A half-smile creeps across my lips. This woman doesn't know I exist—doesn't know we are connected by isolation—yet the sight of her sends a tendril of contentment through me. I'm suddenly grateful she has decided to stop and look out her window. I need the sight of a fellow rooftop dweller to bolster my courage as I say farewell. The memory of her pain gives me the courage to climb up on the rail and sit for one more moment.

Balanced on the metal bar, I study my neighbor. I am memorizing the color of her hair when she lifts her chin. A tingle runs up my spine as our eyes meet. Her expression doesn't change for a moment, then shock flickers over her face like summer lightning.

Our gazes lock. I wait, half expecting her to break contact and run for a phone, but she does not look away. Her lips part; her eyes widen.

I am watching her, wondering if she will urge me to jump and end my portion of our shared pain, when a now-familiar voice speaks from behind me: *You were created for more than this.*

On the off chance that my father has materialized on the rooftop, I turn my head slightly. "I don't understand."

Speak to Samuel.

More surprised than frightened, I turn to look behind me. Carefully, I survey the rooftop—I am still alone, sharing the square space with only a rusty chair, a few broken pots, and a pair of pigeons.

But the door, which I did not prop open, is opening.

"Hello?" This voice is less authoritative, more human, and decidedly anxious. "Aurora, are you up here?"

A figure intrudes on my field of vision; after an instant of squinting I recognize Phil. I see him tense when he spots me on the rail. Before I can call out, he is sprinting toward me.

The sight of him and the vibrant urgency of my father's voice send a rush of longing through my veins, and suddenly I don't want to answer death's summons, I don't want to disappear, I don't want oblivion.

I turn and clamber to the safety of the solid rooftop, and Phil is there, pulling me away from the edge with a rough grip.

"Rosie, are you *crazy?*"

I have never seen him be anything but gentle, but his frantic efforts slam my wrist against the wall and I wince. "What are you doing?" I yell over the wind.

"That's what I should be asking you!"

I'm safe in his arms, but he glares down at me. "Aurora, I need to know—do I need to take you to the hospital?"

"I don't see why you should."

"But . . . what were you *thinking*?"

A dim section of my mind—one not occupied with physical pain or suicidal thoughts—speculates that the truth will not serve at this moment. "I was . . . watching a friend." I gesture toward the penthouse across the street.

Phil's eyes fill with the dullness of disbelief, but he turns to look. I follow his gaze, but the woman has left her terrace and disappeared into the depths of her glass tower. Either she has gone to call 911 . . . or she has indulged in disconnection, a state of mind endemic among New Yorkers.

Phil's stare drills into me. "I'm not playing games, Aurora. I want you to give me straight answers."

I tilt my head as his words sink through my confusion. "How'd you know I was here?"

"You left your apartment door open and you weren't on the stairs. Where else were you going to go?"

I shrug.

"Who's up here with you?"

"No one."

"Don't play games with me now, Rosie. I heard him."

A sense of unreality settles over me. "You heard someone?"

"As I came up the stairs, I heard a man's voice."

"Do you remember what he said?"

The corner of his mouth twists with exasperation. "I'm not kidding, Aurora. What happened? Did you send the guy down the fire escape or something?"

"There is no fire escape . . . and I'm not kidding. But it's important, Phil—what did you hear?"

He stares at me a moment, his jaw clenching, then he closes his eyes and shakes his head slightly. "Something about Samuel. That's all I remember."

I press my hand to his chest as the world goes soft all at once.

"Is the coffee all right?"

"It's fine."

"Good." Phil sinks to the edge of the table in front of the love seat where I have curled with a mug between my chilled fingers. The fragrant brew has warmed my body but failed to alleviate the chill that has settled around my bones.

"Let's start at the beginning." Phil lifts his own steaming cup. "You said you heard something on television about your father."

"An interview. He said he wrote another book, a novel outside his genre. And I've read it."

Phil sips his coffee, then nods. "Okay, I suppose I can see why your father might try to reach out through a book—after all, he's a writer; it's what he does. But you have to admit that's a long shot."

"That's why it doesn't make sense. If he really wanted to reach me, why didn't he call or write?"

Phil doesn't answer for a long moment. "Norquest is in the hospital now?"

I nod as unexpected tears blur my vision. "That's what the woman said. I got the impression he's about to die. That's why they were airing the footage of his interview."

"So you went up to the roof . . . why?"

I swallow hard, feeling my cheeks blaze. "Because I didn't have any other options. My father tried to reach me. I think you were right, I think Mother and Clara lied, but what can I do about that now? He's dying, I can't leave, so I . . . gave up."

He looks at me, his eyes soft with pain. "You *do* know suicide is not the answer, don't you?"

"I . . . don't know what I know. I only know I can't go on like this. I was hoping to begin a new life, but how can I do that now? Clara's gone, and the one thing I wanted is slipping away . . ."

The empty air between us vibrates; the silence fills with dread. When I look at Phil, his long face and blue eyes are filled with beaten sadness, and when he speaks, his voice is rough. "Maybe not," he says. "Maybe there's hope."

"You mean . . . Samuel?"

One corner of Phil's mouth twists, and in that instant I realize I have not responded with the answer he wanted. He is hoping I'd find a reason for living in *him*. But I can't contemplate a love life now. If I can't make myself happy, how could I possibly bring happiness to someone else?

Unable to stand the wounded look in his eye, I lower my gaze.

"Why not?" he says, glibly overlooking the injury I've inflicted. "Maybe Samuel holds all the answers."

"That's crazy." I am so burdened by guilt I can barely lift my head. "Besides, I thought we agreed I've been hearing things."

"I heard it, too."

"It could have been someone's radio or television caught on a wind or something. You never know what can happen in these tall buildings."

He turns the cup in his hand, then looks at me. "Are you familiar with the story of the prophet Samuel?"

I make a face. "Was he like Nostradamus?"

Phil laughs. "No, Samuel was a prophet of Israel. But when he was a child, a voice woke him in the night; someone called his name. He assumed it was Eli, the old priest who acted as his mentor, but when he reached Eli's bed, the old man insisted he hadn't called."

Though the hair at the back of my neck is rising with premonition, I don't interrupt.

"Twice more Samuel was awakened by the voice, and twice more Eli insisted he didn't call. By the third time, Eli realized something else—voices in the night don't have to have reasonable explanations. Though we can't comprehend everything about God, we can *apprehend* things that lie outside the realm of natural law. So Eli told Samuel to go back to bed, but if the voice called again, to say, 'Yes, your servant is listening.'"

Cold panic sprouts somewhere between my shoulder blades and prickles down my backbone.

"I think that's the issue." Phil meets my gaze. "Someone has been speaking to you, Aurora—have you been listening?"

The question hangs between us, pregnant with possibilities. "It's my father," I tell him. "I heard him on the television. I'd swear it was the same voice."

Phil strokes his chin. "Your father is talented, but I don't think he's mastered transatlantic ventriloquism."

"Then who?"

"Maybe . . . God?"

"You think *God* has been speaking to me? Whatever for?"

Phil tilts his head and smiles. "I think he wants to speak to everyone. With most people, though, he tends to use more conventional means of communication."

I push at my heavy bangs. "I don't get any of this. Why would God—the master of the universe, right?—why would he give a flip about me?"

"God loves everyone, Aurora; we're all created in his image. And I've heard that people tend to view God in the same way they view their fathers. You've never thought much about your father, so you've never thought much about God."

"I've thought about my father." My mind drifts back to nights alone in my bed, when I closed my eyes and pretended to go for long walks on my dad's arm. "In secret."

"Ah." Phil shrugs. "But now your views of your father are softening . . . and so are your views of God. Or maybe God has orchestrated everything because he knows your views of God and your father are all mixed up—"

"That's quite enough, Dr. Shrink," I snap. "What you're saying makes no sense at all."

"Doesn't it?" Phil folds his arms and grins. "What'd the voice say tonight?"

"He told me to speak to Samuel. I don't even know any Samuels."

We are interrupted by a buzz at the door. I glance at the clock— seven fifteen—then frown at Phil. "I'm not expecting anyone."

"I'll get it."

My heart begins to pound in honest fear as he strides to the door. What if the penthouse woman called the police? They could be outside now, ready to take me away. A knot of apprehension rises in my throat, making it difficult to breathe or swallow . . .

I rise and tiptoe to the doorway, then peek around the wall. The man at the door is wearing a uniform, but it's red, not blue.

"Clarence." Sighing, I go to the door, where the night doorman stands with his arms filled with mail.

"Sorry to bother you, Ms. Norquest." He gives me a sheepish smile. "But Mrs. Bellingham didn't pick up your mail today, so I thought I'd better bring it up."

Startled by the bundle in his arms, I step forward. "I'm sorry, I didn't even think about mail today."

Phil leans on the door, studying the man in uniform, then he thrusts out his hand. "I don't believe we've met. I'm Phil Cannon of 15B."

The man grins. "I didn't think I'd seen you yet, Mr. Cannon. I come on at seven, so it takes me a while to meet most of the new folks."

"Especially those who don't go out much." Phil's shy grimace acknowledges his lackluster nightlife. "Has anyone ever told you that you bear a striking resemblance to the doorman who works mornings?"

A grin overtakes Clarence's features. "Yes, sir. And that's natural, sir, because Mr. Booker is my father."

"Really!"

"Yes, sir. He's been on the job since '57, and I came on in '81. Seems like someone from my family has always worked at the Westbury Arms."

Phil stares at the doorman for a moment, then presses a finger to his lips. "Clarence—would you happen to know anyone in the building named Samuel?"

Clarence nods. "Yes, sir. No tenants, sir, but that's my father's given name. Samuel Booker."

Phil tosses me a pointed look, then grins at the doorman. "Will he be in tomorrow?"

"Yes, sir. He comes on at six. He works six to one, then he takes off—short hours, you see, on account of his age. My son Thomas covers the desk from one till seven, then I pull the night shift."

"Wonderful. Would you leave Samuel a note, please, and let him know Ms. Norquest would like to meet with him tomorrow? Maybe at one, when he gets off?"

Phil says this without so much as a glance in my direction, but I'm powerless to stop him. Suddenly it seems extremely important that I talk to Samuel Booker.

The man nods. "I'll tell him, sir."

"Thank you." Phil takes the bundle of mail from the doorman, then piles the mound on the foyer table as I lock the door.

I can't believe there is so much mail—brochures and catalogs and at least three envelopes that appear to be from credit card companies. "What on earth?"

Phil casts me a curious look. "More than usual?"

"Loads more. I usually get maybe five or six catalogs. All the bills and things go to my accountant."

"I think"—Phil slips his hands into his pockets—"Clara has been screening your mail."

I stare at him as his words take hold.

"You asked why your father never wrote," he says.

I wince. "You think Clara pulled his letters?"

"Maybe," he says. "But I think tomorrow Samuel Booker will be able to explain everything."

33

APARTMENT 15A

I wake after a long and deep slumber. As I slipped into my pajamas last night, I worried that the events of the evening would trouble my rest, but the embracing folds of sleep buried any disturbing dreams I might have had.

Moving automatically through my morning routine, I shower and dress, then sip coffee in the kitchen as I listen to the morning news. At eight ten a newscaster reports that novelist Theodore Norquest is still hospitalized with pneumonia; doctors say his condition is critical.

My buttered toast becomes dry and tasteless.

After dumping the bread down the disposal, I call the hospital to check on Clara. The receptionist confirms that she is a patient, but when I ask for information, I'm told that privacy laws prohibit the hospital from revealing any details.

"But I'm the closest thing to family she has."

"Unless you signed her in, we are not allowed to discuss her case with you. I'm sorry."

The woman thanks me for calling, then hangs up.

I sink into a chair at the kitchen table, still unable to believe Clara could be struck down so suddenly. She was the picture of health, as active as a woman of her age could be.

Though part of my brain wonders why Clara has been deceiving me all these years, we do share a common history. And she needs help, so who else can give it?

I reach for my address book when the answer comes to me. Bert Shields was Clara's lawyer, too, so he would have her living will and perhaps even a power of attorney. If the hospital won't talk to me, surely they'll talk to Clara's legal representative.

The lawyer isn't in yet. After speaking to Mr. Shields's secretary, I lower the phone to the cradle, satisfied that I've done the best I can do for now. I hope Clara isn't suffering.

My thoughts drift to my father, who may be struggling to breathe as he holds on for the daughter he has never seen.

I sit in silence, feeling as if strong hands are slowly twisting every last drop of life from my heart. How much loss is one person supposed to be able to bear?

Before I can pursue the thought, the phone rings. "Miss Aurora?"

I recognize the scratchy voice. "Booker?"

"Yes, ma'am. My son said you wanted to see me."

"If it's convenient. Could you come up after work?"

"Yes, ma'am." A moment of silence, then, "Have I done something to upset you, Miss Aurora?"

"Oh, no, Booker, don't worry about that. I wanted to talk to you about my father. Since you knew him—"

"Well, glory be!"

"I beg your pardon?"

"This is wonderful news, Miss Aurora, just wonderful. Let me call my wife and have her bring the things over."

"What things?"

"Excuse me, Miss Aurora, I've gotta run. You take care and I'll see you this afternoon."

The line clicks, and I am left with more questions than before.

I spend an hour mopping the kitchen floor, then find myself studying Mother's room. I still need to call a local thrift shop and the medical supply company, so I might as well get started.

An hour later, the arrangements have been made. The hospital bed will be picked up before week's end; the thrift store will come tomorrow for any furniture I don't want.

My hand is still on the phone when it rings again. Bert Shields is on the line, his voice properly somber. "I had to go to the hospital and file papers to establish my authority," he tells me, "but all that has been settled."

"How is she?"

He hesitates. "The outlook is not good, Aurora. She's had a stroke and she's in a coma. The doctor says she may linger a week or a month, but she's not likely to wake up again. I have a letter here with her final wishes regarding the funeral—would you like me to have everything lined up for when the time comes?"

I swallow hard. "Thank you."

"Clara was a sharp woman. She'll have everything arranged, so you don't have to worry." He clears his throat. "I know this must be rough for you, losing Clara so soon after your mother."

"I'm okay." I force the words over my tongue. "I'm kinda numb, to tell you the truth."

"Time has a way of healing all wounds," Shields says. "As I'm sure you'll discover—"

"Did you know," I interrupt, "that my father is in the hospital with pneumonia?"

"No . . . I'm sorry. I hadn't heard."

"He's in London."

"Yes . . . and that's quite a distance, isn't it."

I wait, hoping he'll say more, but he remains quiet.

"Did you know my father, Mr. Shields? I mean, more than just as his attorney?"

"I knew him well."

"If you were me, would you go to him?"

The lawyer is a man of careful words and cautious habits, but he doesn't hesitate: "I wouldn't delay a moment, Aurora. In fact, should you decide to go, I'd be happy to expedite your passport. We can get it for you in two weeks."

I thank him and hang up the phone, then stand and pace in the kitchen. How hard can leaving an apartment be? I was ready to jump off the roof last night; leaving the apartment can't be as hard as that. Last night I looked death in the eye with a steady gaze; why can't I step aboard a 747 with the same resolve?

Phil arrives a few minutes before one. I haven't invited him to sit in on this meeting with Booker, but I'm glad to see him. "Come on in," I say, leading him into the living room. "Did you eat lunch?"

"Caught something at school, then hurried over. I knew I wouldn't want to miss this."

I prop my hand on my hip, both irritated and touched by his interest. "Booker may not know anything, you know. He may come up here and tell us my father is the monster Clara said he was."

"Maybe." Phil's eyes are gleaming. "But maybe not. In any case, I'm eager to hear him out."

He eases himself into the corner of the sofa, then crosses his leg the way men do, his ankle resting on his knee. He taps his hands on his leg, then grins at me. "Got anything to munch on while we wait? That sandwich didn't fill me up."

Grumbling good-naturedly, I head into the kitchen and open cupboards, peering into their depths for anything that resembles potato chips, salted nuts, or pretzels. I'm taste testing a box of cheese crackers when the buzzer sounds.

"Phil?"

"I'll get it."

I hear the murmur of voices, followed by the rumble of masculine laughter. Samuel Booker, obviously. And he might be hungry and thirsty.

While the men carry on at the door, I pour the cheese crackers into a bowl, then fill three glasses with ice cubes. All I have on hand is diet soda, but water would probably be just as welcome . . . the crackers are a tad on the stale side.

For some reason, my hands shake as I fill the glasses with water.

After setting the bowl and three glasses on a tray, I cross the foyer and head into the living room. Because I'm concentrating on not spilling the drinks, I am five feet into the room before I glance up and see what Samuel has brought—

Boxes. Over a dozen. They range in size and most are taped shut, but someone has written my name on each of them, along with a date: 1975–77, one box says. The one next to it is labeled 1980–82.

I slide the tray onto the coffee table, then sink into the nearest chair. "What is this?"

"Your packages." A wry smile flashes briefly beneath the doorman's tidy mustache. "I've been collecting 'em ever since your mother said I wasn't to bring anything up to you. She told me to have everything returned, but I couldn't do that—especially when Mr. Norquest told me to hold 'em for you. He said you might ask for them one day."

Ripples of amazement are spreading from an epicenter in my stomach, prickling my scalp and tingling my toes. "This—all this—is from my father?"

"Uh-huh. It's mostly letters, but there's gifts, too—your birthday and Christmas, I think. I think some of them are toys—a shame they're not much use to you now. But at least you'll know he was thinkin' of you all that time."

I reach for the nearest box and rip the thin strip of sealing tape away. The top of the box is covered in a film of dust, but I don't care. I lift the flaps, then plunge my hands in and withdraw letters—more than two dozen, all written in the same distinctive scrawl.

I look at Phil. "My father wrote me."

Booker chuckles. "Yes, ma'am, as regular as clockwork."

"He didn't forget me."

"No, ma'am."

I shift my gaze to the doorman's broad face. "Why didn't you tell me?"

His expression twists in a small grimace, as though I had suddenly struck him. "Don't be holding that against me, Miss Aurora. I was torn, you see. I had your mama telling me never to let a single letter or box make it past the front desk, and I had your daddy telling me to keep an eye on you. He called me fairly regular, always asking how you were doing and if you were happy."

I take a quick, sharp breath. "He *called*?"

"He called me, ma'am, at the desk. I don't think he ever called your apartment. He said he didn't want your mama cursing at him anyplace you might hear. He said she'd done enough damage."

"*She* did the damage? I knew they were angry with each other, but the way I heard it, *he* caused the problems in their marriage. I heard he had a mistress in London."

"Oh, Miss Aurora." The doorman closes his eyes, squeezing them so tight his face seems to collapse on itself. "Mr. Norquest was afraid you'd hear something like that. Truth is, your father was always a gentleman, ever since I've known him. He didn't meet his English wife until long after the divorce. But he traveled a lot while he was married to your mama, and she didn't like being left alone. I probably shouldn't speak ill of the dead, especially bein' a doorman and all, but when your father was traveling, your mama was entertaining all kinds of fellows.

"Anyway, one night Mr. Norquest came home from London and found her with . . . well, this is gossip for sure, but I don't mean anything malicious by it and I know it's the truth. He found her with another man and she asked your father to leave. He did leave the apartment—he came downstairs to sit with me—and when the fellow left, he went upstairs and told your mother she needed to be faithful. He didn't ask much, but marriage requires faithfulness and your mama didn't want to give it. So he left the apartment and the next morning he came back to find all his things sitting in boxes out in the lobby."

I listen in silence, comprehension seeping through my astonishment. Knowing Mother, I find it easier to accept her infidelity than my father's abusiveness. She always wanted to be adored. That's why she loved Clara, who willingly played second fiddle.

"So . . . my father left after that?"

"He did. And later he found out about you. He came back to the Westbury to present her with legal papers demanding custody, but that lawyer, Mr. Shields, caught him and told him the courts would never take a baby away from its mother. He tried to see you when the divorce was settled, but Mrs. Norquest wouldn't allow it. He was afraid a nasty court fight would hurt you—New York gossip bein' the way it is. He figured if you came to him, you'd have to come by your own free will. So Mr. Norquest said he was going to do whatever he could to pave your way . . . bein' that he suspected your mama might try to stop you. And that"—Booker spreads his hands, indicating the boxes around us—"is what this is all about."

Unable to answer, I slip out of the chair onto the carpet. On my knees, I open the second box and find more letters. The third box reveals the same, an absolute hoard of riches, dozens of affirmations of the one thing that matters:

My father loves me.

With trembling fingers I pull a random letter from the stack and rip it open. The message, dated October 14, 1995, is written in a strong, sloping script:

> *My darling Aurora:*
> *This morning finds me hoping and praying, as always, that you*

are well. Yesterday at the park I found myself watching a young woman of about your age—she had two small children, but Booker tells me you have not yet married.

Your devotion to your mother is admirable, Aurora Rose. Though I have never had the chance to see you in the flesh, through Booker I feel I know your character and would recognize it anywhere. And while my heart breaks for the distance between us— and the falsehoods that undoubtedly separate us in other ways—my soul thrills to see your strength of spirit.

And my hope is strong. Though I love my other children dearly, my love for you has grown deeper and more desperate through the years. So hope feeds me, nurtures me, and compels me to write, trusting you will read my words and see my heart.

Your loving father,
Ted

It's only one letter amid hundreds, but it's enough. Through tear-blurred eyes I look up and meet Phil's gaze. "Help me." My voice is a ragged whisper. "Help me get to London."

A glow rises in his face. "I'll make the reservations. We'll do whatever it takes, Rosie. We'll get you there."

Samuel Booker slaps his leg. "My wife will be glad to hear we kept these boxes, glad to know Mr. Norquest didn't misplace his trust in us."

"No," I manage to whisper, "he didn't. Thank you, Booker, for making this day possible."

He grins like a scout who's just done a good deed, and Phil helps me to my feet. "You see Mr. Booker to the door," he whispers in my ear, "and I'll go online to check out the flights."

In the foyer, I lock my arms around the old man's shoulders, breathing in the scent of his wool coat and the faint hint of aftershave. I try to control myself, but my chin wobbles and my eyes fill in spite of my intentions. "Thank you," I tell him. "You've made me very happy."

"Your daddy did the real work, Miss Aurora." He pats my shoulder. "Now you scoot on over to London and tell him so. He's waiting."

I pull out of his embrace and meet the old man's gaze. His eyes are dark brown, soft with kindness, and in them I see no uncertainty at all. The future may hold fears I must face, but right now I cannot consider anything but the father who has spent half a lifetime trying to reach me.

Desperation drove me from this apartment to the rooftop . . . surely love can transport me from the Westbury Arms to London.

I rise on tiptoe, kiss Samuel Booker's whiskered cheek, then close the door and hurry to find Phil.

We have some major baby stepping ahead of us.

34

I am sitting beside Phil in the back of a London taxicab. My heart is racing along with the traffic, and Phil must know that I am nervous. He squeezes my hand, then leans over and presses a kiss to my cheek. "You look lovely," he says, and though I'm not sure I believe him, I'm glad he thinks so.

Our plane landed at Heathrow over an hour ago. I'm a little groggy from the time change and jet lag, but my blood brims with anticipatory adrenaline.

I am going to meet my father today.

Overcome with emotion, I bury my face in the soft shoulder of Phil's wool coat. I feel him shift slightly, then his head tilts to rest upon mine.

He's been beside me throughout this adventure, and I don't know what I would have done without him. Clinging to Phil and a bottle of Valium, yesterday afternoon I boarded a British Airlines jet. Because of Phil's steadying influence, however, I didn't take a single pill.

Defeating my fear of leaving home hasn't been easy, but Phil helped me see that I'd already begun to beat it when I ventured down to the lobby and up to the roof. In the two weeks it took for my passport to arrive, Phil escorted me to several meetings with a psychiatrist and an agoraphobia support group. The first time I attended the group session, I felt like I'd stumbled across a group of long-lost cousins. They spoke my language; they understood my fears in a way no one else could.

As a reward for taking a few giant steps, Phil also took me out to buy new luggage, new clothes, and a winter coat. Each excursion pulled us a little farther from the Westbury Arms entrance, and each success raised my confidence level.

One afternoon we took the subway to visit Clara in the hospital. I sat by her bed and held her hand for an hour, silently saying good-bye. Oddly enough, I couldn't be angry at Clara for the way she'd deceived me. The lies had originated with Mother.

With my arm firmly wrapped through his, Phil escorted me to Clara's funeral at St. Pat's. She died without ever regaining consciousness, and I wept for her.

Clara is part of my past, and I buried my nightmares with her. I am ready to move forward.

I was tense when we boarded the plane and downright nervous when we landed in London, but Phil has negotiated every aspect of our journey. He and Bert Shields took care of details I have been too scattered to consider, including passports, tickets, and our need to let Father's family know we are coming.

At first we planned to stay in a hotel, but Hilly Norquest, my father's wife, insisted that we stay with the family. "All the children are home," she told Bert Shields, "and we've always room for two more. You tell Aurora and her gentleman friend to plan on staying at least a fortnight."

So Phil took a leave of absence from the college—claiming he needed a vacation anyway—and we booked open tickets. If my father does not pull through his illness, we'll return to New York after the funeral.

I have braced myself for the worst. Two people in my life have died in as many months; I may lose a third. But I am doing everything within my power to be sure I arrive before it's too late.

I lift my head and look out the wide window of the boxy taxi. We are riding on the left side of the road, the driver sits on the right side of the car, and this backward situation seems perfectly normal for a country on the opposite side of the ocean. I close my eyes as we speed through a roundabout without stopping, then I lean back and tell myself to relax.

I learned a remarkable lesson on the plane. When I was housebound, the thing I feared most was the sense of being out of control when a panic attack struck. But I didn't panic on the flight because I have never felt more in control of my life. For the first time in years, I made a decision independent of my mother's influence, and the resulting confidence has carried me safely into a foreign country.

The taxi pulls into a driveway in front of London Bridge Hospital. Phil pays the driver while I step onto the curb and blink up at the morning sky. A moment later, the driver sets our luggage on the curb. I pull one of the smaller pieces onto my shoulder, then follow Phil toward an information desk.

He pauses a moment to drop the luggage, and I surprise myself by approaching the woman at the counter. "Hello," I tell her, a little intimidated by the mound of sternly coifed hair supporting her cap. "We're looking for Theodore Norquest."

"You an' everybody else," she says, lacing her fingers. "Mr. Norquest deserves his privacy."

"I'm part of the family," I answer. "Hilly Norquest is expecting us."

I have uttered the magic words. The aide writes a number on a slip, then points to an elevator down the hall. "Take the lift up one floor, turn right. You'll most likely find the others waitin' in the family room."

I take the slip and turn to reach for Phil's hand, but he has bent to lift our luggage. And so, feeling suddenly alone, I follow the hall toward the elevator as Phil follows.

My heart is hammering my ribs again, but this time my fears are grounded in reality, not imagination. What if Hilly Norquest takes one look at me, sees my mother in my face, and turns me away? What if her sons resent my sudden appearance? What if we're too late?

I step into the elevator and hold the door as Phil staggers forward with our bags. Other people board the car—a young woman with a tangerine pouf of hair holds the hand of a little boy. An older woman follows them, an expression of dread on her face.

I know how she feels.

No one speaks as the elevator rises. A bell chimes when the car stops, and the sound makes my heart skip a beat. When none of the other passengers move, I step off and turn right, knowing Phil will be right behind me.

The paper in my hand says my father is in room 267. A woman sits in a chair outside that room, but this is no femme fatale. This woman looks more like a sixty-year-old Betty Crocker.

I approach slowly, then stop. "Hilly Norquest?"

The woman, who is plump, soft, and rosy-cheeked, stands and opens her arms. My stomach churns as I move into her embrace, but she kisses me on both cheeks, then steps back to squeeze my hands. "We are so glad you have come." She looks past me and sends Phil a smile. "You must be Philip."

"Phil," he says, stepping forward to shake her hand. "Phil Cannon."

She ignores his outstretched hand and embraces him, too. I'm wondering if she will pepper us with polite questions about the trip, but she seems to sense my urgency. Swiveling her hazel eyes in my direction, she asks, "Are you ready?"

I answer in a weak and tremulous whisper. "Yes."

Hilly Norquest takes me by the hand and leads me into my father's room. The man I have seen in black-and-white photographs is propped against two pillows and lying within the rails of a hospital bed. His hair is combed, his eyes closed, and an open book rests upside down in his lap.

Somehow I push a question past the lump in my throat. "Is he better?"

Hilly's smile blazes in the dim light of the room. "Much improved. He took a turn for the better right after we heard you were coming."

I am about to suggest that we not wake him, but Hilly has already placed one hand on his shoulder.

"Teddy?" she whispers. "Another of your children has come home."

My father opens his eyes . . . and those dark depths snap with love and boundless joy.

"Aurora."

Hilly steps back as he lifts his arms. Careful of the wires and tubes, I sink into his embrace, letting my tears speak for me.

We are people who love words, but words are not necessary in this moment. Still, I need to confess something. "I'm sorry," I whisper when I finally find my voice. "I'm so sorry for believing the lies."

His strong hand falls upon my head. "I have always loved you." His voice, so warm and familiar, shivers the skin of my arms. "Welcome to the family."

I feel like a child who has stumbled for years in darkness and suddenly finds a lamp. I feel joyful and complete, but most of all I feel . . . free.

Epilogue

Christmas Day, and I keep pinching myself to make sure this isn't the mother of all daydreams. I'm wearing a paper crown in the dining room of my father's London house and grinning like the Cheshire cat as I survey the long pine table.

Phil sits next to me, his hand occasionally reaching over to squeeze mine. We have grown closer during the past two weeks; the English air has been good for our relationship. Now that I understand my past, I feel capable of looking toward the future.

Next to Phil sits the oldest of my four younger brothers, John, who bears an uncanny resemblance to the Lord John of my dream. My father's house, come to think of it, looks a great deal like the Castle of Aragon, minus a few turrets, the moat, and the gate.

My other brothers—Andrew, Louis, and Edmond—are also at the table. Edmond, like Phil, is a bit of a computer geek, and the two of them have spent hours discussing bits and bytes and the future of wireless communications. Their conversations are pretty much Greek to me, but they seem to enjoy their talks.

The greatest surprise of the journey sits across from me—Alice, my twenty-year-old sister. Like me, she shares my father's dark eyes and love of literature. Her room, one of many in this rambling old house, is as littered with books as my apartment.

Theodore Norquest, looking every inch like Father Christmas, sits across from Hilly at the opposite end of the antique table. My siblings call him *Papa*, so now I do, too.

In view of the chill, Alice has tucked a plaid blanket over Papa's shoulders, but he is proudly wearing a new Eddie Bauer flannel shirt (a gift from Phil) and new puppy slippers (a gift from me and Macy's). Bert Shields had our gifts shipped from New York when we called him with news of my father's recovery.

As we smile at each other over the ravaged remains of a turkey, Hilly carries a steaming plum pudding to the table. "Watch out for the coins," John warns, lifting his chin to peer at me over Phil's raised knife and fork. "Wouldn't want you to chip a tooth on a penny."

I nod, content to continue in this happy daze. My new family has been warning me about cultural differences ever since my arrival, but never have I felt less than absolutely welcomed.

Now my father raises his mug, steaming with wassail. "To family." He looks around the circle with a smile that is both pleased and proud. "And to love."

As one, my brothers and sister echo him. I lift my drink and catch Phil's eye as my mug clacks against his.

I'm not sure what the future holds. Alice is talking about opening a writers' retreat at the house in France, and she says she'd love to have a partner. I've considered the idea, but I keep remembering how close I came to ending my life before it actually began. If not for my father and Phil, I wouldn't be here.

I can't imagine the next chapter of my life without either of them as major characters.

I lift my mug and drink deeply of the spiced cider. Last night Papa and I were sitting by the fire, not saying much, just enjoying each other's company. But beneath my happiness I was beginning to feel the stirrings of anger. How could Mother have kept me from this kind of joy? Why did she force the pain of separation upon me?

By the light of the blazing fire, Papa's eyes seemed to examine the deepest part of my soul. "I know the pain she caused," he whispered, "but to completely break free of the past, you must forgive her."

Hatred, Papa went on to say, is not easily satisfied. It grows and devours everyone it touches unless quenched with love. If I continued to resent Mother, I would prolong the power of her hate. So if I am ever to be liberated from fear and anger, Papa said I must forgive.

For a moment I could do nothing but sputter in disbelief. But after sleeping on his advice, I think I understand his reasoning. I want to be free. Others do, too.

As the sweet wassail warms my core, my thoughts drift back to the Westbury Arms and its rooftop view of another woman who has been imprisoned by circumstance and loneliness.

Will the penthouse princess be eating alone this Christmas? Somehow I doubt her clients will drop in on a day designed for families. Even if they do, what they offer is not love. Those men are a lot like Mother, trading in counterfeit emotions and lies as they seek their own pleasure.

She is as much a prisoner as I was, trapped by her choices, perhaps, instead of her fears. But if I can break free and reach out to my father, she can, too.

The world is filled with women like me and my friend in the glass house. And though I have no idea how to help them, I have Papa, Hilly, four talented brothers, and a sister who will give me direction. I have a trust fund to underwrite any number of philanthropic enterprises.

And I have Phil, who has helped me discover who I am meant to be. As I smile at him, he leans toward me. "You know," he says, his warm breath tickling my ear, "now that you're mobile, we're going to have to look into getting you a laptop."

Discussion Questions
for Readers' Groups

1. Angela Hunt has described *The Awakening* as a parable, a story designed to illustrate a spiritual truth. What truth(s) do you think the story illustrates?

2. Do any of the characters in *The Awakening* have spiritual counterparts? Do you think it's possible that Theodore Norquest, a horror novelist, could represent God? Why or why not?

3. Is God horrifying? What aspects of his character could be terrifying?

4. At one point Aurora recalls something she once read about an ancient means of execution—how the Romans strapped a dead body to a living one. Why do you think this image resonated with her? How is it reflected in her dreams?

5. Read the following paragraph and discuss how it relates to the gifts God has given his children. How has he endowed us? And what sort of responsibilities does that endowment entail?

Still . . . something in me yearns to know the man whose image I bear. . . . And he named me as an heir to so many of his copyrights— an act that could mean more than his monetary endowment. I'm no expert about copyright law, but I know he is entrusting me with the fruits of his creativity, allowing me to control and reap benefits from his work. With that responsibility comes the power to prevent his works from ever being published again . . . or ensure that they are published throughout the world.

6. "The important thing," Phil tells Aurora, "is knowing your father remembered you. If your brain is conjuring up memories instead of dreams, maybe he thought of you every year but your mother prevented you from receiving his gifts."

7. Has the Father sent gifts to you that, for one reason or another, you've been prevented from receiving?

8. What do you think happens to a child's self-image when one parent teaches a child to hate the other? How is this evidenced in Aurora's life?

9. One of Aurora's more graphic nightmares features cockroaches. If you were to attempt dream analysis, what do you think the cockroaches represented?

10. Of the woman in the penthouse, Aurora says, "I've been trying not to think about the woman in the penthouse, but I keep seeing her in that man's arms. She is Beauty and the Beast, both personalities encased in a slim, golden-haired package. . . . How can a person look so delicate and be so manipulative?" How do Aurora's thoughts about this woman relate to her thoughts about her mother?

11. Aurora has a terrible time writing a letter to her father. How does this compare to the difficulty some people have when they sincerely try to pray for the first time?

12. Though Aurora is joyfully accepted by her father's family, she does have to deal with a few cultural differences when she joins them. How does this relate to what new Christians face

when they join other believers in fellowship? How can more mature Christians help newcomers to the family of God?

13. Do you have any idea why Hunt named the two main characters Aurora Rose and Philip? Hint: think classic fairy tale.

An Interview with Angela Hunt

Wow! This book was really different for you.

(Laughing.) It was, wasn't it? But it's a parable, and those are the stories I love to write.

How do you get ideas for your novels?

Usually I pick up a fascinating piece of a story, then another piece, then another. And when it's time to write a new book, I put the pieces together. For *The Awakening*, the idea came to me in a flash—what would you do if you heard the voice of God?—but in the idea's first incarnation, the voice was speaking to a woman in a T.J. Maxx dressing room, probably because that's my favorite store.

Later, though, I talked to a neighbor who suffers from nightmares she described as occurring in "levels," and by that time I'd become fascinated by the idea of rooftops in New York. So those pieces fitted together and ultimately became *The Awakening.*

How much time do you spend researching and writing a book?

I write at a fairly fast pace, and I tend to research as I go. Each book takes me between three and four months to research and write. I think about the ideas, however, for months before I begin the actual writing. I considered the idea of God speaking to a woman for at least two years before I began to write this book.

You described The Awakening as a parable. How do you "interpret" it?

Well . . . before I answer, let me say that part of a parable's power comes from that "aha" experience a reader enjoys when he or she realizes the meaning of characters and symbols. I don't want to spoil that experience, so if anyone hasn't finished the story, they should stop reading now . . .

Okay—we'll trust they're gone.

All right, then. I see Theodore Norquest, of course, as God. He created Aurora and he loves her no matter how many other children he has. Aurora, of course, represents any person who is living in deception and bound in fear. She yearns for a relationship with her creator, but it's hard for her to approach God because she's spent her life snared in a web of lies.

Mary Elizabeth, her deceptive mother, represents those who reject God. They are loved by the Father, but their unwillingness to love and obey him results in eternal estrangement. Like Lucifer, M.E.'s chief characteristic is pride and her chief desire is adoration, which she exacts from Clara, Aurora, and her lovers. I was surprised when her initials spelled "ME." I was *amazed* when Aurora looked at the monogrammed bathroom towels and saw her mother's full initials: MEN. A telling clue of another major flaw, and one I did not consciously insert into the story.

The books her father wrote? His novels represent the sixty-six books of the Holy Scriptures.

There are other parallels in the story, but one of my chief goals was to illustrate the many ways God tries to reach us. He speaks to us through the Word—-written, spoken, and incarnated in the flesh of his Son, Jesus Christ. He yearns for us with compassionate love. He endows us with gifts, his Spirit draws us even in our estrangement, and when we make the decision to come to him, he welcomes us to the family with open arms.

Will there be a sequel? Will we see what happens to Aurora and Phil in the future?

Don't think so. I think the story offers a certain symmetry. The novel began with an exhausted Aurora burying the past and ends with an energized Aurora facing the future.

What's next for you?

Well . . . tonight is Christmas Eve 2003, so I plan to take a few days off and enjoy my family. And after the turn of the year, I think I hear a few gorillas calling my name . . .

Gorillas? You're joking, right?

(Laughing again.) I think this is where I'm supposed to say, "Stay tuned." Check back with me in about six months.

Look for these other novels by Angela Hunt

The Debt

ISBN 0-8499-4319-1

When Emma first met Abel Howard, she was a woman with a past, a woman who had not always made the right choices. But after twenty-five years of marriage to Able and with his world renowned ministy career at its peak, she doesn't often have a reason to dwell on things of the past.

Until Christopher Lewis—the son she gave up for adoption years before—arrives at her doorstep.

This young man's entry into her life rock Emma to the very core of her being, Challenging everything she's ever believed about God and His Purposes for her.

The Debt is a tender, bittersweet story of redemption and forgiveness.

The Canopy

ISBN 0-8499-4345-0

Deep in the lush and dangerous forests of Peru, Alexandra and her team search determinedly for a cure for deadly diseases. One strain of the disease has already begun the process of ravaging Alexandra's own mind and body. Finding a cure is the only hope for her and for her daughter, Who has almost certainly inherited the same disease.

Alex believes she is searching for a needle in a haystack until she meets Michael Kenway, a British doctor who lost his wife when "mad cow disease" ravaged Britain in the 1990's. He presents her with an incredible story—a patient suffering from the disease was cured by a mythical "healing tribe" living deep in the Amazon Jungle. Reluctantly placing her faith in Michael, who is entirely too religious for her comfort, Alexandra and her team seek out an unreached indigenous group who may hold the cure not only for Alex, but also for the world.

Look for these other novels
by Angela Hunt

ISBN 0-8499-4366-3

The Pearl

She had a perfect life . . . until the accident. Now science offers her the opportunity to replace what she has lost, but at what cost?

Talk-radio show host Dr. Diana Sheldon has made a career out of giving advice to irate daughters-in-law and spurned lovers. But when her whole life changes in one moment of bad judgement, the carefully built life she's built begins to spiral out of control. She'd give anything and everything—to get her family back.

The Note

In the wake of a tragic plane crash, a reporter's life is turned upside-down by the last words of an anonymous passenger.

When PanWorld flight 848 crashes into Tampa Bay killing all 261 people on board, journalist Peyton MacGruder is assigned to the story. Her discovery of a remnant of the tragedy—a simple note:"T—I love you. all is forgiven. Dad."—changes her world forever. A powerful story of love and forgiveness.

ISBN 0-8499-4284-5